HISTORICAL

Your romantic escape to the past.

A Naval Surgeon To Fight For
Carla Kelly

Cativated By His Covenient Duchess
Lauri Robinson

MILLS & BOON

A NAVAL SURGEON TO FIGHT FOR
© 2024 by Carla Kelly
Philippine Copyright 2024
Australian Copyright 2024
New Zealand Copyright 2024

First Published 2024
First Australian Paperback Edition 2024
ISBN 978 1 038 91781 2

CATIVATED BY HIS CONVENIENT DUCHESS
© 2024 by Lauri Robinson
Philippine Copyright 2024
Australian Copyright 2024
New Zealand Copyright 2024

First Published 2024
First Australian Paperback Edition 2024
ISBN 978 1 038 91781 2

MIX
Paper | Supporting
responsible forestry
FSC® C001695

Published by
Harlequin Mills & Boon
An imprint of Harlequin Enterprises (Australia) Pty Limited
(ABN 47 001 180 918), a subsidiary of HarperCollins
Publishers Australia Pty Limited
(ABN 36 009 913 517)
Level 19, 201 Elizabeth Street
SYDNEY NSW 2000 AUSTRALIA

Cover art used by arrangement with Harlequin Books S.A.. All rights reserved.

Printed and bound in Australia by McPherson's Printing Group

A Naval Surgeon To Fight For

Carla Kelly

MILLS & BOON

Carla Kelly started writing Regency romances because of her interest in the Napoleonic Wars, and she enjoys writing about warfare at sea and the ordinary people of the British Isles rather than lords and ladies. In her spare time, she reads British crime and history. Carla lives in Idaho and is a former seasonal park ranger and double RITA® Award and Spur Award winner. She has five children and five grandchildren.

Visit the Author Profile page
at millsandboon.com.au for more titles.

Author Note

I've worked in hospital and hospice public relations through portions of my writing life. I'm a historian by training and practice. Writing was always part of this, thanks to an excellent beginning in, yes, high school journalism. Had I continued beyond my master's degree in history, I know that a doctoral dissertation would have focused on US Civil War medicine.

All this research has taught me a fact of which I have no doubt. Pre-twenty-first-century medicine makes some shake their heads over "primitive" practices and beliefs of the eighteenth and nineteenth centuries, as in "My word, didn't they know better?"

Not me. All my historical research in medicine has given me nothing but respect for those men—they were all men then—*who practiced to the extent of their knowledge.* That's the key. I don't doubt they wished they knew more; their writings sometimes expressed this frustration. Even in our age of amazing medical procedures, I also have no doubt that current practitioners of the healing arts wish they knew more.

Think of it: knowing more. Isn't this something we all wish? I hope my fiction conveys this deep admiration I have for surgeons and physicians of earlier ages.

DEDICATION

In memory of all the men who fought so gallantly at Trafalgar, and the never-mentioned wives there, too.

Also in memory of my dear writing buddy.

Prologue

At the age of nine, Jerusha Langley was no shrinking violet, no meek female, in an age when meek females were highly prized. Children were to be seen and not heard, and females—no matter what age—were never to call attention to themselves.

Jerusha had long been curious about the duck-pond on her father's modest property, or rather, the parish's modest vicarage near Bolling, where the Langley family resided, thanks to a living furnished by Jerusha's aunt, Lady Oakshott, who had the good fortune to marry a baronet. The vicarage in Bolling was small, but ideal for an equally modest clergyman.

For a few weeks, Jerusha had observed tadpoles turning into frogs on the pond's fringe. Mama threw up her hands in exasperation when Jerusha trooped into the house bearing three little frogs. Papa gently reminded her that frogs belonged in ponds, and would she please return them?

She did so with no good grace, because she would have preferred to keep the frogs. Muttering to herself, she carried the frogs back to the pond, leaned over, and released them. In the process, she dumped herself in.

It was early spring, so her coat dragged her down. She sputtered and thrashed into the middle of the pond, which took on the proportions of the ocean so vividly described by her father's discourse upon Noah and his ark. She thought she might

make sufficient headway if she flailed about enough, but that coat was heavy and now waterlogged. She began to sink.

When matters reached their worst, a boy appeared at the pond's edge, older and taller than she was. He hesitated not a moment but plunged in, swimming to her. He grabbed the back of her coat and hauled her to shore.

'You're all right, now then?' he asked finally, in that Scottish lilt of his.

She recognised him. His father was secretary to the solicitor who lived next door. Jerusha didn't know his name—he was a twin and either Douglas or Jamie—but she thanked him for saving her life.

'You should learn to swim,' was his reply.

He walked her home, all sodden and squelching. Mama shrieked and accused him of pushing her in the water. Jerusha protested. The boy calmly assured her mother that he was merely walking by and rescued her. Mrs Langley whisked her inside and slammed the door in his startled face.

And that was that, even though Jerusha protested as Mama dried her off, and stated that the boy had saved her life.

'I've heard complaints aplenty about the secretary's twins,' her mother said, when Jerusha was dry and sent to bed—over further protest—mainly because Mrs Langley had personal tendencies towards hypochondria. 'I know for a fact that one of them stole a pig. That's the rumour, but it came from a good source.'

Jerusha's 'But Mama...' fell on deaf ears.

Mrs Langley carried the news of Jerusha's near death to Vicar Langley, who carried the tale to the solicitor, who grilled his secretary, Daniel Wilson, and then sacked the man over his protests that Douglas, his more obstreperous son, would never push someone in the water just to turn around and appear a hero, and Jamie, his twin, wouldn't, either.

The solicitor told the vicar later that he was happy enough

to see the backs of the whole Wilson clan, because his secretary had a disturbing tendency to correct his grammar and spelling on legal documents, damn the man.

'Douglas or Jamie, those twins will never trouble the district again,' Jerusha's mother announced to her in triumph a few days after the Wilsons were sent packing.

'Mama, one of them saved my life,' Jerusha said.

'Oh, pish posh,' Mama said. 'It is a shallow pond. You could have just put your feet down and waded ashore, I am certain. They're gone and the district is the better for it, I am certain.'

At the age of nine, Jerusha learned three valuable lessons: Life isn't fair, Augusta Langley had a curious grudge against Scots, and she wasn't much of a Christian. When Jerusha attempted a mild protest—'Mama, you should have thanked him.'—Mama gave her a good shake.

A conscientious child, Jerusha nursed her own anguish, mortified to have been the reason a secretary was unjustly sacked. Her only consolation was the Langley's cook, a kindly woman. Jerusha moped in the kitchen until Mrs Pingree allowed her to pour out her misery at the whole wretched business.

'Lovey, the Wilsons will be fine,' Mrs Pingree soothed, wiping away Jerusha's tears and handing her two lumps of sugar. 'I hear that Scots are a tough lot.'

Jerusha did one thing of consequence that she never told her parents: She learned to swim. The whole thing was clandestine, but she had discovered a tendency to go her own way when she was certain she was right. The matter involved watching behind trees in high summer as boys gathered at a deeper pond for merriment.

Her education increased because they swam naked, but never mind that. From her secret spot she watched them push up from the bottom and lie on their backs. It looked simple

and she tried it during late-night visits to the pond when the house was dark. Push up, lie flat, arms out. Easy.

She watched again at actual swimming, and at night repeated that flailing about with a purpose this time, arms moving in rhythm across the pond. She sank a few times, but figured it out.

Swimming was her little secret.

Through twelve years and more, Mrs Pingree kept up occasional correspondence with Mrs Wilson. Jerusha learned that Mr Wilson acquired better employment in the Highlands. As for the twins later on, Douglas took Orders in the Church of Scotland—so much for stealing pigs—and Jamie attached himself to the Royal Navy at age thirteen, not so long after the drowning incident.

'Last I heard,' Mrs Pingree told Jerusha when Jerusha was twenty-one, 'is that Douglas has a fine church in Spring Hill and a wife, and Jamie is a surgeon's mate in the navy.' Mrs Pingree handed Jerusha two more lumps of sugar and they both laughed. 'You needn't trouble yourself about Jamie Wilson.'

Then why couldn't she forget him?

Chapter One

❦

Jerusha's twenty-first birthday had slid by unnoticed three years ago, in the Year of Our Lord 1802, but there was something intimidating about birthdays twenty-two, twenty-three, and twenty-four, mainly because nothing much had happened since 1802. It was more than that. As she sat up in bed on a drizzly morning in February of 1805, now twenty-four for heaven's sake, she knew that life had blown a kiss in her general vicinity and passed her by.

Jerusha's first inclination had been drummed into her since she was old enough to be accountable: Ignore it and find some useful Good Work to do. Typically, that sufficed, but not this time. Looking around Papa's parish, Jerusha saw women her age enjoying life. Liddy, the daughter of a joiner, had recently married an up-and-coming tenant farmer. Maude, widowed young and with a daughter, had contracted an enviable alliance with Bolling's butcher. Sally Brown, she with a large birthmark on her cheek, was anticipating another child with her husband the constable, and positively glowing.

Here I am, Jerusha thought, *with nothing and no one.*

She knew her parents would never countenance self-pity, so she said nothing. In that well-mannered but pragmatic way of hers, she entertained the notion that she deserved a turn of events in her favour.

It would never do to admit something so self-serving to her

parents. Vicar Langley knew he had married a little above his station. He was not an ambitious man, so his parish living sufficed. Augusta Langley, on the other hand, felt worldly things more keenly. In years past, that generally meant a querulous letter to her sister Hortensia, who had done the opposite and married up, no matter that Sir Harvey Oakshott was a squinty-eyed fellow, twenty years older than she. Such a letter to her older sister usually meant a week at the seaside for Augusta with her two children, and childless Lady Oakshott. Jerusha did like the ocean.

That Sir Harvey Oakshott, at his wife's instigation, had provided that living, Mama seemed to consider her due. After all, the Oakshotts did have lovely Oaklands, an estate near Plymouth. What did they know of genteel poverty? Or so Mama reasoned.

Lately, even though Mama still sent querulous letters, nothing came of it. 'The Oakshotts have forgotten me,' Mama announced dramatically over breakfast.

All that earned her from the vicar was raised eyebrows and a return to his perusal of the newspaper, the same paper Jerusha was hoping to pounce upon when both parents left the breakfast room. If she hurried, she could generally snatch it before the housekeeper used it to wrap wet rubbish.

All Jerusha wanted was a glimpse of the wider world beyond the parish. Taking her usual careful inventory of her felonies and misdemeanours, she knew she shouldn't chafe so about that wider world. No ladies of her acquaintance did. The matter came home to roost on her heart when coffins bearing young men were buried in Bolling Parish because of the war against Napoleon.

'I want to know what's going on,' Jerusha had told her mother only last week, when caught with the newspaper. Mama must have tattled to Papa, who must have directed the housekeeper to keep it from his daughter. Jerusha reminded herself that Papa meant well.

Lately, though, his kindness wore on her nerves. When he ventured some admonition, some reflection on her character, he used the same tone he used to speak to children. It grated. 'I am twenty-five,' she wanted to tell him. 'I am not six and recalcitrant. Papa, treat me as an equal.'

Such would never be the case, not in this household from which there was no escape. She remained single and no one's equal.

Then came the moment when she knew what lay ahead as clearly as if it were already written in her book of life. Her younger brother Gerald, a no-hoper currently studying at Cambridge, came home for a repairing rustication after performing miserably in the entire term. As it turned out, he must have learned persuasive argument.

Before she left to deliver soup to one of the least fortunate of her father's parishioners, she saw Gerald standing outside Papa's study, looking less than sanguine. *I would give ten years of my life to have a chance at Cambridge*, she thought, as she passed him in the hall. *What now, you ignorant twit?*

The result of Gerald's supposed dressing-down ended any of Jerusha's possible dreams. By the end of an evening in Papa's study, Gerald came out triumphant. He grabbed Jerusha and swung her around. When she asked what the fuss was about, he gave a modest smile.

'You are looking—or soon to be looking at—the British Army's newest cornet. And all it will cost is five hundred pounds!'

And how is that sum to be obtained? was Jerusha's first thought, followed by a faint, 'My goodness.'

'Papa scolded, but he assured me that he could borrow against our little legacy,' Gerald confided. 'He knew you would not mind.'

Little legacy. Wasn't that what Mama had assured her and Gerald would be evenly divided some distant day? Both of her

parents must have been deficient in simple arithmetic. 'Four hundred for Gerald and one hundred for you,' Mama stated firmly, except all of it went to Gerald. Within a month he was outfitted, commissioned, and on his way to a regiment in distant Canada, with Cambridge a thing of the past, along with any stipend for her to please a possible suitor.

Her anguish increased the night she overhead Mama and Papa quietly arguing in his study. She only heard random bits—'My love, I did not know Hortensia would cut up so stiff about borrowing that money for Gerald.' This from Mama.

This next rejoinder came from Papa after a gasp. 'Augusta, do you mean you borrowed five hundred pounds from your sister? I thought you had kept that money safe all these years as our children's legacy. Did you…had you spent it on furbelows for yourself?'

This was followed by a long silence and then sobs. And this: 'Dear husband, Hortensia will not help me. There is nothing for Jerusha. With any luck, Hortensia will not press me for repayment. After all, we had to help Gerald.'

It was probably no coincidence that Papa's sermon the following Sunday was taken from I Timothy, Chapter Six: In a surprisingly loud voice, Papa thundered from the pulpit, 'For the love of money is the root of all evil!' Too startled to turn her head and stare at Mama, Jerusha's side glance took in tight lips and bright spots of colour in Mama's cheeks. Jerusha trod quietly around the parsonage that week and the next, until she was tired of both parents.

Whatever had been promised to her was gone with Gerald, the Cambridge dropout with empty space between his ears. The reality was that she saw her parents as they really were, vain and silly. The time had come for…something. She didn't know what, at least until a letter arrived from Aunt Hortensia, who preferred that everyone, even her niece, call her Lady Oakshott.

A letter from Mama's sister, Lady Oakshott, was a rare enough event. 'I wonder what Hortensia can want,' Mama announced to Papa at luncheon on a cold February morning. 'Oh, I hope it is not a demand for...' She lowered her voice. 'You know.'

Papa glared at her, after a glance in Jerusha's direction, as if trying to decide if she could hear their obvious conversation. Jerusha decided to ignore them both and leave the room. She could take luncheon in the kitchen with the cook and have more agreeable company.

Before Jerusha left, Mama opened the letter, read a few lines, and gasped, which only made Papa exclaim, 'Has she decided to demand our daughter as partial payment for...you know what? Has the bill come due already?' he asked, perhaps in jest or perhaps not.

Oddly enough for a vicar, Papa's strong suit was not forgiveness. He and Mama still addressed each other most formally, the matter of her borrowing money for Gerald's advancement at Jerusha's expense still a sore spot. Jerusha edged for the door, unwilling to hear another word.

Too late. 'Jerusha, sit down. This concerns you,' Mama said as she waved Lady Oakshott's letter about.

'Aha!' Papa declared. 'She is inviting Jerusha to Oaklands, where she will meet an elderly fellow who will marry her despite her lack of fortune.'

'Francis, that is quite enough,' Mama said, in tones frosty enough to make Jerusha wonder if Papa was sleeping on the cot in his dressing room.

'Here it is, daughter,' Mama said. Jerusha could almost feel her excitement. 'Lady Oakshott is planning to sell a Plymouth property of her late husband's estate. Apparently, she feels she should be there for some necessary repairs and would like your company.'

'She barely knows me, Mama,' Jerusha said. 'I wonder why she feels the need of my company.'

Mama was still reading. 'Here it is: Apparently my sister's lady's companion resigned, and she wants the comfort of relatives.'

Someone who insists her niece call her Lady Oakshott doesn't long for relatives, Jerusha thought.

'She wants someone to fetch and carry.'

Jerusha was not slow; there was a larger matter, the business of Mama's borrowing from her sister and using all that money for Gerald's commission. Perhaps this was Aunt Hortensia's recompense for her younger sister's profligate spending.

Mama's hesitation confirmed Jerusha's suspicion. 'It's not a bad thing, daughter. Perhaps there might be a future for *you* as a lady's companion.'

There it is, Jerusha thought. Still, it could get her out of the vicarage, which suddenly seemed like an excellent notion.

'I can entertain the offer,' she said, matching Mama's casual tone.

She'll tire of me soon enough, Jerusha left unsaid.

'You'll do more than entertain it,' Mama said. 'I shall return an acceptance this afternoon. No one needs you here.'

'True, Mama. No one needs me here.' Or anywhere, for that matter, Jerusha knew, but couldn't say.

No one needs me.

Chapter Two

Lady Oakshott paid Jerusha's passage to Plymouth on the mail coach; not for her a post-chaise as her mama made no effort to add enough Langley funds to make up the difference.

The mail coach it was, but not before The Lecture. Jerusha knew it was coming, even though she was twenty-five and beyond needing it. Her father warned her about the Royal Navy in general and sailors in particular.

It was a concerted parental effort, which relieved Jerusha's mind. At least Mama and Papa were speaking to each other again, even if she was the object of their interest. Mama added nothing to Papa's warnings, but she dabbed at her eyes and appeared concerned.

Finally, it was too much. Jerusha fixed a kindly eye on both of her parents. 'My dears, all I am going to do in Plymouth is see how I can assist Lady Oakshott. I have no designs on the Royal Navy and know it can have none on me.' She shouldn't have, but she added, 'I am still too poor to attract any officer, and probably too opinionated. Let me pack.'

Jerusha swept out of the room, pausing a moment, waiting for regret at her firm words. Nothing happened. In fact, she felt more cheerful than she had in ages. 'I am leaving the vicarage,' she whispered. 'Bravo for me.'

During her remaining days in the vicarage, she made a point to be extra polite to her mother, who moped about with

some drama. She knew her father would find a way to work her plain speaking into a sermon, and she endured a scorcher on 'Children, obey your parents.'

The last night in the vicarage was a trying one, with Mama in tears through most of dinner and Papa opening and closing his mouth, ready with aphorisms, of which he had plenty, but reluctant to share them. She assured them in her quiet way that she would never do anything to embarrass them.

Mama tried once. 'Daughter, if you wear your nicest coat tomorrow and best bonnet, you won't be encroached upon in the mail coach,' she said. 'The other riders will see that you are Quality, and will leave you alone.'

And sit in superior silence? Jerusha thought in horror. No, never that.

'I'll be fine, Mama.'

Mama patted her hand and consigned her darling daughter to the mail coach, as though it was a fixture in Dante's rungs of hell. Perhaps her conscience bothered her. Jerusha almost told Mama that she knew her visit to Plymouth, however long, was a payback, destined to turn her into a lady's companion, since she could hope for nothing better. Her trunk was packed and already deposited at the Fox and Hound, where the mail coach stopped. It only remained for her to follow it in the morning.

When the house quieted, Jerusha tiptoed downstairs and into the servants' quarters, where she knew Mrs Pingree would be seeing to those last things that seemed to fall to a woman's lot.

'Will you miss us?' the cook asked.

'You know I will, Mrs Pingree. I have been welcome here.'

'You always will be,' Mrs Pingree assured her. She put down a half-dry pot. 'What is Lady Oakshott's game, do you think?'

Such a conversation opener would have stunned Mama, but then, Mama was a stickler on separation of upstairs and downstairs, while Jerusha was not. She knew Mrs Pingree well enough to assume she already suspected the deeper reason

for Jerusha's visit to Plymouth. Why not put it to the test? 'I believe I have been summoned to Plymouth in at least partial payment for Mama's mishandling of a loan from Lady Oakshott that went entirely to Gerald. Apparently, I am to become a lady's companion.'

Ah, there it was: Mrs Pingree nodded. 'We have been suspecting that,' she said, then leaned closer in conspiracy. 'The upstairs maid noticed a letter to that effect when she was tidying up in the sitting room.'

Jerusha laughed inside at the euphonism of 'noticed.'

'Do you think I will make a successful lady's companion, Mrs P?'

'I supremely doubt it, Lovey,' the cook replied, using that endearment from Jerusha's childhood when she came below stairs for biscuits and sympathy when life upstairs was too tiresome. 'You're an opinionated lady, and you don't lack for good sense.'

She knew a high compliment when she heard one. 'My pretentious aunt will tire of me, and I will be home before the end of summer,' she predicted. 'Even the Royal Navy will fear me, and I have no fortune to tempt anyone.'

'I'll miss you until you return, but there's no rush,' Mrs Pingree said. She lowered her voice. 'And no fears about the Royal Navy. The men smell of brine and are always at sea.'

Jerusha could tease, too. 'Then I am safe from their machinations,' she joked. 'Gentlemen don't smell of seawater.'

'Here is a novel idea: Plymouth is probably full of ordinary men. Find one.' Mrs Pingree turned serious. 'Trust yourself, Lovey.'

Chapter Three

To Jerusha's surprise, she slept well. She was past feeling dismay at leaving the vicarage; she had resigned herself to being the Good Example. Her own brother had fled such responsibility. For all she knew, he was staring down large bears in Canada. At least he wasn't in Europe, with war on again.

No one will know me in Plymouth, she thought, as she sat on a bench outside the Fox and Hound, waiting for the mail coach, her bandbox beside her. *When I leave Bolling, I am on my own.*

Mama did not see her off. She was no early riser, and besides, enough shards and remnants of her more genteel life as a Pigott of Albemarle would have drawn back in horror at the very idea of waiting for a common conveyance.

Jerusha wore her plain brown wool coat, since early spring was a tease. Her bonnet was more tried and true than stylish, which suited her fine, because so was she.

She knew she still stood out, a youngish woman travelling alone, but obviously Quality. Heading north, the first mail coach that stopped, took away two hopeful riders. When the coach heading south arrived, she was the only boarder. The coachman flung up her trunk to waiting arms on top and opened the door for her when she handed him her fare.

'To Exeter?' he asked.

'Yes, sir. Then I take the local stage to Plymouth.' The idea that she was actually leaving Bolling for who knew how long

struck her forcefully and she couldn't help smiling at him. Mama and Papa would probably have wondered if she had listened to a word of their admonitions. They weren't here, so she smiled.

'Got a sweet sailor boy in Plymouth?' he teased.

'Nothing that exciting,' she replied, knowing that Mama would be stunned at her daughter's easy camaraderie with one lower than she. 'I am going to stay with my aunt.' She wasn't about to mention Lady Oakshott's name and title.

He gave her a hand up, after leaning in first to address the riders. 'Make some room for the lady,' he said.

They did. On one side, she squeezed between a farm wife with a cage of three chickens, none of them happy, and a little boy on the other, with two more chickens. Across from them sat a middle-aged lady who looked up from her book, then glanced away.

None of the others made eye contact with her, confirming Mama's comments about the shield and protection of class. She sat back, preparing herself for silence, then reconsidered.

She, Jerusha Langley, had finally been allowed into the wider world, which obviously meant ignoring others, even though they sat cheek to jowl. If there was a more artificial situation, she couldn't imagine it.

She contemplated the lives of the others. Perhaps the lady only slightly older than she might be a governess en route to a house with people of quality inside it. Another look at the lady seated across from her suggested an old maid facing a change of employment and nothing more.

Perhaps this will be my life, Jerusha thought.

She decided to change the script. Where to begin? She looked at the lad with chickens in a small cage. Jerusha knew he would never speak first. It was her turn.

'Are these your very own chickens?' she asked, six simple words. If he replied, she knew she had changed her world.

As she thought he might, he looked first at his mother, who hesitated. To Jerusha's relief and triumph, the farm wife smiled at her boy and nodded, giving him permission to reply.

'Aye, ma'am, my birds,' he said, giving Jerusha a glance both shy and hopeful.

'Did you raise them from eggs?' Jerusha asked.

He nodded. She knew it could have ended there, but Mrs Farm Wife took her turn. 'One of our hens decided to hide a clutch.' Jerusha saw the pride in her eyes. 'Johnny, here, 'e found 'em.'

'I kept 'em warm and all three hatched,' he said proudly. 'Papa said they wouldn't make it, but Mama and me knew better.'

Jerusha watched with delight as mother and son shared a private glance suggesting they knew more about poultry than Papa.

'Look how fine they are now,' Jerusha said and kept up the conversation.

When mother and son left the mail coach, Jerusha hurried inside the inn, nabbing only a meat sandwich. When she returned to the coach, the silent lady still sat there, feet together and hands folded primly in her lap.

Jerusha decided to take another chance. She handed one half of the sandwich to the lady. 'I almost didn't make it back,' Jerusha said. 'That lunch counter is not for the faint of heart. You were wise not to attempt it.'

If that was your reason, she thought, pleased when the lady took the half sandwich. She finished it, losing not a crumb.

The lady looked around, but it was still just the two of them. 'I have wanted to do what you did,' she said. 'It can get so lonely, at times, sitting in silence.'

That was all she said until it was her turn to get off the mail coach at the stop before Exeter. The lady nodded to Jerusha, then departed.

Never get yourself into such a position, Jerusha told herself. Johnny had his mum and the promise of more chickens. The quiet lady had nothing. Perhaps, just perhaps, being Quality put up barriers. *Let that be a lesson to me*, Jerusha thought.

Jerusha left the mail coach at Exeter, with no fears about boldly asking an older woman how to catch the coastal carrier from Exeter to Plymouth. 'Follow me, dearie,' the woman said, 'I'm going a little farther.'

They were joined by two men. Soon the new coachman snapped his whip and Jerusha settled back, ready for this journey to be over. They meandered over miles, but in sight of the sea now in the gathering dusk. The woman was a widow of some years and well-acquainted with the route. 'Visiting me daughter, I was,' she said. She waved her farewell at Torquay, a village on the bay, with Royal Navy ships at anchorage. 'They come and go and fight Boney at sea,' were her parting words. 'Lonely navy wives on this coast.'

Funny how silent travel can be so tedious. Jerusha wanted more conversation, but the men chatted quietly together. She told herself it wasn't nosiness but boredom that made her mentally dub them Old Traveller and One Leg, because his left leg ended in a wooden peg.

Darkness settled in by the next stop, when a youngish man climbed aboard. There was no place to sit except beside her, so she shifted farther into her corner. His overcoat had a briny odour. Old Traveller and One Leg continued their low-voiced conversation about what she thought was the blockade of the French coast. The young man hunkered down and chewed his nails.

To her embarrassment, Jerusha's stomach protested loud and long against its fading memory of a mere half sandwich.

To her surprise and her gratitude, Old Traveller handed her an apple. 'There miss, we can't have you chewing off your arm, now, can we?'

When One Leg gave her a shy grin, she relaxed. 'It's been a long day,' she admitted. 'Thank you.' She munched her apple dinner and decided to chance some conversation. It had gone well with Johnny, and his chickens, hadn't it?

She had noted from years of observation that men liked to explain things. 'Pardon me, sirs, but I heard you mention a blockade?'

'It's part of war, miss, the boring part,' One Leg said. 'T' Frogs want England, and they can't have it.' He tapped his wooden leg. 'I served, oh, I did, at the Nile.' He explained the blockade as Old Traveller nodded, then closed his eyes for a nap, conversation over.

A few hours brought them to Plymouth, that navy town on the River Plym. It was too dark to see anything, and time for her to wonder how to find number twenty-eight Finch Street.

When the carrier stopped in front of an inn with a creaking sign—the wind was up—the door flew open, and a uniformed man with a cudgel leaned inside the carriage, swore, and shoved the cudgel under the chin of the man who had never spoken.

Jerusha gasped as the uniformed man pulled back the rider's briny coat. 'A little birdie says sailors got on at Exeter,' Cudgel Man shouted, as though they were all hard of hearing. 'Forget goin' home. The king wants ye now!'

With that, he jerked the rider from the coach. Jerusha made herself small in the carriage as two more men in uniform—who were they?—hauled down two more protesting riders from the top of the carrier.

'It's a good haul, sir!' Cudgel Man yelled to a younger man in uniform. Another curse followed a crack on the head to her former seatmate, who dropped like a stone.

Old Traveller pulled the door shut. 'We'll wait here until they leave,' he told Jerusha. 'No good for you to be on the street.'

'I... I wouldn't want to,' she assured him. 'Wh-what has just happened?'

'Press gangs all over Devon and Cornwall are rounding up sailors who try to sneak away,' he said. 'Thank the Almighty *I'm* too old. It's war, miss, and they have no choice but to serve.'

Chapter Four

No one waited for her a few blocks on at the coastal carrier's terminus, which surprised her not at all. Jerusha knew Lady Oakshott well enough not to count on much. She remembered disappointing visits when she was much younger that Mama chose to gloss over, calling them the eccentricities of the wealthy. Jerusha knew selfishness when she saw it, despite Mama choosing to ignore the matter.

When she and the remaining riders finally left the coastal carrier, One Leg came under the press gang's scrutiny. He sent them on with a brusque, 'Carpenter's mate here. I gave all at the Nile, ye fiends of hell.'

'Mind your tongue, anyway,' snapped the young officer.

'Do they just grab anyone that suits their fancy?' Jerusha whispered to One Leg.

'They're not supposed to,' he replied more quietly as the press gang moved on. 'They'll grab sailors off returning merchant ships, claiming the necessity of national calamity.' He chuckled. 'And God help ye if you're on an American ship, minding your own business!'

'This doesn't seem fair,' she said, flinching as a screaming woman ran after the press gang, clutching an infant and raising her free hand, begging mercy where there was none. Jerusha turned away in shock.

'It's war,' One Leg said simply. 'Boney has thousands of men just across the Channel, waiting to invade.'

The three of them stood shoulder to shoulder until the press gang moved off to terrorise another public house. The woman with the baby ran after them, sobbing.

Old Traveller sighed and took out his timepiece. 'Is someone coming for you? It is nearly eleven of the clock.'

'I doubt it. My aunt is…' How to describe Lady Oakshott? 'Let me say that she is scatterbrained. I know her retainers are old.'

'Retainers?' One Leg asked. 'What sort of household is this?'

Better spill the budget, Jerusha decided. 'My aunt is Lady Oakshott of Oaklands, and I am a poor relation.' Blunt but true, and certainly no more shocking than the press gang, which, from the sound of things, was creating merry hell on the next street.

Old Traveller stopped a passing hackney. 'If you have an address, we will drop you off.'

'Thank you, sir,' Jerusha said. She took the address from her reticule. 'Here it is. I am in your debt.'

Twenty-eight Finch Street was not far from the old town. Old Traveller called it the Barbican. The jarvey pulled up sharp and handed down her trunk. She waved goodbye to her fellow travellers, took a deep breath, and knocked on the door of what looked like a dark house.

Nothing. She knocked again, but louder, then once more, and pressed her ear against the door. To her relief, she heard footsteps and stepped back when the door opened a crack.

'Yes?'

'It's Jerusha Langley,' she said through the crack. 'Lady Oakshott is expecting me.'

The door swung open on a man even more ancient than Old Traveller. He was thin and squinty-eyed, which suggested a

need for spectacles. When he straightened up, she knew she was looking at a butler, albeit a superannuated one.

'Jerusha Langley,' she said again. 'Did…did Lady Oakshott mention me?'

'I forget,' the old fellow said. 'I am Napier, and I am seventy-five.'

A little old to be working, she thought, even though what he said amused her.

Or maybe she was tired. She looked into his eyes and even in the gloom saw kindness, something so far in short supply in Plymouth. She indicated her trunk leaning against the bottom step. 'If you help me, I believe we can get my trunk inside.'

They did, after some theatrical grunting on the butler's part. The trunk made it to the foot of the stairs, and the butler stopped. 'I'll get the maid of all work to help me in the morning, Miss Langley. Goodnight.'

With that, he wandered away, after blowing out the candle and leaving her in darkness. Jerusha sat on her trunk and laughed at the absurdity of her situation. In all their admonitions about sailors, her parents hadn't thought to warn her about antique butlers.

Jerusha tiptoed down the corridor, peering into rooms, until she found one with a promising sofa. A pillow from a wing-back chair met her approval. With a sigh, she took off her shoes, removed her overcoat and bonnet and lay down. She was asleep in moments.

I would give my left testicle for a good night's sleep, James Wilson thought, as he stared at his dark house.

Sound asleep inside was his housekeeper, Margaret Mc-Donald, widow of a bosun who had extracted a promise from his surgeon as he lay dying of an unidentified tropical fever. 'Take care of her, laddie,' his fellow Scot had demanded with his last breath.

True to his word, James found her in a rooming house in Plymouth, delivering both the news of her husband's death and his offer of employment as his housekeeper. She was as Scottish as he was. When she finished crying, she gave her shoulders a shake, packed her bags, and followed him to this little house.

Mags was a jewel and a wonder, and James had no regrets. Now, his sole aim was to get inside, upstairs, and in bed without waking the old lady. She was used to his weird hours, most of which he blamed on his profession. Only an idiot among the Stonehouse surgeons would ever have declared that he never got seasick, and sea duty suited him fine. His cheerful statement led to an epiphany among senior surgeons. As the most junior of surgeons currently working in the hospital, Jamie Wilson found himself sentenced to ship *and* shore duty, shuttling between the blockade and Stonehouse with medicine and patients.

He had to agree it was a good system before the Treaty of Amiens, which halted warfare and meant he had no sea duty. After the treaty broke in 1803, he resumed sailing with a messenger ship, going back and forth to the blockade to return any badly wounded back to Plymouth's naval hospital and deliver medicine.

Jamie would have been the first to admit that his was a thankless business, but better than letting the seriously wounded languish on the blockade. Because one badly wounded lieutenant required around-the-clock attention on the return trip, usually three to five days, depending, James couldn't remember when he had last put his head on a pillow.

He was tired beyond belief. After he found his bed, he lay awake only a few minutes, doing what he always did, because medicine was his calling. He thought back over a few thorny cases, analysed them, and wondered what he would do different.

The mattress felt good, but his mind refused to let him go.

Since he knew he would rise early, he let his mind wander to a small success, one that never failed to assure him that not all his patients died. He settled in to remember rescuing the vicar's daughter in Bolling, where his father had briefly clerked for a solicitor. He had rescued her from a duck-pond, pulling her out by her cloak and nearly strangling her in the process.

He set her on her feet, but not before extracting a promise that she would learn how to swim. He remembered her eyes, so big and blue, with a little mole beside the left one that acted like a directional sign pointing to those memorable eyes.

She nodded so solemnly, fixing those eyes on his with no hint of guile. 'I promise to learn,' she told him, then, 'Thank you for saving my life. You are my hero.'

James knew he was nobody's hero. That title belonged to the iron men of the blockade, who in all weather kept their wooden walls between Napoleon and invasion. It was a harmless memory that sent him into the arms of Morpheus more content with his lot.

And so he slept.

Chapter Five

'Lady Oakshott, I have only misplaced her temporarily. She is here somewhere.'

Through her sleepy fog, Jerusha recognised the voice. She squinted at the clock on the mantelpiece then opened her eyes wider. Half twelve? A glance out the window confirmed that she had managed a long slumber on a lumpy sofa.

She sat up and stretched, her bones protesting from a night spent…she looked around at shelves of books…in a library.

There are worse places, she thought, glad she had at least removed her bonnet, and happy there was likely no press gang roaming Finch Street, at least not in broad daylight.

She tried to smooth the wrinkles out of her travelling dress, and gave it up for a bad business, opening the door and peering out instead. 'Um, good morning, Lady Oakshott.'

When her aunt glared at her, Jerusha suspected it was not going to be a good visit. However, the glare modulated into something resembling a smile. 'Left to my own devices, Jerusha, I never go into the library.' She held out her hand to her niece, who didn't know whether to kiss it, shake it, or genuflect.

Jerusha attempted humour. 'You never would have found me then?'

Lady Oakshott cleared her throat in most impressive fashion. 'Not until a stench arose.'

Jerusha laughed, but her aunt frowned, opening the possi-

bility that Lady Oakshott did not possess a sense of humour. Napier managed a butler smile, which gave nothing away. When neither of them made a move, Jerusha cleared her throat. 'Aunt,' she began, and was frozen in place by a glance. 'I mean, Lady Oakshott, if someone would show me to a room, I can unpack and perhaps be ready for luncheon.'

'Abbie!' Lady Oakshott called. 'Tiresome girl, where are you?'

Silence, then the sound of someone running. 'Just dusting, my lady,' the girl said, out of breath. Jerusha thought she didn't look a day over eleven.

What sort of place is this? she asked herself, surprised. She remembered a much earlier visit to Oaklands when Sir Harvey was alive, when there were servants enough to trip over. Obviously, things had changed.

'Abbie, take Miss Langley upstairs to the blue room.' Lady Oakshott dragged out a timepiece from somewhere in her bosom. 'In thirty minutes, luncheon will be served in the breakfast room.' She left the room, sweeping out grandly, Jerusha thought, for someone in a nightgown and shawl. What a strange household.

Jerusha followed Abbie to the next floor, while Napier thumped her trunk up behind them, wheezing as he followed. She picked up the other handle on the trunk. 'This will be easier,' she assured the old man. 'Better still, just rest a moment until you feel like it.'

Abbie waited impatiently at the top of the stairs, or was it impatience? Jerusha took a closer look. *She's afraid*, she thought. 'My dear, tell me which room, if you need to be elsewhere.'

Abbie's eyes softened.

No one has ever called you 'my dear,' have they? Jerusha thought, as her heart softened, too.

'The blue room,' she announced, and opened a door.

Perhaps the wallpaper had been blue at one time, but everything had faded. The room smelled unused and somehow sad. 'I don't suppose anyone has lived here for a long time,' she said.

Abbie shrugged. 'I've never been in here. 'Course, I was raised at Oaklands.' She went to the window and after a struggle, raised the sash. 'Let's get some air. Smells like a wet dog in here.' The maid leaned on the windowsill. 'And lookee, you can see the ships.'

Jerusha saw more ships in the distance. 'My goodness. Is everyone at war?'

They stood in silence at the window until Abbie turned away. 'I have to help the cook now. You'll be all right?'

'A basin of water would be nice.'

The frightened look returned to Abbie's eyes. 'I… I don't have time.'

'Then don't worry,' Jerusha replied. 'I can see to that later.'

Abbie darted for the door. 'One moment,' Jerusha said. 'How many of you does my aunt employ?'

'There's old Napier, and René the cook, 'cept we are to call him a chef, Lady Oakshott's maid, and me.'

We have more servants in the vicarage, Jerusha thought, startled.

'You are a busy girl. Hurry on. I'll manage quite well here.'

Abbie pelted downstairs, gathering speed for a run down the hall. Abbie sat beside Napier until he recovered, then helped him get her trunk up the few remaining steps. She thanked him and closed the door, wondering why her aunt had left everyone else behind at Oaklands.

She went to the window again, looking out until the alarm bells in her brain stopped. Or did they? She leaned out a little farther, hearing real bells to the west, and wondered about them.

Her clothes quickly went on pegs in the dressing room that

needed a swipe with a duster. She knew a basin of water could wait. She shook out a simple muslin dress, tucked in her stray curls here and there, and took her own time down the stairs, observing dingy walls. The house was old and ill-used. Jerusha thought of Lady Oakshott's letter to Mama, something about improving the house to sell. Her aunt must have been here several months now, but nothing appeared to have happened.

The breakfast room was no grander than the blue room, with faded walls and the general sad air of a grand lady down on her luck. Still, no one could fault the menu of toast, shirred eggs, and bacon on the sideboard. She filled her plate and sat down, all under the watchful eye of Lady Oakshott, who sipped tea.

'You would have a trimmer figure if you didn't pile your plate so high,' her aunt commented, after another parsimonious sip.

'All I had yesterday was one apple.'

'One should always travel light.'

The eggs turned into boulders, Lady Oakshott eyeing every forkful. Jerusha thought better of that second strip of bacon and drank her tea instead, weak tea, as though the tea leaves had been used too many times.

I will starve here, she thought.

When she put her napkin beside the plate, Abbie whisked it away. When the door closed, only she and Lady Oakshott remained. Her aunt looked her over in silence. Jerusha felt her heart begin to fail her. Was conversation also rationed here? She cleared her throat, determined to maintain her equilibrium in the face of what looked like disapproval.

'Lady Oakshott, I'm delighted to be here,' she began, immediately recalling Papa's frequent sermons on the sin of prevarication. 'Your letter mentioned something about renovations here so you could sell this house?' Nothing. 'Wh-when are you planning to begin the work?'

'I have changed my mind,' her aunt said, then managed a laugh. 'Silly me, I have already let Oaklands for the summer to an enterprising man who smells of the shop, but who won't irritate my neighbours.'

'You've *rented out* Oaklands?' Jerusha asked in amazement. She met her aunt's gaze, prepared for a sharp reply. 'I mean… I suppose it is a big property to rattle around in, and this might be cosier, even if it is only Plymouth and…' She stopped, aware that she was babbling, but still, renting out an ancestral manor?

'Precisely,' Lady Oakshott said. 'I had intentions of doing as I said in the letter—by the way, your mother uses such poor stationery—but I am reconsidering.' She managed a laugh with no mirth in sight. 'Since I have let Oaklands, I will have to live here for the term of that lease. Such a bother, but there you are.'

'What…what am I to do for you here?' Jerusha asked, more curious than afraid. With its press gangs and general air of the commonplace, Plymouth did not seem to hold much attraction for a late baronet's widow. *Plymouth?*

'You strike me as the useful sort,' Lady Oakshott said. 'Biddable and quiet, so your mother describes you, and someone not unfamiliar with light housework.' She cleared her throat, as if to drive a point home. 'And you're not getting any younger.'

'That's true,' Jerusha said. 'I can polish silver with the best of them, even if I am an antique,' she joked, and regretted it.

Lady Oakshott merely raised her eyebrows at this feeble attempt at humour. 'We can include that in your duties, along with sweeping and tidying. The walls need washing in the entryway. Hopefully you can climb a ladder without getting dizzy. The walls should probably be attended to first. Did you bring along an apron or two?'

'No, Lady Oakshott, I did not,' Jerusha replied. She remembered overheard conversations about turning into a lady's companion for her aunt.

Am I to be a common servant, too? she thought.

'There should be aprons in the pantry.' She rose, and glared at Jerusha until she stood up. With a nod, Lady Oakshott made her stately exit, pausing in the doorway. 'It's nothing onerous, niece. I am preparing you for a life of service to others.'

Aren't I the lucky one? Jerusha thought, angry, but at whom?

She reminded herself that she was twenty-five, without a dowry or prospects. But in what universe was a lady's companion also a drudge?

Her cheery nature attempted a recovery with the thought, *We can laugh about this when summer's over and I am home.* Still…

She looked up from her contemplation of her hands at a scratching on the door. 'Yes?'

Abbie opened it, carrying an apron over her arm. 'Lady Oakshott says you are to begin with me right now in the sitting room.'

'Certainly,' Jerusha replied, amused at what had to be a little mistake on her aunt's part. Imagine what Mama would say to all this. 'I am puzzled about something.'

'Yes, miss?'

'Abbie, you told me there are four servants here—you, Napier, and René the chef, and Lady Oakshott's maid. When am I to meet *her*?'

It was Abbie's turn to stare at her. 'Lady Oakshott meant you.'

Chapter Six

Lady Oakshott most certainly did mean her, a matter made amply clear, as March passed into April. Jerusha vacillated between asking her aunt when she might learn about being a lady's companion and whining to Mama. She knew she could have whined, but something odd happened: Working for Lady Oakshott came with a measure of freedom she hadn't reckoned on. She liked it.

Jerusha knew this was better than whining to Mama. Besides, she knew how to clean a room within an inch of its life.

She was ready to at least masquerade as a maid. A long moment staring into the mirror in the shabby blue room made her look deep into her own eyes and acknowledge that there wouldn't ever be a husband, and certainly not a surprise inheritance from an unknown relative to allow her any independence. Whatever tiny pittance might have tempted a would-be suitor was gone with the purchase of her brother's commission.

Jerusha reconciled herself to the prospect of eventually turning herself into a lady's companion. She would have a home, and it was a genteel occupation. She never had been one to put herself forward, so blending into the background posed no difficulties. Why, in no time at all, she would turn into wallpaper. *That* thought made her look away from the mirror.

As she dusted and cleaned that first afternoon, she resolved upon the truth, with variations as needed. Abbie was gullible enough to believe a slightly manufactured tale of an impov-

erished relative of Lady O, even though Mama would never see herself in such a light.

'It's this way, Abbie,' she said, as they polished the fireplace attachments. 'Lady Oakshott will eventually find me a situation as a companion someday. In the meantime, it never hurts to make things tidy.'

'You don't really mind this sort of work?' Abbie asked, sounding dubious. 'I mean, a lady's companion would never have to do *this*.'

'I don't mind cleaning,' she replied, thinking of floors she had mopped, and corners dusted in homes of the deserving poor of Papa's parish. 'I've had plenty of practice…uh…working in a vicarage. It's our Christian duty to be of service.'

'Hmm,' was all Abbie contributed. 'If you say so.'

'I do,' Jerusha said, and it was no lie. Yes, she was under another's thumb, but she was free from the tyranny of a complacent parish with judgemental ladies who pitied their vicar's unmarried daughter. 'Things change. Just wait.' Maybe they would, maybe they wouldn't. There was no harm in hoping.

Her only hesitation came on that first supper below stairs. Heaven knows she had been below stairs in the vicarage, but never to actually eat with servants. Two deep breaths and down she went. There they were, waiting for her—Napier, the antique butler; René, the chef whom she had yet to meet; and Abbie. Obviously, Abbie's duties included the kitchen, as well as everything else. Napier nodded, René winked, and Abbie shyly passed her the potatoes.

Napier introduced René des Champs. 'He cooks very well and he hates Napoleon.'

René bowed from where he sat. 'Mademoiselle Langley, you are welcome to this household.'

René sounded no more French than she did. 'Thank you. Umm…'

René looked at Napier and shrugged, then both men chuck-

led. René leaned forward with a smile in his eyes. 'I am no more French than you are, but Lady Oakshott doesn't know that.' He smoothed his eyebrows. '*Mademoiselle*, I can put on zee accent as required, and *allons*, it got me a job.'

Jerusha laughed.

'I trust you will overlook our various eccentricities.'

'If you will overlook mine,' she replied, which made Napier nod and look heavenward.

What sort of place is this? she asked herself again.

They ate in silence, then Napier cleared his throat. 'Miss Langley, Lady Oakshott assured us that you are a useful sort.'

'All my life,' she said cheerfully.

'We haven't too many rules.' He held up one finger. 'First, the cardinal rule: There will be no noise of a housecleaning nature before twelve of the clock. Lady Oakshott rises at noon. She is adamant about this and there are no exceptions.'

Jerusha wanted to ask that if someone broke that rule, did it mean the rack or drawing and quartering, but she prudently didn't. Napier seemed entirely serious.

'Lady Oakshott specifically wants you to attend to her in the evenings in the sitting room.' When his lips twitched, Jerusha suddenly realised she might like her social descent into the bowels of number twenty-eight Finch Street, where people at least had a sense of humour, unlike upstairs. 'She likes to play Patience and she cheats.'

René rolled his eyes in most Gallic fashion, and Abbie laughed. 'Sir, perhaps this is part of training me to be a lady's companion someday,' Jerusha said calmly, wincing only a little at that social descent.

Napier continued his list of dos and don'ts. He gave her a kindly look, which seemed like permission to ask her own question. Why not? The worst that could happen would probably be a sorrowful headshake from Napier, who had obvi-

ously had years of experience as a butler, assuredly in grander homes than this.

'Why is Lady Oakshott so intent on maintaining the sitting room impeccably and the entryway, when other rooms need more attention?' Jerusha asked. 'I heard from…a source that she plans to sell this house. Shouldn't she be employing restorationists?'

'It is not our position to divine Lady Oakshott's intentions,' Napier replied. He said it kindly, which barely embarrassed her. My, but he had a knack.

René was another matter. Perhaps Lady Oakshott didn't pay him enough. He gave the butler a glance, and her, his attention. 'Shall we say, Lady Oakshott is working herself into the good graces of the local grand dames, such as there are in a navy town. She wants the sitting room to look up to the mark, and the foyer, certainly.' He looked around at what Jerusha suspected were already co-conspirators. 'We planted flowers in the front after dark a few weeks ago. Can't have the neighbours thinking she cannot afford a gardener.'

'Oh.' Jerusha could think of nothing more profound than that. 'Frugal zinnias?'

Everyone laughed, and Jerusha knew she was now a co-conspirator, too.

She reminded herself that her tenure here would likely be for the summer only, but then what? And if her aunt needed a lady's companion, or even a maid, Jerusha didn't have a better plan.

The thought stayed with her as she and Abbie cleaned and polished. By unspoken consent, it became her duty to deliver her aunt's breakfast to her promptly at noon and listen without comment to her various complaints. Jerusha delivered mail then, too. She noticed bills from tradesmen, but Aunt Hortensia usually brushed those aside and pounced on invitations to take tea.

She waved those at Jerusha in triumph, when they came. 'See there, I had feared that once Sir Harvey shuffled off his mortal coil I might be forgotten, because we did not spend much time in Plymouth—Lord, these people are common—but such is not the case.' If there were no invitations, she made herself comfortable in the sitting room, waiting for visitors to materialise, which they often did not.

It wasn't the sort of news she thought Mama would like in her weekly letter to the vicarage. She reasoned that Mama would also not care for what else she discovered she was enjoying: going to the market in the Barbican with René and Abbie.

She had not thought she would ever be in a market by the docks with a basket on her arm, haggling over the price of potatoes, but there she was, triumphant over five pounds of potatoes, with three leeks thrown in because she smiled at the vendor.

Her delight was overshadowed by the clanging of the bell she had noticed earlier. 'René, what is that?' she asked, after he paid the vendor.

'War against an evil man,' he said. He pointed west. 'Stonehouse is a few miles that way in Devonport, a hospital for Royal Navy and Marines. When ships make their way to Stonehouse Creek with their wounded, the bells summon the surgeons.'

'Ha…have you ever been there to see it?' she asked.

'Once.' He looked out to sea. 'It is a terrible sight.'

She looked around the market—the women bargained for chickens, teased the grocers, asked for samples—and wondered how easy it was, even in Plymouth, to see nothing of war, and only hear distant bells.

She thought of Jamie Wilson and wondered where he was, on what ocean he sailed. She stood still, her hand on an onion, and wondered if he even lived. 'René, do you think that someday there will be a way for people to know where friends and families are by…oh, it would take a magic potion.'

'You're missing someone?' he asked, taking the onion from her and adding two more to his basket.

'Not really,' she admitted. 'I owe someone an apology. That is all.'

'Hopefully he has long since forgotten and you needn't fret.'

'*I* didn't forget.'

Chapter Seven

Lady Oakshott could never be accused of patience. Mama had told Jerusha of times when her older sister would threaten to hold her breath until she exploded, if she did not get her way. Jerusha noticed how her servants tiptoed around her when she sat and stared with a certain steely-eyed calm they found unnerving.

Apparently, Lady Oakshott could not manage without attention. When day after day passed with no invitations, her aunt began to snap at Abbie over trivialities or glare at Jerusha and demand to know if she were hiding the mail.

It's only for a summer, Jerusha reminded herself, even as she wondered about that. Did Mama tell her she could come home in autumn, or was that merely something Jerusha hoped? Ah well. She could clean the house to a fare thee well, and ready it for the time when the mouldering old place actually went on sale, once the lease on Oaklands concluded.

She and Abbie had advanced beyond the sitting room to the dining room and the tedious task of polishing chairs that had not seen linseed oil in years. The long-neglected wood soaked it up like thirsty mariners abandoned in lifeboats to float for months at sea.

She had come to appreciate Abbie's nearly constant good cheer, and even more, her tenacity. As they scrubbed and polished, the little maid told Jerusha about running away from a

workhouse at age eight, wandering the streets in Plymouth, then curling up on the doorstep at number twenty-eight Finch Street because she was tired.

'Mr Napier found me, and I stayed,' she said simply. 'Pass the linseed oil.'

God forgive me when I whine, Jerusha thought.

'Here you go.'

When the post delivered the mail this morning, Jerusha set it beside the breakfast tray after a glance. There were the usual bills, which would likely join the pile of bills beside Lady O's bed, ignored, and two cream-coloured envelopes that looked like invitations. That should sweeten up the old rip.

She carried breakfast and letters upstairs at precisely noon, let herself into the darkened room, and pulled back the draperies on a lovely Plymouth morning. She knew better than to speak. Everyone knew to tread lightly before that first cup of tea.

Such a tyrant, Jerusha thought, as she closed the door. *If I am ever an actual lady's companion, I pray it will not be for someone like my aunt.*

She was down the stairs, heading for linseed oil and dining room chairs when she heard a mighty shriek, loud enough to stir Napier from tidying the already immaculate, if shabby, foyer, ready for visitors who seldom materialised.

Fearful, Jerusha took the stairs two at a time. To her enormous relief, she opened the door on Aunt Hortensia with a huge smile, fanning herself with one of those cream-coloured envelopes. To her further astonishment, her aunt patted the bed in an invitation for her to sit, a liberty Jerusha couldn't imagine.

'What on earth, Lady Oakshott,' she managed. 'You frightened me, but you look…'

'…over the moon,' her aunt supplied. She clutched the letter to her breast and looked heavenward for a moment. 'I have

arrived, Jerusha. Finally.' She patted the bed. 'Sit. Who knew that war could lead to something so good for me?'

Horrors, Jerusha thought. Was war something to send any-one into ecstasies of delight?

'Admiral Stoppard's wife is organising us to take comfort baskets of food and special treats to wounded officers at Stone-house,' Aunt Hortensia said, barely able to contain her glee. 'I am numbered among them!'

'Such an honour,' Jerusha murmured. 'But don't the offi-cers already receive the best of everything? What about the ordinary seamen?'

Aunt Hortensia fixed her with a steely-eyed glare that Abbie said made her want to void. Jerusha tried to maintain the neu-tral face she had been nurturing in the past few weeks under her aunt's thumb. She must not have succeeded.

'You are an idiot,' her aunt said. 'It is the *officers* who mat-ter to an admiral's wife.' She shoved the letter towards Jeru-sha. 'Here is a list of items for a basket. Assemble it and take it to Stonehouse.'

'Me?' Jerusha asked, surprised. 'The honour is yours, Lady Oakshott.'

'The credit is mine, my dear slow-top, the credit,' her aunt said. 'Mrs Admiral Stoppard writes here that servants are to deliver the baskets.' She jabbed her finger at the beautiful script. 'She wrote this: "I won't have you frighten yourself, dear Lady Oakshott, so do appoint a servant."' She turned kindly eyes on Jerusha now, the look someone would give the mentally deficient. 'You will take it. Here is the list. There must be a basket around here somewhere.'

There was, a dusty one in the pantry that smelled of smoked oysters, which Napier set Abbie to cleaning. René took the list with a straight face. 'Calf's foot jelly, a bottle of spirits, tea, slippers, cod liver oil'—the chef made a face—'sweets, an

improving work by a distinguished author, comb and brush. Useless.'

'I brought along Shakespeare's sonnets,' Jerusha said.

Napier found an even dustier bottle of smuggler's sherry in the nearly depleted wine cellar and sent Jerusha with a pound note to the apothecary for cod's liver oil and calf's foot jelly. René shook his head over the whole thing and said he would bake macarons. 'Men who are wounded surely deserve something better than what is on this list,' he told Jerusha as she left. 'They will be boxed and ready tomorrow morning, or my name isn't René.' He laughed. 'Which it isn't!'

She stood a long moment on the front step, aware, even if the others weren't, that this was her first unaccompanied trip to the markets. She savoured the moment, choosing not to dread it. She didn't feel the same disquiet that followed her below stairs with the servants for that first meal, or the mop and bucket in the sitting room, or linseed oil to tackle the dining room chairs.

This was different. In her heart, this was no descent. She was walking independently somewhere by herself, something thousands did every day. She could dawdle if she chose, even flirt with the tradesmen or sit in the sun with nothing more in mind than enjoying the day. If there was a penny or two to spare, she could buy a sweet or hand the penny to a beggar. No one would scold her or give her that patient look destined to keep her biddable and obedient. Those days were done, and she seized the moment for what it was: liberation.

As she came closer to the Barbican, that warren of narrow, crooked streets familiar to many a mariner since Alfred the Great, for all she knew, Jerusha realised she had no plans to do other than what she was here for.

You are a dull dog indeed, she scolded herself as she opened the door to the apothecary and the bell tinkled.

The thought had made her smile, which meant the apoth-

ecary had a smile for her, too. She placed her little order, and he delivered it. Only a few months ago, that would have been that. Things were different now. She told him what it was for, which made him nod and add another jar of calf's foot jelly, think a moment, then stick in a package of throat lozenges.

'On the house,' he said with a grand gesture, which made Jerusha laugh.

'Thank you, sir. Lady Oakshott says it is for officers at Stonehouse.'

The apothecary shook his head. 'Lass, they're fawned over enough by the uppity ups. Take it to Block Three or Four, where the ordinary seamen are.'

'I'd like to, but I have my orders,' Jerusha told him.

He winked at her. 'Lady Oakshit…'

'Oakshott,' she corrected, determined not to go into whoops over that.

'Oakshit… Oakshott… She'll never know.'

He looked out the shop window, seeing something far distant, which made Jerusha wonder if he had served his own rough apprenticeship at sea in some long-ago war. 'Aye, miss, now that the treaty's broke, we'll be hearing that bell day and night.'

'Ships fighting in the Channel?' she asked.

'Everywhere. The sea can be cruel, and not as forgiving as land battles.'

She took that thought home and below stairs, where René was already working his magic with macarons, explaining to Abbie—standing by his elbow, her concentration fierce— how critical the right temperature was in the oven. Jerusha breathed in the fragrance, thinking of all the years when she had no idea just how divine a kitchen could smell.

The macarons were boxed and ready to go in the morning, long before Lady Oakshott was up. Napier appointed himself her escort. 'You've never been to Devonport, and there are all

those sailors,' he said firmly, as if he saw a scoundrel behind every coil of rope.

The hackney took them past rows of houses, then warehouses, and a long building the butler identified as a rope-walk, then dry docks and ships half built. The area buzzed with the commerce of war. Jerusha looked down at the basket, wondering how something as silly as calf's foot jelly and throat lozenges would appear to the surgeons and physicians at Stonehouse.

'This is a fool's errand, isn't it?' she asked.

'Lady Oakshott and her friends don't see it that way,' he replied. 'There is no harm in wanting to do something.'

She nodded, unsatisfied with his answer. She thought of her useful years in Papa's parish, and wondered at the baskets she had delivered there. 'I would like to do more,' she said, but softly, not certain Napier would understand.

The jarvey let them out in front of a massive series of buildings, individual blocks forming a courtyard around a park with trees and benches. Her heart sank with the realisation that such a hospital was needed, as Napoleon continued to rage on the continent and the waters around their island.

'I wish I knew where to go,' she whispered to Napier.

As she stared, she noticed a middle building at the top of the courtyard with a more elaborate entrance. 'Let us start there,' she said.

Between them, they carried the heavy basket towards what she hoped was the administration building. Napier began to flag, so they stopped several times. Finally, he gave up and sat down on one of the benches for convalescents, some of whom sat here and there on other benches.

She left him with the basket. 'I'll find someone to take this…this thing,' she said, happy to abandon the basket that seemed to grow larger and heavier and more ridiculous by the moment.

She wasted no time hurrying up the steps and opening the door to stand in a hall with many doors. *Now what?* she asked herself. Maybe she could leave the basket on the lawn like an old, abandoned dog. She could stow away on a ship and move to America.

'Jerusha Langley, you are an idiot,' she whispered under her breath. 'This is not the wicked stage, and you are not emoting in a melodrama.' She stood there and took another deep breath.

Or I can knock on a door until I find someone willing to help me.

She walked down the hall, peering in open doors at men in uniform writing or talking to other men. No one looked up when she passed. Everyone was busy. She reminded herself there was a war on.

She passed another door and paused a moment. Two men in uniform stood with their backs to her. She heard a Scottish accent and smiled, remembering another accent like that years ago. One of the men turned part-way around and she hurried on.

When she was halfway through the width of the building, she saw a man sitting behind a higher desk. Perhaps he was an information clerk. She couldn't be the only one who ever got lost in a place this huge.

He looked up when she came closer, but seemed to be looking beyond her. In another moment she heard behind her, 'Miss Langley, did you ever learn to swim?'

Chapter Eight

It was only the briefest of glimpses, a woman in a dark dress and plain bonnet, but there was something about her. James Wilson couldn't have explained to a jury why that glimpse captured him, especially since he was wrangling with the purser over how much calomel and catgut a surgeon needed. The man had no imagination and he had never been to sea.

Still, the rustle of skirts caught his ear and he turned instinctively. He quickly turned back to the business at hand, which he knew he was losing. Too bad that a surgeon was not allowed to be a purser. There would be no question about what drugs and splints and bandages a surgeon needed when he shipped out on a water hoy or Fast Dispatch Vessel to take water or messages from ship to ship on the blockade, plus a surgeon was used to emergencies.

It was a strange duty, but he enjoyed it. He loved the sea and was never seasick. He liked patch-up surgery because he was a problem-solver from childhood. He also knew unerringly when a wounded man needed a hospital, and fast. So far, there was always a sloop carrying messages back to Portsmouth or Plymouth, which meant faster travel. There was also a satellite hospital at Gibraltar, if these were Mediterranean casualties. Most larger ships of the line had a surgeon, but sometimes needed more help.

Some of the wounded men died. Others survived with bet-

ter care in a hospital and not a ship's sickbay. The odds were in no one's favour, but James trusted to chance and faith in a God who had no use for Napoleon, or so he reasoned, in his logical, Scots way.

'I'll be back, sir,' he told the purser, who gave him a gallows smile. 'Another matter calls me.'

But why this? He watched the woman walk towards the clerk at the end of the hall, who spent his days fielding questions about who was where in this enormous hospital dwarfed only by the larger one in Portsmouth.

He knew he was right as he watched her gait. She was quick of step, but some oddity at birth must have rendered her right leg slightly longer than her left leg, creating a barely noticeable limp. He was aware of it because years ago he dragged her out of a pond when she was much younger, and he noticed the hesitancy of her gait on land when he walked her home.

'What in the world are you doing here?' he asked under his breath. He followed her and stopped once. If he was wrong, he was going to make a complete fool of himself. In the greater scheme of things, that wasn't so awful and wouldn't be the first time. She'd likely tell him what she thought, and he would go back to the purser's office to fight a little more for supplies. The woman would never see James Wilson again, and she could go about her business wondering about cheeky Royal Navy men.

He paused behind her, searching for the best approach. Nothing witty or debonair came to mind, so he cleared his throat and took a chance.

'Miss Langley, did you ever learn to swim?'

He was right. She gasped and turned around, reminding him all over again why he remembered her: With those big blue eyes, she was even lovelier now than soaking wet, nine years old, and yanked out of a boggy pond.

What to say now? Make a joke. He staggered back and put his hand to his heart. 'I was right. Miss Langley, how are you?'

To his complete and total amazement, she started to cry. If he hadn't been a surgeon, he probably would have turned and run. After years of fraught events and people falling apart in front of him, he knew better. He gently took her by the shoulders. 'Miss Langley, I hope I didn't frighten you. Do you remember me?'

She nodded and her tears flowed. He whipped out his handkerchief and gave it to her. She held it to her face while he admired her dark hair.

He led her to a bench away from the clerk, who watched this whole exchange with rapt astonishment. A door had opened across the hall. When he frowned and shook his head, it closed.

He let her cry, because there wasn't anything else he could do. He knew she would dry up eventually. When she did, she blew her nose, tried to find a dry spot, and dabbed at her eyes. He took out another handkerchief. She smiled at that.

'Two?'

He reached inside his uniform coat for a third, and she managed another watery smile.

'It's a medical thing, Miss Langley. Why the tears? I didn't mean to frighten you.'

She took a few deep breaths, which meant he had to admire her bosom just a little. 'Jamie Wilson,' she said, and he heard all the wonder. 'I doubt anyone calls you Jamie now.'

'James,' he said. 'What are the odds I would ever see you again, and here in this place?'

'Miniscule, I am certain,' she said. 'For fifteen years at least, I have wanted to apologise to you.'

He heard all the uncertainty and shame. 'Why?'

'I know I was responsible… It was my fault your father was fired from that odious squire's employment.'

She said this in a low voice, her head down, as if she were remembering the whole event. He remembered the matter much differently.

'Nae, lass,' he said in his best Scots accent. 'Nae.'

'I told my father what you said about teaching me to swim, and he carried the tale to the squire.'

'Everyone should know how to swim,' he told her. 'I would give the same advice to you today.'

'Papa told me the squire got all indignant, called you a bad name, and swore to be rid of the Wilsons.'

Your father told you all that? James thought, startled. *How unkind to push the blame onto your shoulders.*

He remembered the squire's visit to their cottage. The man pointed his finger at James and declared, 'Your son is a menace!' Then the awful man had noticed Jamie's twin, Dougie, who did like a little mischief. '*Both* your wretched sons!'

The story *he* told was of a no-good youth leering at a young girl and telling her he could teach her to swim, but she'd have to take off her clothes. James shook his head at the memory. He tried to explain to the squire that he told Jerusha she would have to remove her coat for a swimming lesson. That was all.

As he looked at the pretty Miss Langley, who regarded him with shame in her eyes, he knew she wasn't someone he ever wanted to lie to, not then, not now, not ever. 'The squire accused me of wanting to take liberties with you and he sacked my father on the spot.'

'All you did was yank me out of a duck-pond and tell me I should learn to swim,' she said. 'I am so sorry it came to that. I truly am.'

'I hate to think that you fretted about the matter for fifteen years,' he said. 'Here's the irony: My father was heartily tired of the squire. He had been in correspondence with a laird in the Highlands, who offered him a position as steward. Da was composing a letter of resignation to the squire when he burst

into our house.' He touched her cheek—couldn't help himself. 'We were gone in a week, and never looked back. You stewed about this for naught, dear lady.'

'Surgeon Wilson!'

James glanced towards the office he had left. 'Duty calls. Follow me?'

You either will or won't, he reasoned. *Please do.*

To his delight, she came with him. He wanted to ask her if she was looking for her husband. She was of an age to have one of those, and with such a lovely face, there must be someone in Stonehouse—damn the man—eager to see her. Perhaps an officer. But no, she had answered to Miss Langley. Not that it was his business, but here she was, hurrying to keep up with him. He slowed his steps, remembering that he was not due to sail for another week.

'Wait here, please,' he said, pointing to a bench outside the purser's office. 'I must do battle with the thief and rascal who controls the supplies.'

She smiled at that. 'Both of my parents warned me about the Royal Navy.'

'And here you are? You had better explain yourself, Miss Langley.'

He went into the office, ready to surrender and sign anything, if she would still be waiting on the bench when he finished. To his amazement, the purser declared, 'You win. Take the additional laudanum and silver nitrate. I'd rather lose my soul than argue another minute with a Scot.'

Pursers have no souls, James thought, but he did not say it.

He signed everywhere indicated and told the purser's mate to box the medicine and deliver it to Number Eight Quarters within the hour. His housekeeper, Mags McDonald, would stow it with the other supplies destined for the blockade when he sailed again. He had five days.

To do what? he asked himself.

He had no idea, really, beyond the pleasure of seeing a half-forgotten face in an unexpected place. He was far too busy to be lonely, wasn't he?

Well, wasn't he?

Chapter Nine

Jerusha knew it wasn't too late to hurry outside where Napier waited. She glanced inside the office, thinking for a moment that this was impossible. No, there Jamie stood, leaning over to sign some papers. She reminded herself that fifteen years had passed, and she didn't know a thing about *this* James Wilson.

She looked again. He was taller, certainly, and well built in that way of solid men. Capability came to mind, which was the one thing that she remembered from her childhood. He had just waded in and plucked her out of the duck-pond. He didn't waste a moment. No surprise to her that he was a surgeon.

I daren't waste his time, she thought. *I'll leave now.*

She couldn't. She waited, for what she couldn't say, but she couldn't leave. A few minutes would catch her up on his life. She could answer any questions he had, and that would be that.

'I'm glad you didn't run away,' Jamie said.

Startled, she looked up from an in-depth study of her hands. He had a satchel slung over one shoulder, which he pulled aside when he sat. She didn't move over to give him more room. She smiled to see freckles still on his nose, that brand of a Scot.

'I wasn't going to run away,' she told him. 'Do you remember Mrs Pingree? She was the vicarage cook.'

'Aye, she and me mum stayed in touch for a few years. Alas, Mum died four years ago. Is Mrs Pingree still there?'

'She is. Years ago, Mrs Pingree told me she thought you

were the twin who had joined the Royal Navy at thirteen years of age. She heard you were a surgeon's mate.'

'I passed my exams and orals four years ago, and I am a surgeon now.' He touched the caduceus outlined in green on his collar. 'How is it that you are here?'

She remembered Napier and stood up. 'It's a long story, but right now I need to rescue an old gentleman.'

'Did he fall into a duck-pond?'

She laughed and felt immeasurably better. 'No! He is a butler for Lady Oakshott, who is my mother's sister.'

He raised his eyebrows. 'I thought you were a vicar's daughter.'

'I am. My aunt married well.' She reconsidered and settled on the truth. 'I doubt *I* would have chosen an older man with bad breath and of staunch opinion, but she likes being called Lady Oakshott.'

He smiled at that. 'Let's find this butler. I'd like to know why *you* are here.'

Napier sat where she had left him. He was far enough away, giving her time to explain Plymouth. She didn't know why Jamie got a little tight about the mouth when she told him she was working as a maid for her aunt who insisted upon being addressed as Lady Oakshott.

He seemed equally unhappy that her mother considered her stay in Plymouth as good experience for a lady's companion, which was likely her fate, since no suitors ever came 'round. He opened his mouth to make a comment, then closed it, so she didn't have to explain her lack of dowry and embarrass them both.

She almost hated for the meander to end, but here was Napier. She introduced him and knew it was time to explain the basket. Since the whole business seemed faintly silly to her, she couldn't imagine how silly it must sound to someone who actually treated grievous wounds with items beyond cod's liver oil and throat lozenges.

'We are here to deliver a basket for poor, suffering officers. An admiral's wife engineered this scheme. My aunt is trying to work her way into Plymouth social circles before she sells the house where we are staying now.' Oh, dear, that was blunt.

'May I?'

She nodded. He lifted the cloth and chuckled. 'Looks harmless enough.'

'Will it do anyone any good?'

'My, but you go to the heart of a subject, don't you?'

She felt her face grow red. 'P'raps I am as opinionated as Lady Oakshott's late husband.'

'There's no harm in having an opinion. What this will do is cheer someone to know that his country cares about him. Would you consider taking it to one of the enlisted men's buildings? Mine, perhaps?'

'I would, but Lady Oakshott would not.'

Jerusha was certain her statement would create a sudden chasm between them, hers of gentle breeding and his, son of a steward. She decided to speak her mind. 'I would prefer that, too, but you of all people know that orders are orders.'

'Aye, miss.' He picked up the basket. 'On the condition that I drop it at Block One, then you come with me to Block Four, and see my bailiwick, at least when I am not at sea. Napier, would you care to join us?'

Please don't, Napier, Jerusha thought. *I want to walk with Jamie Wilson one more time when I'm not soaking wet and nine years old.*

Are prayers ever answered? As the child of a vicar, she hoped and was rewarded. 'I will enjoy remaining here, Jerusha,' Napier replied. 'There is a pleasant breeze and no one needs me.'

'I'll bring her back soon, Napier, and hail you a hackney,' Jamie promised.

They started across the quadrangle, Jerusha suddenly feel-

ing too shy to do more than enjoy the lifting of fifteen years of guilt. It was a slow walk, one that included a stop where one convalescent with a leg *in absentia* sat in a wheeled chair, and another man with a bandaged eye was seated on a bench.

Jamie introduced her most properly. 'This is an acquaintance of mine from years gone by,' he told the men, then lifted the bandage on the partly absent leg. 'Looking good, Barlow. If we fit you with a peg leg, d'ye think ye might like to spend some time with the apothecary, learning a different trade?'

'Could I?' he asked. Jerusha heard the hope, and it touched her.

'Why not? You can fight Boney medicinally. I do.' Jamie glanced at Jerusha. 'It had to be medicine for me, Barlow. Firing your big guns would give me the shudders. That's why I cower on the orlop deck and take off legs.' His patient grinned.

'And me, sir?' the one-eyed patient asked. 'Is there something?'

'We'll find something,' Jamie assured him. 'I know you read, write, and cipher. If we put you with a purser, you can check *his* mathematics and keep him honest.'

The one-eyed man laughed. 'Really?'

'All it takes is one eye. You'd be rendering the Royal Navy a real favour. I'll do what I can.'

'I know you will.' The man looked at Jerusha, then back at Jamie. 'Is she your bonnie lassie?'

'Your imagination's runnin' away wi' ye,' Jamie said. He looked unperturbed, when all Jerusha could manage was to look away, her face flaming again. Did *nothing* disturb his goodwill? Then he compounded the felony. 'I dragged her out a duck-pond when she was a wee lass, and she's finally come to Plymouth to thank me.'

The one-legged patient threw back his head and laughed. 'Aye, miss, but the surgeon has a quip for everything.'

It was another one of those moments. Jerusha knew pro-

priety suggested she return some wooden answer. She was a genteel lady, after all. She chose another path again. 'Between you and me, he lays it on a bit thick with his Scottish trowel, doesn't he?'

The patient gave her a little salute. 'Right so, miss, right so.'

They walked to a three-storey building with Block One over the entrance. 'Wait here,' he told her.

He returned minus the basket, good cheer still written all over his expressive face. 'Have you a moment for Block Four?'

'Certainly. I don't precisely understand what you do,' Jerusha said. 'You tell me you are at sea, and now we are going to Block Four.'

'I do both. As I mentioned, we are again blockading all ports in France. This means warships sailing back and forth just out of the reach of their shore batteries. The Frogs' ships are bottled up and they watch for a change of wind and our inattention to break free. It is tedious for us, and that makes it dangerous, because crews get careless.'

'These ships have surgeons, I assume,' Jerusha said. 'Then why…'

'It's a new idea, tried first at Haslar Hospital in Portsmouth. The smaller ships of war and some bomb kedges don't have surgeons. My sea duty is to travel with what is called an FDV, a Fast Dispatch Vessel, which takes messages from Admiralty to the fleet. I go along to deliver medicine and see to any emergencies.'

'Goodness.' She stopped. 'Does this sort of duty ever frighten you?'

'Always,' he said. 'I never know what to expect. Sometimes I can save a life, sometimes I can transport a grievously wounded man to a ship of the line with a surgeon, and sometimes I chance a return to England with a patient.'

How can you look so good-natured? she asked herself.

'How do you…?'

'Miss Langley, I love my profession and I love my country. Well, Scotland, and I suffer you English.'

She couldn't help her laughter. It ended when they walked up the steps into Block Four. She sniffed the odour of strong carbolic and washing soap, but it wasn't powerful enough to mask the rot underneath. She put her fingers to her nose and hesitated at the door. Jamie reached in his pocket and handed her a small jar.

'It's camphor. Dab a little under your nose. It helps.'

She did as he said, blinking at the equally strong disinfectant.

'Better?'

She nodded. She followed him up to the first floor. 'Jonathan Kidwell is chief surgeon in this block,' he said. 'I make it about one and a half when I am here. There are hospital stewards, one to a floor, plus a matron. Here we are.'

He opened the door on rows of iron bedsteads. All eyes turned towards them, even the bandaged ones. Jerusha pressed her lips tight to keep from bursting into tears.

Then an astonishing thing happened, something that made her take Jamie Wilson's hand like the commonest woman in Plymouth. They whistled at her. 'Three cheers!' someone shouted, and huzzahs rang out.

The surgeon squeezed her hand. 'You are an instant success, Miss Jerusha Langley,' he said quietly. 'Above and beyond throat lozenges for officers, will you come here and do some real good?' He leaned closer until his lips nearly brushed her ear. 'Um…perhaps this is how you pay me back for saving your life in that duck-pond.'

Chapter Ten

It was a quiet ride home in the hackney with Napier, until the butler's curiosity got the better of him. 'Miss Langley, kindly tell me what is going on.'

Oh, you mean when our heads were close together? she thought, wondering how an obedient, biddable young lady could for even one second consider James Wilson's suggestion.

'Nothing of consequence, Napier,' she lied, then regretted her lie immediately. As she saw the disappointment in his eyes, it occurred to her forcefully that servants, and she must remember to include herself, had so little to look forward to. Life with Lady Oakshott was nothing but dull.

There may have been a time when Sir Harvey Oakshott was still alive and there were parties, but those times were over. Lady Oakshott, always imperious, seemed oddly adrift. If she had an ally, it might be Napier.

Either trust him or don't, Jerusha told herself, and took a leap of faith.

'Napier, James Wilson asked if I would come to Block Four several times a week and write letters for his patients,' she said. 'Some are blind, some are illiterate, and others have missing hands. He...he said it would do them no end of good.'

'Lady Oakshott would never allow it.'

Jerusha knew that already. As she listened to the patient clop clopping of the horse, she asked herself how long it would

take until she became like the horse, calmly plodding along the same roads until it died in harness.

Which is it to be, Jerusha? she asked herself. *You have only one life.*

That was her answer. 'Napier, I believe I will take the chance.'

She waited for him to object, but he did not. 'There was a time after I entered service for Sir Harvey Oakshott's that I thought I might take the King's Shilling,' he told her. 'There were wars in Germany, and I wanted excitement.'

'You, Napier?' she asked, then reminded herself that he wasn't always old.

'I was ready to run away from Oaklands.' He sighed, and she heard the regret. 'I lost my nerve, stayed, and here I am.'

Jerusha wanted to tell him that he probably made the prudent choice, and look, he was a butler, but she couldn't. 'This might not end well for me,' she said. 'I doubt Lady Oakshott will approve.'

The butler shrugged and turned his attention to the view. When the jarvey tugged back on the reins and spoke softly to his horse in front of number twenty-eight Finch Street, Napier helped her from the hackney and paid the man. They spoke for a few minutes and the butler indicated she come close.

'Jerusha, this is Jake O'Toole. He promised me that he will be here tomorrow morning at seven of the clock. He will also be at the head of the quadrangle at ten of the clock.' He noticed her hesitation. 'I will pay your fare until we at least decide if this is the course you wish to follow.'

'Oh, but…' she began.

He shook his head with a smile. 'If you don't take a chance, you will end up like me.'

Tears rose in her eyes. This kind man she barely knew was going to do something bold for her. The least she could do was match his kindness with courage. 'If I end up like you, Mr Napier, I will be a kind person.'

'You already are.' He stepped back. 'Mr O'Toole, stop at the corner tomorrow morning at seven.'

The jarvey touched his whip to his hat, then set his horse in motion, off to find another fare. 'Thank you, Napier,' she said simply. 'I don't have much money…'

'I have no family, Jerusha. Let me do this for you.'

'Why?' she asked simply.

'I have a good feeling about it.'

James Wilson watched the hackney leave Stonehouse and stood a moment in thought, hands in his pockets, wondering what Jerusha Langley would do tomorrow. He marvelled that his day had begun as all days did at Stonehouse, a quick breakfast, and a fast walk to Block Four, where he knew that once he stepped inside 'his' wards, there would be no peace or time to reflect upon anything except the duty before him.

The only change came when the bell clanged in the jetty to announce the arrival of the wounded, who were deposited in the quadrangle for a grim sorting. He went immediately to work, concentrating on the mayhem before him and doing everything in his puny power to alleviate suffering and keep Hippocrates content.

It was midnight when he walked back to his house, hands again shoved deep in his pockets. He guessed and second-guessed and told himself that Miss Langley was too smart to take him up on his generous offer to overwork her.

'You have some nerve, Jamie boy,' he muttered as he walked along. He wondered all over again how he had recognised her after so many years. It was only that slight limp, because he barely glimpsed her face. Why had he even remembered such a tiny detail? He smiled to himself, recalling a lecture at the medical school in Edinburgh where he had spent a spare six weeks, before heading to sea to be taught on the job by surgeons on the orlop deck.

The lecturer had spoken briefly of the brain, only enough to assure them that too much injury to the head warranted setting the poor sod aside in a quiet spot on a noisy, creaking ship with guns at play, to die, because die he would. 'Lads, we know nothing of the brain,' the instructor told them, then pointed at each student in turn. 'What goes on inside *your* brain will probably always be a mystery, especially during our oral tests.'

He smiled at the good-natured laughter that followed.

My brain is remembering something about Jerusha Langley, he settled on. *Thank you, brain.*

His was a short walk to the modest row of houses behind the administration building. There were two grand houses there for the physician in charge and a surgeon in residence. The four smaller quarters were for each block's chief surgeon, and two more for clerks. One of those last two had been allocated to him, since he had no family and required little space.

As small as it was, the house was his alone, an unheard-of luxury for a steward's son who went to sea and moved up the ranks because he had medical skills even he only dimly suspected, at first.

He had no hope that Mags, his housekeeper, would be awake when he returned, but somehow she was, properly nightgowned and robed and her hair in neat braids, ready with a mug of steaming cocoa. With no fanfare, they sat down in the tiny dining room and he told her about his day. 'The nameless blind man still refuses to consider sending for his wife, there's a double amputee from York and too much diarrhoea.' He sipped his cocoa and felt himself relax.

'There's more,' she told him. 'I see it in your face.'

How did Mags do that? He drained the cocoa and told her about Jerusha Langley. 'She was a drowned rat and I yanked her out of a duck-pond,' he said. 'I doubt she was more than

nine years of age, and there she was, in the Admin Building this afternoon.'

While Mags looked at him with lively eyes, he told her he had asked her to return to Block Four and write letters for the wounded men. 'I am an idiot,' he concluded.

'Do you think she will show up?' Mags asked. 'Thousands wouldn't.'

Would she? He felt his eyes growing heavy as the twelve-hour day took its toll. 'Would you?'

'That would depend.'

'On what, Mags?'

'On how I felt about you.'

He laughed. 'I have no idea what Jerusha Langley is thinking.'

'And what are *you* thinking, James Wilson?'

He had no answer, even as he felt heat move north and bloom on his face. Hopefully, it was too dark in the kitchen lit with only a branch of candles for Mags McDonald to see a surgeon blush.

Chapter Eleven

I am a thief in the night, Jerusha thought, as she dressed quietly.

The sun was already up and Finch Street looked as prosaic as usual. There weren't any squeaking steps to avoid. No suspicious persons lurked.

Napier met her in the foyer and opened the door on the beautiful day. He looked at his timepiece and nodded approvingly when Jake O'Toole pulled up at the end of the street.

Jerusha hesitated as the butler prepared to give her a hand up. 'Napier, this could backfire spectacularly.'

'Lady Oakshott is fixed in her habits,' he assured her, 'and we know that Abbie and René will never cause you grief. Go do some good.'

She doubted Plymouth and nearby Devonport ever slumbered during wartime. The dry docks already hummed with the sound of hammer and saw. As she watched, her mouth open, a gang of men stepped a mast in place. She held her breath as it quivered, then sank into its slot.

When the hackney stopped at the foot of the quadrangle, Jerusha lost her nerve.

What am I doing here, alternated with *Aunt Hortensia will never approve.*

She stared down at her hands as Mr O'Toole opened the door.

'Miss Langley?' he asked, when she didn't move.

'Mr O'Toole, I shouldn't be here,' she said, barely above a whisper.

'Miss Langley, listen now,' the jarvey said. 'My only child went to sea and died in a battle with the Frogs in the Mediterranean. He was buried at sea.' He took a deep breath. 'I think of him every day. Somewhere is a mother or father thinking about a lad here. They probably wish they could be where you are. Just give it a go this once, miss. Do it for Billy O'Toole.'

She let him help her down. 'For today. Then we shall see.'

He touched his whip to his hat. 'That's all I ask.'

She stood there, too afraid to move. 'This will never do,' she scolded herself, after looking around to make sure no one was listening. 'You are twenty-five. Move!' She moved, unaware that she was under observation on the first floor of Block Four, by Surgeons Wilson and Kidwell.

'Is that her?' Jonathan Kidwell asked.

'The very same, sir,' James assured his chief. 'I did not know if she would do this.'

'Encourage her.'

There she stood in the open door, which warmed his heart in ways unimaginable. 'I nearly turned around,' she admitted. 'I'm practising a great misdemeanour, being here.'

He motioned her closer, wanting to hurry her upstairs to his chaotic world. 'How so?'

'My parents made me promise to have nothing to do with the Royal Navy,' she told him, 'and Lady Oakshott said the same thing.'

'Wise of them,' he said, then couldn't help his laugh. 'Miss Langley…'

'Jerusha,' she said quickly, which warmed his heart another notch.

'Very well then, Jerusha.' He was so pleased he could have wriggled like a puppy, but he knew better. 'Let me assure you there isn't any patient in Block Four that you can't outrun.'

What she said next put him on notice. It was nothing he expected.

'Does that include you?' she asked, and gave him a clear-eyed look.

There was only one thing to do, because her plain speaking surprised him. He started to limp, which meant a hearty laugh from that person he saved years ago from a duck-pond. It was no simper, but the kind of belly laugh that made him laugh, too. Good God, she was perfect for Block Four.

He took his chances on the stairs, since she seemed determined now. 'There are between twenty and thirty patients per floor, Wards A and B. Some will recuperate and some won't. The ones who won't are on Ward B, and you needn't go there.'

'I might cry.'

'Then you'll join the rest of us,' he said without hesitation. 'Paper and pencil?'

'I brought some,' she said. 'Lady Oakshott will never miss it. I need a writing board.'

'I'll find one.'

As they approached Ward A, he thought to offer her more camphor from the jar in his pocket, but changed his mind. She needed to get used to hospital odours.

He opened the door and ushered her inside. Jon Kidwell turned from the window and executed an elegant bow, considering that he only had a leg and a peg. Jerusha dipped a curtsy and came to him, a nicety that made the older man nod his approval.

'Miss Langley, this is Chief Surgeon Kidwell,' James said. 'I believe he has forgotten more than I will ever know about medicine.'

Jon tapped his wooden leg. 'I earned this is an earlier war against the Dutch. The Powers That Be turned me out to pasture, but were happy enough to see me here at our sick bay

that doesn't float, when our troubles began with Boney.' He gestured to James. 'This lad is faster on stairs than I am.'

'What *he* is, is superior to us all,' James said, in his Scots way, never comfortable with a compliment. 'Let me introduce you to our motley crew.'

He hadn't expected what followed, but there was Jerusha Langley, walking down the rows by herself. She stopped a moment by a one-armed Marine, who was trying to take a jar lid off with his teeth. She sat beside him and held out her hand. He handed it to her with a grin and she quickly removed it, then peered inside.

'You're the lucky one,' she declared. 'Cubes of sugar?'

'My wife sent them,' he said. 'She lives in Dover.' He popped a cube in his mouth, then held out the jar to her. James smiled inside when she popped a cube in her mouth, too, then rolled her eyes. 'Divine. She must really, really love you.'

The sergeant of Marines laughed. 'Aye, miss, she really, really does.' His face fell. 'Maybe. She…she knows about my arm, but I haven't written to her yet.'

Jerusha leaned closer to the man. James could only admire her animation. The Marine's arm, what remained of it, was bare and stitched with black sutures, but she did not falter. 'Are you right-handed?' she asked. 'I can write for you.'

'I'm left-handed, but th-that's not it. I'm just…' He looked away.

'Maybe a little nervous to write?' Jerusha asked, her voice gentle, but in no way condescending. 'It's probably a little hard to hold down a piece of paper and get properly situated, isn't it?'

He nodded, thought better of it, and shook his head. 'Maybe I'm a little afraid, too.'

'You tell me what to write and I'll do it for you this time,' Jerusha said. She removed her bonnet. 'You can write to her

the next time.' She turned to James. 'Surgeon Wilson, could you find me that writing board?'

'I'll go.' Surgeon Kidwell limped away and returned with a tray. 'We were going to introduce you to these miscreants and malingerers, Miss Langley.'

'This comes first, sir,' she said. She returned her attention to the one-armed Marine lying in the iron cot, who, to James's amazement seemed to lie there a little straighter, and certainly more alert. Jerusha uncapped the ink, positioned the paper, and began.

The Marine opened his mouth, closed it, looked at his little secretary, and began to weep. Surgeon Kidwell leaned forward to take charge, but James put a hand on his arm.

'She has good instincts, sir,' he said. 'Let's step back.'

Praying he was right—how well did he really know her?—James watched as she put her hand on the Marine's remaining arm. When he stopped weeping, she took a handkerchief from her sleeve and wiped his eyes.

He gathered himself together, then must have remembered that he was a Marine. 'Miss… Miss…'

'Jerusha will do,' she said quietly.

James was suddenly aware that the entire ward had gone silent. No one was slapping down cards and there was no coarse laughter. Were they *all* listening? By God, they were.

'Jerusha, if my Marines ever find out what I just did…'

She laughed. 'It's our little secret, Sergeant.'

To James's delight, one of the sergeant's Marines called out, 'Three cheers for Sergeant Mulvaney!'

After the hip hips and huzzahs rang out, everyone returned to his bedbound business. The cards slapped down again and someone burped. The picture of serenity, Jerusha dipped her pen in the ink. 'What's her name, Sergeant Mulvaney?'

'Sylvie,' he said, his voice assured now. 'I met her in Montreal. We have three children.'

'Dear Sylvie?' Jerusha prompted.

'Dearest,' he replied, and began to dictate. 'My love, I know you already have the news…'

Surgeon Kidwell took James by the arm and led him to the matron's desk. 'She has a sure touch, James, my lad. How did you know?'

How indeed? he asked himself. His only association with Jerusha Langley had been a brief one at a duck-pond. A man of science and not of religion, he had no rational explanation.

'Dumb luck, sir.'

The letter took a lengthy time, with pauses where Jerusha simply sat there and held his hand while the battle-hardened Marine wept. When he finished, he looked at peace. In a few minutes, he slept. Jerusha carefully folded the many-page letter and handed it to James.

'He said you have Sylvie Mulvaney's direction,' she told him.

'I do. This will be posted today,' James told her. 'Let me walk you through the ward now. There will be time to meet the men tomorrow.'

'Wednesday,' she corrected. 'Three times a week. I daren't take more chances than that, and besides, Abbie and I are cleaning the downstairs rooms. I think Lady Oakshott is going to invite some guests for dinner. I have to help Abbie with the rooms.'

It seemed strange to James that Lady Oakshott was so short of domestics, but it wasn't his business to question Jerusha. Still, there was one pressing matter.

'I suppose your jarvey is waiting below,' he said. 'It's half ten of the clock.'

'Oh, my, yes,' she said, and put on her bonnet, which made the more alert patients practically sigh in unison. James put up his hand. 'Gentlemen, Jerusha has other commitments, but she will be here on Mondays, Wednesdays, and I think Fridays. Fridays, Miss Langley?'

'Aye,' she said. 'Always.'

Aye or nae? He paused at a cot with a long list of surgeons' notes, his among them. 'I doubt this man will make it to Wednesday. Please say hello to him. He's been watching you.'

'I can't imagine why.'

Have you no idea how lovely you are? he thought.

'Jerusha, you're so pretty. Don't blush; it's true.'

'Surgeon Wilson, you are a flirt and a danger to society,' she told him, which made him grin, something he never did at this particular bedside.

'Sit here a moment,' he whispered, before putting out a chair for her. 'Corporal Meade is another of Sergeant Mulvaney's men. They were mauled in a sharp fight before Brest, when their bomb kedge exploded. I doubt he had another day left in him.'

She sat without question. He knew then what it was he remembered about her, from the duck-pond. Her eyes met his and he saw all the determination in her. This was not a woman to be trifled with.

'Corporal Meade, Miss Jerusha Langley wanted to meet you,' he told the dying Marine. 'She's from near Bolling, which I believe isn't far from your home in Dalton.'

Corporal Meade managed a smile. 'Not far at all.'

'Perhaps you know my father,' Jerusha said, her hand on the corporal's arm. 'He is vicar of Bolling Parish.'

'Never went to church,' he said. 'Never had good clothes. Mam has a Bible, though.'

James saw a shadow cross her face, making him wonder if Vicar Langley was the sort of clergyman who differentiated between the poor and the deserving poor. He thought he knew the answer.

'I am certain she read it to you,' she told the corporal. 'Would you like me to read to you tomorrow?'

'But, Miss Langley, you told me you couldn't...' James began.

'I mixed up my days,' she said, silencing him. 'I will most certainly be here tomorrow. Until then, Corporal Meade.'

Chapter Twelve

'You're late,' Mr O'Toole told her when she ran to the hackney. She didn't think he was angry, but she burst into tears anyway.

He neither flinched nor faltered but clapped his arm around her shoulders. 'Hospitals are tough places, Miss Langley. D'ye want me to run Surgeon Wilson down in the street on some dark night and put you out of your misery?'

That brought a welcome chuckle. 'No, Mr O'Toole. I do need to be here tomorrow morning at seven of the clock. Someone needs me.'

'I hope you don't get in trouble with Lady Oakshott. I'm not supposed to pick you up again until Wednesday,' he reminded her, sounding remarkably like a parent.

'She is never an early riser. Tomorrow, please.'

She was back at number twenty-eight Finch Street before eleven, Napier watching for her at the open door. She didn't know him well enough to interpret his 'butler face,' but his 'No worries, Miss Langley,' set her at ease. She was soon dressed in what she thought of as her 'biddable dress,' a plain dark blue cotton with a modest lace collar, grand enough to greet mostly non-existent visitors, but with an added apron, good enough for helping Abbie with their latest task, washing windows inside the sitting room while René balanced precariously outside and did the same.

At precisely noon, she carried breakfast and the day's mail to her aunt's bedroom and opened the draperies on a day she was already quite familiar with.

What a lazy aunt you are, she thought.

As she plastered on a smile, she discovered that she didn't really care for subterfuge. It was not her first twinge of conscience about the matter, but she subdued it, considering all the good she might do at Stonehouse, whether Lady Oakshott liked it or not.

She spent this afternoon in trivialities. Her aunt had exclaimed over her excellent penmanship, so it became Jerusha's duty to answer all correspondence. This meant dictated letters to Admiral Mrs This or That, or a Lady Beecroft that Aunt Hortensia already informed her was a vulgar woman married to a wealthy merchant of marine goods whose title came from Prinny because he provided a loan that turned into a gift. Jerusha was wise enough not to comment that the late and mostly unlamented Harvey Oakshott had a similar background.

Wonder of wonders, there was even a visit from Admiral Mrs Stoppard, bubbling over with self-congratulation over the delivery of the baskets to Stonehouse officers' blocks. Jerusha listened from the desk by the window, where she attempted to translate her aunt's nearly illiterate scrawl unto lovely prose.

'Jerusha, how was your delivery received?' Aunt Hortensia asked.

'I took it to the front desk in Block One,' she said. 'I assume it was delivered appropriately.'

'You were supposed to speak to a physician and deliver the basket to an officer yourself,' her aunt reminded her.

'I apologise then,' Jerusha said. She tried to resist, but couldn't. 'Aun… Lady Oakshott, I wonder if any future baskets might be better appreciated among the ordinary seamen. Their families are not so likely to have the ability to travel to bedsides as easily as officers' families.'

Both ladies looked at her as if she was wanting, indeed. 'Rabble,' Mrs Admiral Stoppard said.

Rabble? Jerusha thought. *Your captains and admirals would never leave port without those rabble.*

She pasted on an apologetic smile, even more determined to hold that dying rabble's hand tomorrow, provided he survived the night.

'We deal *only* with officers and their families,' Aunt Hortensia reminded her. Mrs Admiral Stoppard nodded vigorously, which set the feathers on her bonnet expressing themselves, as well.

How will I survive a summer here? Jerusha asked herself below stairs that evening as they ate.

She told her below stairs companions of the Royal Marine sergeant who was so grateful she wrote a letter for him to his wife, and the others who flirted with their eyes, which meant that they would probably live to fight another day.

She dreaded another evening in the sitting room, knitting and listening to her aunt go on and on about life at Oaklands and wondering what crisis the Cit she had rented it to for the summer was causing among the neighbours and staff.

Jerusha looked up from her knitting. 'Why did you let it out in the first place?' she asked, and got a glare for her pains.

'Simple girl, I told you I am preparing to sell this place,' Lady Oakshott snapped. To Jerusha's relief, she turned her attention to her card table, where she played Patience and cheated. Eventually she flounced upstairs and Jerusha followed without the flounce. Another boring night at number twenty-eight Finch Street.

It was even easier to slip out of the house at half past six the next morning. No one was awake, not even the ever-watchful Napier.

'Mr O'Toole, am I crazy to do this?' she asked as Mr O'Toole nodded a greeting to her from his perch.

'You're entirely sane, in a world gone mad,' he assured her.

She thought about that as the jarvey made his way to Stone-house. She leaned back, enjoying the momentary peace and thinking of all the times her mother had insisted, for form's sake, that even a visit to the local grocer's in Bolling included taking a maid along. To be by herself felt like liberation. True, the responsibility seemed to increase, but she welcomed it because she suspected she was a woman of good sense.

As they pulled up to the quadrangle and circled around to the ward blocks, Jerusha wondered if Jamie Wilson would understand what she was only beginning to learn about herself. *I could use a friend*, she thought, as she thanked Mr O'Toole, and paid him for the journey this extra day.

As she watched Mr O'Toole drive away, she noticed bits of what looked like bloody bandages littering the courtyard's grassy expanse. She saw stretchers leaning against the buildings, and men slumped beside them. She sucked in her breath, thinking they were dead, until she heard snoring as she hurried to the entrance.

'I wonder...' she said out loud. The jetty bells must have rung last night.

There were more bloody stretchers inside, two of them with their occupants still in place, but shrouded now, their journey over.

You are right, Mr O'Toole, she thought. *This truly is a world gone mad.*

'Miss Langley, I didn't expect to see you today,' she heard over her shoulder, and looked around to see a bleary-eyed Jonathan Kidwell.

'What has happened here?' she asked, turning aside his question. 'Perhaps you should sit down, sir. Here's a chair.'

My, but I am commanding, Jerusha thought, as she pushed a chair forward.

The one-legged surgeon sat, and she saw the relief.

'The jetty bell rang at midnight,' he said, accepting a glass of water from her that she found on a nearby table. 'We have been sorting the wounded and stashing them here and there.' He set down the glass. 'Why are you here? Unless the ordeal was longer than I thought, it's not Wednesday yet.'

'It's for Corporal Meade,' she told him. 'I...held his hand yesterday, and I don't think I am done yet.'

He smiled at that, which threw off the years from his lined face. He nodded towards the stairs. 'He's behind a curtain now. James is with him.'

She hesitated on the stairs. 'No fears, Miss Langley. There's nothing as welcome as a kind touch.' He smiled and looked away. 'Be it for Corporal Meade or Surgeon Wilson, who doesn't like to surrender patients to death. None of us do.'

She lifted her skirts higher than she usually would on stairs, because these treads still were bloody in spots, waiting for the morning clean-up crew perhaps, or maybe for someone to have a moment to swab away.

The ward was silent. She passed the Royal Marine sergeant, asleep, who twitched as he slept, perhaps in the thrall of battle dreams. She hoped his letter to Sylvie would bring a prompt reply.

There was the curtain, navy blue with a fouled anchor in faded yellow. She drew the curtain aside and knew beyond question that she was needed. Corporal Meade looked at her, his eyes barely open. He managed a smile. He looked at her, then glanced to his left, not moving his head, to the sleeping surgeon who held his hand.

'I think he's had a night of it, Corporal Meade,' she whispered.

He nodded, then closed his eyes. She thought for one terrifying second that he was dead. In a panic, she watched his chest, then breathed out herself when it rose and fell again.

There was a basin half full of water, and a clean rag. Un-

sure but certain she could never hurt someone already so far gone, she wrung out the rag and wiped the corporal's face. He didn't open his eyes, but his sigh sounded contented, almost as if she was doing something useful and restorative, even though she knew that wasn't the case.

James's eyes opened. 'You came.'

Jerusha saw all the exhaustion in them and knew it had been an endless night. 'Said I would. Let me sit here a while beside Corporal Meade,' she whispered.

He stood up and she took his place, holding the dying man's hand. Corporal Meade opened his eyes and gave her a slight nod. 'Softer,' was all he said.

She stroked the man's hand as he breathed, forgot to breathe, then breathed again until the next time. For a few minutes she was Maudie, then pretty Maudie. As death pressed down, and as James Wilson watched from the chair next to hers, she turned into Mam, and then Mama, over and over.

'They always ask for their mothers when they are *in extremis*,' Jamie whispered. 'Even the lads who came to the navy from workhouses and probably never knew their mothers. I'll never understand it.'

They're only going back where they began, she told herself.

She held Corporal Meade's hand, then pressed it to her cheek, letting her tears water his fingers. She held her breath when he patted her cheek once, then again. Who comforted who? 'Sleep well, son,' she told him, and he died.

James dragged out his timepiece as if it weighed ten pounds and stared at it. 'I call it at zero eight one five,' he said, then reached for the chart, writing the time of death, and adding his initials. Without a word, he rose and pulled back the curtain, leaving her there alone.

Startled, she frowned at his coldness, then held her breath as his shoulders started to shake. 'Poor, poor man,' she whispered.

Imagine doing this day after week after year, Jerusha Langley, she scolded herself.

She had no idea of the usual protocol, but did it matter? She carefully straightened the collar on Corporal Meade's nightshirt and wiped his face again. Where she had seen pain, she saw only calm. 'Where are you now?' she asked him. 'I would write to Maudie, but I haven't an address.' She pulled the sheet over his face. Rabble, indeed.

Mrs Terwilliger, the matron, had watched the whole matter from her desk, her face impassive. Jerusha still had the washcloth in her hand. 'If you tell me where I can get more water, I can wash a few faces,' she said. She looked around at cots that were empty only yesterday. 'I'm not skilled for anything else.'

Mrs Terwilliger looked at James Wilson, who had walked to the end of the ward and stood there leaning his forehead against the wall. 'That one will be all right in a few minutes. I'll get you water.' She pointed to the new residents. 'These are the latest, courtesy of the jetty bells.'

Jerusha wiped away grime and dirt from drowsy men's faces. She shook her finger at one man who, livelier than most, patted her breast. The others were respectful and told her 'Thank 'ee,' as if she had done something miraculous. One sailor tugged at her skirt, and she sat beside him until he closed his eyes with something close to contentment and died.

James was nowhere in sight now. Surgeon Kidwell appeared to be setting a bone. Jerusha retrieved her bonnet and left the ward and then Block Four. She hadn't told Mr O'Toole when she might need him, so she walked back to Finch Street, arriving after eleven o'clock. She had moved along purposefully, so no one bothered her.

She didn't think the distance was much more than two miles. She passed men and women engaged in building, buy-

ing, haggling, and selling, as if this were an ordinary day, and not the day when she, Jerusha Langley, knew for certain there was work to be done that had nothing to do with Lady Oakshott.

Chapter Thirteen

'You weren't afraid to walk from Devonport?' Abbie asked, her eyes wide with worry. Watching from the window in the foyer, she opened the door before Jerusha could raise her hand to the knocker and dragged her inside.

'No pirates swooped down and carried me off,' Jerusha assured her, then couldn't resist. 'Someone must have told them I'm all of twenty-five with no dowry. What is the alarm? I know it is not noon yet.'

'I heard her moving around and muttering to herself,' Abbie whispered, as if Lady Oakshott stood in the next room.

In odd confirmation, the bell from that upstairs chamber jangled below stairs. 'You'd better hurry,' the young one said.

Jerusha looked down at her walking dress in dismay. 'I haven't time to change.'

'Just put on an apron. You'll think of something,' Abbie said. 'What can she want so early?'

Jerusha did as Abbie said. She hoped her aunt hadn't seen her from an upstairs window. As she climbed the stairs in some dread, Jerusha knew subterfuge did not sit well with her, even when the cause was most noble.

She opened the door to see her aunt sitting in bed, looking perturbed, out of sorts, and mostly spoiled. 'I cannot sleep in this wretched house,' she announced, then took a closer look at Jerusha. 'Where have *you* been?'

Tell the truth, Jerusha told herself, but could not. 'I went for a little walk,' she lied, hushing her conscience, for it was sort of true. 'It's a fine morning, Aunt Hortensia.'

'You are *not* to call me that.'

'Beg pardon, Lady Oakshott,' she said promptly, crossing her fingers that would be enough inquisition.

It was. Her aunt squinted at her bedside clock. 'Silly girl, why didn't you bring me the mail?' she asked. 'Add a biscuit to the chamomile tea. Go on now.'

She did as she was bid, grateful to escape without any more questions or scrutiny. 'I can't keep up this pretence,' she told René as he prepared two biscuits and Abbie poured tea.

The cook shrugged, a Gallic affectation he had mastered well. 'The old rip ain't much given to contemplation on any subject that does not involve her directly.'

But I know better, she wanted to tell him, then considered the source.

'René, I already know that you are not really French. Where are you from? What is your name?'

He snapped a towel at her. 'From Manchester. Me, work in the mill? Never. I ran away. I'm Robby Blair.' He bowed and she laughed. No, this wasn't a man to be concerned about anyone's false impression. Maybe she needn't give the matter another thought.

She did, though, all the way upstairs, and it weighed heavily on her, at least until she set down the tray and her aunt pounced on the cream-coloured letter with elegant calligraphy. She tore it open, read it, and clutched it to her bosom, her eyes gazing heavenward. 'I am saved!'

Jerusha stared at her. 'What…'

Aunt Hortensia held out the invitation to her. 'I have been invited to dinner at Sir William and Lady Beecrofts' house tomorrow night!' She pulled the invitation back as Jerusha reached for it. 'I suppose this means someone else turned her

down at the last moment and she reckoned I would be doing nothing.'

'Still, Aunt… Lady Oakshott, this is an honour,' Jerusha said, happy to shove her lie somewhere in the back of her mind.

Her aunt held out the invitation again. 'She wants me to bring my lady's companion. That is you, of course.'

'Lady's companion?' Jerusha asked in surprise. 'Already?'

'Your mother knows. Do as I say, and you will end up working in one of England's great houses. How good that you are so biddable, niece! You'll give no one any trouble.'

There it is, Jerusha thought later, as Lady Oakshott busied herself in her closet, searching for the perfect dinner gown.

Her future stretched before her as this new development sank in. Lady's companion? She knew it was coming, but now, and so suddenly, when she had work to do in Block Four? She chafed silently at the unfairness of it.

She mulled over the matter that evening, counting the hours as Aunt Hortensia carried on about the treat awaiting them both tomorrow evening. 'If we play whist, remember that you are to lose, if a gentleman plays opposite you. Your mother has told me how you've beaten everyone in your small circle of acquaintances. It is no wonder that you are twenty-five and single.'

Jerusha lay in bed wondering if she should ask Mr O'Toole to direct her to the nearest mail coach stop. She could be home and better off, a declared spinster. Two things stopped her: She hadn't enough money for a return to Bolling, and James Wilson needed her.

She pounded her pillow, which seemed to hold equal parts rocks and lead bars. Before she closed her eyes resolutely, determined to sleep, the unwelcome thought struck her that perhaps *she* needed Jamie Wilson more. Thoroughly unhappy with all her lies, Jerusha, daughter of a vicar, knew she was still an honest soul—hopefully. She asked herself why *she*

needed Jamie Wilson, a lad in her life fleetingly, gone so long and now a man.

'I am living in a world at war,' she decided on, which seemed more honest. Almost but not quite. 'I want to help.' That felt better, but still… 'I like him.' She said it softly, waiting for it to sound weird. It didn't.

Jerusha Langley must think I am a mutton-headed cry-baby, James told himself, as he ward-walked past sleeping men, his slatted lantern held high, looking for trouble before he sat down, because he knew he would fall asleep immediately.

Not this time. He sat beside Blind Man. His chart even said Blind Man, because he had been fished from the waters off Brest with the usual piecemeal uniform of a Royal Navy man long on the blockade. Some catastrophe had left him blind. He had no identifying papers on him and he refused to speak.

Trauma did that to some. It had been James's experience, though, that once a man was fished out, dried off, and fed, the mind began to right itself. Not in Blind Man's case, however. He spoke, and his accent was the slow drawl of the Cornishman, probably not so far from Plymouth. As the days passed, he sank into total silence.

They tried. The only thing in his pocket was a water-soaked miniature of a pretty woman and a baby. 'We know your wife is wondering where you are,' got them nowhere, except a tightening of Blind Man's lips. 'I wouldn't burden her with a blind man,' was all anyone could coax from him. That was it.

Surgeon Kidwell thought he was barmy. 'James, you have too much to do as it is.'

But James found himself sitting beside Blind Man when he had a free moment, and telling him about his day and the war, and the damned jetty bell. He discovered that Blind Man didn't approve of ribald commentary, oh, no. James had told him of one newly married surgeon in Block Two who came

grumbling from his quarters as the bell rang, pulling on his trousers and grousing, 'I get my eager willy in me bride and that damned bell ends it. I'll never be a father.'

'Coarse humour is a curse,' Blind Man informed him, turned over and gave him the cold shoulder. The blind prude somehow knew who was who, and for too many days he had turned away when James sat down. Was it his accent? Just the fact that he sat down?

An apology from James ended the cold shoulder last week, so James sat now. But what to talk about, even if he talked to himself? 'I'm tired,' he said simply, which earned no response. Undaunted, he told Blind Man about Jerusha Langley sitting with the dying man that morning.

'She sang. I heard her,' Blind Man said to James's amazement. He heard something in his voice, a certain longing. Hopefully, he wasn't imagining it. Using a shred of wisdom—the kind that sometimes surfaced around midnight of an endless day—he stopped himself from leaping into what he knew by now was unwanted interrogation.

James groaned and stood up. 'I crack and pop when I get up. Goodnight.' He walked away, gratified by 'Goodnight,' from Blind Man, the first time he had said that.

He had one other stop before he lay down for one blissful hour, and the steward came to take over.

Sam Wycherly was a Welsh carpenter's mate, done in by the carelessness of another sailor, bored with the tedium of the blockade, who slammed down a maul on the mate's wrist when Sam held a wedge to shape a chair leg. When the mangled man arrived three weeks later at Stonehouse, amputation was the only recourse, even though Sam objected in two languages.

James discovered that Sam held no grudges. The matron wrote a letter Sam dictated, telling the man who mauled him not to dwell on the matter. James wasn't sure he could have been so forgiving, and admitted as much to Sam. All Sam

did was ask James for some paper. 'I like to draw. I'm pretty good with either hand.'

Sam drew his first image of a patient across the aisle who had just drawn his last breath. He sketched quickly, but with a sure hand. 'It will bring comfort,' was all he said when he handed it to James. 'Give it to his wife, please.'

James sat a moment beside Sam, who reached for his latest work of art on the other side of his cot and held it out. 'If you know this lad's next of kin, send it on.'

James looked and looked again. It was Corporal Meade, with Jerusha Langley seated beside him, her hand in his. 'Hands are hard to draw,' Sam said. 'I can learn. Give me time.'

Time. Surgeon Kidwell had given him a memo, stating in two days he was to sail with a Fast Dispatch Vessel back to the blockade. This time, James Wilson had no urge to go, necessity be damned.

He glanced at the drawing again, absorbing some of the serenity emanating from the simple sketch of a lovely woman seated beside a wounded man, now dead, but ushered from mortality by the comfort of soft hands. The lovely woman was Jerusha, and that made all the difference.

He didn't want to go to sea, at least not so soon. He wanted to stay in Jerusha's peaceful orbit. It was a jolt of a thought: Didn't he tell her only yesterday that he loved his sea duty?

You are a drooling idiot, he told himself.

'Sir?'

James recalled himself and nodded to the artist who held out his hand. James returned the drawing with what he hoped was casual disinterest, nothing more. In this he failed. Maybe artists, even mangled carpenter's mates, heard beyond words and into the heart. James hoped he wasn't *that* obvious.

In this he failed, too. 'Sir, I'll dress it up a bit and you can send it to the corporal's widow.' He didn't stop there. James

saw the Welsh shrewdness in Sam's eyes, or maybe it was understanding. 'I can draw you another picture of Miss Langley.'

There was no point in trying to bamboozle a Welshman. 'I would like that. She's a pretty lady.'

He looked up from the drawing when the door opened, and the steward stood there, looking bright and cheerful and ready for the night duty, generally peaceful enough because patients on the mend slept.

Still he waited, hoping Jerusha would somehow arrive a little early today—midnight now, if he wasn't mistaken. Lord, he *was* an idiot. She would be here in the morning! *I want to see her now*, he thought, reminding himself of a two-year-old.

'Sir?'

'Aye, steward?'

'Go to bed, sir. I'll watch them for you.'

James handed him the slatted lamp. Let the steward think he was only concerned about his patients, and not thinking of a child from his past who had come into his life again, grown up now and troubling the still waters of his bachelor complacency.

Baffled by his own foolishness, James walked the length of the ward, pausing as he always did by Blind Man, then letting himself out into the hall, down the stairs and into the cool of night. With any luck, the jetty bell would be silent and he could sleep. With even better luck, he would see Jerusha tomorrow, before he sailed for the damned blockade.

Chapter Fourteen

He overslept and woke up, his heart pounding, when Mags McDonald knocked on his door. 'Breakfast, sir.'

'You don't oversleep often,' Mrs McDonald observed, when she set porridge in front of him fifteen minutes later. She looked at him closer. 'Dab at your chin, James Wilson, for I see shaving soap.'

'What would I do without you, Mags?' he asked as he bolted his food.

'You'd be an untidy mess, unfit for a gentle companion,' she retorted, 'someday,' and made him blush, which made her laugh, a welcome sound. Maggie didn't laugh much. He knew she still missed her own companion, that red-faced, rough-hewn bosun.

James ate fast—a requirement for any surgeon or physician in wartime, he was certain—then sat back with a novel thought. No one better to ask than Mags, who knew him well.

'Margaret McDonald, do you see anything repellent about me?' he asked. 'My ears too large? Poor hygiene?'

Thank God she didn't laugh. She regarded him seriously, but he saw the lurking smile behind her eyes.

'Such a question, sir! Your ears are fine. I think you have all your teeth, and personally, I like to see a few freckles on a man's nose. Just enough, though. Some poor men have too many, in my opinion.'

He didn't tell her about the freckles on his shoulders and back, but Mags wasn't done. 'I don't recall that you have ever been drunk, in my presence, anyway. As for vices...' She plunged ahead, as any good Scotswoman would. 'At least you don't drink to excess, and you don't chase hoors.'

'No to that one! My mother warned me.'

He kissed her cheek and she cleared the table, her thoughts her own, until she sat down and laughed.

'What now, Mags?' he asked, enjoying this cheerful side of his housekeeper.

'Laddie, I was thinking of that patient of yours last year. The one wi' two wives.'

'Oh, aye,' he said, laughing, too, as he remembered Reggie Roundtree, he of the handsome visage and a leg broken in two places. It was a never-to-be-forgotten scene in Ward A, where two wives converged on his bed at the same time, took one look at each other, and fell to, shrieking and scratching at each other's eyes and rolling on the floor, affording amazed patients and surgeons alike bare-bottomed glimpses of which most women are more discreet about.

Once James separated them—getting a black eye and scratches for his pains—he gave them each a good shake and told them to sort it out or go to the brig. To his further amazement, they did as he asked, settling down, sniffling, and wiping noses on sleeves.

He should never have turned his back in them. Arriving at some mysterious comradeship, they took their understandable umbrage out on their 'husband,' who came out of *that* scrape with two black eyes and a broken nose, a wiser bigamist he.

'Reggie Roundtree! I never saw a sailor so eager to return to sea! Mags, he *was* a handsome man, and he had a way with women.'

It never failed, that tender moment when Maggie McDonald reminded him of his own dear mother, dead these four years,

she with her own brand of good nature. 'Jamie, I have no idea how you are with the ladies, but I know you haven't much opportunity to find out because there is a war on.'

'Wish I did,' he said as he buttoned his uniform jacket and headed to the door.

She didn't stop there. 'You have someone in mind?'

Was he so obvious? 'I might,' he said. 'It's early days, though, Mags. Leave it at that.'

To his relief, she did, joking at him to mind his manners. He was still smiling about it when he entered Block Four and took the stairs two at a time, energised by good humour.

And there Jerusha Langley sat, giving her attention to the powder monkey who had followed her with his eyes yesterday as she moved among the patients, then sat with Corporal Meade until he died.

Her consolation now appeared as paper, pen, and ink, the very excuse he had used to enlist her help in the first place, since he admitted to himself now that he wanted to see her again and again. How else could he do it?

'I didn't know if you would come today,' he said.

'It's Wednesday, sir.'

'So it is,' he replied, professional again. He continued to his desk and the eagle eye of Mrs Terwilliger, who handed him the daily report. He looked over it—or overlooked it, because his mind and heart were both fastened on the pretty scribe at the powder monkey's bedside—until Jerusha finished, tucked the young boy's blanket higher to cover grievous wounds, and joined him at the desk.

'Who is young Michael writing to?' he asked. 'He's another product of the workhouse.'

She blushed. My God, what a lovely woman. 'I… I noticed him watching me yesterday.'

'A lot of men watch you.' James took a huge chance. 'I am not immune, either.'

Did he *say* that? She astounded him then, completely, utterly. 'Jamie, women look, too.' She smiled down at the floor. 'I happen to like freckles.' Then she hauled them both back to the business at hand. 'Mikey said he wanted to write to someone of my choosing, so he could tell his story.'

Professional again, he looked towards the powder monkey, knowing the extent of his injuries under that blanket. 'I doubt it is a cheerful story.'

She shook her head, and he saw all the sorrow of a caring person. 'It must take strong boys and girls to survive a workhouse. We both cried, and he was kind enough to hold *my* hand for a moment.' She looked at him out of lowered eyes, probably not aware of how attractive that was. 'I promised Michael Summer I would send his letter to Mr William Pitt, himself. That was who I chose. "I hope he reads it," was all Mikey said.'

'I will see that it gets to Downing Street, Miss Langley.'

'Better add a note of explanation,' Mrs Terwilliger said, from her desk. He saw she was visibly moved, and the matron was a woman who had seen everything.

'I will do that, too.' He glanced at the reports on her desk, the additions, the deletions, either because his patients were pronounced fit to serve again, or they had changed venues forever. He sighed at some of those names, wishing—as he always did—that medical knowledge was greater. With others, he felt relief that their pains were done.

He glanced at Jerusha, surprised to see her eyes on his face. He saw understanding and compassion, and he took heart for another day of this work. She held out Michael Summer's letter.

'I corrected some of his grammar as he dictated to me,' she said, 'then I decided, no, our Prime Minister should hear what I heard.' She looked into that far distance that only those at war saw, which startled him, then humbled him. He had in-

troduced her to dying men, and she now saw what he saw. He looked down at the letter, knowing it would break his heart. He could read it later, and he would, but not now, when this kind lady stood before him, as brave as any of his patients.

'Where do they get such bravery?'

'I don't know.'

Ah, but you do, even if you don't know it yet, he thought. *Courage comes from within, that mysterious place where no matter how the enemy rages, we will defend our homeland.*

As for now, 'Please continue what you're doing,' he told her. 'Let me introduce you to our biggest question mark. Over here.'

She followed him to the bed of the blind man who seldom spoke. He wanted to explain this man, even though he had nothing to tell her. No one did.

'We know nothing,' he whispered. 'Before he turned silent, he told Surgeon Kidwell that no wife needed the burden he would be. They found him floating in the water, nary a ship in sight, after a minor fleet action near Ferrol.'

'So sad,' she whispered back.

'I cannot predict what he will do, but he is harmless. Sit down for a moment and acquaint yourself with him. We've tried everything else except a lovely lady.'

She smiled at that and sat, looking at Blind Man with more curiosity than fear. James watched as she dipped a cloth in warm water, unbuttoned the top two buttons on his nightshirt, and wiped his neck and then his face.

Blind Man opened dead eyes shot with blood until there was no white to the cornea, a sight that still made the night steward flinch.

James almost pulled her back when he cleared his throat, fearing Blind Man was going to spit at her. Instead, he sniffed and relaxed. 'Claudy, *est-ce toi*?' he said in a voice rusty with disuse. 'You?'

Chapter Fifteen

'I wish I were, but no,' Jerusha replied, hardly knowing what she said, but aware of what he had done. 'Does…does your wife wear scented talcum powder, too?'

He nodded and said nothing more. In another moment, he turned away from them, from everyone, burrowing against the place where the blanket and sheet met his pillow, a safe haven.

She had known a parishioner's cat who did that whenever anyone came to call on his mistress, an old widow supported by the parish because all her means were gone. The cat trembled and tried to squeeze himself under her armpit as he shook. 'He's shy,' the widow excused. 'He came to me a stray.'

Jerusha was only a little girl then, and Papa wanted to raise a useful child. She petted what she could reach of the little beast. It growled at her, but nothing more. Every visit, she did that, but nothing changed. She tried it now, putting her hand gently on Blind Man's shoulder. 'I wish she were here, too,' was all she said, before she rose and went to the next bed.

'This is Sam Wycherly,' James said. 'He is our resident artist, at least until his captain misses him and away he goes.'

Jerusha heard the affection, a welcome antidote to Blind Man. 'What do you draw?'

The man eyed her, not in a way to embarrass her, but to regard her as an artist would. He tipped his head this way and that. 'You, for certain,' the man said. 'It's something I picked

up on long voyages, after water starts to stink and you've heard everyone's stories. Aye, Sam Wycherly's the name.'

Jerusha thought of the time, years ago, when an itinerant pot mender told her that if she stood still long enough, some-one, someday, would surely want to paint her. She mentioned that to Mama and Papa over supper. Mama gasped. 'We're not supposed to sit still in this life of toil and woe!'

She told Sam Wycherly what her Mama had said. He laughed, filling the otherwise silent ward with something unexpected. Jerusha saw smiles on faces that likely hadn't found much to laugh about in recent days, not with war and wounds in plentiful supply.

'Therefore, I do not sit still for portraits,' she concluded.

Sam winked at her. 'I'm no Rembrandy,' he confided. 'I draw fast and make allowances for a ship goin' up and down. You keep busy, miss, but I might snatch a sketch here and there. You'll never know.' He looked beyond her to James. 'In fact, he has one of my drawings already.'

'Aye, Sam, I do,' James said.

A quick glance showed her a red face, and she was too wise to remark upon it, or more likely, too shy, except that she was curious. 'I... I believe I would like to see it, too.'

'Wait here then.'

Everyone in the nearby beds seemed to wait, as well. Jeru-sha sensed a good-natured silence, as if the sailors around her were healing and reaching that stage of boredom with sick-ness and were on the mend.

I wonder, she thought, *would you like me to read to you?*

As she considered what book might be appealing to rough and ready men sidelined by wounds, Jamie returned with the little drawing. His face was still red, as if he had been caught in some misdemeanour, but she chose to ignore it. She had never before seen her own likeness, so she held out her hand.

Her eyes widened. 'Sam, you are a man of some talent,' she

told him, as she looked at her likeness on the back of a patient chart, her hand resting on the shoulder of the sergeant of Marines. Her image sat in profile, looking down.

'Not so hard, missy, when I have a pretty subject,' the Welshman said, grinning as her face warmed. 'God blast and damn, you can rosy up!' he declared, which meant smiles from nearby beds. Even Mrs Terwilliger, the matron, traded her usual serious scrutiny for something that softened her eyes.

'I'll draw another,' Sam said. 'Surgeon Wilson, can you find me a larger sheet of paper, maybe thicker, too? I'll only wish I had coloured pencils.'

'Paper, yes, but I doubt I can cajole coloured pencils from the purser,' James said.

Sam shrugged. 'How else can I capture those blues eyes?'

'Really, Mr Wycherly,' Jerusha said. She knew it was time to get her bowl of warm water and cloth and start wiping faces, even if too many of them seemed determined to keep smiling. She reasoned that wasn't a bad thing, not at all.

She devoted herself to the task, not looking around until she thought a glance wouldn't seem out of place. Jamie was nowhere in sight, which made her sigh.

'He'll be back, miss, never you fear,' said a sailor, with his face fine drawn in pain and a leg in an elaborate system of pulleys that made her shudder inside. She sat with him until he slept, then glanced at the watch pinned to her apron bib and turned last to Blind Man.

She sat beside him and did nothing more than wipe around his eyes which he kept closed, even though she knew he wasn't asleep. 'I could read to you,' she said finally.

'You could also leave me alone.'

'Very well,' she replied, determined not to let his words flay her, because she could see and had no worries worse than approaching spinsterhood and employment as a lady's companion, if Aunt Hortensia had her way. He ignored her, but

she remained beside him until she knew Jack O'Toole would be waiting for her in his hackney.

Well aware that Sam Wycherly was drawing her, she made a face at him, which made some of the others laugh. She tried not to be obvious as she looked around for Surgeon Wilson, who was nowhere in sight. Ah well. He was a busy man.

Everything followed its normal course at number twenty-eight Finch Street when she returned with the usual luncheon and mail for Lady Oakshott, just roused from slumber. Later, she and Abbie began their onslaught on the sitting room, polishing chairs and the whist table. She heard Napier down the hall, arguing politely with Aunt Hortensia. The tense encounter ended with her aunt muttering something about stuffing bills away if she felt like it.

Who to ask the impertinent question that had been dogging her for days? There was no one to ask but Abbie, currently applying linseed oil industriously to the remaining chair.

'Abbie, it seems to be that Napier and Lady Oakshott are wrangling over unpaid bills,' Jerusha began, in her most neutral voice. 'Has she always done this?'

Abbie was a trusting sort. 'Only since t'master died. Ooh, the wrangles we used to hear from both Oakshotts, coming from the book room then! Now it is Napier reminding her about unpaid bills.' She returned her attention to the chair leg.

'Um…can he exert any influence?'

Abbie shook her head, her eyes sorrowful. 'He's just a butler. He can only remind her.' She leaned closer. 'Between you and me, I don't think Lady Oakshott has paid a bill in donkey's years.'

'But…'

Abbie gave an airy wave. 'I'm sure she knows what to do. Don't the rich always know what to do?'

Possibly not, Jerusha wanted to say, but to what point?

She continued polishing, wondering if her own mother had any notion of affairs at her sister's house.

I doubt we will all be on the street tomorrow, she reasoned finally, because try as she might to manage it, there was no way any of this was her business.

As recently as this morning's return to Finch Street, she had watched a woman with a bleak expression, two small children beside her, sitting upon a well-worn trunk in front of what looked like a boarding-house, probably one of many in a navy town like Plymouth.

Was the lady with sorrow etched on her face a new widow? Perhaps her husband had died at Stonehouse. Where did they go? She knew in her heart that it mattered now, where it hadn't mattered before.

She kept her thoughts to herself as she scrubbed at the sitting room furniture with Abbie. By the time afternoon began to wane, she knew she wanted to spend all day, every day at Stonehouse. The idea was preposterous, of course. Here she was, a gently reared woman destined to remain a spinster and strongly suspecting that a career in nursing was lowbrow and out of the question. Maybe in another generation, but not now, where the only path was marriage.

She asked herself again, *Why am I here? Mama and Aunt Hortensia both seem to think I must become a lady's companion.*

Mama had hinted she could return at the end of summer, but for what? The pity of well-married parishioners? She knew her aunt wanted to turn her into a lady's companion.

No one had ever consulted me, she told herself, as she dressed for dinner at the Beecrofts, an invitation that had sent Aunt Hortensia into ecstasies. *What do I want?*

Jerusha thought about that as she and her aunt walked the two streets farther away from the bay, which gave Sir William Beecroft a commanding view, almost the same view that

Sir Francis Drake enjoyed some two hundred years ago as he bowled and watched the Spanish Armada approach.

So many years had passed since that fraught time, and here they were at war again. 'Amazing what happened here so long ago,' Jerusha said to her aunt, who blew off her enthusiasm with a wave of her hand and one pithy word, 'History,' as if it was something unmentionable.

She slowed her steps, well aware of a deepening chasm between herself and Lady Oakshott, no matter that they were aunt and niece.

I don't know this woman, she thought, and took a careful breath. How to phrase this?

'Au… Lady Oakshott, what do the Beecrofts know of me?' she asked as they turned onto Launch Street. 'I mean, do I address you as Aunt Hortensia or Lady Oakshott? Who am I here?'

'I have told Lady Beecroft that you are the child of my sister, who didn't marry well.'

'Papa is a vicar, aunt!' Jerusha said.

Lady Oakshott gripped her arm. 'At one time, your mother had a baronet mooning over her, and what did she do but marry a penniless cleric in Orders? If my Harvey had not arranged a parish for him, I do not know what would have become of my sister!'

In a startling moment of reflection, Jerusha understood. 'So I am already the poor relation to people in Plymouth.'

'Poor but biddable,' Lady Oakshott told her and released her arm. 'You are along tonight to fetch and carry and arrange shawls that fall off shoulders and help the servants prepare tables for whist. Smile and say nothing. There will be a lady in attendance looking for a lady's companion for her mother. Pay her particular attention and mind yourself!'

What could she say?

'Remember who you are,' Lady Oakshott said, as she turned

around to simper and smile at other arriving guests on the street.

Who was she? Jerusha had a fair idea by the time the endless evening ended. She noticed a lieutenant who spent a moderate, polite time chatting with her, then turning the pages for her when she played a modest Scottish piece on the pianoforte with a fair amount of skill. When she finished to polite applause, she joined the ladies and watched as he chatted with Lady Beecroft. After that little chat, he did not engage her attention again.

Jerusha felt herself sinking inside. She did as she was bid, adjusting shawls for ladies who complained—but politely—of a slight chill. She arranged the whist tables and set the chairs just so.

And she died inside.

Chapter Sixteen

Jerusha cried herself to sleep that night. When she woke, she stared at the ceiling a long while and decided not to cry again. Only a foolish woman would have looked at last night's treatment—polite, yes, but putting her firmly in her place—and felt anything but the hard reality of her future.

She had no doubt that the young lieutenant had expressed some interest to Lady Beecroft and wanted an introduction, and the admiral's wife had set him straight. As for the lady who wanted help with her shawl, or the one who needed lemon in her tea just so, she also had no doubt that Aunt Hortensia had set the record straight there earlier. No one was rude. No one treated her unkindly. They had all passed judgement, but politely.

Jerusha decided that morning to not waste another tear on Plymouth society. She lay there thinking deep thoughts about Bolling, where she had been born and reared. Papa's parishioners already knew her circumstances; she knew word had already circulated that any dowry left to her had been spent on her brother's commission in the army. She could go home, but she didn't want pity from Papa's parishioners.

A dilemma raised its hand and waved it about, demanding that she respond.

Where do you belong? was the question.

The obvious answer was nowhere. She was too poor for the

genteel society in which she had been raised and too superior to the rabble below her to want to mingle there.

That annoying hand kept waving about. 'Very well. What is your question?' she asked herself out loud and answered it. 'Do I really want to be a lady's companion? No, I do not.'

But you are biddable, her other self, that annoying self, reminded her.

It was a fair comment. Jerusha knew she was a quiet sort, obedient to doing good works, because that was what her parents did, and she liked doing good works. It wasn't her fault that she was pretty. Her practical side knew that a wealthy duke or earl, or even a Cit, would never suddenly swoop down and declare that lack of dowry was no impediment. That only happened in bad novels. The plain truth, bold and unvarnished? Gentlemen wanted money, too.

Over breakfast that morning with her companions below stairs, she hadn't intended to whine over the hand fate had dealt. Somehow though, she blurted out her dissatisfaction, then felt deep shame. 'Forgive me. This is a stupid concern,' she said, wondering what these good souls must think of her. They surely already thought of her as privileged. She sat there, wretched with fear that she had ruined her friendships below stairs.

'Jerusha.'

She shook her head, unwilling to look up, even though Napier sounded so kind. 'I'm sorry for whining.'

She heard the butler's chair scrape back, and in another moment felt his hand on her shoulder. He gave her a gentle shake, and she looked up. 'You have our friendship,' he said.

Abbie leaned close to her. 'Maybe things aren't as bad as all that,' she said, the little girl who had fled the workhouse barefoot in winter and was found sleeping by the servants' entrance at twenty-eight Finch Street.

'Maybe things aren't,' Jerusha agreed, heartened to a degree she had not expected.

René cut through any remaining tension in inimitable fashion. 'I'll be happy to spit in Lady Oakshott's soup for you,' he declared, in his finest faux French accent. Jerusha laughed along with the others, relieved that she had burned no bridges below stairs.

If only it were her assigned day to visit Block Four, that safe haven where, for a few hours, she was useful, even if what she did was puny by anyone's standards. Instead, she and Abbie cut up strips of newspaper, dampened them, then scattered them around the venerable sitting room carpet.

She thought of the times she had watched Mama's servants do this. She asked to help once, but Mama firmly stated that her duties didn't include sweeping away carpet dirt with damp newspaper. Mama wasn't here, so she swept and thought of nothing more gratifying than seeing dirt and dust attach itself to the newspaper.

Honest work with Abbie was better than the charade of appearing at Aunt Hortensia's bedchamber at precisely twelve of the clock with mail and a cup of tea, only one cup because Jerusha was never invited to join her.

Aunt Hortensia pounced on the mail first, holding up a letter. 'From Lady Beecroft,' she said, then read it, pausing only to exclaim that Lady Beecroft had addressed her as Hortensia. She shook her head. 'You made a profound impression on Lieutenant Bracknell last night.' She read a little more and chortled. 'Never fear. Lady Beecroft set him straight. I trust he will recover. Isn't that droll?'

Jerusha had no difficulty finding other tasks around the house to occupy her for the day that involved no interaction with her aunt. By evening, Aunt Hortensia was now in transports of delight over another invitation to take tea. To Jerusha's relief, she was not included.

Sleep came easier that night, knowing she would see James Wilson in the morning.

And tell him what? she asked herself, even as she knew the answer was *Nothing*.

She couldn't tell anyone what happened, but she knew it would be enough to see Jamie and the men on Ward A.

Even the hackney ride from Plymouth to Devonport convinced Jerusha it would be a good day. People and commerce were unvarying, which soothed that part of her heart that craved order. To her additional relief, there were no stretchers or bits of bloody bandages on the grass, telling her the jetty bell hadn't rung last night. It was easy to wave goodbye to Jack O'Toole, smile when he raised his whip in return, and hurry inside.

Mrs Terwilliger smiled at her from the matron's desk, where reports piled up and probably always would. Surgeon Kidwell gave her a wave from a bedside where he sat. One of the naughty boys, probably the double amputee at the end of the first row, started a 'Hip-hip hurrah,' at the sight of her that the others joined in.

Jerusha laughed and looked around. Mrs Terwilliger cleared her throat and stacked a few reports, unwilling to meet her gaze. 'Surgeon Wilson left with the tide last night. He's on his way to the inshore station off Brest.'

The sun went out of the day as though Atlas himself had picked up the earth, toyed a bit, then tossed it over his shoulder. Jerusha looked down at the papers the matron had set aside.

He said that would happen, she thought. *Take a deep breath.*

'Then I had better get busy washing faces,' she said. Hopefully, Mrs Terwilliger was a silly woman who would never notice her dismay.

She looked at the matron, who would never be a silly woman. To her relief, Jerusha saw understanding and not derision. 'I wish he were here, too,' the matron said.

Mrs Terwilliger pointed towards the second row. 'This is a stinky bunch,' she said, loud enough for the stinky bunch to hear and laugh and cover Jerusha's disappointment.

'Then that's the row,' Jerusha said.

So there, Jamie Wilson, she thought. *I hope you're seasick.*

It was one thing for the bosun on the sloop *Harmony* to mop sweat from his face and mutter, 'I'm too old for this.' James Wilson felt precisely the same way when the slightly larger *Fleur de Violettes*—such improbable French names—rose out of the fog, so close to the French shore.

Harmony's gunners were better. Trust the Frogs to back off after one well-aimed volley. The only injury on the *Harmony* was to the cook, who scalded his shoulder when he crashed into the stove, extinguished as soon as the *Fleur* hove into view, but still hot. Would that wounds from all sea actions were so easily treated.

Foggy it may have been, but the crossing from Plymouth to Brest had been helped along by a stiff wind. Royal Navy frigates came and went, with the *Harmony* hailing those who were recipients of mailbags. From the grins on the faces of men who received the toss, James knew how welcome mail was to the crews that tacked and wove back and forth across the entrance to the Brest anchorage, with its French and Spanish allies bottled up inside and unhappy.

He watched the mail being handed around. For a brief moment, he wondered what it would be like to receive a letter from Jerusha Langley. Any daydream ended when a sailor tossed him a small package that tinkled alarmingly. To his relief, only one vial of laudanum was broken. The bosun gave the tar a ferocious scold, ending with, 'Suppose you had needed that laudanum after some Frog cannon took off your leg! Ye *hand* stuff to the doctor, idiot.'

So it went as *Harmony* approached the Channel Fleet. Prog-

ress slowed as the Fast Dispatch Vessel raised flags signifying Surgeon on Board, sometimes to hand over requested pharmacopeia, and other times to answer signals for help.

There wasn't anything drastic on the voyage out, beyond one duty that always made him shiver. The captain of *HMS Calliope* requested dental assistance, which meant highlining in a bosun's chair across a daunting space to the deck of the frigate. Because of the disparity in the two ship's sizes, this included a climb, with his dental kit slung over his shoulder. That was the easy part.

The captain waved him away. 'Not for me. For my servant,' he said hastily, and led him to his own quarters. There sat the Old Man's terrified servant, his jaw swollen, and his eyes filled with horror.

James assumed a studied air, because no patient liked to see that same horror mirrored in the surgeon's face. It wasn't that he couldn't do the simple procedure. It was the pain he knew he was about to inflict, and the noise, which rivalled that of a man screaming as some assassin ran him through with a dull blade.

The captain had already vacated his own quarters.

Coward, James thought, with an inward smile.

'Open up,' he said.

The servant did as requested. James took a good look, satisfied to see the offending tooth presented no more challenges than usual. He swallowed a few times because this was never easy.

James put his hands on the trembling man's shoulders. 'This will go fast, but you'll think you're going to die. You won't. Open up.'

Startled there were no preliminaries, the man opened his mouth wide. James clamped the business end of the dental key around the tooth, and gave a twist and massive tug. The servant screamed as James yanked, pulling out the inflamed

tooth, roots and all. The servant slumped back as his mouth poured blood.

James staunched it quickly with a wad of cotton and pressed down. 'Clamp down hard,' he ordered.

'Ah oo doon?'

'Aye, lad. You were a prince. You and I will sit here a minute. I will change that wadding a few times. I'll tell the captain no duties for you for twenty-four hours.'

He finished in half an hour, satisfied when the hole stopped bleeding. 'Keep the wadding in place,' he directed. He handed the now harmless tooth to the servant, who took it warily with thumb and forefinger, as if expecting the tooth to snap and snarl. 'It ooks oosluss,' he said.

'Aye, it is useless,' James said. 'It will do you no more harm.'

'Ank oo.'

'You're welcome.'

Chapter Seventeen

And that was the worst so far. Happy to leave the servant's drama on the *Calliope* behind, James spent some time on the *Harmony*'s quarterdeck, because he knew the sailing master. He knew him as the proud possessor of a massive suture in Sumatra a few years ago, when the ship fell afoul of pirates and the outcome was in doubt until another frigate hove in sight, belching fire. The master lifted his pantleg and showed off the neat line of fading stitches that James had applied in such a hurry because so many needed his attention.

James remarked on the number of blockade ships he had seen on the way, sailing west, and the sailing master nodded. 'There's been a breakout. Happened during a storm when our inshore fleet crossed the channel to anchor in Torbay.' He shook his head. 'Frankly, I didn't think the Frogs were that brave. Apparently they joined with ships from Cadiz, which meant our little Nelson is tracking them into the Atlantic.'

'Where away?'

The master shrugged. 'Explain the French mind to me, laddie. There's a grand chase on in the Atlantic and we're stuck here and bored.'

They watched the *Calliope* heel to the wind and sail towards France. James stayed on deck when his friend went below, enjoying the lull in duties, the same duties which had no lull at

Stonehouse, where there were patients and the dreaded jetty bell to summon more.

He surprised himself. Usually, the only thing filling his mind were those same patients.

He draped his arms over the *Harmony*'s modest railing and thought about Jerusha Langley instead. The more scientific side of his brain, the side that had bustled in and shooed away anything else, relented enough for her to sidle through the opening. He missed her. Gone only five days, and he missed her.

No one needed him right now, and they were under sail towards the inshore blockade to deliver messages and mail. All he wanted was to return to Stonehouse and see a pretty face in Block Four.

And here he had thought Jerusha Langley would be a real treasure to wounded men who needed to write letters and see a lovely woman. As he stared towards Europe, James Wilson admitted to himself that he wanted to see Jerusha as much as his patients. In fact, he wanted to see more of her.

He knew what women looked like. God knows he had delivered babies at sea and in port. When opportunity presented itself, he had never resisted the charms of the ladies. Now he wanted to know, really know, this charming creature he had met in a fraught moment, then not seen again for years.

James wondered how some sequestered part of his brain had retained that brief encounter, then brought it back with the sight of her walking down the hall in Admin. He shook his head, aware that if he hadn't turned around at the sound of a skirt swishing, he never would have found her again.

The possibility of time with Jerusha sooner rather than later died the day after, as the *Harmony* heeled towards the frigate *HMS Avenger*, answering the messenger's Surgeon on Board flags with, Come on. Urgent.

As he handled the transfer in the usual way, this time carry-

ing his full satchel because he had no idea what the emergency was, James had a moment to consider: Didn't the *Avenger* have its own surgeon?

To his dismay, the answer was yes and no. The surgeon's mate met him on deck, introducing himself only as Silas.

'Where is your surgeon, Silas?' James asked. 'I know you rate one.'

'Just...just come below with me, sir,' Silas said. 'You'll see.'

He followed the surgeon's mate down into the murk and stink of a ship too long at sea, with lanterns giving off a fitful light because the oxygen below deck was limited. Silas opened a hatch where lay the surgeon sprawled on a cot, wearing only a shirt and dangling a bottle in a limp hand. The stench was overpowering. There he lay, utterly useless to the fleet.

'I don't know what to do,' Silas said. 'Please help me.'

With relief, James closed the hatch on the insensible surgeon and followed Silas to another room off the officers' wardroom. There lay his real patient, a man no older than James, but with a leg that had been removed too late. A flick of the sheet covering him showed red streaks moving north from what had been a knee once. They had travelled into his belly, and he was full of death.

'Is...is there anything you can do?' the surgeon's mate asked, even as his eyes told him he already knew James's answer.

'Nay, lad,' James said in a low voice, on the chance the man sinking fast could hear the worst news. 'It's too late. What happened?'

The surgeon's mate turned away. 'Men get careless, sir.'

'Call me James, please.' It was a simple thing, but this overwhelmed man didn't need the bother of protocol. 'What did he do?'

'It wasn't him. T'luff was minding his own business. The

Frogs came out and caused a bit o' trouble. Sent some wounded men below and we was busy.'

'I've seen it, too.' The exhausted look the mate gave James was also familiar. 'Say on, Silas.'

'T'middie in the crow's nest was fooling around and he fell. The lieutenant tried to catch him—a fool move…'

'But a natural reaction.' James could see it all, because he *had* seen it all before. 'The midshipman died, didn't he?'

'Bounced and died. The luff's leg broke in two places. When the surgeon sobered up a day later he took off Lieutenant Gibbon's leg below the knee. Shoulda gone higher.'

'Aye, lad, but even then…' He remembered a similar case near Borneo, only the surgeon had been sick, did his best for another, then both men died, and there he was, James Wilson: young and unprepared.

Silas looked at his patient, who stirred and moaned. 'He's in terrible pain and I can't do anything for him, God damn me.'

'No. God damn the war and gross incompetence from someone who could have done better,' James assured him. 'It's not your blame. Let's see what we can do.'

They returned their attention to the dying man. James took a page from Jerusha's book and washed the man's sweaty face, then his chest. The lieutenant opened his eyes. 'I hurt everywhere,' he said simply. 'End it.'

'Aye, sir,' James replied, as the chill of death settled in his own marrow. There was one thing he could do, and *he* would do it, not leave it to some bewildered surgeon's mate. He opened his own satchel and took out a vial of laudanum.

Silas stepped back in alarm, then seemed to consider the matter. 'There isn't anything else we can do?'

'Nothing.' He leaned over the lieutenant. 'Sir, do you have someone you would like me to write to?'

'Mary Sheffield, number eleven Water Street, Portsmouth,' the man said. He never opened his eyes again, but dutifully

drank all the laudanum James poured down his throat. He said something more, and James knew, as he listened close, his ear nearly to Lieutenant Sheffield's lips, that it was meant for him.

'I have…wife…daughter. Mary due again.' He seemed to relax as the laudanum did its duty, as the lieutenant had done his. 'Soon.' More quiet breaths, each with a longer space between. 'Married?'

'No.'

'Good. Don't.'

Shaken, James took out his watch. The lieutenant's face grew slack as the tension melted. He breathed quietly for another ten minutes then stopped.

James called it at fourteen hundred hours, and Silas wrote the time in the dead book, his face calm. As James watched, the mate wrote the lieutenant's name, then his wife's name and address. 'I'll take it to the captain. He'll write her a letter.'

Silas laid a gentle hand on the dead man's chest. 'We'll get him ready for the sea.' The mate's voice hardened. 'Can we get rid of that useless surgeon?'

'We can and will. I'll make my report to your captain and the Navy Board,' James assured him. 'This was a hard school today.'

Silas nodded. 'Did I pass my exam?'

'Quite well,' James said, recalling all his similar trials by fire. 'I can't take the surgeon with me, but he can be confined to quarters. It's all on you now, Silas.'

'I know.'

James found the captain, suggesting—he had no power to order—that the surgeon be confined and not allowed to inflict any more damage. He could do no more for Silas or the lieutenant.

Or for himself. The lieutenant tried to warn him, but no. James Wilson knew he loved Jerusha.

Chapter Eighteen

The dying lieutenant's words lingered in his mind. He was not the first man that James had sent to an early grave, when he knew death was certain. He regretted not one single assisted death.

He had seen other likenesses of wives and children aboard ship, but only now, when there was a woman he cared for, did it occur to him that the misery didn't end with the final breath for married men. Now he knew their agony at abandoning their loved ones, because they had been foolish enough to love in time of war. James knew because now he loved.

He thought of Blind Man in Block Four, the one refusing to tell anyone of his wife's whereabouts. After the death of the lieutenant, James understood it as the desperation of a man completely altered and well aware he could neither support nor perhaps fully satisfy a wife ever again. Whether that was true or not remained moot. The blind man must believe his wife would be better off thinking him dead, and perhaps remarry.

James decided he would be selfish, indeed, to continue his interest in Jerusha Langley, someone beyond his social sphere anyway, even if she didn't quite fit in another, because her undoubtedly respectable parents had not provided any sort of marriage portion. That was her bad luck. His misfortune was to love her during a time of war, when not even he could guarantee he would not end up like the blind man.

And yet… He knew Jerusha was far above the fetch and carry existence of a lady's companion, no matter what her thoughtless aunt imagined. He had to smile when he knew that, provided she was willing and provided he had the courage to *ask*, for God's sake, their only escape was to run away to the United States, where one's social sphere didn't matter. They could find a parcel of land beyond the Allegheny Mountains, maybe on the western frontier in Ohio, and wear themselves out cutting down trees and planting corn. Just the idea made him chuckle and go about his business of healing the sick. He had his life; she had hers.

He won't be there, Jerusha told herself every morning she smiled at Jake O'Toole and let him hand her into his conveyance.

Sure enough, Jamie wasn't. Early in his absence, she attempted what she thought was an offhand remark to Mrs Terwilliger about how long Surgeon Wilson usually spent in his sea duty. What she got was a straightforward answer: 'Hard to tell. One month? Maybe two?'

If Surgeon Kidwell hadn't been there with his affable demeanour and real understanding of his and Jamie's patients, she would have never darkened the door of Block Four again, as one week passed and then another. The one-legged surgeon saw to it there was warm water, washcloths, soft soap, and towels available on the mornings when she volunteered her services. She couldn't call it work. On many mornings he moved from bed to bed behind her, so she was always in his sight, which reassured her.

Sometimes new patients—the Royal Navy had a well-earned reputation—needed to be reminded that she was a lady. One admonition generally served, she noted, especially the morning when a cheeky patient on Monday was a subdued fellow with a black eye on Wednesday. No one ever confessed and Jeru-

sha was wise enough not to ask. Her task of washing faces and writing letters varied little, as the weeks without Jamie Wilson passed. Jerusha worked with a willing heart.

She knew she would always remember the first emergency. She had finished washing the Blind Man's face, humming softly but saying nothing because he had told her not to speak to him, as he told everyone.

'Miss Langley, I need you now. I wouldn't ask, but the steward is elsewhere occupied.'

Surgeon Kidwell's voice was calm and almost conversational. She hurried to his side, aghast to see blood pouring from the arm of a sailor with terror in his eyes. He couldn't speak, even as his mouth open and closed in fright.

'Jerusha, put your finger right where mine is,' the surgeon told her. 'Press down and don't let up.'

Without a word, she did as he said. He quickly tightened down a tourniquet and the flow stopped. To her relief, the patient fainted, which seemed so sensible to her that she almost wanted to try it, too. As she watched in fright, her interest grew.

Surgeon Kidwell threaded a needle with a length of catgut and carefully trimmed the artery, moving aside her finger and sewing the ragged sections together with tiny stitches. 'This happens sometimes, when there has been too much trauma near a vein or artery,' he told her, explaining as he worked. 'Nothing we can't repair.'

She watched in amazement as he sewed and surprised herself by matching her calm to his. 'Surgeon, you can't imagine the tears I shed over embroidery. My mother gave up in utter despair.'

He laughed, pointed to his work, and held out the needle, still attached to the thread and arm. 'Put in two of your own. I'll show you how. Mind you, no fancy embroidery stitch.'

She hesitated until the one-armed man in the next cot

cheered her on. 'Very well,' she said. She took the needle, forcing herself to remain serene. 'I loop it?'

'Yes. That's right. Do it again, then I'll tie it off. Well done, Miss Langley. You have the magic touch. Such a pity that ladies aren't ever surgeons. Now I'll unleash the tourniquet a little at a time and we'll see how good we are.' He looked at his work in quiet satisfaction. 'This will hold now.'

'Aren't ship surgeons any good?' she whispered, not wanting to terrify the sailor regaining consciousness and send him back into oblivion.

'My dear, consider doing what we just did on a ship heaving up and down and maybe dodging about, wearing and tacking, with cannon roaring and a sick-bay full of men just like this one, and worse,' he pointed out. 'Consider that and ask yourself why any sailors at all survive to see us in Stonehouse.'

He touched her cheek, even though his hand was bloody. 'Miss Langley, you're a good person to have around in a crisis.'

'I wanted to faint,' she admitted. 'At least until I discovered how interesting this is.'

'Bravo, little one,' Surgeon Kidwell said. 'I'll send that in a letter to James. I write him every week.' He shrugged. 'Maybe the letters get to him, most often not. I number them.'

Jerusha had to bite her lip to keep from leaping about like a child, tugging on his arm, and asking if you could add a note, too, just a little PS from a friend. She reminded herself how improper that would be.

Still, her minor part in saving a sailor's life warmed her all the way home. So did Blind Man. When she passed his cot, he reached out and tugged on her skirt. That was all. Nothing said. How did he even know she was there? She took a chance and touched his shoulder, then continued on her way, wondering how in the world to convince him to tell them something about the lady and boy in the miniature.

Everything was the same as usual at twenty-eight Finch

Street—Lady Oakshott still abed, and the others dusting, cooking, and managing, as if the house belonged to someone of note, and not an encroaching widow determined to squeeze her way into Plymouth's limited society.

Thinking of the good she did this morning, Jerusha went through the charade of her day, bowing to Lady Oakshott's demands, even as she wondered how to help Surgeon Kidwell the day after tomorrow, when she could return to Block Four and make a difference.

She smiled her way through a boring whist party that evening at someone's house, playing a stupid hand because that was what ladies were supposed to do, so gentlemen partners could 'rescue' them. She arranged shawls, she nodded when expected to, and voiced no opinions of her own when the men discussed the war, even though she had opinions.

The only one who would have enjoyed hearing how she helped Surgeon Kidwell was at sea. She silently admitted to herself—no one would ever know—she needed him, his warmth, his protection, his heart beating next to hers, even as she saw no way in any universe for this to happen. 'Maybe someday' became her mantra, until she tired of it, because it was completely out of the realm of possibility.

True to her upbringing as a vicar's daughter, she petitioned the Almighty for help. Her father had taught her from early childhood that the Lord was available for consolation and remedy. Nothing happened. She knew it was past time to understand that the Almighty had more important petitions to consider, especially with a war on.

Failing that, she wanted to discuss the matter with someone earthly. She came close on the morning of her next visit to Stonehouse, when Jake O'Toole was stalled in traffic. He shook his head and stared at the tangle of horses and wagons, with a street full of chickens in cages dumped from one

of the wagons. The drivers had squared off in front of each other, ready to fight.

Jerusha leaned forward, wanting to tell him her dilemma, then sat back, because she had no words for what she was feeling.

Saying, *I am in love with a man inappropriate for someone in my social sphere to even consider*, would probably send him fleeing from his own hackney.

She smiled to herself at her folly and the moment passed. Two stout men in the crowd separated the belligerents, even as several nimble sprites snatched up the chickens, to the crowd's approval. Mr O'Toole laughed and snapped his whip over his horse's head, and they moved on.

Almost to her disappointment—not quite but almost—there was no emergency of wounded men on the grass in front of the admin building. No one needed her to join emergency care on the lawn, which, while terrifying, gave meaning to her belief that this war was her war, too.

But wait. Something she couldn't explain told her something was going on in Ward A. She wasn't wrong.

'There she is!'

Jerusha looked behind her. The good-natured laughter that followed her involuntary action made her laugh, too. They must have been waiting for her. Maybe she was wrong about no one needing her. She put her hands on her hips, saw no Mrs Terwilliger, so exclaimed in her best imitation, 'What are you miscreants plotting?'

Sam Wycherly, the one-armed former gunner, put his finger to his lips, then beckoned her closer. He held out another drawing, this one of Blind Man asleep and facing Sam, whose cot was across from his.

'I want you in the drawing, too,' Sam continued, 'plus a few other, ahem, miscreants. You know, to set the stage this is a hospital.'

'It is,' Jerusha agreed, wondering what the man had in mind. 'What will this accomplish?'

'Mrs Terwilliger—God bless the ladies—thinks we can put two or three such drawings in prominent places in markets where women assemble.' He grew serious then. 'Granted, it's a long shot, but someone might recognise him.'

'What would you write on the picture so people will know what to do?' Jerusha whispered back.

'Surgeon Kidwell said simplicity is best. Something like, "Do you know this man? Please come to Stonehouse Naval Hospital,"' he said, with an enquiring look at her, testing her reaction.

Jerusha considered the matter, unable to avoid her hesitation. 'Sam, I do not wish to be recognised on a poster.'

He frowned. 'Not ladylike, is it?'

'No.'

On the other hand, she considered her small circle of acquaintances among people of her sort in Plymouth. Those friends of Lady Oakshott's did not frequent markets, and this might be the only way to find out anything. 'I will help,' she said, after more thought. 'How do we do this?' She glanced at the sleeping man. 'He mustn't know.'

'Agreed.' Sam motioned to three miscreants who could walk. 'You, you, and you. Miss Langley, you sit over there, and they will group themselves around you.' He gestured to his drawing, propped up before him on his cot. 'I will add you four to what I have already drawn. No one will know you're not beside his bed, even as he faces me.'

Why not? Mrs Terwilliger returned from business in Ward B upstairs and helped arrange them. 'I should be doing something in the drawing,' Jerusha told her, 'something I would usually be doing.'

'I kn...kn...know,' said a patient, who everyone said had

never stuttered before the fleet action that put him here. 'Re... read to us.'

'I haven't a book,' she said.

'I... I...have.'

With some effort, he took a small volume from under his pillow and handed it to her.

'Oh, my,' she said. 'I do like Shakespeare's sonnets.'

Someone groaned. Someone else laughed. 'Hush,' Jerusha said and smiled at the patient. 'You show excellent taste in literature.'

'Yes. He. Does.' Mrs Terwilliger frowned at the lot of them, and the teasing ended promptly.

Jerusha smiled inside. 'Sir, do you have a favourite?'

'Sonnet Eighteen,' the man declared, after a pugnacious look around at his more subdued fellow invalids, now that Mrs Terwilliger had given her opinion.

'My favourite,' Jerusha declared, and cleared her throat, 'Mr Wycherly, are you ready to draw?'

'Aye, miss,' he said.

'"Shall I compare thee to a summer's day? Thou art more fair and temperate..."'

She stopped when Blind Man woke up and rolled over, regarding them out of sightless eyes. 'Good God, can't a man sleep?' he asked the room at large.

'Mr Whoever-You-Are, I have decided to read Shakespeare,' Jerusha stated, impressed with her own firmness.

He sighed. 'Whether we like it or not?'

Blind Man swore fluently, then closed his eyes, resigned to his lot.

Sam Wycherly grinned and picked up his pencil.

Chapter Nineteen

Jamie Wilson never paid much attention to correspondence received at sea, unless it came as a stamped, sealed dispatch from men farther up the chain of command, which was nearly everybody. He did keep a memo from Admiral Lord Collingwood himself, thanking him for curing his dog Bounce after Bounce ate one too many rats from the hold.

This voyage—perhaps like Collingwood's dog—he would happily have pounced on every memo or note with his name attached. Alas there were none, because the *Harmony* itself was delivering mail and not receiving any, except to forward to ships on the blockade or to the occasional frigate moving towards the Mediterranean fleet.

When they delivered mail to the larger slips, he envied complacent married men who received several letters. He tried not to remember the agony of the dying lieutenant who dreaded the awful letter his wife would receive, noting his death and expressing official sympathy.

Damn him, even with *that* memory, he also tried to forget how much he wanted to court and marry Jerusha Langley, someone who had come out of his past and made him wonder if he had ever really and truly forgotten her, even though he was twelve at the time. He knew enough about the brain to be well acquainted with how little anyone understood that jumble of matter that sat atop everyone's head and dictated…what?

He had no answers, but in a few days, he had a letter. It was one of those rare moments, so unexpected that he stared like an idiot when the captain called out his name after rummaging through a canvas mail sack from another Fast Dispatch Vessel like theirs.

'Ahem, you *are* Surgeon James Wilson?' the captain asked with a grin. 'You *do* read?' He sniffed the envelope. 'Not from a female.' He laughed and handed it to James. 'Go below and read it.'

James needed no more encouragement. He was only slightly disappointed to discover that Surgeon Kidwell had written. He propped his feet on a sack of corn destined for the mynah bird belonging to Captain Hughly of the *Prometheus* and started reading.

To his utter delight, the letter dealt mainly with Jerusha, which made him wonder for an idle moment if Jon Kidwell was interested in her, too. Surely not; the man was a confirmed bachelor and old, nearly forty.

Who could not smile at a letter like this? 'So, Surgeon Kidwell, you taught Jerusha to splice an artery?' he asked out loud, wishing he had been there to watch her eyes. That was what he remembered most about the duck-pond: her determined eyes, as she flailed and tried to reach the edge of the pond, one that probably looked as wide as the Mediterranean to someone whose feet didn't touch the bottom. He imagined that determined look directed at an offending artery.

The letter was mostly taken up with Sam Wycherly's excellent plan to sketch four drawings of Blind Man, with Jerusha behind him, reading to three or four other patients. Sam thought it a brilliant stroke to write in big letters *Do You Know This Man? Contact Stonehouse*, and then distribute the drawings to the four largest markets in Plymouth and Devonport, where ladies shopped.

He wrote:

Some housewife or servant might know this man. Look how carefully Gunner Wycherly drew him, with a face to be recognised.

James put down the letter, remembering Sam's first little sketch of Jerusha Langley. He pulled it out of his uniform pocket, the one where he stored lint and gum plasters. Sam drew her looking down at a patient. Sam had captured the softness of her lips and the wrinkle of concern between her eyes. Sam drew that certain youthfulness about her, the look of someone untouched by war, which seemed to take the softness out of men and women alike. He wanted her to remain like that forever, even though he was pretty sure Stonehouse was already changing her.

Back went the image into its nest of lint. He finished Kidwell's letter, which was surgical business, then followed the little arrow to the other side for a postscript.

The oddest thing. Perhaps Gunner Wycherly should be flattered. Apparently someone stole one of the four images of Blind Man and Jerusha.

Surgeon Kidwell had drawn a little frowning face.

We needed that missing picture. It might be our only way to identify this stubborn man. Imagine a world where such images could be churned out in seconds and plastered everywhere. Ha-ha. I know. Almost as fanciful as your wish for operating theatres so bright that we could work at night.

Jamie wanted so badly for the *Harmony* to sail for home, but there was more medicine to deliver farther south, now that blockading ships also lurked around Ferrol in Spain.

The only excitement came when *Harmony* was singled out, because of size and dexterity, to move close enough to Ferrol to pick up a spy and get his report to the frigate *Naiad*, which would put on full sail for the Mediterranean and Nelson's fleet.

It was a successful manoeuvre, done in dark and silence. 'I have such news,' the spy said, before he was rowed to the *Naiad*. 'Won't our Admiral Nelson do a jig to know that the Combined Fleet of Frogs and Spaniards is bottled up at Cadiz?'

Three more days—they had been gone six weeks—they delivered mail and medicine and added to the *Harmony*'s growing stack of dispatches for Admiralty and Horse Guards.

Home, please, James thought. *Now.*

If there was anyone more eager to see Plymouth again, James had no idea who it was. Somehow, some way, he needed to find the time—always his chief enemy—to court Jerusha Langley. He closed his eyes to the still-vivid sight of the dying man's regret he had ruined the life of the woman he loved. James decided it would be different with him somehow.

James blamed himself for the next delay. With fire in his eyes, the captain of the *Harmony* woke him too early. 'Get your carcass on deck! Captain Beck of the *Bonne Chance* wants you. It had better not be what it was the last time!'

But it was. 'Bring your little clippers and hurry,' was the message that made James groan.

Shoot me now, he thought, as he pulled on his pea coat, found his thickest gloves and the clippers, and was soon dangling between ships.

At least he thought to bring along twine.

Captain Beck shook his head over the twine when James, soaking wet, was admitted to his cabin on the *Bon Chance*, a frigate captured from the French, which came with a cat that refused to be dislodged. The Royal Navy surrendered meekly enough, and Captain Beck, the ship's next commander, found himself the object of adoration from the French cat.

The cat, now named Booty, as in, prize of war, followed Beck everywhere. The captain succumbed to such devotion, which his crew had to admit, softened him up a little. No harm there.

Six months ago, Captain Beck asked James to clip Booty's nails. The following bloodbath left James with permanent scars, but the deed was done. Booty's nails were trimmed.

Now it was time for another trim. Captain Beck had got word from another blockading ship that James was aboard the *Harmony*.

'Sir, I'm tying this twine around Booty's jaws,' James said firmly. 'Please note that I am soaking wet because your crew dropped and dragged me twice between ships. I am cold.'

'No twine,' Captain Beck said just as firmly. 'Booty will be a perfect gentleman.'

Good kitty, my arse, James thought.

'Twine,' he repeated.

'No.'

When James returned to the *Harmony* an hour later, his cheek bloody and forearm throbbing, Captain Ames clucked his tongue.

'It's just a cat,' he said. 'I know you doctored Admiral Collingwood's dog. That's how the word got around the fleet, eh?'

'I don't want to talk about it, sir,' James said.

Weeks away from Plymouth had never mattered before. He knew Surgeon Kidwell, despite his missing leg, was perfectly capable of managing Block Four. Perhaps that was an exaggeration. Jon Kidwell did tire sooner.

James Wilson knew he was known as a man dedicated to medicine and the fleet. However, he didn't need to look in the mirror to see the longing there for Jerusha Langley. Was he crazy? He barely knew her. Then why… There it ended every time, since love was not scientific and he didn't understand it.

So he thought. Captain Ames disabused him of that fool-ishness on the voyage home, when the captain joined him at the rail and asked, 'What's her name?'

'Jerusha,' James said without thinking, then stared at the captain. 'How did you know?'

'I looked like you five years ago,' came the captain's dry answer.

'You didn't try to talk yourself out of marriage, war, and leaving her a widow with small children and no income?'

Captain Ames shrugged. 'I tried, then decided I deserved to be as happy as the next man. Marry her. Goodnight, James.'

I wonder, James thought, as he stared after the captain. *Does she even have the slightest idea how much I care?*

Chapter Twenty

Jerusha had no qualms about increasing her mornings at Stonehouse from three days to five. Since Lady Oakshott's staff were by no means unintelligent, they had long known how easy their mornings could be, with Lady Oakshott asleep until noon. Going to the market could become a leisurely thing, which meant that René was able to develop a promising friendship with Dolores, a sultry-eyed Spanish candle-maker who sold her wares near the greengrocer.

'I kissed Dolores behind the green beans,' the chef confided to Jerusha as she prepared to leave for Stonehouse. He blew a kiss towards Lady Oakshott's bedchamber. 'No one's the wiser.'

'Thank goodness,' Jerusha said. 'René, for the first time in my life, I am truly useful. If I were not part of Block Four, I wouldn't have known how something as simple as a clean face can change someone's whole day. And a letter? So many of those letters I have written for the men have been answered.'

'No one ever wrote me a letter,' the chef said.

Jerusha laughed. 'Go to sea, receive a grievous wound, and I will write you one.' Her reward was a great rolling of eyes.

She thought her expanded schedule might get an argument from the jarvey, Jake O'Toole, but he gave her none, merely said, 'Five days a week instead of three seems right to me, too. No worries. I'll be here.'

His willingness to help coincided with the day weeks ago that he dropped her off as the jetty bell rang. With no hesitation—even though she knew she would never get over the terror—Jerusha leaped from the hackney and ran to the quadrangle. In a moment, Jake passed her carrying a little powder monkey in his arms. The little lad still clutched a bagged powder charge he had been carrying up to the gun-deck when all hell broke loose. No one had been able to coax it from his grip.

Jake O'Toole helped all morning that day until it was time for him to pick her up for the return trip to Finch Street. 'As God is my witness, I had no idea,' he said as he helped her into the hackney. 'If I hear that bell, wherever I am, I will come.'

Jerusha could have given him several disputes, principal of which was that he needed to work to provide for his family. 'I only hope your kindness isn't taking food from your children's mouths,' was her only attempt, which brought a wistful smile.

'We only had the one son, and he is gone. We'll get by, Jerusha.' He cocked his head towards hers. 'May I take a liberty and call you Jerusha?'

'It's no liberty,' she assured him. 'You're a kind man, Mr O'Toole.'

'You could call me Jake.'

She held out her hand. Only a few months ago, she would have hesitated and wondered if this was a step down from her precarious enough social rung. She knew it for what it was now, a bond with another person trying to live a good life, the same as she was, society be damned. 'Jake, we're equals.'

'I never shook a lady's hand,' he said, the hesitation his.

'Then would you shake a friend's hand?' she asked.

'Aye.' He shook her hand, then stepped back in fake surprise. 'The sky didn't fall!'

She had a friend. Still, five days a week… 'Jake, I can't afford to pay you for five days.'

'No fears! I've noticed that if I drop you off here three days

a week, I find more fares on this side of Devonport and Plymouth. Five days will be even better.'

He tipped his hat to her and rode away, his back straight. She watched him a moment, then entered Block Four, moving quickly up the stairs to Ward A, ready to work.

As always, she stood in the door of Ward A for a moment, wanting to take a quick census and see if anything had changed since her visit two days ago. She looked first at Blind Man, wishing that somehow his wife would have materialised overnight. Maybe those paltry four posters hadn't provoked a response.

What are we going to do with you? she thought.

She continued her assessment down the row. The two crushed ribs in Cot Thirty was still there. She sighed with relief to see an older couple sitting beside him, a great hamper between them. Usually that meant food, which somehow managed to be shared around the ward, if there was enough.

Cot Fifteen was empty.

Oh, please, no.

She turned away, determined not to cry this time, as she had last week when a powder monkey died of sepsis. He'd been ten, and had fled a workhouse to join the Royal Navy. As a vicar's daughter, she knew the little fellow was out of pain. As Jerusha Langley, she had wept on the landing, so as not to disturb the others.

But the empty Cot Fifteen meant Sailing Master Kent was no longer. She hadn't thought his injury so serious. Please God, not Master Kent, who, with his rank could have gone to a ward for warranted officers. 'No, Surgeon,' he had told Jamie firmly. 'These are my men. I was one of them once, and here I belong.'

She went to Cot Fifteen for a closer look, in that way of shoppers seeking out a certain produce, who stand there, star-

ing at the place where it should be, even though it is obviously not there. She dabbed at her face with the end of her shawl.

'Missy, that's not it,' she heard from Sam Wycherly, her artist across the aisle. 'Master Kent has been reassigned to a frigate. He told me to tell you ta-ta.'

She closed her eyes in relief.

'Here's something to cry about—a night steward told Mrs T that one of your posters was pinched from the great market on Albemarle Road.'

'Who would do such a thing?' she asked in distress.

'Some bloke who likes a pretty face,' he teased.

'Sam, really.' She glanced at Blind Man and lowered her voice. 'I wonder…we've never told him what we are attempting.'

'Maybe it's time we did,' Sam said. 'I mean, he lies there somewhere between awake and asleep, and he says nothing. Find Surgeon Kidwell. See what he thinks.'

'Where…'

He pointed overhead. 'Ward B.'

'I've never been there. Will it frighten me?'

'It might,' he told her honestly. 'No-hopers upstairs.'

Funny, she thought, as she climbed the stairs. *A month or so ago I would have thought that nothing could be worse than Ward A. Stonehouse is a lesson to me.*

The door was closed. She raised her hand, wondering if she should knock or just run downstairs and out the front door, becoming the biddable almost-servant her aunt already thought she was.

Open the door, she told herself. *Walk in.*

The room was a duplicate of the ward downstairs, except that most of the draperies were drawn at least half shut, turning the bright morning sun dim. The odour was no worse or better than downstairs.

She was startled to see nuns gliding down the rows, stop-

ping here and there to wipe a face. Jerusha looked closer, then turned away in shock—or what passed for a face. She took a deep breath, and another, aware she was far out of her sphere.

She focused on the nuns, remembering them from the jetty bells, and occasional glimpses. So this was where they laboured, attending those far gone but not quite dead, men with no hope, as Sam Wycherly said. No-hopers.

'Yes, miss?'

Chills ran down her spine as she thought for a small moment that one of the almost-dead had spoken. But no, it was a nun, a sort of person she had never spoken to before.

She saw an ordinary face enclosed in a white wimple and wearing black. 'I was looking for Surgeon Kidwell,' she stammered. 'I… I…'

The woman laid a gentle hand on her arm. 'These are God's children, too. We pray for them.' She gestured down the row to a bed with a curtain around it. 'He is in there, where a man is finally dying. Please follow me.'

The aisle was narrow so she walked behind the nun, seeing with horror the worst of what war could do to the men who fought. She saw vacant eyes and no eyes, one poor boy with no arms or legs, another with his mouth open in a silent scream. Another muttered to himself and kept rubbing at a missing leg.

The nun stopped. 'I'll ask Surgeon Kidwell if he has a moment.' She pulled back the curtain and Jerusha looked at the floor, suddenly ashamed that she had all her parts, a good mind, and a future, no matter how humble it had become since Lady Oakshott took her in hand.

'Jerusha, what are you doing here?' Surgeon Kidwell came out of the tent.

'Sam Wycherly t…told me about the missing poster. We got to thinking that maybe Blind Man doesn't know what we are trying to do for him. Sam thinks I should tell him.' She

put her hand to her mouth. 'Surgeon Kidwell! I had no idea about Ward B!'

He regarded her patiently. 'They have nowhere else to go. The Sisters of Mercy tend them until they die.'

She nodded as her mind calmed. 'Should I say something to Blind Man?' She clutched his arm. 'I mean, he could end up here!'

'Do what you think best, Jerusha.'

'That's no answer!'

'It's all you need. I trust your judgement.' He touched her cheek then returned to the curtained off area.

He trusts my judgement? she asked herself in anger. *I don't even trust my judgement.*

She stared at the curtained off area, then looked around and saw the devastation of war. Maybe she could return here another day. Surely that was enough.

She started towards the door, stopping as someone grabbed her skirt.

Don't disappoint Jamie, she told herself.

In that split second, she knew that even beyond Jamie, she didn't want to disappoint herself.

'May I help you, sir?' she asked, surprised at how calm she sounded, when her stomach was doing handsprings. 'Let me get a chair.'

Chapter Twenty-One

Jerusha looked down at a man not much older than herself, but with a massive scar on his forehead. She gently released his grip on her skirt and sat beside him. To her relief, those imps screaming inside her head, telling her to run away, must have sped ahead. Sam Wycherly could wait for an answer. Blind Man didn't want her around anyway. She had time and little else to offer this wounded man.

She held his hand. 'I'm Jerusha. Who are you?'

'T'best foretopman who ever lived,' he said, his words slow and dreamy, as if he were remembering better days at sea. 'Billy Barton is my name. The *Undaunted* was my ship.'

'Billy Barton of the *Undaunted*,' she repeated.

She saw that his eyes were sunken. He opened them as best he could and spoke with intention. 'You won't forget my name and ship?'

'I won't, Billy,' she told him, her voice firm because she understood herself a little better. 'I'll remember you always, you and the *Undaunted*.' In the deepest part of her heart, she knew she would remember.

The look in his eyes changed from urgent to peaceful. His shoulders relaxed and he died. Jerusha stayed where she was, thinking that a Jerusha Langley she barely recognised any more would have run away. Papa told her once that a dead person's spirit lingered after the last breath, which she doubted.

As she sat there quietly, rejoicing in the peace around Billy Barton, *HMS Undaunted*, foretopman, her doubt changed to belief. Papa was right.

She did jump when someone touched her shoulder, except that it was Surgeon Kidwell. 'Everyone else is so busy. What a blessing you were here,' was all he said, before he closed the foretopman's eyes. After consulting his timepiece, he wrote on Billy Barton's chart and pulled a sheet over the best foretopman who ever lived.

'Billy Barton of the *Undaunted*,' she said. 'I promised him I would remember, and I shall.'

'Jerusha, you amaze me,' he said as they walked downstairs to Ward A. He stopped at the door and considered her earlier question. 'Tell Mr Blind Man what we are trying to do for him. I don't care how blunt you are.' He managed a smile. 'He ignores the rest of us. At least he growls at you.'

She gave him The Look, something she borrowed from her mother. He laughed. 'You could chastise children with that someday.'

'My mother excelled in it.'

'Didn't they all?' he commented. 'You seem so obliging, especially when we are making demands.' He looked at the ceiling. 'Or when others feel safe enough to surrender to death, thanks to your serenity.'

Ha, she thought to herself. *Ha-ha*.

He opened the door and ushered her in. Her fear left her as she approached Blind Man. Hadn't she just guided Billy Barton to a peaceful place? She sat beside his cot in silence, wondering if anything could shock her now.

'I know you're there,' he said finally. 'You're wasting your time.'

What to say to this man? 'No, sir, you are wasting *our* time,' she settled on, cringing because it sounded harsh to her. But having said it, she knew this was no time to back down. 'I

doubt you will approve of this, but Sam Wycherly across the aisle from you drew your likeness, plus mine and some of the others.'

'Damn him,' Blind Man said under his breath.

'No, bless him for thinking of a way to get your appearance out. Someone, maybe your wife—I think you have one—will see it in the market and find you.' It was the most she had ever said to Blind Man at one time. She didn't hesitate to put her hand on his arm. Billy Barton of the *Undaunted* had so recently offered no objection to that.

She waited for him to shrug off her hand. When he did not, she took heart. 'She needs to know.'

He said nothing for a long time. Jerusha watched his face, tried to look at him as a wife might. She had become used to the scars around his right eye and the longer one that crossed the bridge of his nose and disappeared into his left eyebrow. How sad that affecting one eye affected the other. Perhaps a surgeon—Jamie Wilson?—could explain that to her someday. There was so much she wanted to know.

Blind Man stirred, but still he did not move from her gentle touch. 'Don't you know I want to spare her! Look at me. I am a freak.'

'I've been looking at you,' she replied. 'I think you're a rather nice-looking man. Your ears don't stick out, I like auburn hair, and I like the cleft in your chin. My brother has one of those. Do you have any children, sir?'

'Two,' he said automatically, then cursed. 'I don't want to tell you anything.'

She shrugged, aware suddenly that the ward was quieter than usual, everyone listening. 'Whoever they are, I hope they have your hair colour. It's nice.'

'Mary does. Go away.'

'Very well, sir. I'll leave you in peace. I promised to write some letters. Anyway, someone stole one of the pictures Sam

drew, so our chances are lessened.' Oh, why not? She leaned closer. 'Between you and me, I am a raving beauty. I am a bit offended that *all* the drawings weren't stolen. Good day to you.'

Take that, she thought, pleased when he smiled for the first time.

Maybe someday she would write a treatise on managing difficult people. Between Blind Man and Aunt Hortensia, she had plenty of experience.

She finished off her morning taking dictation and wishing Jamie Wilson would suddenly materialise to heal the blind and raise the dead. Surgeon Kidwell took a moment to walk with her from Ward A. 'Did Billy Barton of the *Undaunted* have a family?' she asked, as they walked to the quadrangle, where Mr O'Toole waited for her.

'Not that we know. He came to us as you saw him.' He paused and she saw that faraway look that all men at war seemed to possess. 'We will bury him with others like him, with name, ship and date of death, and we will curse Napoleon and blind ambition.'

He walked her to the street, where Jake waited with his patient horse and hackney.

'One moment,' the surgeon said. 'I should tell you that the *Harmony* is headed back to Plymouth. G'day, Miss Langley.'

She walked away quickly, aware that her face felt warm.

You've been gone too long, Jamie, she thought. *I think I'm finally growing up, after all these years.*

The house on Finch Street was quiet as usual. She wondered what it would be like to sleep until noon, spend an afternoon in idleness, followed by an evening at a dinner, or perhaps only cards, which she feared was her fate this evening. Her aunt confirmed it.

'It is cards tonight at Sir William and Lady Beecroft's,'

Lady Oakshott reminded Jerusha when she brought the mail and breakfast upstairs. 'Sit a moment.'

Jerusha's first thought was that someone had tattled on her mornings, spent in a place forbidden to her, helping, in her minor way, the men of the Royal Navy, also forbidden. Maybe now was the time to own up to her deception, silent and harmless, in her opinion, but deception, nonetheless.

Aunt Hortensia, you would never approve of how I spend my mornings, she almost blurted out, but stopped herself in time.

She poured tea, still only one cup because her aunt had never requested a cup for her, too.

To her chagrin, Lady Oakshott followed her first sip of tea with a command. 'Sit.'

'Yes, Lady Oakshott?'

'Tonight, you will be under scrutiny.'

'Beg pardon?'

'Scrutiny,' Lady Oakshott said, drawing out the word, until it seemed to stretch into four syllables of vast importance. 'Dear Jerusha, Lady Beecroft informed me that she is considering you as a suitable lady's companion for her mother, who lives a restricted life in Yorkshire.' She waved her hand, as if shooing away a fly or a nuisance. 'Apparently her lady's companion eloped with the local butcher, if you can imagine.'

'I can imagine it,' Jerusha said. 'Yorkshire is probably a dreadful bore.'

Lady Oakshott stared at her. 'I told your mother in my last letter that I would find you a suitable arrangement. The Beecrofts are above reproach in Plymouth. For all that Sir William is in commerce, he is a favourite of the Royal Navy apparently.'

She wrinkled her nose, as if the very idea reeked. Perhaps this was Jerusha's moment. 'Mama might not approve of commerce, Lady Oakshott, and I have no desire to go to Yorkshire.'

Lady Oakshott's eyes narrowed. 'Niece, since it is highly un-likely any suitor will appear, Yorkshire is the next best venture.'

'But…'

'Tonight! Do your best to please.' She waved her away. 'Lady Beecroft already told me she was regarding you with great favour. Don't disappointment me, Jerusha.' She delivered the final blow. 'I don't think you have a choice.'

As if to soften the blow, her aunt smiled, perhaps in what she thought of as sympathy, and concluded with this confidence: 'My dear niece, I believe Lady Beecroft is soon to address me by my first name. You may congratulate me.'

Jerusha heard the implied threat, even in its soft form.

I had better not disappoint her tonight, she thought.

Chapter Twenty-Two

Jerusha Langley was made of sterner stuff. She did not disappoint.

Her first inclination was to pack her bags and go home to Bolling, for better or worse, because she knew Papa's parishioners. Bolling already had its share of spinsters. She would eventually fit right in. But there was the matter of coach fare, which she did not possess.

Dinner was a headache, spent in the dining room with Lady Oakshott. Jerusha held her tongue as her aunt reminded her yet again how to behave. She cringed inside at the usual warning: 'I needn't remind you that if there are any young gentlemen, do not encourage them, because you have nothing to offer.'

No, you needn't remind me, Jerusha thought.

She tipped her ear towards Lady Oakshott's continuous flow of advice and quietly shut her mental door on it, thinking instead of Billy Barton of the *Undaunted*, who had died so peacefully. Blind Man had at least admitted to a daughter with his auburn hair, but no, he provided no other useful information.

'You're not listening to me,' Lady Oakshott accused, as Aggie removed the remaining biscuits and stuck out her tongue at the widow behind her back.

'I will be everything you would like me to be,' Jerusha said. 'If Lady Beecroft mentions Yorkshire, I promise to go into raptures.'

The evening went as expected. Jerusha swallowed her heart, soul, personal feelings and performed to admiration as Lady Oakshott's interim lady's companion. She fetched, she listened, she nodded in all the right places and made herself agreeable, not for any hope of employment in an occupation not to her liking, but merely to prove to herself that she could endure anything.

She began to worry, as the evening progressed. She had expected scrutiny because she knew Lady Beecroft was considering her for a paid companion for her mother. This pointed observation was oddly menacing. As she serenely went about helping the older women even before they knew they needed assistance, Jerusha tried to think how she might have offended Lady Beecroft. She could think of nothing, so shrugged off the feeling, or tried to.

The matter didn't keep her awake, except to exult in Lady Oakshott's obligatory self-congratulation on her slow but steady rise in estimation of Plymouth's better citizens. She seemed so pleased with herself that Jerusha asked, 'Did Lady Beecroft suggest that you had arrived at a first-name friendship?'

The self-satisfaction dimmed. 'No, she did not. I thought she would,' her aunt said, then changed the subject.

Before she slept, Jerusha took another look around the mental room where she stored other treasures of the heart. She thought of the pressure of Jamie Wilson's hand on her shoulder as she sat beside Blind Man two months ago. She sighed over his cheerful farewell as he left Block Four for the blockade. Since there was no one around to scoff, she asked out loud, 'Tell me how wives manage such separations?'

Even in the solitude of her room, she blushed to speak of such things. She brought herself to earth quickly with the knowledge that she would never know the answer. She was

twenty-five, with no man likely to go beyond smiling and moving on to someone eligible.

'It's a pity,' she said, after she blinked back tears. 'I would have made some man a wonderful wife.'

The matter of employment occupied her as she left the quiet house that morning. Usually she drank tea downstairs first and visited with her friends, but today she wanted her own time and space to consider an occupation, of which there were few for ladies.

She also began a mental letter to her parents, requesting a small amount to get her home. She hesitated over explaining her reasons, and decided the matter could wait. What would have been the harm in Jerusha simply remaining at home, to fade into old maidhood?

As I see it, Mama, she told herself, *you are still mortified at the disappearance of whatever money might have gone to some gentleman as a dowry, because it all went to Reggie. We could have talked about this.*

If she was more quiet than usual on the drive through neighbouring Devonport to Stonehouse, Jake O'Toole made no mention. He addressed his horse instead: 'Walk on, Noble Beast, and we will hope the jetty bell is as silent as Miss Langley.'

She knew he wanted her to at least smile at that, but it wasn't in her this morning. He shrugged and dropped her off with his typical, 'See you at half past ten.'

There was something in the air besides decay and carbolic as she started up the stairs to Ward A. Her first thought was death, followed by the hope that she would see Jamie Wilson sitting with a patient or writing on a chart.

She held her breath as she heard loud sobs and took her hand off the doorknob, not ready for sorrow on Ward A, where she had come to know the inhabitants. She finally opened the door and peeked in, startled to see the stoic Mrs Terwilliger in tears.

'M-M-Mrs Terwilliger?' she asked. 'Who this time?'

Mrs Terwilliger grabbed her and sobbed. 'It's Blind Man.'

'Oh, no,' Jerusha said, burrowing closer to the stiff and professional ward matron, who suddenly seemed as vulnerable as she felt.

She sniffed back her tears. 'See what you and Sam Wycherly have done. Don't be afraid.'

Jerusha took a deep breath and looked down the row, where Blind Man sobbed and held tight to a bonneted woman who sat on his cot, her hands straining as tight as his.

'She was waiting outside Block Four when I arrived,' Mrs T said in a low voice. 'I think she was waiting to speak to a woman.' Her voice hardened. 'The uppity ups in this block probably ignored her.' She gave Jerusha a little push. 'Go on now.'

'He'll tell me to go away. He always does.'

'Not now, he won't.'

Mrs Terwilliger's push moved her towards the sobbing blind man. Jerusha edged closer until the woman looked up, first in surprise, then in recognition. Her expression softened and she held out a shaking hand. 'I know you,' she said.

Jerusha grasped her hand, no words spoken or necessary. Blind Man must have felt her presence. He reached for her skirt and dabbed at his blind eyes with it as his wife scolded so gently.

'Mind your manners, Hal. I *do* know you. You're the lady in the poster,' his wife said. 'There you were, looking down at a book and reading to my Hal. I found the poster in the Great Market in Devonport.'

'Hal?'

'He is Henry Porter,' she said, 'and I am Claudine. He called me Claudy.' She brushed the hair back from his forehead. 'We met in Toulon, back when it was a safe harbour for the Royal Navy.' She made a face. 'It was before the Corsican Mon-

ster. He needs a haircut. No, no, not Napoleon. *This* man, this
stubborn, foolish man who thought he would disgust me. I
hope your husband is wiser,' she concluded, looking fondly
at the shaggy man. 'Hal, how could you ever think I would
not love you?'

'Claudy, I'm blind!' The words seemed torn from him, as
he surrendered the last of his dignity and the rule of society
that man earned the living and woman did everything else.
'Don't you see—I hate that word—that I was trying to spare
you from all this…this…' He gestured around the ward.

'I'm looking,' she said, her words full of love. 'All I see is a
room full of what look like kind people.' She took the folded
poster from her grocery basket and spread it open on the bed.
'See here, Mrs… What is your name?'

'I am Miss Jerusha Langley. My father is a vicar in Bolling.
I came to Plymouth for…for a reason I have yet to determine,
except that I come here as a volunteer to write letters and wipe
dirty faces. My aunt Lady Oakshott doesn't know.'

It seemed to pour out of her in one breath. Claudy stared at
her with her mouth open and the Blind Man started to laugh.
Jerusha sat back, stunned, to hear his laughter, the anguished
man who had held them hostage with his silence. She listened
to his laughter and knew there was nowhere else she would
rather be in all the world.

The feeling grew stronger when she glanced at Claudy Por-
ter, who held her husband's hand to her breast. In another
moment, she released his hand and gave her the poster. 'Usu-
ally my neighbour goes to the market for both of us while I
watch her twins. She likes to get out more than I do.' Claudy
ducked her head. 'I am sometimes teased about my accent.
There are widows in Plymouth who have lost their own hus-
bands to the French.'

'I like the sound of it, Claudy, *ma cherie.*'

Claudy leaned closed and kissed her husband's forehead,

murmuring something to him that was soft and gentle and not intended for anyone's ears but theirs. 'I went instead this morning early, because her little ones are teething and cross.' She gently outlined her husband on the poster. 'Otherwise, I would never have seen this… And here I am,' she said simply to Jerusha.

When Surgeon Kidwell joined them, Claudy gave him her full attention. 'Sir, please may I take him home with me?' She held Hal's hand to her breast again. 'I promise to take excellent care of him and…'

Hal did not withdraw his hand. 'Claudy, I am blind and useless.'

'You are my husband. We will find something for you to do,' Claudy replied emphatically. She spoke to Surgeon Kidwell. 'Hal comes from a family of millers in Kent. We will find something there.'

'I expect you will,' the surgeon said. 'I'll make the arrangements, if you wish.'

'But I… You can't…' Hal began. Even to Jerusha, inexperienced in wounds and healing and convalescence, his protest sounded hollow. Gone was the angry man who could not see, all because he was with the woman he belonged to, all his ill nature and protestations aside, which were merely barriers against rejection. It was that simple.

Jerusha spent the morning washing faces as usual, then taking dictation from a newly arrived Marine, pale from blood loss. He had come out of that odd sort of half-awake and half-asleep state of the badly wounded and beckoned to her. 'Please, miss, a letter to my sweetheart,' he told Jerusha. She obliged, her heart heavy, as she watched him struggle to say something coherent. Finally, she wrote what was in her own generous heart to Betsy Strider, who need never know that she, Jerusha Langley, had composed it.

She could nearly feel the Marine's exhaustion. He directed the letter to Betsy Strider, Strider Farm, Roads Cross, Yorkshire. 'She'll be here as soon as she can,' he assured Jerusha, then closed his eyes in death. Jerusha sat beside him until her anger at Napoleon subsided into deep hatred. When she rose from the Marine's bedside at Surgeon Kidwell's quiet reminder that Mr O'Toole was waiting outside, she nodded, took one final look at the sergeant whose name she did not even know, and knew she was born for hard things.

And joyful ones, too. By now the Blind Man, a.k.a. carpenter's mate Hal Porter, was sitting up, dressed, and being fussed over by his wife. 'His father is a mill owner,' she said to Jerusha. 'I will write a letter. In a few days I know we will be on our way. Mr Porter will find something for Hal to do.'

Jerusha told Mr O'Toole about Blind Man on the drive to Finch Lane. 'Surgeon Kidwell tells me that such moments as those are the salary he cannot spend,' she said. 'That could have gone so differently.'

The jarvey nodded, as he slowed his horse in front of Lady Oakshott's house. He turned slightly to regard Jerusha with what looked to her like the sort of satisfaction she would have enjoyed seeing on her own father's face, were he a man given to admiration. 'You are doing a great work. See you tomorrow?'

She waved to him from the kerb, ready to take Aunt Hortensia's letters to her and tuck away her deception until tomorrow. Afternoons and evenings belonged to Lady Oakshott, at least until she finished that letter to Mama. It wasn't going to be an easy letter.

Napier must have heard her come in, even though she was ever so silent. Maybe he had been waiting for her, something he never did, because she knew he did not entirely approve of her actions, which he preferred to ignore.

'Napier, see? I am here and your employer and my aunt are none the wiser,' she said, until she took a good look.

The butler was as pale as the Marine. He took her arm and gave her a little shake. 'Napier?' she said again, as a great dread grew in her.

'She knows!' he whispered to her, giving her another shake. 'She knows! Who should storm in here an hour ago but Lady Beecroft herself.'

Jerusha gasped, her stomach dropping somewhere near the vicinity of her shoes.

'She went upstairs with not so much as a by-your-leave, waving around a smudged poster from some market or other!'

As he paused to collect himself, Jerusha saw, through her own sudden fear, an old man grown suddenly older, and knew it was her doing. 'Napier, I didn't mean to cause trouble,' she began. 'I only want to make myself useful. I will explain myself to her.'

He nodded, his eyes troubled. 'Explain to Lady Oakshott why she isn't going to be received in any more drawing rooms in Plymouth, according to Lady Beecroft, who is lording it over her right now! Go explain that away, Miss Langley.'

Chapter Twenty-Three

Jerusha climbed the stairs slowly, hand over hand. She paused outside the door, unable to knock as she heard snatches of '…foolish and stupid…' and '…vulgar behaviour…' and '…nurturing a viper in your bosom…' and '…tending sick men like a common drudge…'

To Jerusha's sudden remorse, she heard her thoughtless, selfish, unkind aunt weep. She realised, to her horror, what she had done to a foolish woman, yes, but not something she deserved. Scathing mortification washed over Jerusha, bringing along its near relative: shame. She opened the door.

Two women stared at her. Lady Beecroft's face registered a cold disregard. Lady Oakshott's eyes were red with weeping, as though a beloved relative had died. As Jerusha looked at her aunt, she knew she stared at social ruin.

'Please, Aunt Hortensia, let me explain…' she began, and was stopped immediately by Lady Beecroft, who crossed the room quickly, waving the poster in her face.

'I knew it was you last night. I knew it!' she crowed in triumph. She held the poster up to Jerusha's face. 'See there, you foolish woman. *This* is your niece. You have harboured a viper in your bosom!'

Lady Oakshott wailed. 'I had nothing to do with this! You say you saw this in the market?'

'I did nothing of the kind,' Lady Beecroft roared back.

'You think I would go to market like a common fishwife? How dare you?' She turned her attention to Jerusha, who up until then hadn't known a person could actually feel blood draining from her face. This woman, screeching like a banshee, terrified her. She edged closer to her aunt, who, to her further dismay, backed away and wept. She stood between them, a target for both.

'I only…how did you find out, Lady Beecroft?' Jerusha asked.

Lady Beecroft turned to glare at Lady Oakshott, returning the poor woman, weeping, to her sodden handkerchief. 'Hush, you old fool! It was a maid who accompanied the chef. She saw you at an earlier whist party, and told the chef, who…er… appropriated the poster. She told me yesterday.'

So that is why you stared at me last night, Jerusha thought.

Lady Beecroft tossed away Sam Wycherly's wonderful poster that had brought together a blind man and his wife only this morning. 'My maid left this on my breakfast tray this morning and I knew it was you,' she said in a softly sinister voice more frightening than her previous sound and fury. 'Lady Oakshott, how could you be so common as to let her do this in a hospital full of…of…'

'Wounded men,' Jerusha concluded. 'My aunt had no idea what I did each morning.'

Lady Oakshott gasped, perhaps wondering if she could work her way back into Lady Beecroft's fast-vanishing good graces. 'Deceiver! You told me nothing of this! You…you… took advantage of my great leniency…'

'I took advantage, yes, of the fact that you never get up before noon each day, to do something useful in a place where *you* sent me initially, to deliver a basket of useless things,' Jerusha said in a firm voice, even as her insides roiled about.

Both women were silent, so she continued, knowing in her heart and mind that neither would understand what it meant to

be useful. 'I wiped off dirty faces. I held the hands of dying men. I wrote letters on behalf of those unable to write, either because of wounds or because they never learned.' She forced herself to cross the room to pick up the discarded, forlorn poster. 'One of the wounded men—he has only one hand—drew this, in the hope of putting several like it in the markets in Plymouth and Devonport to help locate a blind man's wife.'

Silence, then, 'Oh, good for you,' Lady Beecroft said, and Jerusha heard all the venom. 'I suppose there was a touching reunion.'

Jerusha chose to ignore cruel sarcasm. 'As a matter of fact, there was. The poor man had not wanted to be found, because he knew he would blight her life.'

'I don't care,' Lady Beecroft said. 'It was beneath you. For shame.' She came closer to Jerusha, who dug her toes into her shoes, determined not to let this woman frighten her. 'I was going to offer you a position as my mother's companion in Yorkshire. I wouldn't dream of it now.'

'I couldn't dream of it before,' Jerusha replied calmly. 'I would never have accepted.'

Lady Beecroft gasped as if Jerusha had struck her, then Lady Oakshott stuck in her oar, too, perhaps in a vain attempt to remain in that vile woman's good graces. 'Jerusha! Apologise!'

'Never,' Jerusha replied. 'I never wanted to be a lady's companion, Aunt Hortensia. That was your idea.' She should have stopped then, but she couldn't. 'I have done more good on Block Four in three months than either of you have done in your entire lives.'

'Leave this house at once,' her aunt said.

'I wipe my hands of both of you,' Lady Beecroft announced. She narrowed her eyes as she glared at Aunt Hortensia. 'To think I was going to address you by your first name.'

'She's only my niece…barely a relative,' Aunt Hortensia

stammered. 'A few months ago, I wouldn't have recognised her on the street!'

'I doubt another door of any consequence will open to you.'

Lady Beecroft marched across the room to the door. She slammed the door, the feathers in her hat also trembling with righteous indignation.

Jerusha knew she owed her aunt a massive apology. She had been deceitful, without question. Perhaps Lady Oakshott meant well by seeking out gainful employment for a lady gently reared, but with no prospects.

'Aunt Hortensia, I am so sorry,' she said, and she meant it.

'That is supposed to make everything right?' Aunt Hortensia replied, biting off each word.

'I know it cannot.'

'You have ruined me forever in Plymouth,' her aunt said.

'Send me home,' Jerusha said quietly, even as her heart broke. She knew she belonged in Block Four.

To her astonishment, Aunt Hortensia grabbed her arms in a grip that belied her age. 'I wouldn't spend a penny on even the mail coach, you fool,' she hissed. 'Get out of my sight!'

Jerusha left the room, closing the door quietly behind her. She stood there a moment, listening to Aunt Hortensia weep. She put her hands over her ears and stood there until she knew she could go to her room, where she sat as the afternoon passed.

What to do? Aunt Hortensia had turned her off. She had no money. She had no doubt that her aunt was even now composing a letter to her easily influenced little sister in Bolling. Papa might take her back, but preach a sermon about ungrateful children, because she already knew he was somewhat lacking in forgiveness.

Lady Oakshott would probably return to Oaklands when the tenant's lease ended. There might be enough society there to

placate her, if the word did not spread of shameful goings-on in Plymouth.

When shadows lengthened, Jerusha washed her face, tidied her hair, squared her shoulders, and made her way below stairs, uncertain of her reception there. There they sat in the servants' hall. Jerusha stood there, waiting for Napier to motion that she join them. When he did not, every fear returned.

'I caused a terrible scene upstairs,' she admitted. 'I am certain you heard it.'

'I think the neighbours heard it, too,' Napier replied, sounding like a stranger.

'Lady Oakshott and I were never close, but I do regret what happened. I suppose now she will return to Oaklands as soon as the lease is up.' Their expressions were unreadable. 'Have you been keeping something from me?'

Again the others looked at Napier, who appeared years older since this morning. 'Lady Oakshott did not lease the house to that mushroom from the City,' he said. 'She sold it to him.'

Jerusha couldn't help her intake of breath. Napier stared straight ahead. 'Sadly, the old place was already deeply in debt. It took nearly all of the purchase price to pay off her creditors.'

She saw a spark of anger in his eyes, this man who had probably been trained from birth to show no emotion. 'Sir Harvey gambled, wenched, and drank. He ruined whatever prospects either of them had. Lady Oakshott only has this house and a small pittance.' He looked at his co-workers. 'None of us have been paid in months.'

'I had no idea,' Jerusha said, when she could speak. 'I suppose my situation is not important to you, is it?'

'Not really,' René agreed, but not unkindly. 'You at least have a home to go to.'

I doubt it supremely, Jerusha thought.

'We shall see. Excuse me, please.'

She went upstairs again, as an idea took hold. She squelched

her thought of borrowing money from Napier to get home; they had less than she. Lady Oakshott told her to leave.

What to take? She had come with a sturdy grip and her portmanteau, which would have to remain behind, because she could not afford to cart it anywhere. By folding and rolling, she managed to get two dresses, petticoats, camisoles, nightgown, robe and shoes into the grip, plus smaller items, and her treasured hospital aprons, given to her by Jamie Wilson, who was somewhere between here and France.

There was only one place to go. No one enquired after her as the sky turned dark. When she knew no one would notice, she moved quietly down the stairs and out the door without a backward glance.

She avoided Devonport's streets with grog shops where sailors hung out, and which Mr O'Toole drove past with no qualms. It was strange to hear only silence from the dry docks where warships came for repairs. She walked with purpose, as she watched Mrs Terwilliger walk, confident in appearance, even as she quaked inside, wondering if she was doing the right thing, but knowing she had no choice.

The front door of Block Four was locked, but her momentary panic left her when she saw one of the nuns from Ward B coming out of a side door. When the woman was out of sight, she tried that door, sighing with relief when it opened. It was an easy matter for her to store her grip in the broom cupboard by the morgue.

She put on her apron and walked upstairs to Ward A, where, to her relief, Mrs Terwilliger was supervising the end of supper. Quickly and quietly, she explained her unexpected appearance. 'I will do tonight what I do during the day,' she said, 'if you will let me. Do I know the steward who will be on duty?'

She did, an older fellow who put her to work tidying the men she already knew so well. Sam Wycherly, her dear artist, swore a mighty oath when she told him what had happened.

The word passed quickly, and soon she was left to tend these friends.

Blind Man's bed—no, Hal Porter's—was already occupied by another patient, a frightened powder monkey. She found a book to read to him, loud enough for all to hear. Little by little, she knew that somehow, someway, this would work out.

Chapter Twenty-Four

Jerusha knew Mrs Terwilliger left at seven of the clock. She had no idea what tomorrow would bring, when Surgeon Kidwell returned, and the admin building filled up with men who made decisions. She could think about that tomorrow.

I am in everyone's black books and I have become a burden, she told herself.

When the powder monkey slept, she washed faces as the hospital steward helped the patients who needed urinals. For a rough-looking fellow, he was delicate in his duty and also careful to make sure she did not see anything a tender young woman should not witness. She silently thanked him for this kindness.

On the steward's advice, she took dictation on a letter from another new arrival, who wanted his mother to know where he was, and how fast she could bring a hamper of food. They both laughed over that one.

'Gor, miss,' the gunner said. 'I didn't think I'd laugh again.'

Neither did I, she thought.

When she finished and the ward was full of drowsy men, or patients dosed with laudanum to stop pain for a few hours, Jerusha sat at Mrs Terwilliger's desk. She leaned forward and rested her head on her arms. What a dreadful day this had been, a day when she declared a small measure of independence, with little, really, to show for it.

She started in fear when a firm hand rested on her shoulder.

'No worries, Miss Langley,' she heard, and sighed in relief. Surgeon Kidwell stood there, Mrs Terwilliger beside him. 'Mrs T told me of your dilemma.'

'Had to wait for him to leave Ward B,' the matron said. 'Don't mind admitting that Ward B gives me the willies.'

Personally, I feel closer to God there, Jerusha wanted to tell her.

But that would be presumptuous, and she had caused enough problems for herself and others today. Better to remain silent. God knew she was penitent.

The surgeon sat down with his own sigh of relief. 'Long day. Good night, Mrs T. I'll take it from here. I promise her back to you in the morning.'

'Verra well, sir. G'night, you two.'

'She told me what happened,' he said, with no preliminaries. 'You're in a bad spot, but I can help.' He appraised her, as if searching for courage. 'Or rather, Surgeon Wilson can help, even though he doesn't know it yet. Come along.'

She followed him without question. He waited while she retrieved her grip by the morgue, then followed him out the side door.

'Surgeon Wilson and I are quartered in two houses behind the Admin Building,' he said. He held the lantern higher. 'See there?' He stopped before the second house. 'It would be highly improper for you to stay in my house.'

She nodded, grateful the darkness hid her rosy face, which turned even warmer when he gestured to the other house, lit inside. 'Surgeon Wilson is still at sea, so we are going to take a chance for a few days. You may stay here. I've already discussed the matter with Margaret McDonald, his housekeeper.' She saw his smile. 'Mags found the whole thing entertaining. There is no accounting for the Scots, is there?'

She had no way of knowing any such thing, but she nod-

ded, suddenly aware of just how tired she was. It had been a long, awful day.

She stood back as he knocked on the door, which opened almost immediately to reveal a short and plump woman, neat as a pin and wearing an apron.

'Here she is,' Surgeon Kidwell said simply. 'I know you'll make her welcome.' He nudged Jerusha. 'I'll stop by tomorrow morning at eight, and we can walk to Block Four.'

'I am a lot of trouble, Surgeon Kidwell,' she said. 'I didn't know what else to do.'

'You're only a little trouble, not much over five feet, I think,' he said with a smile. 'I can use your help, oh, my word, I can.'

'But when Jamie—Surgeon Wilson—gets here?'

'He and I will arrange something. Goodnight, Miss Langley.'

He left, then turned back. 'My mother used to say to me, "Things most generally work out." I still believe her.'

'Miss Langley, are you hungry? I am,' Mags McDonald asked, also with no preamble. Jerusha was discovering that medical personnel didn't waste words.

She doubted she would ever eat again, but the chicken stew was perfection. And since Mags—she insisted Jerusha call her Mags—always took a little grog before bed, Jerusha did, too.

'Two parts water and one part rum,' Mags told her. 'Simplest recipe I know. You'll feel better after a snootful of this.'

Jerusha doubted this, too, but her shoulders did relax after she downed the grog, and her eyes grew heavy. Dutifully, she followed Mags up the stairs and into one of three rooms. 'I'm downstairs, and there's only that one small chamber off the kitchen,' the housekeeper explained. 'You'll be fine here.' She gestured. 'The surgeon sleeps across the hall, and he has a wee office in the other room.'

Jerusha looked around the small chamber, with its bed,

bureau, and washstand. 'I'm so tired,' she admitted. 'This will never *ever* do once Jamie—Surgeon Wilson—returns...'

'Then it's a good thing he's not here,' Mag concluded cheerfully. She shook her finger, but Jerusha saw nothing unkind in the gesture. 'Remember what Surgeon Kidwell told you?'

'Things most generally work out?'

As she closed her eyes mere minutes later, Jerusha sincerely hoped they were right.

The deck of a Fast Dispatch Vessel like *Harmony* was no place for a worried man to walk back and forth, but Jamie Wilson had done it before, stepping around rope and other deck accumulation. This time the worry was a lieutenant of Royal Marines below deck with a broken leg that might set correctly with proper pulleys, if he could get him to Haslar Hospital in Portsmouth soon enough.

The wrinkle in that plan? Stonehouse in Devonport was closer, but *Harmony* also carried dispatches from Admiral Nelson cruising off the Strait of Gibraltar, with orders to get them as soon as possible to London. The leg had to wait to Portsmouth.

The able seaman with the shattered collarbone died last night and had been given a burial at sea this morning.

You should have lived, Jamie thought, as he bowed his head with the others and sent the man sewed into his hammock to the depths.

It was a careless accident, as so many were on the blockade, when the tedium of service made crews lax and silly.

But orders were orders. The amputation was doing well, with no red streaks or bad smells to warn of worse to come. The ensign still had most of his lower right arm. He could be fitted with a hook and continue his career on the quarterdeck. He seemed content, and more to the point, alive.

James still wanted to pace back and forth on the deck,

and not solely because of his miniature floating hospital and its patients. Only yesterday he had received a note from Jon Kidwell, tossed aboard *Harmony* with a bag of mail from an outgoing messenger sloop. The message had ended up in the water, and the ink ran. All he could make out was:

Jerusha...bad spot... We're making...

Making something? The rest was illegible except for either *tears* or *fears*.

Although not a message designed to comfort him, it meant Jerusha was still in Plymouth, and must have reached out to Jon Kidwell for something. He added Jerusha to his long list of worries. The longer he practised medicine, the longer that list grew.

Even worse was the overwhelming, all-consuming exhaustion that worked its way into his mind and body never to leave. He had forgotten what a peaceful night's sleep felt like. By the time he returned to Plymouth and saw to his patients aboard the *Harmony*, he would be away again to the blockade.

Usually, his wishful thinking ended right there. This time was different. Nobody on board *Harmony* had any idea he was wondering how nice it would be to lie down with Jerusha Langley, her head tucked into his chest, his arm around her, and sleep. Nothing more. He had never been a man to ask for much, not during this generation of endless national emergency.

And there was this: What could he possibly offer the gently raised daughter of a parish vicar and his well-bred wife? Jamie knew his origins and they were humble; Jerusha knew them, too. She had already told him she had no dowry and was destined for the single life. He also knew her dilemma was none of his business. Better he look forward to a deep sleep in his own bed, and not a hammock that swayed.

To his relief, no fickle wind or additional duty stopped *Harmony* from Portsmouth. The sloop sailed into the bay and the dispatches for Admiralty were handed off to a courier. Captain Ames took *Harmony* directly to Haslar. God bless the architect who knew precisely where to put a naval hospital. Hospital runners waited with stretchers for the broken leg and the amputated arm. Jamie saluted both men, and returned to *Harmony*, where Captain Ames slept on the deck next to the mast.

And God bless you, Captain Ames, he thought, looking down at a man who had come up through the ranks, same as he.

No wonder *Harmony* suited him. There was none of that posturing plaguing other ships. Everyone aboard *Harmony* was as common as ducks in a pond.

A day later in the waning afternoon, the sloop docked in Devonport, snugging right to the wharf because of its small size, and not anchoring in the bay. A bleary-eyed Captain Ames already had orders to sail in two days with the tide. Jamie had prepared his list of medications for the next voyage. He would slip it under the apothecary's door in Block Four and hope it would be ready in two days.

Jamie started towards his quarters behind Admin, ready to collapse in his bed, when the jetty bell began to ring. Too tired to even curse, he turned towards the quad, where the newest crop of wounded would soon litter the ground.

He raised a tired hand to Jon Kidwell, coming slowly from Block Four on crutches, telling Jamie worlds about his fellow surgeon's own exhaustion, when his peg leg pained him. He started towards Jon, until he was grabbed by his night steward and directed towards The Hopefuls, as he called those likely to survive. He worked without stopping.

Two hours later, Jamie pressed his hand into the small of his back and watched the hospital administrator finish assigning the wounded to wards. With a sigh, he turned towards The

Hopeless, to see what, if anything, he could do for those who would never find a bed inside.

In the near darkness, he stared in open-mouthed amazement to see Jerusha Langley, her dress and apron stained with the blood of The Hopeless. Surely he was imagining things, but no. He watched, humbled to the dust, as she carefully wiped what remained of a sailor's face, and held his hand. Her own face was calm. She had eyes only for the dying man.

'Come along. I'll tell you what happened to her,' Jon Kidwell said behind his back. 'She's been staying in your quarters. Her aunt turned her out.'

'What on earth…'

Jon stopped him. 'If I'm misreading the signs, I'll find another place for her tomorrow,' he said. 'If not, then you have been given a rare opportunity.'

If he had been more alert and less exhausted, Jamie would never have said what he did. 'This is war and no time for… for what I am not certain of.'

'It's all the time you have, James,' his superior said. 'Think hard.'

Chapter Twenty-Five

Bless her heart. Mags McDonald had bean soup and bread ready when Jerusha dragged herself back to Jamie Wilson's quarters. It was a simple matter to strip naked in the kitchen and wipe herself free from the blood and unmentionable debris of the dying.

So tired, she barely watched as Mags pocketed a note and turned a cheerful look her way, which startled Jerusha. Surely the old lady had heard the jetty bell ring? To her further surprise, Mags took the comb from her hand and extracted the rest of the detritus of war and wounds from her hair.

'There now,' the housekeeper said in her usual brusque way. 'I'll get my robe. You look too tired to climb the stairs.'

The robe was miles too big, but Mags helped her by tying the belt snugly enough and then touching up her hair again. 'Sit and eat,' she said when she was apparently satisfied. 'If I don't help you up the stairs, someone will.'

It was already their little joke. Mags had assured her it was the joke in many a British household where the men were at war, and wives and daughters left to fend for themselves.

She was halfway through the bowl of beans—vaguely surprised that she could tend to dying men with unspeakable wounds and then knock back a meal—when the front door opened. 'I hope to goodness that isn't someone needing me,' she said to Mags.

'I think it is,' the housekeeper replied, then went into her quarters off the kitchen and closed the door.

To Jerusha's delight, agony, consternation, joy, relief, longing, and total confusion, Jamie Wilson came into the kitchen. As she watched him, her hands folded in her lap, he leaned against the doorframe and smiled, as if he could not get enough of merely seeing her sitting in his kitchen. She knew she was no prize at the moment, but it didn't seem to bother him.

She remembered her manners, as in, 'May I get you a bowl of beans?' and then forgot beans when he wrapped his arms around her.

'I am so tired,' he said, which did not surprise her, not after his weeks at sea. Then she wondered. 'Were you…were you in the quadrangle?'

He released her, which she thought a good idea, since Mags's robe was starting to gape a bit. He sat down, looked at her bowl, and appropriated it without asking, which touched her heart. 'Mags makes the best bean soup,' he said. 'And I have rag manners.'

'You're hungry.'

'You have no idea the depth of my hunger,' he told her.

To her heart's delight, she understood him perfectly because she saw it in his tired eyes. Still, he needed to know. 'My aunt turned me out because she found out my deception.'

'You mean the deception of becoming indispensable to Wards A and B in Block Four? That one?' She heard the tease, despite the exhaustion.

'Aye, that one,' she replied. At least Jamie Wilson might not scold her about the mess she created, all by herself. 'I was wrong to deceive her, when everyone told me to avoid the navy.'

'Would she have given permission for you to help us on Block Four?'

'Certainly not. She considered it beneath me.' He might

as well know more. 'Jamie, she was training me to become a lady's companion, since no man of my society would ever want a wife with no dowry.'

'Men need that bride money, I suppose,' he told her.

Her heart failed her at that simple statement. Better not to show it, so she turned towards the kitchen range. Maybe something needed stirring, except that it was midnight and the stove was clean.

He needed to know everything. 'The worst part is that my deception ruined her in the eyes of those fribbles she has been toadying up to, seeking entry in Plymouth high society.' She had to smile. 'Plymouth *has* no high society.'

'Not that I've ever observed,' he agreed.

'I ruined her, nonetheless,' Jerusha concluded. 'She turned me out. She was counting on her inclusion amongst the wives of admirals and bankers, I suppose.' Oh, why stop there? 'She hid from me that she sold her late husband's country estate, and the purchase price was just enough to discharge Sir Harvey's great debts. All she has is the house on Finch Street and a pittance left for her to live on and no, she has no friends, thanks to my deception.'

That was the worst of it. She dabbed at her tears with the end of the tie on Mags' robe. 'No matter how she treated me, she is worse off because of me.'

'Those friends would have turned her off anyway, once they discovered how poor she is,' he said reasonably. 'It's hard to keep secrets when you're broke.'

'Custom and tradition, Jamie. She tried to hide her ruin, and I made it worse,' she said, tired now and wanting her bed.

'That's out of *my* social sphere,' he assured her. 'Surgeon Kidwell told me how you and Sam Wycherly found the blind man's wife.' He sighed. 'I doubt Lady Oakshott would have approved.'

She felt on safe ground, now that the talk had turned to

Ward A and not her predicament. 'Jamie, he was so determined that his wife not know he was even alive, and she was so happy to find him. Why would a man do that?'

'He wanted to spare her the burden,' he said too quickly, which made Jerusha wonder if this long-forgotten, apparently never-forgotten friend of hers had considered the dilemma himself.

He stood up and held out his hand. 'Let's sit on the back steps. It's chilly out there and I'm falling asleep in here.'

'Then go to bed,' she said, practical again, now that he knew the worst about her. She could figure out where to go in the morning. Mags might know of a position.

'Not yet,' he told her.

She suddenly felt too shy to question him. Maybe he wanted to tell her of his weeks on the blockade, going from ship to ship.

'Why this?' she did ask, when they sat on the outside steps. She had no plan to ever tell him that all she wore was Mags's robe, and the cold from the stone step cut right through. He at least wore a wool cape.

'I like the peace and quiet back here. Nothing is creaking or moving, and no one is going to ask me for anything.'

Oh, dear. This squashed her tentative plan to ask him for mail coach fare home to Bolling. Still, he was probably the only one she knew well enough to help her. She realised she had nothing to lose in the asking. Perhaps she could joke about it.

'Jamie, your statement entirely ruins my feeble plan to ask for the loan of mail coach fare to Bolling. I cannot stay here and...'

'Why not? You're so useful in Ward A, according to everyone,' he said. 'Even our dragon lady, Mrs Terwilliger.'

She looked at him in amazement. 'Mrs T said something nice? Surely not.'

'Surely yes. She told me you are fearless.'

If I never get another compliment in my life, I can die content, she thought.

'I had no idea.'

'What will happen if you go home?' he asked, when she was starting to wonder if he had fallen asleep. He seemed to be leaning against her, or maybe she was leaning his way.

'Mama will weep and sigh, and Papa will deliver a lengthy sermon about the sins of deception and ingratitude.'

'That's wicked,' he said in a tone of voice that made her never want to cross him.

'I will find out when I get home.'

His arm went around her and she leaned in. 'Jerusha, do you really want to leave?'

The question hung in the air, delivered in total seriousness. Something sweet and certain told her he was really asking, 'Do you want to leave me?'

Did she want to leave him? Never.

Jerusha Langley took a deep breath and changed the course of her life. She held his hand to her cheek and kissed it. 'No, I do not,' she said firmly, the right answer.

He tightened his grip on her shoulder, which more than suggested that for the rest of their lives, this man would protect her, and if she was lucky, love her.

'We'll manage, Jerusha,' he replied. 'We'll manage.'

He relaxed his grip, and she burrowed closer. 'I have to return to the blockade immediately.'

When she started to cry, he handed her an already used handkerchief, all he had. 'Blow your nose. I can get a common licence for eight shillings today. I believe it is after midnight.'

'But the banns...'

'Nae, nae lassie, listen a moment. The Royal Navy has certain prerogatives. Banns don't matter.' He held her off and took a good look at her. 'Are you prone to seasickness?'

'I have no idea,' she answered honestly.

'No matter. Whatever ship I am on is my parish. Right now, it's the *Harmony*, Captain Ames commanding. I am going to pay a persuasive visit to Plymouth's bishop, whose son I tended successfully at the Battle of the Nile. I think I can convince him to marry us on the deck of the *Harmony*. That is another prerogative. I'll help you down the gangplank like a real gentleman, and I'll sail away like a cad. What an offer! Aye or nay?'

She smiled at that, then watched his face, seeing exhaustion. Perhaps when he had some sleep, he might shake his head at this folly and call the whole thing off. Until that happened— if it did—she was ready and willing. 'Aye.'

He pulled her up and kissed her soundly, which did amazing things to her body. He led her up the stairs and pointed to the left. He went to the right.

'Lass, when you come down for breakfast, I'll be gone,' he said. 'Go to Block Four and help all you can. Can you locate Mr O'Toole?'

She nodded.

He seemed to understand her shyness. 'Ask him to meet us at the dock and come aboard, too.'

'Surgeon Kidwell and Mrs Terwilliger, as well?'

'They'll probably have to do a coin flip, one or t'other.' He kissed her. 'Find a better dress. Mags's robe is a little casual for a wedding.'

With that, he yanked the tie off and chuckled as she tried in vain to cover herself. 'G'night, my bonnie lassie.'

Chapter Twenty-Six

H e had huge doubts the next morning; maybe that was what two hours sleep did. In the middle of the night, Jamie opened his bedchamber door several times to stare at Jerusha's closed door, but went no farther. He lay down again, revisiting the sight of Jerusha's beautiful body in the half-light of the upstairs corridor, then went over every medication he needed to cajole from the apothecary. He scolded himself for thinking a wartime wedding like this was even remotely a good idea. His doubts didn't vanish, but did slink away to a dark spot, maybe to jump out later and yell 'Boo!'

Mags didn't seem surprised at his announcement. 'I thought this would happen.'

Between toast and tea, he told her about his and Jerusha's back step decision, which made her laugh. On her advice, he gathered up his papers identifying him as a naval surgeon, place of birth, and other proof that he was not a drooling idiot. With those, and a visit to the bishop, who remembered him and couldn't stop thanking him, he acquired a common licence. Minus eight shillings, he arrived at Block Four a few hours later.

He nodded to Jerusha, who sat beside one particularly obnoxious purser's mate who was barely wounded and taking up bed space, then sat down to write a quick note to Captain Ames aboard *Harmony*. He sealed it and before he lost his

nerve, handed it to the runner who had followed him into Block Four and now relieved him of another shilling as he darted away.

He wanted to sit down with Jerusha Langley, apologise for his hasty proposal last night, and see if she felt the same way. They could end this mad business with no one the wiser. On the other hand, his Scottish soul reminded him that he had spent eight whole shillings on permission to rapidly wed and eventually bed a wife.

A moment came during the noon meal, when Mrs Terwilliger and her assistants passed around food, helping where needed. He rose to seek out Jerusha, but annoyingly, she was helping someone already. He got close enough to see that her eyes looked tired, suggesting that she had suffered a restless night, too. He needed to say something to her. No time.

Then it was an afternoon of setting bones, and performing an amputation there in the ward with a curtain separating them from patients probably trying to studiously ignore the noise, tears, and rasping of saw. At least it was quick.

He was assisted by Jon Kidwell, who looked at him with merry eyes once the worst was over, and the patient, lighter one foot, dozed with the blessing of Surgeon Laudanum. Still behind the curtain, Jamie poured out his doubts. Kidwell stopped him. 'This is the smartest thing you have ever done.'

'What? Ruin someone's life? I could die at sea tomorrow.'

Kidwell shrugged. 'War is the hand we have been dealt, I would remind you, Surgeon Wilson. Look around you.'

Jamie had one last, weak card to deal in that hand of death, something feeble about sparing the woman he loved. He thought about a sweet face on a crowded dock, waiting for him to return, a sight he longed for, if he was honest, because he had no one, either. Was it fair, though?

'I'm a coward,' he said simply.

'Hardly. You see right here the consequences of war. That

doesn't make you a coward, because you *are* going to marry Jerusha this afternoon, in spite of what you know about suffering and death.' Kidwell clapped a hand on his shoulder. 'I envy *you*.'

Jerusha bided her time quietly all that long day, with Jamie so close but busy, and when he wasn't busy, in intense conversation with Surgeon Kidwell. She knew he must be having second thoughts, and she did not blame him. She took her own census of her defects. All she brought to marriage was a pretty face. Yes, there was silliness about a dip in the duck-pond, possibly the only thing they had in common. She thought of all the reasons this was nonsense.

She told herself to stop. There was work to do, and time between their walk from Stonehouse to *Harmony*'s dock to sort this out and end it. He would sail away.

The matter became simpler. Cot Fourteen's mother enlisted her to hand out soft bread and jam to those who could eat it. Jerusha marvelled at such goodwill in a sad place. She glanced at Jamie's broad back a few times—he had a marvellous back—and knew this turmoil would amount to nothing.

She had distributed the last of the bread and jam when Jamie gestured to her by Mrs Terwilliger's unoccupied desk.

This is it, she thought, because he had removed his surgeon's apron.

She glanced at the clock and knew it was over.

You're not waiting to walk me to the dock.

He spoke with no preamble, because that was Jamie Wilson. She braced herself, then wondered. 'I am to supervise my pharmacopeia order immediately,' he told her. 'There's no one else to get it to *Harmony* and I need it. I must leave now.'

Over and done, and neatly, too. 'I hope you have a successful voyage,' she said.

He gave her a strange look. 'What I mean is, I won't be

able to walk with you to the dock. I'll meet you there. Do you need directions?'

She shook her head. He handed her directions anyway, written on the back of a prescriber's pad. 'Your handwriting is illegible,' she said, which made him chuckle.

'Just look for a small ship with one mast and a quantity of naval stores being loaded aboard. See you in an hour.'

And he was gone like that, a surgeon intent on getting his medical supplies on board his second home, doing battle with Napoleon. She returned to her duties, well aware that if she didn't show up at the dock, *Harmony* would sail anyway, no matter what. He might be at sea for another six weeks, and she could be home in Bolling. A grovelling letter to Mama would provide mail coach fare.

Except for one thing. She surveyed Ward A and found herself looking at Blind Man's cot, occupied again. Still, the sight remained of Blind Man and his wife, their arms around each other, ready to do battle with an enemy besides Napoleon, but together for the fight. In that moment, Jerusha Langley knew that if she did not walk to the *Harmony* and know for sure, she would regret it the rest of her life.

She walked by herself, head up, shoulders back, and no target for lounging sailors. The air was brisk and cold, and the water had a chop to it. The sight of a row of docked ships stopped her. She looked in the bay where the larger ships of war anchored. It was a world foreign to her, but she felt the energy and the need for speed, with the turning of the tide soon.

There was *Harmony*, so small that it dismayed her.

A big wave will swamp this wee thing, she thought. *What can the Royal Navy be thinking? That's my man on board.*

She stood still with that realisation. *Her man on board?*

She saw other women waiting, some with little ones, some

alone. She was about to join a sorority of those who waited, feared, and hoped.

How do they do it? she asked herself, even as she knew she had committed herself.

Uncertain, she stood by the ship, watching the loading of the last cargo, winched up efficiently, the ropes soon to be stowed. Men were already climbing the rigging, heading to furled sails. Was she too late?

'Jerusha.'

James stood near the wheel. He motioned her closer and started for the gangplank, a narrow affair that made her frown. When she hesitated, he came down as calmly as if he strolled along a wide boulevard. He held out his hand and she grasped it.

'Watch your step. They're still stowing things,' was all he said.

'This boat really looks too small for the ocean,' she said. He ended all argument by holding her close. She turned her face into his uniform, which smelled of brine and camphor.

'It's a sloop, not a boat, dear lubber,' he said.

She remembered something she wanted to tell him from their first encounter since Bolling and a duck-pond. She held herself away from him, noting his disappointment at that, but wanting to see his face. 'I should have told you this sooner,' she said, laughing inside at his wary look.

'Should I worry?'

'Not at all,' she replied. To her delight, Mrs Terwilliger came puffing up the gangplank.

'I taught myself how to swim,' she said quickly. 'I can float and paddle about. I promise I won't sink ever again.'

He laughed and gave her a loud smack of a kiss, then turned her around to face Captain Ames, who eyed them with a smile of his own. The bishop stood beside him and opened his prayer

book while the first lieutenant bellowed, 'Stow the noise, ye fiends of hell!'

'I don't have a ring,' Jamie whispered in her ear.

In sudden, unexpected silence on a ship preparing to get underway with the tide, they were married. It was a brief ceremony. A sail thundered down as the bishop said, 'Kiss your wife, Surgeon Wilson, then see her over the side.'

He kissed her and held her close. 'I had the coldest feet this morning,' he told her. 'All day, if I'm honest.'

'So did I,' she said. 'I changed my mind three or four times.'

'And here you are anyway. I'll see you who knows when,' he told her, after they signed a registry and then the sailing master's log. 'There's a war on, my love.'

'Say that again,' she asked impulsively.

'A war on?' he teased.

'Oh, you...'

He pulled her close and put his hands on her neck. 'My love,' he mouthed, then kissed her, to the general enjoyment of the crew, the bishop, and Captain Ames.

He helped her down the gangplank as the ship's crew cheered. 'I'm a particular favourite,' he confided, 'except when I wield a dental key or treat one of them for the clap.'

'That's hardly loverlike conversation,' she told him, even if she wanted to tug him back to his house and see what happened in that bedchamber across the hall.

'Wait till I come back,' he replied, his face serious now.

Sniffing back tears, Jerusha stood on the dock until *Harmony* sailed out of sight.

Mrs Terwilliger walked her back to Stonehouse, then told her to go home.

Home.

She looked down at the wedding papers Jamie Wilson had put into her hands, along with a pouch. She opened it, looking

inside to see shillings, a key, and a note, which was—true to form—scribbled on a prescriber's pad.

She read it.

This is your house. My bed has an excellent mattress.
Remember me, my dearest duck-pond girl.

Chapter Twenty-Seven

Jerusha set about becoming a wife without a husband, a husband she knew she wanted more every day. She lay in bed the next morning after her hurry-up wedding, hands folded together, watching the day come. She enjoyed the luxury of there being no one in the house, Mags a possible exception, to tell her what to do.

That realisation lasted briefly because she knew duty summoned her from Stonehouse. There were never enough people to help Mrs Terwilliger, an awesome dragon who frightened pursers and bosuns, but was tender enough to sit beside a frightened Marine until he died.

And those letters Jerusha wrote for others weren't going to write themselves. She got up, made her bed, then padded across the corridor to her husband's empty chamber. She was almost afraid to open the door, so palpable was his presence.

'Such a tidy man I married,' she said, marvelling at the order. The bed was neatly made. It touched her heart to see that his pillow still bore the indentation of his head, telling her he must have lain down for a moment after he made his bed.

She came closer to observe the book on his bed, with a folded note on top. There it was, addressed to *Jerusha Wilson*.

She sat down and read it, her hand to her cheek, whispering the words.

Dearest Jerusha,
If you wish, read this book first. It's basic and contains
information to begin your own medical education, if I
am not overstepping any rights and privileges I might
have as a husband. I regret that likely no one will allow
your intelligence to be considered in its true light, but
you will be knowledgeable all the same, and surpass-
ingly useful.

She followed the arrow with her finger, laughing softly as
it meandered all over the page, then indicated she turn it over.

> *Or don't read it. The choice is absolutely yours. If you*
> *wish to stay here and tend our home, I will be equally*
> *satisfied. The choice is yours and no other's.*
> *Love,*
> *Your husband*

'You dear man,' she said, and ran her finger lightly over
those three words. 'I will always be safe with you,' Jerusha
said.

She kissed the letter and put it in the book. She dressed and
went downstairs, hoping not to wake Mags, but pleased to see
her in the kitchen anyway, porridge and tea ready.

'Mags, I could do this, and you could sleep,' she said, which
earned her a stare over the older woman's spectacles, followed
by a finger-wag and a smile.

'It's what I do for the master,' Mags said. 'You are his mate.'

'I am, aren't I?' she asked, still filled with the wonder of
it all. She blushed then, aware in her mind at least, that she
might be married, but she wouldn't be Jamie's wife until there
was time to consummate the matter.

Mags seemed to understand her red face. 'Give it time,
lovey. He'll be back.'

Without asking, the housekeeper fixed her a luncheon of meat and cheese, with one apple, and wrapped it in a large handkerchief. 'I'll tell you what I tell the master: Take the time to eat and don't just throw it away on the way home and tell me a fib.'

'Surely he would never...' Jerusha started, then laughed. 'I promise.'

She began her morning as she usually did, cleaning up after breakfast and washing faces, Mrs Terwilliger supervising, which meant that the matron looked up from her paperwork every few minutes and stared intently.

Letters came next, which more and more led to quiet time to merely sit and listen as some of the wounded sailors told her how they earned their cots in Stonehouse. Some were matter of fact and cheerful, others embarrassed that the hated Frenchies caught them off guard. Still others tried to tell her, but ended up in tears. She cried with them.

She made herself eat her sandwich and apple, then asked Surgeon Kidwell what he wanted her to do. 'Jamie said I should make myself useful,' she explained. 'He...he even left a book for me to read.'

The surgeon considered her request. 'Follow me. Watch. Then read for an hour.'

And that became her day, and then her week. After lunch, she followed and watched, eyes filled with sympathy and sometimes horror as the one-legged surgeon stumped from cot to cot, tweaking there, mending here, observing everywhere.

Her test came at the end of the first week of her marriage, when he drew the curtains around a man with burns on his leg. Jerusha knew him as Hank from Sheffield, a bosun who had tried to drag out one sailor too many from a burning bomb kedge before it exploded. Two days before, Jerusha had watched Surgeon Kidwell and his steward remove the dead

tissue with tweezers. She winced as the burned man winced and sniffed back her own tears when he cried.

'Here,' the surgeon said, handing her his tweezers. She looked around for the steward. Nowhere in sight. She took the tweezers from Kidwell, and then looked into the eyes of the bosun. 'I... I really don't want to hurt you,' she said. 'I promise you.'

'Pluck away,' he told her cheerfully, 'as long as you promise me a kiss when you're done.'

She smiled at that, imagining what Jamie would say, and began her work gently and carefully. She pulled away the burned skin as the bosun swore quietly under his breath. He grabbed at her hand once and she turned her hand to hold his, fingers twined together.

Surgeon Kidwell watched the whole thing, guiding her hand where needed, then readying the ointment when she finished. 'Spread on a light coat, and we'll cover it with this gauze.'

She did as he said, relieved to be done. Hank lay there with his eyes closed. She kissed his cheek. 'There now. I'll do better next week.'

'I have a daughter. She's about your age now.'

She kissed his cheek again. 'This one is for her,' she said, then moved to the next cot with Surgeon Kidwell.

'You're a cool one,' he said.

'Thank you, Surgeon Kidwell,' she said, feeling far from cool.

'Call me Jon,' he said, which meant Jerusha gained admission into the society of suffering.

She wrote about it that evening in what became her nightly letter to Surgeon James Wilson, Ship FDV *Harmony*. Channel Fleet, Ship to Shore.

Mags reminded her to put a number on the back of each. 'That way the men know what has gone astray, as most do.'

Every morning Jerusha took each letter to the Administra-

tion Building and left it in a box marked Channel Fleet. Once
she learned that there was something to write about every day,
she hoped she wouldn't make her husband the fleet's laugh-
ingstock. She said as much to Jon Kidwell.

'He's the envy of nations, providing any of the letters find
their way to a little sloop always on the move.'

She contented herself with that, and so she told the coma-
tose man in Ward B, where she always ended each long day.
'I don't know what they hear, if anything, but sometimes I
think I see a spark in their eyes,' Jon told her earlier on a ward
walk through cots with dead men still alive. 'Talk to them.
What can it hurt?'

She lost her fear of death in Ward B. The nuns kept the
men clean and fed the ones who could eat. The others died
quickly enough. The comatose man—according to his chart
he was a gunner—lay there with his eyes open, blinking now
and then. Feeling like a silly woman complaining, Jerusha told
him what had happened to her at number twenty-eight Finch
Street. Now and then he frowned, and she wondered.

Something happened as she told her own story to him.
The sting of her rejection by Aunt Hortensia left her, as she
realised that her trials were nothing compared to what these
heroes, these men who kept her safe from Napoleon, had suf-
fered. 'I'm sorry I complain so much,' she whispered to the
gunner as she said goodnight at the end of her second week.

It must have been her imagination, but she thought he man-
aged a slow wink. 'What you must think of me,' she told him,
and left after straightening his coverlet, all with the approval
of one of Ward B's Sisters of Charity.

That next evening, she came home to two letters addressed
to Mrs James Wilson, Stonehouse, Quarters D, Devonport,
England. Mags, all smiles, had set them beside her dinner
plate. They were number One and Four. She read them in si-
lence while Mags busied herself in the kitchen. 'He hopes

you are doing well, Mags,' she said, after blushing over Letter Four that ended with his longing to see much more of her anatomy in a few weeks.

'Mags, how do people manage when they are so far away?' she asked. 'How did you manage with your foretopman gone so often?'

'The same as you're doing.' Mags's voice lost that brisk tone, which threw off years and miles as nothing else could have. 'I kept very busy. Eat your dinner now, or I'll scold!' Her tone softened again. 'Mark my words. He'll show up when you least expect him.'

Chapter Twenty-Eight

I am a well-trained surgeon, professional and concerned about my patients to the exclusion of all else.

Over a tankard of *all* parts rum—no one's idea of navy grog—Captain Ames had so expressed himself to his first mate and Surgeon Wilson one night after a near collision with a frigate in a freezing rain off the Brest blockade. Of course, Captain Ames had said 'captain' and 'crew' instead of 'surgeon' and 'patients,' but Jamie heard the message clearly. All *he* wanted to do—professional or not—was to go home and crawl in bed with his wife.

'We're to do our duty, gentlemen,' Captain Ames added, raising his middle finger to that careless frigate that nearly mowed them down. 'What do you say, gentleman? Shall we not leave HMS *Brawler* any mail?'

They all laughed, men well acquainted with both danger and duty, and now it was definitely pea coat weather on deck. Jamie draped his arms over the railing in lubber fashion, impervious to hoots and catcalls from his fellow seamen.

Captain Ames joined him at the rail. 'Heading home and high time, Surgeon.' He nudged Jamie. 'I reckon you are more eager than most.'

For six weeks he had been teased about his remarkable wedding on the deck of HMS *Harmony*. There were no blushes left

in him. 'I am not the only eager husband aboard this sloop,' he corrected.

'Perhaps, but you are the envy of all. How is it that you get a letter or two with each passing messenger sloop?'

'She likes to write to me,' Jamie said. 'She writes every day.'

'How she can possibly think of something to write about every day is beyond me,' Captain Ames said. 'My wife can only manage a letter or two a month.'

'Anyone working at Stonehouse always has something to write about,' he replied and stared at the water again. He could tell the captain about her latest medical education, but would he understand? Jamie read Letter Number Twelve several times, marvelling to himself how someone so quiet, shy almost, could debride a burn and not slump into a dead faint. It was not women's work, not at all. She wrote how it terrified her, but she learned anyway, because Surgeon Kidwell was overworked, and the jetty bell rang all the time.

The *Harmony* worked her way through the fleet, laden with dispatches and mail and bound for home. They were five days out from England when Lieutenant Simpson, grimmer of face than usual, burst into the sick bay as Jamie was tying off a final stitch on a gunner's laceration.

'Topside!' he shouted.

Jamie followed him to the deck, where a frigate was backing her sails. 'Look.' Simpson pointed to the signal flags snapping in the cruel wind that seemed to roar down the Channel.

Extreme Distress flew. There was more to follow, and he waited for it, knowing that one captain's idea of extreme distress differed from another.

'What is it?' he asked the bosun's mate, who stared in surprise.

'I'll be damned, sir. It's Baby.'

Jamie grabbed his satchel and rooted about for some cloths.

He had no small blanket, but he found a towel. He mentally rehearsed what to do, since it had been three years since he had delivered a baby. Still, babies were babies.

On deck, he slung his satchel across his body and wrapped the cloths under his new pea coat, a gift from a grateful Dutch mariner he had cured of piles. He wasted not a moment in settling into the sling and nodding to the bosun's mate, who lowered him always too close to the water.

The distance was short. As soon as he was aboard the frigate *Naiad*, the *Harmony* backed off and waited.

The captain himself waited on the *Naiad*'s deck. He took Jamie by the arm and hurried him to the companionway. 'It's a damned sad business,' he said, his voice soft. 'The wife of our sailing master is dying in childbirth.'

'Let's hurry then,' Jamie ordered.

He ran down the companionway with the captain and into the wardroom. 'This is Master Whittier,' the captain said, motioning to a man with sorrowful eyes who stood by an open hatch in the wardroom.

'Please, surgeon, can you do anything?' Master Whittier said. 'Our surgeon is in the middle of a malarial relapse—damn the Caribbean anyway.' He started to cry. 'Maudie insisted on coming along to the blockade. She's done it before, but this time… Oh, God. In here.'

Jamie stared down at a woman mere seconds away from death. Her eyes were already sinking back into her head. Ear to breast, he listened for a heartbeat. As he listened, it stopped.

He waited not a second, pushing the master and captain out of the stateroom and slamming the hatch shut. His concentration fierce, he whispered, 'I will save your baby,' and went to work with his capital knives.

Not until the infant was out and screaming at the top of her lungs and the cord cut, did he close his eyes for a tiny moment of peace. Not until he opened them did he notice a

wide-eyed young man crouched in the corner. 'Are you the surgeon's mate?'

The lad nodded, tears on his face. 'I tried to help. There was nothing I could do.'

'Nay, lad. It was a terrible presentation. I want you to wrap this little lady in that blanket over there and take her to her father. Don't let anyone in here.'

The mate did as asked, and hurried with his screaming bundle through the hatch. Jamie sewed up the woman. He made her presentable by smoothing back her still-sweaty hair. He marvelled at the peace on her face now, as if she somehow knew her baby was alive and well and noisy. Such a pretty lady. He thought of Jerusha and vowed she would never follow him to sea, as some wives of masters did.

In another moment he had bound the pretty lady into a blanket and knotted the ends. No need for the sailing master to see anything. He washed his hands, removed his bloody apron, and stowed it, then opened the hatch.

The sailing master, tears streaming down his face, held his daughter. 'My wife was a bonnie lass,' he said. What he said next did not surprise Jamie. He knew sailing masters were generally the smartest men on a ship. 'Surgeon, obviously I cannot take care of her, but I have a sister and brother-in-law in Cornwall who would love this little one heart and soul, because my sister is barren. Will you get her to them for me?'

'Aye, sir,' Jamie said.

'Thank you from the depths of my heart. I... I don't know how you're going to feed her, even with the—what—four days from here to England,' the father said, as he held his daughter close to his chest. 'I just don't know.'

Beyond the fact that his daughter was alive and well, there was another good piece of news Jamie had for the bereft man. 'I'm on a Fast Dispatch Vessel. We have, of all things, a mama goat aboard.'

'You're jesting me.'

'You would be amazed what we haul back and forth,' Jamie said. 'It belongs to a lieutenant aboard a warship at Ferrol whose goat ate his captain's best wool stockings. It was apparently the last straw.' No point in telling a sorrowing man that the lieutenant sneaked the goat and her kid aboard the *Harmony* before his captain ate the thing in revenge.

The master managed a smile. 'I suppose we have seen it all, on blockade.'

'Aye, sir. Your daughter will be in good hands from here to Cornwall. Just give me the address,' Jamie said, his own heart full to bursting. 'I have eyedroppers and syringes. No fears, sir. No fears.'

And so it was that Jamie Wilson carried a baby to his house a week later in the middle of the day. Between his medical duties and 'round the clock tending of an infant on a dispatch vessel, he could not remember when he had slept last. Captain Ames gave him a long and mournful look as they disembarked from *Harmony*. 'Four days only and we sail again. I'll expect you back from Tweazel.'

'Aye, sir,' Jamie said. He understood duty, as much as he sometimes hated it.

'If I were a braver man, Jamie my lad, I would apologise to your new bride myself. She still isn't going to see much of you.'

Mags McDonald met him at the door, her mouth open and her eyes wide. Barely able to keep his eyes open, Jamie told the whole, sad story to his housekeeper.

When he'd finished, she held up her hand. 'Wait right here,' she said. 'Don't move.'

'I probably couldn't,' he said, mystified. Still, he had grown somewhat attached to the little one, who was stirring now, probably hungry, and ready for goat's milk through an eyedropper.

Mags darted out the door, moving faster than he had ever

seen. He watched her out the window as she ran towards the littlest house on the row, the one belonging to a hospital steward on Block Three.

She came back more sedately, arms linked with the wife of the Block Three steward. He opened the door for them. 'Well, Maisie Brower, you've been kidnapped,' he teased.

'Aye, sir,' she said, and took a long look at the infant, wrapped in a towel, that he held close to his chest. 'What's she been living on?'

'Goat's milk.'

'Hand her over. I have plenty.'

He stared in amazement as Mrs Brower opened her bodice, gave the little one a nudge, and smiled as she latched on. 'There now, there now,' she crooned.

'I still have to get her to Tweazel,' Jamie said. 'In God help us Cornwall.' He sat down, his eyes closed, and his head dropped forward.

'Don't be so certain about that,' his own dear Jerusha told him only spare minutes later, as she arrived on the run, breathing hard. She shook him awake, gave him a smacking kiss, and blew a kiss to Maisie Brower now burping the baby.

He doubted he had ever seen a more beautiful woman, and she was his. 'I wish I could stay here, my love, but I have four days to get this babe settled. Then it's off to the blockade again.'

As tired as he was, he saw the silent message pass from Mags to Maisie Brower to Jerusha, the secret code of women that he knew he would never understand. He knew enough to gently remind them that the baby was promised elsewhere and he had a duty to get her there.

'Of course, dear man,' Jerusha said. 'Can you, Mags? And you, Maisie?'

'I'll go home and bundle up my little one,' Maisie said. 'There's milk aplenty for both. Keep your goat.' She handed

the sailing master's baby to Jerusha and was out the door in a moment. Jamie could only stare at them in befuddled, exhausted amazement.

Jerusha took charge, the baby asleep on her shoulder now.

'Surgeon Kidwell can make arrangements for a post chaise. You know how he is. Mags, you'll be on your way within the hour. Go pack. I'll tuck in the surgeon.'

'Wait… I…' He what? Jamie couldn't think of how to end a sentence. 'But…'

He wasn't sure how Jerusha steered him upstairs, but he made no objection when she pulled back the bed covering and helped him from his clothing. When he was bare, she kissed his shoulder and pulled up the blanket.

'Nighty-night, sleep tight,' was the last thing he remembered.

Chapter Twenty-Nine

Jamie Wilson slept for twenty-four hours. Jerusha watched him for an entire luxurious hour, sitting in the comfortable chair in his bedchamber, knowing that when she looked up from the medical text she read, he would be there. In itself, that was bliss.

The silence of the house was also bliss, not that she or Mags McDonald were noisy women. She tried to imagine how peaceful this must seem to a man either at sea, with the constant creak of a ship, or in a hospital, with people moaning in pain.

The exhaustion on his face saddened her. She knew he must be twenty-eight or so, if she was twenty-five, but between ocean winds and constant medical emergency, he had earned the lines on his face. She thought of other sailors she tended on Ward A, and silently thanked them—and this man asleep before her—that she and others like her were kept safe from the warfare on that tortured continent across the English Channel.

She watched his whole body relax as he stretched out on his back. She watched the rise and fall of his chest and found herself breathing along with him in perfect rhythm. She found herself relaxing, too.

There was work to do. She returned to Block Four, explaining the situation to Surgeon Kidwell, requesting he arrange a post chaise now and assuring him that she would return in a day or two. 'When he wakes up, he will want to attend here,'

she told him without a blush. She added, 'I intend to be an obstacle for his appearance in Ward A. I offer no apology.'

Surgeon Kidwell nodded, grinned, and started for the stairs. 'Post chaise first,' was all he said.

'My husband is back,' she told Mrs Terwilliger. 'He is mine for a while.' This earned her an unexpected smile and a shooing motion towards the door, which made them both laugh.

She spent the afternoon and evening reading and taking notes, pausing when Jamie muttered to himself, disturbed by dreams. With humility, she wondered how any man in a world at war could escape the danger and terror, even in slumber. She thought of the letters she had written for her wounded patients, letters that spoke of amusing incidents and mundane duty. She had watched enough of them to know their nightmares belied all the simplicity of their letters, written to reassure loved ones. She thanked God for their resilience.

Jerusha thought he might wake up as night fell, but he slumbered on, telling her worlds about his need for rest. When it was full dark, she stripped and put on her nightgown. She knew she would never get to sleep, but she did, lulled to slumber by the warmth of another person so close.

At some point during the night, she draped her leg over his legs. He murmured something, but did not wake up. Neither did she, until morning. She woke up to stare at his back and admire the width of those shoulders. She smiled to see freckles there, as she thought she might.

After breakfast of boiled eggs and toast, Jerusha washed herself thoroughly, wondering if she should take a tin of water upstairs. Jamie was bound to wake up eventually. As it was, she marvelled at the sturdiness of his bladder.

Not inclined to ever wake a sleeping person, Jerusha made herself comfortable in Jamie's chair again, continuing her vigil. It lasted until mid-morning, when he opened his eyes at last.

'Oh, Jerusha,' was all he said. He closed his eyes, then opened them. 'You're still here,' he joked, which made her laugh.

'Let me give you a moment's privacy,' she said, much as she would say to a patient in Ward A, where Mrs Terwilliger told her not to attend to anyone's pissing.

'I've heard you say that a time or two.' With no embarrassment he got out of bed and went into the adjoining room.

Jerusha set aside the book on her lap. The wave of shyness that washed over her surprised her. This beautiful, naked man belonged to her. She considered the matter in her practical way and knew what to do.

When he returned, she ushered him back to bed, fluffing the pillow behind his head. Amused, he patted the space beside him. She sat, after bringing over that tin of now warm water from the kitchen and a cloth.

'See here, this is what I do, because Mrs Terwilliger has trained me well.' As he smiled, she washed his face. 'I'm good around the ears,' she told him. 'You get a neck wash, too. Mrs T only lets me wash a man down to his waist, because she is circumspect.'

'Aye, she is. We can't have any wild notions,' he said. His smile widened. He stretched, then grabbed her and rubbed his unshaven face into her neck, which made her shriek and then laugh. 'What follows?' he asked. 'She's trained you well.'

You dear man, she thought. *You are putting me at my ease.*

'That's simple,' she said and went to his desk, returning with paper and pencil. 'You tell me what I am to write to a loved one. Don't be shy.'

He put his hands behind his head. 'How about this? *Dearest Jerusha, I love you more than I can express in mere words.*' He looked over at her. 'Well?'

Her face rosy, she wrote what he said. 'That's a short letter.'

'There's more.' He regarded the ceiling. 'Add, *Kindly re-*

move your clothing and get into bed with me. Yours most sincerely, Jamie Wilson. Will that do?'

She set down the pen and pencil, stood up, and slowly unbuttoned her bodice, her eyes on his. Her dress crumpled at her feet. Her camisole came off next, after a little hesitation. She knew how abundant she was, and she hadn't bothered with a corset today. From the sigh she heard, her favourite surgeon didn't seem to mind, even if fashion dictated smaller bosoms.

Like most women, she only bothered with small clothes during her monthly flow, so when she slid off her petticoat, that was that. She looked deep into her husband's eyes, liked what she saw there, and got in bed when he raised the coverlets.

At first he did nothing but hold her close, running his hand down her hip. 'You're wondrous soft,' he said. 'You realise this entire thing is preposterous and unbelievable and yet here we are together.' He kissed her breast, then raised teasing eyes to hers. 'And glory be to God, you can swim!'

She laughed then, and gave herself completely to him, her shyness gone, unable to resist a lover with a sense of humour. She touched him, admired him, held him close and made room for him inside her when he stretched out on top of her. Joy had never been something she anticipated, especially since she had given up on any man wanting her. Joy was the only thing she could think of now.

He was gentle, but equally focused on filling his needs, and hers, too, even though she didn't really know what those needs were until he was deep inside, and they were doing a rhythmic slow dance. 'I love you,' he said into her ear. 'Hug me with your legs.'

She did and felt her own urge mount. 'I'm feeling distinctly unladylike,' she managed to say between gasps and a moan that surprised her.

'Good! And you know I'm not a gentleman,' he replied.

Then he was past words as his love for her spilled out of him and she felt like the most privileged woman in the universe. She wanted the feeling never to end. When he finished, spent, she urged him to a little more effort and he obliged, until she truly knew what it was to be complete.

'My word, Jerusha,' he said. He didn't move from her body, and she didn't want him to. He kissed her hair, sweaty now. 'Here's the nice part: we can do this again and again.'

He stayed where he was, growing heavier as he returned to sleep. She ran her hands over his back, enjoying the rhythm of his heart as it slowed to normal cadence. Heart to heart, she loved him in silence now, where before love murmured to them both.

At least we didn't keep anyone awake here, she thought, enjoying the bliss of solitude with the one person in the universe that she knew she could not do without, not ever.

She edged out from under him and moved him onto his back. She washed him below the waist this time, admiring his now peaceful anatomy. Amazing. She wondered how to inform Surgeon Kidwell that washing down to a wounded man's waist was still her limit. This man sleeping soundly was all she ever wanted to see. 'I am yours only,' she whispered.

There didn't seem to be any point in putting on her clothes. The house was empty, and she knew this man would want her again when he was able. She curled up beside him and slept, too, even though the sun was high in the sky. She willed the jetty bell to remain silent, and it did.

Jerusha woke up and found herself gazing into blue eyes. She kissed him, which began all manner of tumult. She was no more of an expert than she had been the first time, but it hardly mattered. Jamie was slower this time, almost leisurely as he caressed her body, then covered it with his. She was better at the rhythm of love this time, her senses more alert to what was happening. She savoured every moment, knowing

in her heart that her man was only here for another day or two, then it was back to the blockade.

Go away, war, she thought, as he kissed her here and there. *Go away.*

Later, lying beside her, he was inclined to talk, his arms around her as her head rested on his chest. 'Jerusha, don't let me embarrass you…'

'I am noticeably past embarrassment, you might have observed,' she teased.

'The sight of you coming out of that camisole nearly made my heart stop,' he said.

'I think we'll muddle along, whenever you make port.'

'I'll be a source of envy when I'm back aboard the *Harmony*, a husband with a stupid smile on his face.' He turned serious. 'Too many men are too long gone on the blockade.'

Too many, too long. 'But you are here, and I rejoice,' she said simply.

Chapter Thirty

Jamie knew he would cherish forever the fluttering of Jerusha's eyelashes against his chest. Her words touched the deepest part of him. He looked down at her, marvelling over sudden joy in his life, where before there was only duty and hard things. She was right; he rejoiced, too.

Duty tugged at him to go to Stonehouse. Jerusha's long lashes tugged at him to stay in his bed. He stayed where he was, content this time to remain awake and watch the loveliness of his wife in slumber. *How often will this happen?* he asked himself, and knew the answer.

Stonehouse could wait, except he knew that it shouldn't. He didn't usually resent his duty, but he resented it now. Jon Kidwell was overworked and should have retired years ago. Mrs Terwilliger was overworked. The stewards were overworked. What right had he to dawdle here and delight in soft eyelashes against his chest? At least he had the good sense to store up that little detail about her to comfort him when he was at sea again, stewing over some medical problem, wishing for more knowledge, craving an end to war: Jerusha's eyelashes.

He patted her on the bottom—storing up that little pleasure, too. 'Up and at 'em, wifey,' he said, sounding cheerful when he knew precisely what he wanted to be doing. 'I propose two things today.'

'Oh, do you?' she asked. Her drowsy voice suggested there hadn't been much sleep involved recently. 'Suppose I disagree?'

He clutched his chest in mock surprise. 'What? Dissension in the ranks?'

'Aye-aye, sir,' she teased back. 'What is your wish?' She sat up and stretched, not remotely shy about showing her assets this time.

'That we stay in bed and pleasure each other,' he said promptly, 'except that I believe we need to pay a visit to your aunt.'

My, but that changed things. She lay down again and curled up close to him. He kissed the top of her head. 'Dear lady, I want her to know that I am not an ogre. True, I am no gentleman, but I should meet your relative. Do you think she is amenable to change in her society?'

'I do not think that is a wound we can heal,' she said, her voice muffled against him. 'I have written to my parents, and they have returned no reply.'

'You're cut off from them as well?' he said. 'I am so sorry. Jerusha, it might take years. It might never happen, but I don't want anyone to think we did not try.'

She was silent and he knew she was thinking over the matter. He got up, found his clothes, and dressed as she stared at the ceiling and thought. When he tried to tackle his neckcloth in a room without a mirror, he heard a rustle behind him. Dressed as far as her petticoat and camisole, Jerusha finished tying it for him, her eyes half slitted in that determination he remembered from the duck-pond.

Her shyness returned as they left the house. 'It is midday. People will know what we have been doing,' she whispered to him, her face rosy.

'That makes me the envy of nations,' he replied. 'Let's stop first on Ward A. I want Jon to know I will be back here soon.'

It was his turn to blush when Mrs Terwilliger looked him up and down. 'I believe you are the last person I expected to see here,' she said, and returned her attention to the papers in front of her. 'Before you leave, sign here and here and here. Jerusha, sit down a moment.'

Jerusha remained at Mrs T's desk, their heads together in a whispered conversation. At the end of the first row, Jon Kidwell debrided a nasty leg wound. He nodded when Jamie said he had an entire day to spend here.

'Jerusha, too?' John asked. 'Someone has been asking for her on Ward B.'

'I doubt you could keep her away.'

But first, Lady Oakshott. Jerusha wanted to walk to Plymouth. Although new to marriage politics, Jamie understood she was trying to put off the ordeal of Lady Oakshott. He agreed with her. They walked slowly past Devonport's dry docks, noisy with hammering and sawing, and the long ropewalk, where men twisted cotton cords, turning it into rigging.

She slowed down, the closer they came to Finch Street. She stopped altogether at the front steps of number twenty-eight. 'You're never alone, Jerusha Wilson,' he told her as he knocked. 'Remember that.'

The butler—Napier? — answered, drew himself up, and announced, 'Tradesmen go through the servants' entrance below.'

Jamie stepped aside so the butler could see his wife. 'Good day, Napier,' she said, crowding close to him. 'This is my husband, Surgeon James Wilson. We want to speak with Lady Oakshott.'

He gave her points for including his rank. After an intimidating glare on the front step, the butler motioned them in. He drew himself up, stared over their heads, and announced, 'Lady Oakshott has told me to say that she is not receiving visitors.'

'I'm her niece,' Jerusha said quietly. 'I am going upstairs anyway. Please don't try to stop me.'

You're braver than I am, Jamie thought, as she released his hand and climbed the stairs.

He waited below with the butler, who wouldn't look at him. It was too much, finally. 'Napier, I am a good man, serving a useful function in the Royal Navy,' he said. 'My father is a respected steward of a laird in the Highlands.'

'You are not good enough for Miss Jerusha Langley,' Napier replied. 'You are no gentleman.'

Jamie strained to hear some sympathy, and there was none. He heard a loud voice drifting down from upstairs. 'Excuse me, Napier,' he said. 'I believe I need to rescue my dear wife.'

'But...'

Jamie took the stairs two at a time, listening. He opened the door on a woman who might have been beautiful at one time, berating the dearest person in his orbit.

'Who are you, to barge in here?' Lady Oakshott demanded.

He was at Jerusha's side in a moment, hauling her close, saddened to feel her trembling, angry that a witch in a dressing gown was making her cry.

'Let's go to work, Jerusha,' he said. 'Let's go where we are both wanted and needed.'

She nodded, calmed herself, and took a step towards the old woman. 'Aunt Hortensia, my only regret is that I did not tell you immediately what I was doing. That was deception and I apologise. I will never apologise for marrying the dearest man in my universe.'

'Your parents have washed their hands of you, too,' Lady Oakshott retorted, her eyes blazing with indignation. 'Augusta is beside herself. Selfish, foolish girl!'

'I know my own mind,' Jerusha said in a calm voice that Jamie knew he could never begin to master, in the face of such

vitriol. 'Good day. I wish you well.' With that, she turned on her heel and head high, left the room holding his hand.

Down the stairs in silence and out the door. He could only walk beside her in amazement at her courage. At the corner, she stopped and looked back at the house. 'I would rather know than not know, and now I can continue with my life,' she told him. She accepted his handkerchief and blew her nose. There in the street she put her hands on his arms. 'I love you, James Wilson. Yes, let's go do some good.'

Her husband was a man of good sense. He hailed a hackney, helped her in, and let her sob into another of his handkerchiefs. He apologised for dragging her to Finch Street. 'I should have listened to you, but I wanted to know where we stood,' he told her. 'Now we know.'

'I might cry about this again,' she admitted to her man, 'but I will mend.' The look he gave her she knew she could store up in her heart against the hard times.

Ward A was quiet, some patients napping while others stared into great distances that disturbed her at first, until she realised the wounded belonged to a fraternity of warriors.

'I am to assist with two amputations,' Jamie told her. 'Someone upstairs on Ward B wants to have a word with you.'

'I heard too many words on Finch Street,' she said.

'I'll go upstairs with you.'

She saw Jon Kidwell beckoning to him. 'No need. I can outrun anyone on Wards A and B,' she reminded him. She blew him a kiss that made a sailor put his hand to his cheek and flop back on his cot.

'You rascal, you're ready for discharge,' Jamie said, but his voice was mild. The others laughed and Jerusha went upstairs to another place that both frightened and humbled her.

She had been away from Ward B for two days, enjoying

herself in the arms of her husband. As she looked across the aisles of quiet men, she knew her heart lay here, too.

My darling could be here someday, she thought, dismissing the Aunt Hortensias from her life. *I must serve where other ladies cannot.*

A man sat beside her patient that she told about her day, every day. He had opened his eyes now and then, which startled her at first, but no longer. The visitor had opened the book of Shakespeare's sonnets that she kept beside the bed.

Should I bother him? she asked herself.

She came closer and cleared her throat. 'Sir?'

'You must be Mrs Wilson.'

She hesitated, then covered her mouth to hide her smile. 'You see, sir, I haven't been Mrs Wilson too long. I... I'm still getting used to it.'

He pulled up a stool from the bedside of another silent patient, and she sat. 'This is my son,' he said. She clearly heard all the pain.

She put her hand on his arm, then hoped he didn't think she was a forward little piece. 'I read to him nearly every day. I talk to him, as well. He knows everything about me.'

'Then I thank you. I am Sailing Master Roger Kent, and this is Alec. I have been on the blockade for months and this is my first opportunity to see him.' She knew better than to interrupt his thoughts as he looked at his son. 'He was a sailing master's mate in the Baltic, learning the family trade. Then this happened.' He bowed his head.

She understood. 'I wash his face and talk to him. I am not a medical person. I come to wash faces and write letters and read to them. It isn't much.'

He covered her hand with his own. 'It is everything. Keep doing it, please.' He managed a smile. 'No one will ever recognise your service, but Alec knows somehow, some way.'

'Yes, sir.'

'No medals for you.' He kissed his silent son.

She walked him to the door of Ward B. When she promised, 'I will tend him,' the sting of Aunt Hortensia vanished. 'I will return the favour someday.'

Chapter Thirty-One

September began with a gust of wind that blew Mags back to Plymouth two days later, minus a baby, and her own story of the sailing master's sister in tears when she put the infant in her arms. 'You know I am not the tearful type, Surgeon Wilson, but that whole village was full of gratitude. Two of her friends lined up for wet nursing. You did a kind thing.'

Jamie nodded and walked upstairs, while Mags unpacked and asked Jerusha to tell 'that silent boyo' thank you for her adventure. 'Maybe I needed to get away for two days, myself,' she confided. 'I trust you and t'master used your time well.'

'That we did, Mags,' Jerusha said. She heard the door to his study close. 'Now he has turned quiet.'

'He sails in the morning. He always turns quiet.'

'Mags, I've never sent a man to sea.'

'It's hard. Just remember to cry after he is gone.'

Jerusha debated only a moment. She went upstairs to knock on the door cautiously, wishing she knew what to do for this man suddenly silent.

'Come in, Jerusha. You never need to knock.'

He leaned back in his chair with his feet on the desk and his hands behind his head. She came up behind him and he stared up at her breasts.

'Now that is a sight to behold,' he said and put his feet

down. He patted his legs and she sat, her arms going natu-
rally around his neck.

'I have lots of similar wonderful sights,' she told him, which
made him chuckle.

'I need to see every one of them between now and tomor-
row morning.' He put his hand against her head in a protec-
tive gesture, this man of hers. 'We had a meeting in Admin
after you left the ward, someone from Admiralty telling us
what lies ahead.' He looked around elaborately. 'If you share
any of this with a spy, I will have to shoot you.'

'Cross my heart.'

'I'll cross it for you.' He ran his hand across her breast.
'Sworn to secrecy. It seems that our little admiral is deter-
mined to dislodge the French and Spanish ships from Cadiz.
Napoleon is jumping up and down in Boulogne, trying to pry
Villeneuve—he of the Combined Fleet—out of Cadiz.' He
tightened his arms around her. 'The Frogs are ready to take
small boats across the Channel to our fair sceptred isle. And
the blockade of Brest wears on. It's unfair that such nice peo-
ple as we are must live in perilous times, eh?'

She put her hands on his face. 'The only place in the world
where I feel safe is right next to you in our bed.'

'That's a simple solution to England's problems!' he said,
and kissed her palms. 'We'll get in bed and hunker down. I
like it, too.'

He held her close for a long and satisfying moment, then,
'But we must sail. I doubt you will see me again until winter,
or until after Villeneuve decides to peek out of Cadiz.' He
sighed. 'That's why I turned quiet. I would rather be here, too.'

How did one say this casually? She had no idea. 'There
will be a battle?'

'Everyone wants it, except perhaps Villeneuve.' He looked
around again. 'Spies say Napoleon is sharpening a guillotine
himself for Villeneuve. I suppose that particular naval Frog

is trying to decide who he fears more: Old Boney or Admiral Nelson. It will be a huge and decisive battle.'

'So it makes you quiet.' She kissed her husband, thinking of the night to come. 'Remember this: I will always be waiting here for you.'

'I hope I will return. There are no guarantees.'

If she lived to one hundred, Jerusha knew she would never forget that final night before her husband sailed back to war. At first, she hoped they weren't noisy and disturbing Mags below stairs, and then she didn't care. 'Good heavens,' she said once, after a particularly exquisite moment that left them both exhausted and sweating. 'Where do you *learn* this?'

'Wifey, you forget I am an anatomist,' he said. 'I must also admit to prior experience. I am a Royal Navy man after all, and we do have a certain reputation.' He returned to kissing her in places she never thought to be kissed, and forgot any commentary.

They must have slept a little, but only enough to regroup and return to that exquisite place, forgetting everything except each other, two insignificant people in a world gone mad. She knew the pleasure ended when he cuddled her close as the sun rose, and turned practical.

'Dearest, you will find all my important papers in the second drawer of the desk in my office,' he told her. 'There is a letter explaining who you are to see to release my savings into your custody, should the matter arise.'

'I don't want to think about it.'

'You must. Everything is in order. I've accumulated some prize money through the years, and I've been frugal. So must you be, as well. Be wise and you'll never be destitute.'

'Please stop,' she whispered.

'Don't hesitate to remarry, should you find another fellow as charming and wise as I am.'

He held her close as she cried. 'There now. Don't see me

to the docks. Just stay here and let me imagine you cosy in my warm spot.'

He dressed quickly, then flicked a little water on her from the basin, which catapulted her out of bed to thrash him with her pillow. As a consequence, they were both laughing when he shouldered his medical satchel and slung his duffel across his back. She followed him into the little street that ran behind the administration building, grabbed him for another kiss, then covered her eyes until he was gone.

Mags was banging about in the kitchen when Jerusha dried her tears, squared her shoulders, and stood in the doorway, feeling both amazingly shy and so sad. Mags handed her a cup of tea.

'Nothing makes it easy,' Mags told her. 'Get to work.'

Surgeon Kidwell helped the time pass. Every morning, he knocked on the door, and Mags ushered him in, serving him breakfast, too, over weak and then no protestation. He walked Jerusha to Block Four, discussing his cases with her as if she were Jamie. She found the notion flattering.

The real test came when he asked her to assist in an amputation. 'We see this too often,' he told her as they walked to Block Four in the rain, moving slowly because Jon couldn't move fast anymore. 'A surgeon at sea is too busy to notice what needs to be done in the moment. Part of him wants to wait and see, but he hasn't that luxury. We must do what he should have done.'

September sped or dragged towards October, depending on how active she was, or how much time she spent brooding on the empty space in their bed. She couldn't help her tears when Surgeon Kidwell handed her a note with familiar handwriting.

Mrs Terwilliger sent her into the linen closet for a quiet space.

Dearest, I am in Portsmouth, delivering patients to Haslar. I have no time to take a coastal carrier to Plymouth. Keep that cosy spot warm. With love, your surgeon.

'I hate the navy,' she told Mrs Terwilliger when she came out of the closet, the note stuffed down her bodice, and her arms full of sheets. Her work went on.

She had to credit her mother, quiet self-effacing Augusta, with giving her something else to worry about. Mama showed up, proper and unannounced, on Block Four.

Jerusha saw her as she finished wiping the face of a new patient from Ferrol, where more Royal Navy blockaders sailed, reinforcing what Jamie said about Admiral Nelson tightening his grip on the enemy coast.

'Mama?' She hurried to her mother, a women used to doing good for others that required no exertion, standing bewildered in the middle of a ward reeking with exertion. Jerusha gratefully accepted Mrs Terwilliger's offer of her little cubbyhole as a refuge for two.

Jerusha braced herself for a scold and Mama wasted not a moment, berating Jerusha for her slapdash marriage. To Jerusha's surprise, Mama abandoned the topic almost at once and moved to what Jerusha discovered was the real reason for the visit: her sister, Hortensia.

'Daughter, last week a Young Person named Abbie—I suppose she has no last name—arrived at our house.'

'Abbie?' Jerusha repeated, startled.

'She had a letter from my sister, Hortensia,' Mama continued. 'I won't bore you with it, but Hortensia went on at length about your deceit, consorting with a person beneath your notice.'

'Surgeon James Wilson is my husband.'

'Don't remind me,' Mama snapped.

Jerusha rose, her mind calm. 'If you have come here to scold me, kindly leave.'

Mama put a hand on her arm. 'No! It was a wild letter, full of vituperation and malice, then vast self-pity that no one cares about her and that her prospects are ruined.'

'She blames me. I have apologised to her for my deception,' Jerusha told her. She sat down again. 'Mama, did she tell you that she sold Oaklands, the family estate, because her late husband's debts were alarming? She is eking out the barest living in her last remaining property, and trying to hide it.'

'It all came out last night when we arrived. She showed me mounds of unpaid bills and cried, blaming everyone for her trials,' Mama said. 'It is vexing.' Mama regarded Jerusha with something that at least resembled understanding. 'She decries your deception, little bothering to mention her own, trying to represent herself as a woman of wealth and position.'

'Did she fool you, too, Mama?' There. She had to ask.

'She did, and for years,' Mama admitted. 'I suppose I have always been a little afraid of her. You know how she is.' Her tone hardened. 'Now she is an embarrassment.'

Poor mama. Jerusha regarded her with more compassion than she might have imagined only weeks ago, when Mama didn't bother to answer her letter. In a flash of recognition, she saw her mother as she was, a lovely lady who managed life well, as long as there was nothing to disrupt her ease.

And she saw herself, too, someone willing to break rules to follow her own path and forge a different life. Whether that was wise or not, only time would tell. 'What will you do about Aunt Hortensia, Mama?'

'Your father is here, too, talking to an estate agent to sell that property on Finch Street,' Mama said. 'Papa has a bilious stomach. You know how he hates to be troubled.'

'I do,' Jerusha said with serenity, certain now that she had

chosen a far better path, even with all its uncertainties. Poor Papa. 'What will happen to Aunt Hortensia?'

'She is coming home with us. No one need ever know how poor she is.' Mama sighed, and Jerusha heard all the resignation. 'I suppose this is my penance for spending what money I had entirely on your brother and leaving you in a situation where, in desperation, you had to lower yourself in society.'

Mama would never understand. Ah, well. Perhaps someday she and Jamie would be invited to visit the parish in Bolling, although she had her doubts. 'I am quite content where I am, Mama,' she said firmly. 'Perhaps you had better return to help Aunt Hortensia pack. What happened to little Abbie, who brought the message?'

'She is a jewel and will work for me,' Mama said. '*I* will pay her for her services!'

It was too much to hope, but why not ask? 'And Napier?'

Mama put her hand on Jerusha's arm. 'My dear, he has kept Hortensia out of the poorhouse, paying her bills out of his savings. He is looking for another position.'

'There is a French cook, too.'

'He scarpered off, the scamp!' Mama leaned closer. 'Napier said his name is Robby Blair and he is a scoundrel.'

'He will land on his feet, I have no doubt.'

'And you?' Mama asked, her face anxious.

She didn't have to consider the matter, even as she mourned that her husband had no time to sail from Portsmouth to Plymouth because there was a war on. 'Mama, I will do very well with the man I love. Depend upon it. Depend upon me.'

Chapter Thirty-Two

Jerusha was never too tired to write to Jamie, no matter how often the jetty bell clanged, or how many wounded men poured into all blocks at Stonehouse. The visit from her mother had been an odd interlude, reminding Jerusha briefly of a life she had left behind, one she did not miss.

In three weeks, she received a hurried note from her husband on the *Harmony*, as it made its way through the blockading ships with medicine and messages.

Tears started as she read that his ship-to-shore life had ended.

I am going to Revenge, a seventy-four whose surgeon has died of disease.

She ran to the linen closet after the last line.

Dearest wife, I do not know when I will see you again.

After weeping every tear in her body, she dried her eyes on a sheet, squared her shoulders, and continued her work.

Wounded men passed though Ward A. Some died, others flourished and left—in her opinion—too soon. 'That is the vexation of writing letters for so many of them,' she grumbled to Jon Kidwell as they walked from their quarters to Block A one morning. She walked slowly to accommodate his painful progress on one leg and a peg, as he put it.

'How is that?' he asked, his eyes merry.

'By writing letters, I come to know the men,' she replied. 'I briefly meet sisters and sweethearts and mothers. I want to know more, and I care.'

She saw the shadow cross his face and wanted to ask about his own life, which he never discussed. She maintained her silence. Jamie had told her once about a wife and child dead of cholera, and that leg gone at the Battle of the Nile. 'That's all he ever said,' Jamie related.

'I suppose there are depths to people I will never know, Surgeon Kidwell. Perhaps I am nosy.'

'Jerusha, you are involved in mankind, and I thank you for your bravery.'

She felt all her bravery desert her the morning she sat beside the comatose son of Sailing Master Kent and watched Alec Kent fade from life. Surgeon Kidwell had warned her he was failing. She could have told him that herself, because she knew the signs—his eyes sank further in his head and he stopped eating. She knew death was only a matter of when.

Alec Kent seemed to know when she was there. How that could be, she had no idea. She had moved from Shakespeare's sonnets to *Pilgrim's Progress*, not that it mattered what she read. This week she brought her Bible.

That afternoon, Sister Mary Martha whispered, 'It won't be long. Please don't leave him,' so Jerusha settled in, knowing she would not leave until he was gone, no matter what time it was.

He died in Micah, Chapter Seven, his breathing softer and slower. She rested her hand on his shoulder, as she often did, and looked at the words, thinking of nations at war and her love sailing into trouble. *"'Rejoice not against me, mine enemy,'"* she read. *"'When I fall, I shall arise; when I sit in darkness...'"* She paused, wondering how or even if his comatose world was

dark. 'Is it dark for you, Alec Kent? What do you see?' she asked the silent man. 'I wish I knew.'

She watched his chest rise and fall and continued, *'"When I sit in darkness, the Lord shall be a light unto me."'* She closed her eyes when his chest rose, fell, and did not rise again. 'You dear man,' she said. 'I hope it is light where you are.'

Later that night, when she should have long been asleep, she sat at Jamie's desk and through her tears wrote a letter to Sailing Master Kent, serving aboard the *Protector*. She assured him that she had been with Alec to the end. She wrote that his son's body had been taken to the family burying ground at Plymouth's oldest church, according to his instructions.

No fears, she concluded. *I did as you wished.*

She wrote a much longer letter to Jamie and took both letters to the usual box in Administration, mindful as she did so of a recurring nightmare, where over and over she dropped letters into a box that opened at the bottom and dumped them into the ocean.

October came with no letters from Jamie, not even a note. Jerusha kept her thoughts to herself as she ran with the others to the quadrangle when the jetty bell rang, and did all that was asked of her, even if the wounds seemed to grow more terrible as each day passed. She soothed her heart with a small thing. Every night after supper with Mags, she took a hot water bottle to her bed and put it on Jamie's side.

When she was too exhausted to do anything else except sleep, she took out that hot water bottle and lay down in Jamie's warm spot. That was the only way she could sleep, and it comforted her…one little warm spot.

Each day turned into the one before, except the day it didn't, the day she received a note from Sailing Master Kent. She changed bloody sheets and forced herself to joke with the patients when she really wanted to go somewhere and hide. Mrs Terwilliger called to her and waved a letter.

Thank God, she thought, running to the ward office.

She grabbed the letter, but she frowned to see Master Kent's handwriting, much neater than her husband's.

Buck up, Jerusha, she told herself sternly. *It's a letter.*

She sat down in Mrs Terwilliger's chair. 'My goodness,' she whispered, and read it again.

'What?' the matron demanded.

She handed the note to Mrs Terwilliger. 'Sailing Master Kent is aboard the *Protector*, here in Plymouth! He cannot come ashore—they have to leave again so soon—but if I don't mind being rowed out to his ship, I can hand him a letter for Jamie. He can find the *Revenge* on the blockade and hand it to him personally.'

Mrs T read it quickly, then slapped a sheet of paper in front of Jerusha, and moved over her ink and quill pen. 'Hurry. Tides don't wait.'

Jerusha started to write as the matron read out loud.

'You missed the postscript: *"Look for a little fellow name of Cornell to take you to the* Protector *in one half hour. I hope you are not prone to seasickness."'* The matron laughed. 'I think you can manage a sail in the harbour.'

Jerusha wrote as fast as she could, knowing it might only be a matter of three weeks or so before Master Kent delivered the letter to the *Revenge*. She wanted to add something of a deeply personal nature, but there was no telling how many eager eyes might read the letter, too. It could wait.

Surgeon Kidwell stopped by as she wrote, and Mrs Terwilliger filled him in. 'There's nothing like a little voyage around the harbour to make you appreciate land,' he teased.

Tugging on her cape because the wind blew cold, Jerusha tucked the letter in her apron pocket and hurried to the harbour.

She went directly to the wharf. 'Are you Cornell?' she asked one promising-looking youth. A blank stare sent her to the

next small craft, this one with a sail. Her 'Are you Cornell?' earned her a nod, smile, and a hand down into the dinghy.

'Sit ye in the middle, miss,' was all the instruction he gave.

Cornell navigated expertly between other small craft and gigs, narrowly avoiding a gig filled with crates of chickens loudly protesting. They passed a cow, head down, mooing a sad refrain. This was a sight of the Royal Navy she hadn't expected, although there was the mama goat on the *Harmony*. It was something to remember when Cornell sailed her back to Stonehouse.

The ships thinned out and then she saw *Protector* spelled out in gilt paint on the stern of a two-decked ship of the line. Cornell expertly brought his little craft close to what looked like a wooden swing dangling down from the deck, which suddenly looked so high above them. 'Here ye are, miss.'

She looked at it doubtfully. 'If you tie up, I can hand you the letter and they could pull *you* up instead.'

'No, ma'am,' he said. 'Orders were for you to do it. Master Kent wants to see you.'

'I would like to see him, too,' she admitted. 'Up I go.'

She looked up to see smiling faces, Master Kent's among them. 'Just sit in the swing, Mrs Wilson,' he called down. 'Hang on tight!'

When she was secure, Cornell backed away his small craft. 'Don't go too far,' she called to him, as the men on deck expertly towed her up the side of the ship.

Master Kent reached for her and helped her off. 'You barely weigh a thing.'

'I'll warn you that some ship out here is about to get a load of irate chickens,' she teased back. She reached into the pocket on her surgeon's apron. 'Here's the letter to my Jamie. Thank you so much for doing this, sir. Now if you'll help me back…'

She looked towards land to see Cornell in the distance. At the same time, the sails dropped and filled with a loud *whoosh!*

and the *Protector* started to move. 'Wait a minute,' she said, her heart in her throat. 'What…?'

Master Kent kissed her cheek. 'Jerusha, I couldn't think of a better way to thank you for how well you tended my son in his final hours. I'm taking you to the *Revenge*. We'll be on the blockade in five or six days, if the wind is right.'

She stared at him.

'I planned this with Captain Ames on the *Harmony*. I know roughly when he will pass the *Revenge* on his return to Portsmouth. What's the harm in spending one night aboard with your husband?'

Chapter Thirty-Three

'Are we still friends?' Master Kent asked Jerusha, when the laughter died down and the crew returned to their duties.

His expression was so earnest that Jerusha had only one answer. 'Master Kent, we are.'

'Call this the adventure of a lifetime, and something to tell your children. Come below. I'll find a spot for you in the wardroom.'

She followed him below deck, picking her way past coiled rigging and mysterious bits of equipment. The rocking motion of the ship was making her queasy, but she told her stomach to behave.

Master Kent opened a hatch and ushered her inside. 'Our second luff is laid up in Stonehouse with a terrible case of hives, so here you are in his quarters.'

She looked around the tiny cabin, touched to see a miniature of an older couple and another of a dog, tongue lolling out, eyes bright. She picked it up. 'Just think, Master Kent: There is a side to every man on board that we lubbers never see.'

'Aye, lass. You're getting a rare glimpse.'

Her rare glimpse expanded during the five days the *Protector* sailed to the blockade. The officers of the wardroom kindly admitted her to their mess table, an offer she declined the first day because she spent it in her cabin, heaving into a vomit tin.

The ship's surgeon, obviously in league with an apothecary

from Hades, concocted a brownish brew that smelled worse than broccoli—her least favourite vegetable—with overtones of rum.

'Hold your nose and drink it,' he said, in the tone of a doctor who seldom heard anyone disagree with him and wasn't about to start with this female.

She drank. To her astonishment, the smelly mass stayed in her stomach. To her further amazement, she felt well enough the next afternoon to come on deck, pleasantly surprised that she was alive.

It was a rare day of sunshine, considering that they were into October now, and she knew the English Channel was fickle. She debated what to do until she saw Master Kent above her on the quarterdeck. She started towards him, but he put up his hand, palm out, to stop her. He conferred with the man with gold epaulets on his shoulders. The captain gestured her up himself.

Jerusha made her careful way to the quarterdeck. The captain was obviously the man to thank, and she did so with a small curtsy. 'I gather I need your permission to be here, sir.'

'I'm happy to grant it,' he said, 'unless you become a managing female who thinks she knows more how to run a ship than I do.'

'I would never...'

'My wife would,' he replied with a smile. 'Welcome aboard.' He glanced at Master Kent. 'Since that man is held in high regard throughout the fleet, you'll always have a welcome on the *Protector*.' He lowered his voice. 'Thank you for tending his son so well, in his final moments.'

'I did it gladly,' she replied.

Jerusha learned other lessons that day, taught by Master Kent, who seemed to have made her his project. She spent a pleasant morning with him at the quarterdeck railing as he pointed out other ships sailing in the same direction, the French coast of embattled Europe. From her hours in Ward A, she

knew enough about sailors who liked to joke when she asked nautical questions.

'Sir, I have been teased by rascals in Ward A,' she told him as they watched the water. 'My questions may seem silly to you, but I am a nautical novice.'

'We all began that way, Jerusha,' he said. 'You…you don't mind if I address you by your Christian name, do you?'

'Not at all, sir.' She looked towards the open sea. 'I would have given the earth to hear your son say it, or say anything. I know he wanted to.'

When he put his hand on her shoulder, she steadied herself. She knew people spoke of iron men in wooden ships, and it seemed a glib statement to bandy about. At this moment, she knew these *were* iron men.

'Thank you for what you do, sir,' she said.

He did not reply, but the pressure on her shoulder increased. Some instinct told her he was struggling, too; perhaps they all were. 'No fears. We'll get you to the *Revenge*.'

Good winds bore them towards France as she remained prudently below deck, helping in the sick bay by rolling bandages and scraping lint. The ship's surgeon was a shy older man with a sure touch. On the third day, Jerusha watched him suture two small wounds. 'Watch closely,' he told her. On the fourth day, he handed her the needle and catgut when a third sailor managed to lacerate his forearm and showed up at Sick Call.

'Such a lovely wound, all neat and orderly,' the surgeon declared, which made his patient stare at him and edge towards the companionway. 'No, lad, come in, come in. I have here Mrs Wilson, who I am instructing in the fine art of suturing. Sit down.'

'Beg pardon, miss,' he whispered when the surgeon turned to his medicine chest to rummage about, humming to himself. 'Can you…?'

'I can,' she assured him. 'I'll probably flinch when you flinch, because I have a soft heart, but I can do this. Steady now.'

The surgeon watched as she dabbed and stitched and dabbed some more. When she said, 'I am not certain of a final stitch to close it,' he took over. She sighed with relief at the same time her patient did. After she bandaged her handiwork, he gave her a small salute and left, a happy man.

'Let's practise that final closure,' her mentor said. 'I have here a slice of condemned beef. I'll slice it in half and you will suture and close. Watch me. It's simple.'

On the fifth day, the *Protector* reached the blockade. Jerusha watched with interest as ships signalled, wore, and tacked. She jumped to hear gunfire, and the first luff was quick to reassure her.

'No fears, Mrs Wilson,' he said. 'The gunners practise all the time. It's our strength.'

Right then, she prayed in her heart that this lieutenant would live long in service to king and country. She had prayed that way at night for years, kneeling by her bed, but as she heard his conviction, she also knew he had a young wife in Hampshire and a son he had not seen yet. She had learned this only last night in the wardroom after dinner.

I have come to know you better, she thought. *I also know what can happen to you, because I run towards the sound of the jetty bell.*

The *Protector* passed one ship, then another. In mid-afternoon as clouds gathered in the west, the first luff handed her his glass. 'Here you are, Mrs Wilson.'

She looked, steadying her arm on the railing, and looked again to see *Revenge* across the stern of the closest ship to port. The lieutenant spoke to the signalman and flags rose in orderly fashion.

'What is he signalling?' she asked.

'Stop. Bosun's Chair. Medical Supplies,' he said. 'Here's what you have to do…'

* * *

'Sir, you're wanted on deck. The *Protector* is dropping off supplies.'

Jamie looked up from his contemplation of an angry tooth in the mouth of a terrified cook's mate. There was no medical matter that bothered him more than the removal of teeth, and this felt like a reprieve for both of them.

Jamie gave his full attention to the messenger, who seemed to be stifling a laugh. 'I didn't know the *Protector* delivered pharmacopeia,' he said. 'Are you certain?'

'Oh, sir…oh, sir,' was all the man said.

Idiot, Jamie thought mildly.

'Seaman Lafferty, stay here,' he said to his almost-patient. 'I am certain you want this tooth removed. I will only be a few minutes.'

'Aye, sir,' his victim said promptly, only it sounded like 'Uh…er…' because of the gauze in his mouth.

'Or this could wait another day,' Jamie said.

The sailor nodded vigorously and began removing the gauze. Jamie unstoppered his oil of cloves and dabbed it on the renegade tooth. 'This will hold you.'

The man beat him up the companionway in his urge to be elsewhere immediately. Jamie followed more slowly, until he saw a cluster of officers around a small person and his heart melted.

His captain was smiling. 'Sir?' he asked, as he hurried to his wife.

'Surgeon Wilson, you are the victim of a conspiracy between Sailing Master Kent, a man I greatly admire, and apparently your own Captain Ames of *Harmony*,' the captain said. He led Jerusha across the deck. 'She is yours until *Harmony* hails us in a day or two to return her to Plymouth.' He tipped his hat to Jerusha. 'Go on, dear, he won't bite.'

He heard the cheers and laughter, and saw Jerusha's smile

so wide that it lit the deck. 'Master Kent engineered this,' she said just before he enveloped her in his cloak and held her close, pressing her head, bonnet and all, tight against him.

He doubted anyone had ever been kissed in the sick bay of the *Revenge*, but it happened as soon as he got Jerusha carefully down the companionway and into his medical domain, which smelled strongly of cloves now.

She sniffed and said, 'You're so sweet, my love,' which made him laugh, then kiss her thoroughly. 'I love you,' she managed, before he locked the hatch, picked her up, and set her down on the cot he used when there wasn't time for a proper rest in the officers' wardroom.

He had no plans at all for a proper rest, and apparently neither did she, considering how eager she was to help him out of his uniform. 'It's easier for me,' she told him as she concentrated on his trouser buttons. 'All I really have to do is raise my skirt and petticoat.'

'Then do it, wife,' he ordered.

She'll think I'm a beast. I've been so gentle with her before, were Jamie's last coherent thoughts, before he performed the most unorthodox bit of medical relief ever attempted in a Royal Navy sick bay, as far as he knew.

There was nothing gentle about it. To his intense gratification, Jerusha matched his own desire, her hands tugging him down onto her, as if he needed encouragement, which he didn't. And thank goodness there were plenty of the usual nautical noises that masked her moan of complete satisfaction, or maybe it was his. He neither knew nor cared. His wife was here and he was the world's most complete man in this longitude and latitude.

When they finished the first instalment of what he hoped were several before the arrival of the *Harmony* to ferry her back to Plymouth, he fetched another blanket and made a more comfortable nest beside the medicine chest. Oh, why

not? He was as bare as a new babe, so he divested Jerusha of all her clothes and cuddled her to him, enjoying every curve, nook, and cranny.

'How in the world…' he started, then listened with growing appreciation as she told him of the kindness of one sailing master.

'He sent me a note telling me to write to you, and that I would have to go on a small boat out to the *Protector*, since he could not leave his ship,' she explained. 'It sounded logical. He kidnapped me!'

He liked the way she burrowed so close to him. His heart broke a little when she whispered to him how she used a hot water bottle every night to trick herself into thinking it was his warm spot in their bed. He couldn't help his smile when she fretted that everyone on the *Revenge* knew what was going on in the sick bay. She was a lady to the end and he adored her.

It seemed a waste, but they slept off and on through the afternoon, lulled by the unmatched well-being of coitus noninterruptus. No one needed his services except his wife, who became insistent, along about time to gather in the wardroom for supper. As it turned out, she was far more delicious than any meal of stringy beef, beer, and hard bread could have been.

By the time morning came many hours later between sleep and utter magnificence, he was ready to tidy up and prepare the sick bay for morning Sick Call. 'I am a surgeon, after all,' he told her. There was no lack of water to clean themselves, and plenty of soft cloths to blot at tender parts, which almost became his undoing, because he wanted to do more than blot.

Duty called; in fact it cleared its throat and tapped its foot, speeding the process of becoming presentable. When he unlocked the door, he saw the usual number of sore throats, lacerations, black eyes and coughs. Morning had come on the blockade.

Another day followed, with equal parts bliss and business.

He discovered how proficient Jerusha was in suturing wounds, a skill he had not expected. He worried, but no one smirked or made snide remarks as Jerusha helped him. She did have a chance to show off her suturing skill on a small wound, impressing both him and the recipient.

And later, when everyone was tended and gone, no emergencies arose to ruin another perfect day. There was more leisure this time to talk. He dabbed at her eyes when she told him of Alec Kent's peaceful death and his father's gratitude.

In turn, she listened to his tally of injuries both real and imagined and laughed when he groused that one of the Articles of War should include a flogging around the fleet for hypochondria. It was the kind of silly talk he never thought they would have time for, not when Napoleon breathed down everyone's neck and they lived in a world at war.

'I will never dare show my face on deck again,' she said, when Jamie opened the hatch to see some kind soul had left them food with a note.

Make sure she eats, Surgeon. You can spare twenty minutes for that. Yrs. sincerely, the Wardroom

The next day began the same as the others, troubling Jamie, as he knew the *Harmony* was due today or if he was lucky, tomorrow, on her return journey through the blockade fleet to England. Jerusha knew it too, because she became more quiet.

In silence, she folded their blankets and set the sick bay to rights as he doctored and admonished today's crop of patients. 'It will be good to put on another dress in Plymouth and wash my hair,' she said halfway through the morning. 'I'm feeling a little dingy.' Jamie's only consolation was that she didn't sound too cheerful about leaving.

He went on deck, thinking to himself why it would be a useful thing to train women for actual medical work in the

fleet. It was wishful thinking—such events probably waited for another, more enlightened century—but it gave him food for thought besides the reality that Jerusha was leaving, and he would be alone again.

He asked for and received permission to climb to the quarterdeck, then wondered at the gathering of officers with their telescopes trained on the nearest blockader, still some distance away.

'It can't be.'

'You're not reading it right.'

'Look again. See there.'

'By God, at last.'

The captain was closest but preoccupied. Jamie looked at the first luff and raised his shoulders in a questioning shrug. The lieutenant motioned him closer. 'As near as we can tell, the dons and the Frogs have left Cadiz and come out to play. Hoorah for Nelson!'

They both turned as a signalman in the rigging shouted, 'Full speed for Cadiz! All haste. Prepare to join battle.'

'There we have it, gentlemen,' Captain Moorsom said calmly. 'Our wait is over. To your stations.' He turned to the Royal Marine sergeant standing alert. 'Tell the drummer it's "Beat To Quarters."'

'Sharpen your knives, James,' the first luff said.

Jamie stood still as the drummer beat out the familiar rhythm.

God help me, I have a wife aboard.

Chapter Thirty-Four

The full implication of her husband's words sank in immediately. 'I'm sailing into battle, too.'

Her covered her hand with his. 'The navy has been waiting for this moment. It will be big and decisive.'

'I'm afraid,' she admitted.

'That's two of us.' With the sound of 'Beat To Quarters' drumming in her ears—she knew she would never forget the steady, unrelenting cadence—he pulled her down the companionway, then farther down, to the deck above the hold, the orlop deck.

She looked around the poorly lit space, crowded with unused sails, tar in buckets, nails, and other naval gear that looked like clutter to her, but she knew must have a purpose. 'Why are we here?' she asked, speaking loudly to be heard above the sounds of men running on two decks to the continuous drumroll.

'This is the safest place. When the bleeding starts, the wounded are taken here. This is my office in battle.'

She didn't mean to start shivering. God knows her husband was soon to be far too busy to worry about her, but she shivered anyway. She had the good sense to keep her lips tight together. There was no sense in giving him one more person to fret about.

She saw his worry for her in his eyes and knew she had to

say something, even as her stomach churned and she wanted to run...where? Deep breath. 'Then it is my office, too,' she told him. 'Tell me what to do, and I will do it.'

That was all her husband needed. He became the reliable, dependable man who had caught her attention in a duck-pond. 'We are aft in the midshipman's portion of the ship,' he told her. 'The only thing below us is the hold.'

Jerusha couldn't help what she knew was her sceptical face. 'I say that in relative meaning,' Jamie said. 'We're in deep water, and we will be fired upon.' He pointed to a mess table. 'That becomes my operating table.'

'It's so dark here. No portholes, no...how can you see to...'

'My mate is gathering lamps.' He pointed to another dim corner. 'Let's clear a wide space to work there.'

'Why so far?'

He took her by the shoulders and gently pulled her to him. 'When the fleet action starts, that is where my assistants and the ship's crew above us—whoever can be spared—will lay the wounded.'

Jerusha nodded, unable to speak.

'You won't recognise it by the end of the day.' He released her and pointed to what looked like sails. 'I have never been to battle in this ship. Hopefully, this is...ah, aye. The surgeon before me knew his business.'

Jerusha knew he was talking to himself, and she listened, sure to glean information and spare him the time of repetition. He raised several portions of sailcloth. 'Aye, aye, Surgeon Westin, you kept it tidy. Jerusha, we will cover this table with one of these sail portions. They're old sails, but clean, and still useful. When I ask you for a new one during battle, toss aside the bloody one and replace it with one of these.'

She couldn't help but suck in a deep breath and another, and he saw it and understood. 'Remember that this is the safest place on board. I'll make you work hard, doing things that

on an ordinary day would terrify you. It's fast work and that will occupy your mind, believe me.'

She didn't, but she nodded anyway, and he saw right through her. He gave her lips a hearty smack and shook her gently by the chin. 'And you're thinking I'm completely barmy, and how can you overlook all the blood and gore, and why on earth did you marry me? Trust me here, my love, you'll be too busy to worry until it's over.' He touched her body in a popular place. 'You know, like the first time we did the marriage dance.'

What could she do but laugh, pat him gently in another popular place, and get to work.

As the *Revenge* raced along with the other blockaders, free at last from their numbing, boring duty in front of Brest, she helped her husband and Paddy, the surgeon's mate, a boy younger than she was, move most of the sick bay's contents a deck above to this tight space below. They were joined by the ship's purser, that officer who doled out supplies with a thimble, according to Paddy. 'He's quiet and a bit barmy, but I trust him,' Paddy whispered.

She helped Paddy clear off that part of the deck by the ribs and piled up more of the sail fragments. 'That's to cover the dead,' he told her, his voice so matter-of-fact. 'We may end up stacking them, too.'

She took his arm, hoping he would overlook how her own arm trembled. 'Paddy, have you been in battle before?'

'Aye, miss,' he said with a grin. 'My first was the Battle of the Nile. I was fifteen.'

'I'll stop complaining then.'

He gave her a wink, the Irish kind she had seen a time or two in Ward A. 'Ye don't complain *now*, Mrs Surgeon.'

The reality of the ordeal to come came home to roost on her shoulder like a vulture when two sailors came below deck, bouncing a canvas sack down the companionway steps. They

lugged it near the table, opened it, and with tin pails started spreading sand.

'For the blood,' one of them explained. 'You won't slip this way.'

Numb with fear, she waited for her husband to return from his summons from the captain, who had ordered all officers and warranted officers to meet him on the quarterdeck. 'He calls it a "consultation,"' Jamie told her as he went topside.

When he returned, he carried some clothing, which he handed to her. 'It's the smallest I could find in the slops chest, but I'd prefer you belay that dress you're wearing for these.' He took a lingering look at her dress, a dark one entirely appropriate for her Stonehouse days. 'I recall undoing all those buttons quite recently.'

She couldn't help laughing, even though she knew that was precisely his intent. She shook out the clothing he handed her. 'I am to wear trousers and a heavy shirt of some sort that will wrap around me twice?'

Again, the reality of what lay ahead brought her down to earth. 'If you end up in the water, it's likely easier to swim in trousers instead of a dress,' he said, and then because he was Jamie, 'You already have your surgeon's apron. Cinch it tight.'

She found a dark corner—orlop decks had plenty of those—and changed into a shirt and trousers that worked well enough when she rolled up the pantlegs and found a length of rope for a belt. When she returned to the improvised operating room, Jamie was leaning on the table, reading what looked like a well-used text. She looked away. There were bloodstains on the pages.

When he finished, he got another bit of sail to cover a smaller table and spread out his capital knives. Paddy brought over a small brazier with a kettle and water. He started a fire and put in a wicked-looking saw. 'Put in two,' Jamie said.

He saw the question in her eyes. 'Lord Nelson's orders.

When he lost his right arm at Tenerife, he said the worst part of the amputation was a cold saw. Hence his mandate to all surgeons: warm saws.'

'I need to sit down,' Jerusha said.

Jamie led her to a stool beside the table. 'That better?'

She had to know, needed to know. 'What will you expect of me today?'

'What you already do best, but this will be hard. When the guns start, every gunner will quickly be covered with block soot from gun discharge. Ah, here it is.' He pointed to another brazier Paddy had toted out from a dark corner. 'This is warm water for you. I know we will run out of towels, but do your best. Wounded men will be bloody and blackened with gun smoke.'

'I'll get them clean.'

'I know you will, my love.' His hand went to her shoulder; she loved the firmness of his touch. 'If we're down to the wire, I'll need you to suture.'

'Oh, my.' What else could she say?

He appraised her, then snapped his fingers. 'One more thing.' He selected a length of muslin from his bandage chest and wrapped it around her hair. 'That'll do.'

'You will never be a lady's maid,' she scolded, and rewrapped the muslin. 'I still refuse to look repellent, and you haven't a clue where to knot anything except a bandage.'

He shrugged. 'I am no hairdresser. I prefer to rumple it.' He held her close. 'My lady, you're amazing. I am going to try you to the limit.'

'Not you,' she said quietly. 'Napoleon.'

Shortly after noon, because of a light wind with greasy swells on the water, Admiral Collingwood's line of battle sailed slowly, majestically, towards the combined fleet of French and

Spanish warships parallel to Admiral Nelson's line. Jerusha sat on the lower deck in her husband's lap.

She had been listening to guns and gunners on the decks above, the trample of feet and gun carriages rolling in and out. 'What will battle sound like?' she asked.

'Loud, so loud. What's harder might be the way the ship will roll with each barrage, in addition to the ship's movement towards the enemy. I need scarcely add that it is hard to amputate limbs or suture under such circumstances.'

'How in the world do you do what you do?' she asked, touching his face, caressing it, even as Paddy looked on with interest.

'To the best of my ability. What else can I say?' He managed a laugh. 'We can both tell our children about this battle outside of Cadiz someday.'

Was this the right time, considering that once the action began, she did not know if he or she would survive? Maybe she should have said something sooner. She knew herself well enough to know that, married or not, she was always going to be a modest woman.

'You should know something,' she said finally, as shouted commands from far above them grew louder.

'Hopefully I'll remember it,' he told her, giving her an extra cuddle. 'Right now I'm wondering if I have enough retractors and if I should have had Paddy roll more bandages.'

'You need to know this. I think—not totally sure, mind you—but I think we started a baby the last time you were in port.'

There was no stunned silence, because the ship noises seemed to get louder, even as she whispered right in his ear. 'You know, in the family way?'

'Oh, Jerusha,' he said, his voice suddenly so tentative. 'Oh, Jerusha.'

'I'm dreadfully inconvenient.'

'I love you anyway. I think both of us are dreadfully inconvenient, unless it was another lucky fellow who surprised you some night when I was gone serving king and country.'

She heard the humour in his voice and marvelled at this man of hers. 'James Wilson, do you have a middle name?'

'Andrew. Is this the dread three-name dress down?'

'It's too late for the tri-scold,' she teased back, astounded at this silly conversation when the *Revenge* could be blown apart at any minute, if things went precisely wrong. 'I was wondering, that's all. Andrew might be a nice name for a son. Aye, Andrew Wilson.'

'And if it's a daughter, I'm partial to Mary.'

She nodded, fearing what was coming soon. She burrowed into his chest and nearly through to his backbone, or would have if she could. She straightened up when Paddy clambered down the ladder into the orlop, his excitement palpable. 'Sir, Captain Moorsom wanted you to know that when the carronades fire, it's the general signal for a broadside.' He rubbed his hands together. 'Sir, looks like we're heading smack in the middle of the southern end.'

'Thank you, Paddy,' her husband said calmly. 'Are you ready?'

'As ever I will be,' his mate said.

Jerusha closed her eyes. If she could have run home to Plymouth, she would have. 'Carronades?' she asked, hoping to sound merely curious, and not terrified, too.

Jamie had no trouble sensing her high reticence for battle. He rubbed her cheek with his. 'Those smaller guns on the quarterdeck. We must be nearly into the Combined Fleet lines. I can't prepare you for the sound of cannonballs hitting the *Revenge*, or maybe sails or a mast struck and falling. Bear it the best you can. That will be followed by men bringing the wounded down here to us and Paddy. We're going to be busy. Hang on.'

Chapter Thirty-Five

Hardly had Paddy assumed his position beside the operating table when Jerusha heard the carronades far forward on the *Revenge*.

'That's it,' Jamie said so calmly. God bless the man she married. The surgeon she adored checked his timepiece, as though pronouncing a death in Ward A, even as she knew they were about to be engulfed by death far outmatching any hospital ward. 'A quarter to one of the clock. Here we go, my love.' He grinned. 'Not you, Paddy.'

The mate laughed.

These men are crazy, Jerusha thought.

She braced herself.

She wasn't prepared. Not at all. Every cannon on the lee side of the *Revenge* blasted death into the enemy. The force of the broadside threw her against the operating table. Jamie grabbed her, righted her, and sat her down on the deck. 'That's going to leave a bruise,' he shouted above the sound of the mighty gun carriages rolling back as gunners swabbed and reloaded.

Her ears rang, but she heard someone on the deck above yelling, 'Fire at will!'

Poor Will, she thought, then realised she had enough lunacy to match that of the man she loved. *Poor Will*.

Jamie was precisely right. Once the wounded men came down, assisted by other gunners or spare men on the gun-deck,

she was too busy to be terrified. It was as though a hundred jetty bells clanged for medical help pouring from Stonehouse to assess, patch immediately, and send wounded men into the wards to live or die. No, a thousand jetty bells, and there were no wards to send the men, only this orlop deck.

In no time, there were ten, then fifteen, then twenty wounded men groaning, crying, and screaming on the sail-covered orlop deck near the operating table where her husband worked with his knives. Some bore their agony silently. She decided silence was worse.

Jerusha wasted not a moment, wiping blood, gun soot, and other bits and pieces she didn't want to think about from those men waiting their turn. She cleaned as gently as she could, which she quickly understood would never do. She increased her tempo of wash and wipe as more wounded surrounded her. On her knees, she moved from one man to the next, cutting off their clothing when she could, at Jamie's command, and wiping blood and bone around shattered arms and legs.

To the side of the orlop deck, she saw where other men were placed, those men who had no chance of survival. She thought of her silent patients on Ward B, Sailing Master Kent's son among them, and wished with all her heart she could sit with them, as she had sat day after day with Alec Kent. Maybe there would be time later.

In a momentary lull, she heard noise of chests being dragged across the deck and looked up. His face grim, his expression set, Paddy tugged three midshipmen's sea chests into the marginally better light next to her husband. The Irishman slung down a bit of sailcloth and nodded to two other slightly wounded men who must have helped take their mates below deck. She couldn't hear what was said, but those sailors carried their wounded to Paddy. She watched another moment. Jamie must have assigned him to suture wounds requiring no amputation.

I can do that, too, she thought. *Maybe when Paddy tires.*

She cleaned the men as best she could, assisted by a uniformed officer she did not know. He must have noticed her questioning look. 'I'm Bailey the purser,' he said. 'Pleased to meet you. I can help here.'

Was this Paddy's man? He sounded like he was addressing her at a garden party. She nodded and returned to her task, and he to his, after he poured out the already bloody water and refilled the brazier from a keg.

After what seemed like hours but was probably only minutes, Jerusha gasped to hear the *Revenge* firing cannon from both sides now. They must be surrounded. She wept in utter terror, stopping only when the wounded man below her put his hand on her arm.

'No worries, missy,' he consoled her, even as his gunnery mate tightened the tourniquet near his shoulder. 'Thank 'ee, mate.'

'But we're surrounded!'

'Never you worry,' the gunner said. He grinned, his teeth white in an otherwise black face. ''Tis the way our little admiral likes to fight. Hit hard, then divide into skirmishes. Pell-mell, he calls it.'

'I think you're all crazy,' she told him, which made him laugh.

As the guns roared, the *Revenge* shook and shivered, and more wounded men joined her sea of patients on the orlop deck. Jerusha ran out of towels.

I haven't a single scruple left, she thought as she pawed through discarded clothing for any cloth that looked remotely clean.

She took solace in watching her husband standing with legs wide apart to balance himself as the *Revenge* did its own battle dance. He barely paused from one patient to the next.

This was no time to complain or hold back, even though

her stomach revolted against the sight of one more drop of blood, or one more man looking at her with hope in his eyes. There would never be enough surgeons for a battle such as this.

To comfort herself, she thought of their baby, nestled deep inside and so tiny, evidence of a wife's love for a husband so often gone, because he had no choice. She wondered if their little one, no older than six or seven weeks, if that, could hear the terrible sounds, or feel the constant shaking of a ship tried to its limit. She hummed a lullaby and realised she wasn't only humming to Andrew or Mary inside her but soothing the Andrews on the deck around her. The notion pushed the heart back into her breast.

When Jerusha began to wonder if every man aboard the *Revenge* was below deck with her, she sensed something different. She became aware that the *Revenge* was not surrounded anymore and the guns fired on one side only, and not as rapidly.

'Jamie?' she said in what she thought was a normal tone of voice. 'Jamie?'

He didn't turn around, so she went back to cleaning dirty men with equally dirty towels and no clean water anywhere now, in hopes that somehow the god of battle would take pity on them.

She noticed that Paddy was rotating his shoulders and turning his head from side to side. To her relief, she saw no new patients on his makeshift operating table. She returned to her duty, aware that the smallest hope was peering at her, its eyes bright, as though it were a living, breathing entity and not just a wish in her heart. She knew she imagined it, but the thought kept her working steadily through the endless afternoon.

When her husband demanded Paddy's aid at his table, Jerusha wasted not a moment, stepping to Paddy's table to continue stitching up what even she recognised as more minor wounds. When Paddy finished, he examined her work and nodded. 'Mrs Wilson, you're amazing.'

'Hardly,' she said. The compliment buoyed her as she returned to wiping away soot and grime.

She finally became aware that she was wiping down one of the remaining wounded, this man a Royal Marine. He seemed alert so she asked, 'Please, sir, what is happening up there?'

'Many ships on fire,' he told her in that cryptic way of the wounded, doling out as few words as possible, because everything hurt, even grammar.

'Ours?'

'Theirs. I pray...'

Suddenly a loud explosion shook the *Revenge* so hard that Jamie threw himself across his patient on the table. Only hours ago, such a noise would have sent her screaming around the orlop. Jerusha waited in silence for a falling mast, or water pouring down the companionway, but nothing happened. Above the appalling odour, she smelled something on fire, and close by.

'Paddy, go have a look,' Jamie ordered, as he continued with an amputation.

Paddy came back soon enough. 'It's a French ship! There's a huge flame!'

'God rest their souls,' Jamie said, he who had been working for hours to save those Royal Navy men near death because of French warships like the one in its death agony nearby.

'It's drifting away from us,' Paddy added. He darted up the ladder again and came down just as quickly. 'Come look, sir!'

'I can't. You go topside, Jerusha.'

Topside was a strange world. Her mouth open, Jerusha stared at bodies in the water, ships dismasted and drifting, others locked together as if in mortal combat. She watched what remained of the explosion, an orange fireball that spread as she stared, transfixed.

But that was almost nothing compared to the death so close

around her on the *Revenge*. She stared at men who never made it to medical aid on the orlop deck.

'Wh-what did you want me to see, Paddy?' she asked, when she could form words again.

'The little ships, one a schooner.' He pointed across the rail. 'It's the *Pickle*.'

'Such an odd name,' she murmured, half to herself. 'Ship to shore, like my husband's usual office at sea?'

'Sometimes. See there? They're picking up survivors.' He squinted in the failing light. 'Good God, they're naked.' To her surprise, Paddy nodded his approval. 'Easier to swim with no encumbrances.'

She jumped involuntarily when more explosions battered her already tired ears.

'No fears, miss,' Paddy said. 'It's just guns still cooking off.' He watched the nimble ships darting in close, too close, to reach for Frenchmen floundering in the water. 'Go below and tell the boss we'll be tending the enemy soon.'

Jerusha stood a moment longer, taking in the sight of so much carnage and mayhem. She gently patted her belly. 'We're still here, little one, you and I,' she whispered. 'Someday, you can tell Admiral Nelson your mama served in whatever place this is.'

She made her way carefully down the gun-deck ladder and farther down onto the orlop deck, slippery with blood. She watched her husband as he put the last few stitches into a flap of skin covering an amputation, and summoned the purser to clear away a spot on the deck for a sailor lighter now than when they laid him on the table.

Maybe Jamie sensed she was watching him. He turned around and leaned against the operating table, where in better times young midshipmen gathered for meals. 'Jerusha,' was all he said.

She came closer, suddenly shy, even though she knew this

man as she had never known another human being before. With humility earned in a terrible afternoon, she thanked God Almighty, Ruler of the Universe and even this sorry spot off the coast of Spain for the best man a wife could have.

He smiled at her, but she could tell he was too tired to move. He looked at the patients on the deck, men he had saved, and men who couldn't be saved. His glance went to the dark corners as if wondering if those men still breathed, those sailors and Marines taken there in the beginning because no power outside of a miracle could save them. She could almost hear his brain working, apologising to the dead that no one alive knew how to heal them.

She came to him and looked, too, where death had come calling, despite the surgeon's best efforts. Jamie's arms circled her from behind.

'What have we been a part of?' she asked.

'Something I hoped you would never see,' he told her. 'But now you know what I do.' He rested his blood-crusted cheek against her blood-crusted cheek. 'We never see the battle, but here we are, fighting the worst of it below deck.'

Her tired brain remembered Paddy's message. 'That explosion? It's a French ship close by. Paddy says you—we—will have more work here soon.'

'I expect we will.'

He spoke so calmly.

How do you manage? she asked herself.

She leaned back against him. For a small moment in a crowded day, maybe it was enough right now to be held close and feel his heartbeat against her back. She squinted into the darker corners where Jamie had looked, and felt an overpowering urge to check on them.

Of the many, she found one still alive, and sat by him. He still breathed, so she sat and took his hand. 'Felicity,' he said, content. 'Felicity.'

Call me whatever you want, she thought, as Nameless One finally breathed a peaceful sigh and left her.

As she sat there, she heard silence, blessed silence. The guns were stilled at last.

'Surgeon? Surgeon?'

Who was calling for her husband? She moved towards him, careful not to step on any of the wounded. She sensed something worse, some news she didn't want to hear. That was folly. What could possibly be worse than this entire day?

Black with gun smoke from hat to shoes, a midshipman picked his way down the companionway.

'Aye, son, what? Who needs me?'

'Captain Moorsom. He's in a bad way.'

'I'll come up now,' Jamie said. 'Move aside.'

'Wait, sir,' the middie said. He straightened up, eyes ahead, as if in recitation. 'One hour ago, our glorious little admiral died on the *Victory*, struck down by a sniper. Lord Nelson lived to know we had won.' He turned away and began to weep. 'What will we do?'

'We carry on,' Jamie told him, a comforting hand on the lad's shoulder. 'As he would wish. Take me to our captain. Now!'

'I don't think I will ever forget this day, sir.'

'None of us will, lad,' Jamie told him. 'Neither will England.'

Chapter Thirty-Six

'Come with me.' Jamie took her hand, so Jerusha followed him topside. She already knew how horrible the deck looked, but barely recognised the congenial captain who had insisted she join the officers in the wardroom when she came aboard—Was it yesterday? The day before?—as part of a good-natured prank. His eyes were two coals in his head, and he was as filthy as his men. She saw the wound by his ear, which seemed to be hanging on by a thread.

He pointed towards the still burning French ship. 'Wounded from the *Achille* are coming here,' he managed to say. Then, 'Lieutenant Hole is now in command. You two there. Take me below deck.'

'Aye, sir.' As two grimy gunners took Captain Moorsom below deck, Jamie went to the rail and stared down as the much smaller *Pickle* and a cutter came closer, carrying wounded men. 'Lieutenant Hole, the quartermaster needs to rummage around quickly for some trousers, at the very least. These Frogs are as bare as Adam in Eden.'

'I've already sent for him,' Captain Moorsom called from near the companionway. Jerusha wondered how he could manage his casual air, with such a wound. 'Close your eyes, Mrs Wilson.'

Where did Jamie find the energy to joke? 'I hope he hur-

ries, Captain. I can't have my wife looking at naked French-
men and making any comparisons. I'd hate not to measure up.'

To her astonishment, Captain Moorsom laughed. 'We do
have a certain reputation to maintain, madam.'

'Do either of you ever lose your sense of humour, Captain?'
she declared, amazed that after all she had seen today, she
could still blush.

'Just exhausted. Get me below deck, gunners.'

She looked across the water to see the *Achille* blazing ev-
erywhere, with burning sailors too done for to jump. She cov-
ered her face with her hands, but that was no reprieve. She
still saw them on fire. 'Will I ever not see them?' she asked
Lieutenant Hole.

'If you are lucky,' he replied. 'Carry on, Mrs Wilson. I have
work to do.'

He looked so young. As Jerusha watched him take calm
charge of the disaster on deck, she knew she was seeing a ju-
nior officer turn into a commander of men, and it humbled her.

Working with Purser Bailey, she scrounged below deck
for more sails. Mr Bailey found a place in her heart forever
when she just stared at the wounded already crowded together
and wondered where to put Frenchmen, too. He brought her
a glass of wine.

'It's a fine Bordeaux from my own stash,' he assured her
with no little pride. 'I'm saving some for our captain over
there.'

It went down her throat like, well, good Bordeaux. 'Heav-
ens, but that was splendid, Mr Bailey. You have a knack.'

He beamed with delight, and casually brushed a bit of
someone's nameless body part off his sleeve like the gentle-
man he obviously was. He flicked something from her hair.
'My pleasure,' he said, as courtly as if he were her host at an
elegant dinner. What a strange place this orlop deck was, she
decided, as she returned to her labours, energised.

To her surprise and then her relief, two other women joined her on the orlop deck. She recognised one as the wife of the quartermaster, and the other as the sailing master's wife. Without a word, they continued her homely task.

She had to know. 'Have…have you ever seen anything like this?'

The quartermaster's wife, whose hair was already greying, shook her head. 'Not in all my years at sea.'

She watched as Paddy and the purser made room for more wounded, Frenchmen this time. In record time, Jamie rearranged and stitched until Captain Moorsom was patched as well as he could manage. In record time, the captain was taken to his own quarters across the *Revenge*'s stern. Over Jamie's protest, Jerusha sat her husband down and wiped his face. 'There now,' she said, hands on hips. 'Time for Frenchmen.'

And they came, some protesting, but more of the enemy from the *Achille* seeing only help and hopefully relief from their burns. Jamie went to work.

He called for her quickly, gesturing her closer for a look. 'Surgeon Kidwell told me he taught you how to debride burns,' he said.

'He did.' She looked and turned her head away. Lacerations were one thing; burns, quite another. 'I've helped with burns,' she managed to say. 'What do you want me to do?' she asked, terrified but game because she had no more choice than the others. He had a good shoulder. She rested her chin on it as he leaned there on the operating table. 'You stink,' she said, which made him chuckle.

'I've stunk worse,' he assured her. 'I sent Paddy to forage for olive oil, any kind of oil. And praise God, I found some gauze. When the burns come in, I want you to put a generous bit of oil on the burn and drape gauze on it. Wait here.'

She nodded. 'I hate war,' she said softly. She knew Jamie's

dreadful task was to decide who of the burned French sailors even came below for such puny aid as they could offer.

She and Purser Bailey stretched the olive oil as far as it would go, helped by the two uncomplaining wives. Hours passed and they were reduced to water only. The more alert among the French prisoners talked, but she could only shake her head and wish she spoke their language.

She thought of all the letters she had written for her patients in Ward A, certain they would be delivered to loved ones. These injured Frenchmen had no guarantee anyone would know where they were. The thought saddened her as nothing else could have.

The purser and quartermaster found trousers and some sweaters, but most of the barely covered patients shivered until their teeth chattered. It went against all her sense of respect for the dead, but she and the wives took the canvas coverings off the English dead to preserve the shivering French.

The moment Jerusha thought she could not stand another patient, a weeping Frenchwoman arrived, towed down the companionway by a Royal Navy officer Jamie introduced as Captain John Lapenotière.

'He skippers the *Pickle*,' Jamie said. 'Who is this noisy baggage?'

'Jamie, don't be rude,' Jerusha scolded.

She reached for the woman, who was dressed oddly in trousers and a jacket with a Royal Navy insignia.

The woman, her black curly hair wild around her face, drew back, then declared, *'Vous êtes une femme!'* She threw herself into Jerusha's arms, sobbing.

Seeing the utter pointlessness of trying to coax rational thought out of the woman, Jerusha did the logical thing and hugged her back. Soon the woman's sobs turned into hiccups, and then she was silent, her head down.

'Captain Lapenotière, why us?' Jamie asked.

Looking as sorely put upon as probably everyone else in the fleet, the captain shrugged. 'I took her to the *Belle Isle* first, but they're in far worse shape than the *Revenge* and they waved me off.' He leaned closer to Jamie. 'She was as bare naked as the others, but some kind soul on the *Belle Isle* gave her some trousers and another man took off his jacket. Surgeon, she has a burn on her neck and back. Can you help her?' He started for the ladder, his mission complete, apparently. 'By the way, her name is Jeannette. That's all we could understand.'

Jerusha coaxed Jeannette to sit on the operating table and held her hand while Jamie probed her burn. She flinched, but did not shriek, and bore it patiently, her eyes on Jerusha's. She talked at length, gesturing with her hands, her face a mask of worry and uncertainty.

Using the slender store of olive oil, Jamie dabbed at Jeannette's shoulder and back and bandaged it loosely. 'I wish we knew more,' he told Jerusha. He cleared his throat. 'Does anyone here speak French?'

No one did, or no one would admit to speaking French, until Mr Bailey returned to the orlop deck, bearing a flask of olive oil. 'I stole this from the quartermaster,' he said. 'QMs are the curse of the world.' Jerusha hid her smile when the quartermaster's wife fixed him with a malevolent stare. He flinched at the stare, shuddered, and turned his whole attention to Jeannette. 'Where did you find her?' he asked.

'She's from the *Achille*,' Jerusha said. 'No one speaks French here.'

'I do,' he said. *'Bon soir, madame,'* he said, which produced more tears and gestures. By the time she finished, they knew Jeannette had been working as a powder monkey with her husband's guns. She gestured a *whoosh* and a *boom*, then more tears.

Through it all, the purser listened intently and with sym-

pathy. When she finished, leaning against Jerusha in her exhaustion, Mr Bailey shook his head. 'The poor dear cannot find her husband.' He was a proper man. He blushed, much to Jerusha's delight. 'She had perched herself near the rudder. When the lead started to burn her, she took off her clothes and leaped into the water.' He spread out his hands. 'My quarters are untouched. I will clear a space for her there. Back soon,' he said, and left as quietly as he had come.

James and Jerusha looked at each other. 'I'm too tired to laugh,' James said at last. 'I believe I will never underestimate pursers again. How does he know French? Jerusha? *Jerusha!*'

She heard his voice from a peculiar distance. Jeannette grabbed her as Jerusha Wilson had all she could manage on this day of crushing, grinding battle. She either fainted or fell asleep. She didn't care which it was. She and either Andrew or Mary were done with this endless day.

Chapter Thirty-Seven

When she woke, Jerusha found herself on a pile of sailcloth, tucked in a dark place. She looked around in wild alarm, wondering how many wounded she had displaced, then took a closer look. Where was she? And what was the *Revenge* doing? She curled up and made herself small as the ship pitched and yawed wildly, caught in the grip of a monstrous storm.

When she cried out in fear, Jamie knelt beside her, gathering her close. She held on just as tight. 'We're all going to die,' she whispered.

'Not yet,' he said, 'although Captain Moorsom muttered something about the wind and waves being allies of the French. And I thought I had heard every curse word possible in the Royal Navy. Silly me. Thank God he is still alive.'

As her vision accustomed itself to the dim lighting, she stared hard at the deck. 'Where have they gone?' she asked, as terrible dread assaulted her. 'The deck was covered with wounded men.'

It was his turn to gather himself together. She had seen him do that on Ward A when something didn't go well; she dreaded it. 'This storm has proved too much for some,' he told her. She rested her cheek against his hand. 'Those men needed a hospital, and not the orlop deck. Look over there, though.'

She looked where he nodded and saw the survivors of rough and ready surgery aboard a ship under attack, some sitting

up, others curled tight as though trying in some weird way to make themselves smaller targets for shot and shell. She heard low-voiced conversation, and to her relief, the quiet slap of cards on the deck. God bless the Royal Navy.

'It's not quite Ward A, but it's close,' she said. 'I should be up and helping. I didn't mean to shirk my duties.'

Her doctor disagreed in firm tones she had heard him use with his patients in Stonehouse, where the floor didn't heave and threaten to toss everyone around. 'You've shirked nothing. No, little mother. You had all you could manage last night. You slept through the day.'

She smiled at that, even as the *Revenge* pitched and tossed like a wild horse unbroken to bit and bridle. 'I know I was tired.'

'Aye, lass. Now will you go back to sleep?'

Not yet. She struggled to sit up, to help, to do a thousand things, because that was what this situation demanded. Drat her sneaky, duplicitous husband. What did he do but what she had seen him do to cranky patients at Stonehouse? He held her close until she felt herself relax in his arms.

'All right, have it your way,' she said finally.

'Why, thank you. That's my intention.'

Jerusha tried to bargain her way to a few more moments of awareness. 'The other ships? Tell me we're not alone.'

He humoured her. 'We're not alone, but several of the Spanish and French prizes of war have escaped or wrecked. Admiral Collingwood is in charge of the fleet and we are heading to Gibraltar to refit.'

'Not home?' she asked, disappointed.

'Some of the larger ships took a terrible beating and will never survive to the Channel without repairs. Admiral Nelson's flagship was badly damaged, and Admiral Collingwood is determined that Nelson will be returned in the *Victory*. First Gibraltar, then home. Go to sleep. You're getting tedious.'

She smiled at that, then closed her eyes. The last thing she remembered was her husband tugging the sailcloth higher on her shoulder and kissing her cheek.

The storm raged for days, so wildly destructive that the cooks couldn't light fires and feed the men anything except ship's biscuit and hard cheese. There was nothing for Jamie's patients except ship's biscuit dipped in wine and then ale, when the wine ran out. Jerusha thought of the low diet that wounded men needed in order to heal, and her heart broke.

Revenge's Lieutenant Hole—obviously cut from the same cloth as his commander—restored all the order he could. The next day, Jerusha heard the temporary walls go up again in the officers' wardroom, which were broken down during battle. She spent a better night in Jamie's tiny quarters, curled up in his swinging cot and prayed not to be dumped out on the deck.

Despite the storm, more order came to the orlop deck. The *Revenge* seemed to have an unlimited supply of vinegar in kegs. Sailors not busy on deck were put to work mixing a little seawater with a lot of vinegar and scrubbing the orlop deck to remove bloodstains.

From somewhere, Jamie managed to actually heat some strong tea, which she managed to keep down. 'I will always smell vinegar,' she gasped, as he held her hair back as she puked into a bucket, because he wouldn't allow her on deck.

Against his protests, she returned to tending the wounded, wiping faces and then simply holding hands with those men as frightened as she was from the storm that continued to rage. Now and then one of the masters' wives joined her, as she soothed and commiserated.

They inched closer to Gibraltar, a wounded, limping fleet that looked nothing like conquerors. Jerusha made her way topside to see the remains of enemy ships, some with men clinging to them, knowing there would be no rescue, no hope.

They may have been the enemy, but this was a cruel death and she couldn't watch.

Jeannette proved to be useless. Even the calm-tempered, courtly Mr Bailey was ready to throw her overboard. 'All she does is weep for her missing husband,' he complained over a luncheon of ship's bread dipped in rum. 'I would happily chuck her over the side, but there is probably a rule of war against that,' he said morosely.

Jeannette cheered up slightly when Jerusha gave her the dark dress she had been wearing when she came aboard the *Revenge* as part of a lovely prank Sailing Master Kent played upon her and James Wilson. It pained her not at all to give away her own dress, because the events of recent weeks faded into nothingness, when the battle they'd been through together loomed so much larger. Perhaps it would stop Jeannette's complaints. It didn't.

In the directive Admiral Collingwood managed to compose, even with his writing desk heaving like a living thing as he put pen to paper, he declared this fleet action to be called Trafalgar, after the nearest cape south of Cadiz and not far from Gibraltar. Jamie told her that some of the officers were already calling this a battle no one would ever forget, when her most fervent wish was to forget it. Men and their battles…

'And here you are, a part of it,' Jamie told her. He kissed her, complimented her on her ability to keep tea and hard bread down in this raging storm, and began his midnight ward-walking among his patients.

No one wants to be here, she thought as she watched him, *but I would gladly stay, as long as you are here, my love.*

She marvelled at her husband, working in a tight, storm-battered space, with almost no medical resources except an active mind and well-honed resourcefulness.

He stayed with her as she wiped down one particularly hard case, a bosun who suffered no fool gladly. The one-eyed

brute glared at her, then his gaze softened. 'Surgeon, who is this pretty lady who winces when I wince?'

'That's my wife,' he told his patient. 'She has a tender heart, and she is mine.'

'I had a wife like that,' the bosun said. 'Gone these five years. Keep blushing, little lady. I'm enjoying the memories.'

'That is more kindness than I have ever heard from him,' Jamie told her later, which only made her sniff back tears and work harder.

At Jamie's insistence, she spent the next day swinging in his cot, blanket warm, her hand resting lightly just below her belly, acquainting herself with her little one. She had no larger task than the greatest task: to simply *be*, so another could grow.

The next day seemed no better than the four that had preceded it, as the storm raged and the fleet limped towards Gibraltar.

She was feeding the wounded their pitiful hard biscuit soaked in only water, when Jamie called to her from the companionway. He draped a woollen cape around her as she came to him. His face expressionless, he led her up to the main deck, cleared now of debris and almost tidy.

'You're going to hate this. You're leaving this ship don't argue with me, Jerusha.' He turned it into one rapid sentence.

He held her close. 'What are you doing?' she asked.

'Sending you home. Back to Plymouth and Mags McDonald and our bed that doesn't move about.' Drat the man; he chuckled. 'Except when we're both in it.'

'I'm not leaving without you,' she insisted, as he carefully edged to the *Revenge*'s railing and braced them both against the storm. Her old friend Panic returned as she stared, wide-eyed, at the boulder-sized waves.

'Admiral Collingwood has prepared a dispatch for the King and prime minister, telling them of Trafalgar,' Jamie said, speak-

ing loudly to be heard above the storm. 'Captain Lapenotière of the *Pickle* is taking it. And you.'

'Please no!' she begged, frightened because she knew he meant it, as sure as she knew how small the *Pickle* was. Compared to the warships around them, it bounced up and down in the water like a toy in a bathtub.

'Shh, shh. He is right now below us, about to transfer a last boatload of French prisoners to the *Revenge*. When they come up, you are going down. I will have not one word of argument, Jerusha Wilson.' He tightened his grip on her. 'I will protect my family.'

When she opened her mouth, he put a finger to her lips. 'My love, the *Revenge* is far less crippled than some of this battered fleet,' he said. 'She might stay right here, or return to the blockade. I will have you safe in Plymouth.'

He was speaking the truth, as little as she liked it. Drat the man again, but she knew he was right. She tried one more time. 'I am no trouble aboard ship,' she told him. 'I know I am useful.'

'Very much so,' he agreed. He seemed to waver and she took heart, then his mouth grew firm again. 'I won't have you in this place of danger while you grow a baby, our baby.'

Jerusha wanted to argue, but he was right. She nodded, unable to speak.

He kept his hand firmly in the back of her trousers as they watched the *Revenge* crew haul aboard the French prisoners, tie them to each other, then herd them in groups of twenty aft, where Royal Marines sat them down on a portion of the deck chained off to receive them.

Lieutenant Hole handed her his own dispatches wrapped in waterproof sealskin. 'Give it to Captain Lapenotière and he'll add it to our admiral's dispatch and other letters.' He kissed the packet. 'There's one to my wife in there, and other men's wives and sweethearts.'

'Aye, sir. That's what it comes down to, doesn't it? Those we love,' Jamie said.

'Aye, it does.' He smiled at her, this iron man who never flinched or faltered, the same as her husband.

England is safe because of you, she thought, and she kissed his cheek.

'Be a good girl,' Lieutenant Hole said as he blushed, that iron man.

'Your turn, Mrs Wilson,' she heard next from her dear surgeon. 'Sit in the bight of the rope and hang on. When you get aboard the *Pickle*, mind your manners and don't think me too heartless for sending you away.'

'Never that,' she whispered, any ill-use forgotten because she knew he was right.

She closed her eyes and gripped the rope for dear life as she swung out from the *Revenge*, then down neatly in the pinnace that she had earlier noticed was tied to the stern of the larger ship. She set her lips tight against any protest as a Royal Marine pulled her onto his lap and wrapped his arms around her. 'Hang on, little lady. We'll be alongside the *Pickle* and underway in no time.'

Dear God, the motion. She gasped as the little boat turned into a wild thing. The little crew struck out with their oars, heading towards another ship that appeared so small. She looked back at the *Revenge* and her husband. She strained to hear him as he cupped his hands around his mouth.

'I'll see you in Plymouth, Mrs Wilson!'

She waved until the *Revenge* disappeared, shrouded in rain. She kept her eyes on the ship and whispered, 'God of war, look kindly on my Jamie. Please, oh, please.'

She was nine days on the *Pickle*, second smallest craft among the victors of Trafalgar, an eighty-foot schooner built for mes-

sages between ship and shore, but even more for speed, if given the opportunity.

With no fanfare, Captain Lapenotière deposited her in his tiny quarters. Sitting her in a chair by the desk, he looked her straight in the eye. 'We're a small ship and we are one thousand miles from England,' he said. 'We are battling a storm of immense proportions and I have no time to coddle you.'

'I don't require coddling,' she assured him, looking him firmly in the eye, too, praying to never do anything to shame Surgeon Wilson.

He pointed to a nest of blankets in the deck by the bulkhead. 'My sleeping cot will swing wildly so you will be safer on the deck and not in it, Mrs Wilson.' He pointed to a bucket with a wooden lid. 'That is your commode. One of the seaman will dump it each morning. You are not allowed on deck unless summoned.'

'Aye, sir,' she said, which made him smile and seem slightly more human.

'It will be a difficult crossing, Mrs Wilson,' he said, his voice less stern. 'The *Pickle* is carrying the most important message to Admiralty and the King that has been delivered in recent memory. There are still enemy warships between us and England, and they have their orders, too. We will do our duty, no matter the danger.'

As soon as the *Pickle* left her relative protection from winds and waves created by the larger ships, the tossing began. Jerusha wrapped herself in a blanket and made herself as small as she could in the corner of Captain Lapenotière's cabin.

Day blurred into night, day after day, broken first by a change in wind direction that turned them back towards the Spanish coast. They struggled through the wind change and were on a course towards England again when she heard the unmistakable sound of 'Beat to Quarters.'

Were it not for a small act of kindness while still on the

Revenge, she would have been at the mercy of her promise to never leave the captain's quarters. A cabin boy had been assigned to bring her meals and empty the slops bucket. She recognised him from a brief stay in Block Four, Ward A, during a relapse of fever. Here he was now, reminding her of their connections.

Jerusha smiled to see that same look of adulation on his stark white face. 'Timmy, pop your head above deck and let me know what's happening.'

'A ship's chasing us!' he said, eyes wide, after a quick turn on the heaving deck.

Please don't blow us out the water, she prayed.

Only to sigh with relief when he came down again minutes later with the information that it was another small sloop, the *Nautilus*.

Even Captain Lapenotière enlisted her help. He sent Timmy down with the order that she find paper, pen, and ink in his desk. 'Mrs Wilson,' the captain shouted down the schooner's single companionway, 'write me a note stating that the Royal Navy was victorious, but we lost Admiral Nelson. Address it to Lord Haybert, British Delegation, Kingdom of Portugal, Lisbon. The *Nautilus* will carry it to Portugal.'

She did as he dictated, trying to time each letter to the rising and falling of the little schooner. When she finished, she dusted it with sand from the shaker in the desk, folded it and took it on deck, where two sailors guided her to the captain as the schooner bobbed about. Through a speaking tube, the two captains coordinated a line and sent the note in a bottle attached to a ring.

'Well done, Mrs Wilson,' Lapenotière said, with a bow to Jerusha. 'Go below and stay there.'

They sailed on through wind and storm that worsened until she saw water leaking into her tiny portion of the wardroom. It rose to her ankles. She held her breath as the bow seemed

to dip lower and lower into the water. The spry little schooner slowed.

Good God, we're sinking, she thought, and held tight to her belly, desperate to protect her unborn baby.

I tried Jamie, I tried, was her second thought.

Her third thought was, *I will not die below deck. I am sorry, Mary or Andrew, that I could not protect you.*

Calmly she mounted the few steps that took her into the storm, the officer's cape tight about her.

Captain Lapenotière picked his way across the slanting deck. She watched him calmly, determined not to be forced below deck. To her relief, he handed her a bucket. 'Start bailing,' he ordered, and she did, bailing until her back ached, doing it for her baby, and not to get some message through, no matter how vital it was. In that awful moment, she bound herself forever to her unborn child.

All night she bailed as some of the crew manned the pump below deck and the rest of them poured water over the side. The effort seemed puny, but she worked until she dropped from exhaustion. Someone carried her to the mast and told her to hang on. She shivered, soaked to the skin. There wasn't a dry place on the foundering schooner.

She woke near morning to the scraping sound of men unbolting the four small but heavy carronades in the bow of the *Pickle*. The guns went overboard with a splash and the ship rose noticeably in the heaving sea.

It made all the difference. The storm raged, but the ship sailed. Someone carried her below deck and she slept, soggy but too exhausted to care.

By noon the storm abated. By the end of the next day, they found themselves in the English Channel sailing on a smooth sea, which earned everyone a tot of rum, captain's orders. On deck again, Jerusha watched the bottle go around. When it

came to her, she tried to pass it on. 'Rum is for heroes,' she said. 'That's what my Jamie tells me.'

'Mrs Wilson, drink up,' Captain Lapenotière said. 'You're a hero, too.'

On they sailed, bedevilled once by no wind at all, which meant the captain ordered his men to pull out sweeps, long oars that bit into the sea, and row. They rowed until the god of wind blew in their direction at last, because apparently the Lord loves effort.

Jerusha saw all the exhaustion around her as men dropped from their labour and slept, waking up only to a prodding boot to keep the sails trim, while other men dropped and slept.

All of them kept a weather eye on the *Nautilus*, the schooner that had taken the message to the British ambassador in Portugal and now seemed to be racing to deliver the most important news of the war at sea to London first.

'Damn the *Nautilus*,' Jerusha heard Captain Lapenotière mutter as he paced the quarterdeck and watched his now-competitor trying to close the gap. Through judicious sailing and seamanship, he pulled ahead of the *Nautilus* and elaborately wiped his hands of the matter.

On November the fourth they made landfall at Falmouth in Cornwall on the southwest coast of England, a long distance from London. 'Why here?' Jerusha asked Captain Lapenotière.

'We depend upon the wind, and it is fickle,' he said, as his crew snubbed his battle-and-wind-tried ship to the dock. 'Now I will depend upon horsepower. I will beat the *Nautilus* to London. I swear I will.'

She watched from the deck as Captain Lapenotière spoke to an interested crowd on the dock, telling them of Trafalgar and Lord Nelson's sad death. Some turned away in shock and sorrow. Some ran to the nearest tavern and shops. She could almost see the word pass through the sleepy town. Bells tolled next.

Within the hour, a post chaise with four horses pulled up to the dock. One of the *Pickle*'s crew tossed in a pouch with precious dispatches and letters from officers to their wives. Captain Lapenotière went on board once more to consult with George Almy, master's mate.

'Mrs Wilson, you will sail with the *Pickle*,' he ordered. 'In a day, maybe two, God willing, you will be anchored in Plymouth.' His tone changed, and she heard the kindness that likely would have been there all along, if not for the terrors of storm and war. He kissed her forehead. 'Bless you, dear Mrs Wilson. If you were a man, I would request your services on any ship I command.'

'I think the surgeon would call you out for a duel,' she replied, which meant he was laughing as he left the gallant *Pickle* after one more long look at the schooner that would make him famous.

True to Lapenotière's words, they made landfall in Devonport on the evening of November the sixth, nine days after leaving the battered victors of Trafalgar struggling towards Gibraltar. Jerusha stood on the quarterdeck of the *Pickle* with Master Almy. She looked around her at the crew, saw their exhaustion and also their pride.

'We did it, Mrs Wilson,' he said.

'That you did, sir.'

'You crewed with us,' he told her, his words sincere. 'Thank you.'

She knew she would never forget his words. She had bailed water with them without complaint. She had doctored a sprain, sutured a laceration, and lanced a boil. Their trials had been her trials. They had passed the rum bottle to her and she measured up. It was enough.

The chill of November settled in her bones. She pulled the dead officer's cape tight around her, mindful, now that she

was on land again and a woman, that she wore the same dirty trousers and shirt and her surgeon's apron, which had come to mean more to her than any garment she owned, or would ever own.

She started for the gangplank, aware that a short walk would take her to Stonehouse and Jamie's quarters. Master Almy put his hand on her arm. 'Listen! Captain Lapenotière must have made his announcement to the king yesterday.'

She heard every bell in Devonport and nearby Plymouth tolling. Tears started in her eyes for the little admiral. 'Victory is hard, isn't it?' she asked.

'Damned hard,' he replied, 'but we got the message here.' She heard so much emotion in Almy's voice that she felt, too. 'We did our duty. You too, Mrs Wilson, although I do not think you will receive any glory for it.'

She wiped her eyes. 'I never expected any. I did it for others, the same as you, sir.'

Chapter Thirty-Eight

Master Almy insisted on hailing a hackney for her. 'Your husband would use that damnable dental key on every tooth in my mouth if I turned you loose in Devonport or Plymouth.'

She didn't protest when he handed her money for the fare. She hadn't a coin on her, and here she was in filthy trousers, a shirt too big by far, and an officer's cape belonging to a corpse thrown overboard during battle.

She said goodbye to the master's mate, who started to help her into the hackney. He was stopped by a noisy, 'Great Neptune's Balls!' The hackney shook as the jarvey climbed down. With a sigh, she fell into the arms of Jake O'Toole, who had helped her carry out her deception against Lady Oakshott. Was that eons ago? No, only since summer.

Jake sat with her in his hackney as she told the story of Trafalgar through tears and monumental exhaustion. 'Just get me home, please,' she said finally. 'I am so tired.'

She slept in the hackney and had only the vaguest memory of being carried inside Jamie's quarters. Mags McDonald, in braids and a ratty robe, took her from Mr O'Toole, scolding and hugging her.

'I'm filthy,' Jerusha said in feeble protest as Mags took her upstairs. 'I need a bath in the absolute worst way.'

The last thing she remembered was Mags assuring her that

she would only drown in a tub tonight, and the matter would keep until she woke up.

Brilliant sun woke her the next morning, only Mags assured her it was the next morning plus one. She made no objection when Jamie's housekeeper helped her downstairs through the warm kitchen and into the bathing room. She sank gratefully into hot water, as Mags scrubbed her thoroughly from head to heels. She washed Jerusha's hair three times, scolding all the while when she wasn't choking back tears.

'Mags, I helped all I could, but there weren't enough of us to save everyone. And Jamie, oh, dear God, he tried so hard.' She wailed then. 'I love him beyond all reason and imagine this? I am with child.'

'That comes as no surprise,' Mags said. 'It's a good thing I'm half deaf. I only heard a little of your carrying on upstairs.' She chuckled. 'Made me a bit envious.'

Jerusha decided to laugh *instead* of blush, letting Mags dry her off and give her another love scold, as in, 'Jerusha, your waist is already thickening.'

'I know. Mags, I'm starving and so is Mary or Andrew.'

After a breakfast large enough to feed the entire crew of the *Pickle*, Jerusha made no objection to a return to bed, this time on clean sheets that Mags must have changed while she was downing a half dozen eggs, bacon and well-buttered toast. She cried because Jamie wasn't with her, then returned to sleep.

She woke in late afternoon to a visit from Surgeon Kidwell, ushered upstairs by Mags, who scolded him, too, for looking so haggard, because she was a Scot and that was the national custom. Mags brought up tea while her other dear surgeon sat by her bed and listened to her retelling of Trafalgar.

'You would have been so proud of Jamie,' she concluded, then leaned forward to touch his hand. 'But you, sir, you've been through it here.'

'The jetty bell is our constant companion. In the last two

days alone, several Trafalgar ships have anchored here and unloaded their wounded.' He shook his head. 'Such a battle. Such loss. Scuttlebutt says Admiral Nelson will be encrypted at St. Paul's Cathedral.'

'But you, sir? Don't change the subject.' Goodness, she was beginning to sound like a combination of James Wilson and Mags McDonald, and she wasn't even Scottish.

He took her hands in his. 'I am shortly to be relieved of duty, dear Jerusha. I have exceeded my limit.'

He said it simply and quietly, but she knew she was listening to a man ready for the peace of the grave.

What has war done to us all? she asked herself, aghast.

'I wanted you to know that I have strenuously recommended to the Sick and Hurt Board that Surgeon James Wilson be named my successor as chief surgeon on Block Four. No one is better trained and no one deserves it more.'

'Thank you.' There was so much she could have said, but she knew that would only embarrass a modest man.

'I have also recommended that you two move into my quarters,' he added as he stood up. 'They're larger, and Mrs McDonald informed me that you will need more room soon enough. Good day, dear madam. Join us in Ward A when you're ready.'

She was ready in the morning, dressed in her other dark dress and surgeon's apron. Mrs Terwilliger nodded to see her and even smiled. Jerusha faced an entirely new bunch of patients, one or two of the livelier ones even whistling their appreciation until Mrs T shut them down with a glare and the comment, 'Mind your manners, you heathens! This is Mrs James Wilson, wife of our other surgeon, who will be here soon enough to thrash you all.' She narrowed her eyes and even Jerusha felt fear. 'Mind. Your. Manners.'

Jerusha returned to duty, even if each day began with morn-

ing sickness. She washed faces, held hands when needed, and wrote letters dictated to her by patients. It soothed her heart.

She spent her afternoons on Ward B, where lay the comatose men, silent heroes existing in that unknown land between life and death. She held limp hands, and talked to these forgotten men, even though she had no idea if anything penetrated. It hardly mattered. Some sixth sense of her own told her that they knew and they understood. It was enough for her.

She thought of Alec Kent, young master's mate following in his father's footsteps, and mourned his loss. 'Master Kent, I hope *you* are alive and well,' she said. 'I hold these hands and think of your son, and you.'

One evening, when the loneliness and longing for some word from or about her husband was scarcely to be borne, she wrote a letter to Mama, who had not corresponded since her rescue of her sister, Hortensia. She wrote of Trafalgar and her puny part. She wrote of her husband's courage, and of their coming child. 'There,' she said to Mags as she sealed it. 'I hope she responds, but if she does not, I know that I tried.'

December came at last, and with it several of the warships from Trafalgar to Plymouth. They carried their wounded, with stories of repairs in Gibraltar, then slow progress through stormy seas. She kept up a good front in Ward A, but poured out her troubles to the gentle souls in Ward B, who comprehended she knew not what.

There was one bright moment. A second luff from one of the ships returning from Gibraltar sought her out on the ward. 'If you are Mrs Wilson, I have a message for you,' he told Mrs Terwilliger, who pointed him to Jerusha.

She listened in delight as the lieutenant gave her greetings from Surgeon Wilson, and the added tidbit that Jeannette, the Frenchwoman found floating bare as Eve in the water, had found her husband, now a prisoner in Gibraltar.

'I saw this, too,' the lieutenant added, laughing. 'She gave him the kiss of the century, then smacked him as hard as she could.' He paused a moment until he could speak again. 'Your husband said, "I have the distinct impression that poor *monsieur* is not going to sea again."'

'He would say that,' Jerusha agreed, happy for any report about her man, and, if the truth be told, a little envious of Jeannette.

On December the fourth, all the bells in Plymouth and Devonport tolled again, signalling the arrival of *HMS Victory* in Portsmouth, bearing the body of the little admiral. Plymouth saw the arrival of the equally battered *Belle Isle*, the dismasted but game warship that blasted the *Achille* into an explosion that still woke her at nights, heart pounding and reaching for the empty space beside her in bed.

In the morning, Mrs Terwilliger greeted her with a letter from Mama. She opened the letter outside the ward and sat on the steps, reading of Mama's relief that she was safe and delight over her news that she would be a grandmama. Some advice followed of an intimate nature, which relieved Jerusha's heart. Mama still loved her.

The letter contained other news. Lady Oakshott had shrugged off her mortal coil.

She died peacefully enough, for Hortensia, Mama wrote, then added primly, *I shan't speak ill of the dead.*

Jerusha chuckled as she read the rest. How Lady Oakshott had sold her Plymouth home to Bedwin Napier, her butler.

I believe he has turned the house into an inn of sorts. A posh one and very discreet, Mama wrote, adding with a bit of fun that warmed Jerusha, *Let me know if there is any scandal attached to Napier's effort, although I am pretty certain he is more proper than all of us put together. Such a snob.*

Mama added a postscript.

*Abbie has scarpered off. I think she found Bolling and
life in the vicarage too dull. Perhaps she returned to
Plymouth.*

Perhaps she did, Jerusha thought.

Curious now, she took a hackney to number twenty-eight
Finch Street.

All Napier can do is refuse me admission.

Her first surprise was Abbie opening the door, then putting
her hands over her mouth in real surprise. 'Miss! I thought you
were Lady Beecroft,' she exclaimed, then lowered her voice
and joined her outside. 'Never tell Napier, but the man she
meets here is *not* Sir William Beecroft, who is thankfully busy
in London. Poor Napier. He would die if he knew, and I will
never tell!' She leaned closer, her eyes bright with conspiracy.
'René will never tell, either. He's returned, too.' She lowered
her voice even more. 'He sports with Lady Beecroft's dresser.'

And that was that. Jerusha waited to laugh until she was
in the hackney.

*Mama will be happier if she doesn't know about this turn
of events*, she told herself. *I will leave this alone.*

She did what she usually did at night, when the house was
quiet. She sat in the window seat in their bedchamber, the
now clean officer's cape around her, hands on her belly, tell-
ing Andrew or Mary about their papa. She concluded as she
usually did, with a little nudge to the Almighty to remember
James Wilson, sailing in the Mediterranean, or perhaps the
blockade off France.

If only I knew, was her last thought each evening. *Do I ask
too much?*

Nothing had changed at sea. The blockade continued, and
Collingwood now patrolled the Mediterranean instead of Ad-
miral Nelson. On land, however, Napoleon had withdrawn his
battle-ready troops from the French coast, ending the threat of

invasion. He turned his attention to Austria, where only days ago, the Grande Armée had defeated the Russians and Austrians near a village called Austerlitz. Her tender heart ached for the death of friend and foe alike, because she understood what surgeons went through on both sides.

Every night, she asked the Almighty God for just one more word from Jamie, well aware that women like her everywhere raised the same petition.

That next morning began as all mornings with a queasy stomach, settled by Mags's dry toast and tea, followed by porridge. As always, she promised Mags she would take moments during the day to rest, although that seldom happened.

On Ward A, Mrs Terwilliger gave her the usual grimace that passed for a smile, according to Surgeon Kidwell.

And there was Kidwell himself, on crutches now and looking more infirm than some of his patients, his body worn out in the service of king and country. Surgeon Kidwell handed *her* a letter this time. 'This came earlier on the *Harmony*. Captain Ames wanted to deliver it in person, but you know times and tides.'

The letter boasted a large number five on the back, so one through four must have gone astray. She read the date first. 'As of November the twenty-fifth, he lives,' she said to the surgeon. She scanned the letter, which felt like a lifeline from the dear man who fathered the child making her waistline vanish. 'He loves me. He says so right here in lots of ways that are for my eyes only.'

Surgeon Kidwell bowed. 'That's all I need to know. I am satisfied that he lives as of November the twenty-fifth.'

She read to herself of Jamie's hurry to get this letter to her before the *Harmony* passed the *Revenge*. His news was heavy, indeed, as she learned of the death of Sailing Master Kent in the thick of it at Trafalgar aboard the *Protector*. '"*My love, I*

hear Master Kent was gallant to the end,''' she read out loud, and dabbed at her eyes.

She continued reading, then gasped, and read the words again. 'Why us? Why us?' she exclaimed.

'What, Jerusha, what?' Surgeon Kidwell asked, alarm in his eyes.

She handed the letter to him. He read it, his mouth open in amazement. 'Jerusha, such a man! Master Kent had no living relatives, so you and your surgeon are to receive his prize money, should something go amiss.'

'Jamie told me about prize money, but…but…'

'Here it is. "Master Kent sent me a note. I quote it in part: 'James, your sweet wife's unparalleled kindness to my dying son will comfort me to my own grave, whenever and wherever that is. At such time, go to the counting house of Carter and Brustein and square up with them. I made arrangements before I left this last time. Bless you both, Roger Kent.'"'

Surgeon Kidwell handed back the letter. 'This makes *my* news paltry.'

'Let me be the judge of that,' she said. She pocketed Jamie's letter, to be savoured over and over again, especially the parts about bone of my bone and flesh of my flesh. Prize money would be wonderful, but the father of her baby meant more.

'Very well, dear Jerusha: When your surgeon makes his way to Stonehouse again, he will be chief surgeon of Block Four.' He touched his chest. 'The Sick and Hurt Board and I came to an agreement.'

She heard a door open behind her. 'I'll miss you,' she said, but he wasn't looking at her now. His smile returned, after a sharp intake of breath.

'Letters one through four went astray, James,' he said over her shoulder. 'You're chief surgeon now.'

Familiar hands went to her waist, followed by a simple word that said everything. 'Jerusha.'

She threw herself into her husband's arms, holding him close, then backing off for a quick assessment. She almost hesitated to touch his face, wondering for the smallest second if he was real, or if her longing had turned her barmy. War could do that to a person. 'You're tired.'

'I'm home.'

Epilogue

June 18th, 1806

Dearest Mama,

Yes, yes! It is Andrew, delivered two days ago by his father, who promptly had to sit down with his head between his legs, once he cut the cord. You would think a man who deals unflinchingly with wounded men daily would not be so tender.

Such a father he is to our Andrew. I nearly have to prise him away from holding our son so I can nurse my wee babe. He's already taken Andrew to Block Four and showed him off to our current crop of patients. You won't believe this, but Mrs Terwilliger cried!

Also, I need hardly add that Mags McDonald is already doing her best to spoil our son. I'm receiving endless advice from her. Tee-hee! His face red, Jamie told me that she got stern with him about leaving me in peace for six weeks. I'll settle for four.

Dear Mama, Jamie was so touched by the letter you sent him last week, when you called him Son. Perhaps James Wilson was not the husband you wished for me, but I know you have changed your mind. For this I am endlessly grateful to you. I predict Papa will hold off judgement only until he meets his grandson in person.

Here's the latest scuttlebutt—my favourite navy word, by the way. Apparently, medals will be awarded to Trafalgar veterans. Jamie told me I would not receive one, because I am a woman. I didn't expect one and so I told him. There are several of us ladies in the Channel Fleet who are equally deserving, but medals are small matters, are they not?

This will make you laugh. I've been hinting for some months now that...ahem... I was promised a wedding ring ages ago. Maybe the promise of a Trafalgar medal for him jolted my dear surgeon's too-busy-with-medicine brain. What should appear beside my bowl of porridge this morning but a gold ring with the inscription 'Trafalgar 1805' inside?

His note to me: I'll put this on your finger tonight, a wedding ring at last and your own medal. Your husband and lover, James Wilson.

Do you know a luckier lady? I don't.

Mama, do come and see us soon, so you can fall in love with your grandson, too.
Lovingly yours,
Jerusha Wilson

* * * * *

Captivated By His Convenient Duchess

Lauri Robinson

MILLS & BOON

Author Note

Welcome to *Captivated by His Convenient Duchess*,
the first book in The Redford Dukedom duet. In this story
you'll meet Myles Wadsworth, the oldest brother, who
must marry in order to secure the future of the Redford
dukedom. He thinks Anita Crawford will make the perfect
duchess, but Anita isn't convinced of that. Taking them
on their journey to happily-ever-after involved healing
the damage caused by old wounds. I inwardly cheered
for Anita every step of the way, because from the first
word I wrote, I knew Myles was there to not only love
her, but help her. I hope you enjoy their story, and enjoy
meeting Wesley, the younger Wadsworth brother, who
will soon have his own story.

A lover of fairy tales and history, **Lauri Robinson** can't imagine a better profession than penning happily-ever-after stories about men and women in days gone past. Her favorite settings include World War II, the roaring twenties and the Old West. Lauri and her husband raised three sons in their rural Minnesota home and are now getting their just rewards by spoiling their grandchildren. Visit her at laurirobinson.blogspot.com, Facebook.com/lauri.robinson1 or X @LauriR.

Visit the Author Profile page
at millsandboon.com.au for more titles.

DEDICATION

To a school friend. I'd always thought her name was pretty, but after learning it was a version of Grace, and a classic name symbolising elegance, vibrancy and strength, I knew it was the perfect name for a heroine. Thanks for the use of your name, Anita, and for your friendship.

Chapter One

Fear and pain had plagued Anita Crawford's life since the age of four. Before then, her life was wonderful. Although she had only a few memories of that brief time, they were ones she'd never forgotten, nor would. Somehow in her young mind, she'd collected them, tied them together and tucked them away like special letters received in the post, bound with a ribbon and hidden away to be reread in uninterrupted privacy. She pulled up a memory every so often but, for the most part, just kept them hidden, safe from the world she'd known since then.

The next twenty years had been filled with fear and pain, and both were alive inside her today as the snow continued to fall, whipped around by the wind that was chilling her very bones. All of her bones. Not just the ones that were normally overly affected by the cold.

Or a storm or even a heat wave. Her left ankle, knee and hip could tell her when there would be a change in weather. At times the ache was so intolerable she wanted to sit down and cry. She never allowed that to happen, because the tears wouldn't just be for the aching. They would be for all the pain that had lived inside her for so long, and she was afraid she'd never stop crying once she started.

The fear inside her at this moment, as she drove the horses through the wintery weather, was not only for herself but for the man inside the coach. Joshua, the coach driver, had never been unkind or cruel to her. Just the opposite was true. He'd always been kind and helpful, and had been at Brunswick for as long as she could remember. The fear of him dying, of freezing to death before she got him to Redford, was overwhelming her aches, pains and other fears.

Mainly, though, she felt the fear of arriving at Redford. Of meeting the man she was to marry—tomorrow! Myles Wadsworth, the Duke of Redford, had purchased her. Of course, he hadn't walked into a store, selected her from a shelf and given the store clerk money like one would for a tin of tobacco or a yard of cloth. No one ever visited Brunswick, nor would they have chosen her given the choice. It was a sight unseen sale.

That Uncle Jerome had sold her hadn't come as a surprise. He'd sold everything else of value, but she was considered by her uncle to be of little or no value. For years, she'd been known as that lame girl. The word *homely* was often included in that description. Anita had long accepted that she was a colourless creature. Her eyes were dull grey, and her thick, coarse hair was neither blond nor brown but a lacklustre shade between the two, with strands of grey that were uncommon for someone of her age.

What had surprised her out of this deal was the Duke. There was no viable reason why he would accept her in any deal. Why anyone would. She had no dowry. Her uncle had used that to pay gambling bills years ago. He'd said the dowry left in her father's will wasn't needed be-

cause she was unmarriageable, that a woman who could barely walk was a sorry excuse for a wife. At twenty-four, she was well on her way to a life of spinsterhood. At least had been, and had accepted that, up until a few days ago.

Although she'd never met him, Myles Wadsworth, the Duke of Redford, had been the talk of many gossip-mongers for several months. Not that she was ever anywhere where gossip ensued. The servants didn't even gossip when she was near. Due to the fact that even though she worked beside the staff more often than not, she was part of the family. In name only. She didn't fit in with the family any more than she fit with the servants. She hadn't fit in anywhere since her parents had died. Since the accident that left her *that maimed girl*.

Her cousins, however, were out and about and collected gossip like bees gathered nectar. Matilda and Irma had brought home many a tale about Myles Wadsworth. He'd been engaged twice already this past year, and both times the wedding had been called off shortly before the event could occur. His former intendeds, both young, beautiful and well bred, from what Anita had heard via her cousins, refrained from saying too much, other than that a marriage to the Duke would never have worked for them.

That left Anita to silently contemplate why? Why wouldn't it have worked? Though she'd never dared asked. Not even after Uncle Jerome had told her about the deal he'd made with the Duke. However, she'd been more curious as to know why Uncle Jerome had offered her and not one of his own daughters.

Matilda and Irma, who were respectively now twenty-

two and twenty, and eagerly seeking husbands, were regularly carted off to London to reside with their mother's sister Rainie to attend balls, theatre performances and other social activities that might gain them possible suitors. Ones of high-enough standards to marry an earl's daughter.

That was what her uncle Jerome was, an earl. The Earl of Brunswick. That had once been her father's title, and she'd been the daughter of an earl, until a dreadful carriage accident had taken the lives of both her parents. She had been in the carriage with them. In that one fateful moment she'd been orphaned and injured and, ultimately, left an outcast.

Her throat plugged and she had to swallow past the lump to encourage the horses to keep moving along. In this weather, on these snow-covered roads, she had to be careful. One slip and they would all be in trouble, with no one to save them. She didn't snap the reins across the animals' backs like some may but instead shouted over the sound of their hoofbeats, the churning wheels, rattling coach, squeaking springs and cold, blistering winds, telling them that they were doing wonderfully, that she was proud of them and to save their strength until the estate was in view. That's when she'd give them their heads, let them gallop. She also told them that it shouldn't be much farther now.

She wasn't sure. Just knew this was the road that led to the Duke's country estate. The owner of the roadside inn where they'd stayed at last night had given Joshua directions to Redford, and she'd been nearby enough to hear. Although the instructions had not been difficult. They'd only had to make one turn off the road, and that

had been right after the bridge where Joshua had fallen into the icy river.

It was always cold in November, but this morning, they'd awoken to gloomy, grey skies and a bite in the air that made her joints ache. Joshua had placed bricks heated by the inn's fire inside the carriage, near her feet, and told her they'd arrive at their destination before noon.

Despite her aches and pains, she hadn't been in a hurry to arrive; however, she also hadn't wanted Joshua and the horses out in the cold for any longer than necessary.

They had barely been on the road an hour when the snow had started to fall. Though it made things colder and damp, it hadn't affected their travels, until they'd come to the bridge. The horses had turned skittish at the ice coating the boards and the sound of rushing water below, and had baulked at crossing. Joshua had suggested they all walk across the bridge.

The cold had made Anita's leg stiff and the ice-coated boards had made each step more difficult than usual, but she and her newly appointed maid, Olive, who had been sent along only because it was expected that she have a maid, had made it safely to the other side.

Her cousins each had a maid, but Anita had never had one, not that she'd ever needed one for anything. Olive was a kitchen maid, had been her entire life of forty years, but was the only staff Uncle Jerome would spare, and between the two of them, they'd managed to get her dressed in what Anita felt was an outlandish outfit that her aunt Tilda had provided for her. It was as bright blue as the wing feathers on a jay bird, and had so many buttons and bows that she and Olive had

laughed themselves nearly silly trying to get her out of it that first night.

It was a pretty enough colour, it's just that so much of it was shocking when she'd looked in the mirror. As she had each morning at the inns they'd stayed at, growing ever more fearful of what the Duke of Redford would do upon seeing her. Would he be shocked? Disgusted? Regretful?

To Olive's credit, she'd also managed to find a way to hide the mass of wayward curls that had fought Anita's attempts to train them for years beneath the white hat that held a single blue feather.

She'd never had a hat before and did like this one for the mere fact it hid a fair amount of her unruly hair.

Aunt Tilda had been more kind than Uncle Jerome, especially back in the early years when Anita had begun living with them, or they with her, since Brunswick had once been her father's estate. Brunswick had also once been beautiful, and despite all she'd tried to do to make the home shine and sparkle like it used to, the paint on the walls was cracked, the bricks on the front steps crumbling, and the windows rattled in the wind. It was as if no one but she seemed to notice those things. The other thing she had noticed was that Aunt Tilda had been as happy as Uncle Jerome over the deal he'd made with the Duke.

Anita wasn't sure where Aunt Tilda had found the blue dress, for she'd never seen her cousins or aunt wearing it, nor the other two dresses that were packed in the small trunk that held all her earthly possessions. She'd chosen to wear the blue one because, of the three, it was the warmest, made of thick corduroy material.

The corduroy was now wet from the snow, as was the

woollen grey cloak she wore over the dress, and her fingers were numb, both from the cold and her grip on the reins.

While carefully leading the horses, Joshua had almost made it across the bridge, too, when Clyde or Clod—or perhaps both, it had all happened so fast it was hard to say—jolted forward, knocking Joshua over the short railing and into the river in their hurry to get across. Joshua had managed to catch hold of a bridge support and got back to shore, shivering so hard his teeth chattered.

Though shaking from the cold and fear for him, Anita and Olive, who had by then been crying fretfully, had managed to help him up the bank and into the carriage. Anita was indeed grateful that the horses knew her so well due to her time in the stables. Upon shouting their names, Clyde and Clod had stopped and settled down since the bridge was behind them, and they had waited patiently until Joshua had been helped inside the coach and she'd climbed up in the driver's seat.

Life had taught her that it wasn't the fittest who survive, it was the strongest. Not even those with strong muscles or even bones, but strong willpower. Strong determination, and she hoped with all her heart and soul that Joshua was as determined to live as she was to get him to Redford.

'Which one of his daughters?' Wesley asked while shaking his head and pacing the floor.

Myles Wadsworth had known his brother would be shocked by the news, as had been his mother and two younger sisters, whom he'd told at breakfast this morning. He also knew Wesley would be the one to question his decision. 'Neither. It's his niece.'

Wesley nearly spat out the whisky he was drinking to take away the chill, having just ridden two hours in a snow storm from London, down the front of his ruffled white shirt. 'His niece! Have you ever met her?'

Myles hadn't met Jerome Crawford's niece, nor the man's daughters, not the he could remember. Neither of the Earl's daughters nor his niece had been on Myles's list of potential wives until Brunswick had sought him out, offering a marriage to either one of his daughters. When Myles had declined, he'd thought it was over, until he'd caught wind of other action the Earl had been taking and had determined to put a stop to it. 'No, I have not.'

Wesley let out a smothered growl.

Myles had no doubt that his brother had heard rumours about Brunswick's niece. The Earl had not been discreet in his spewing. 'Have you met her?'

'No,' Wesley replied, 'but I've heard about her. She's a recluse. Never leaves their country estate. Hasn't for years.'

Myles had heard that, too. Moreover, he'd confirmed it and several other things about Miss Anita Crawford. What he'd learned had cemented his decision to ask for her hand in marriage. Brunswick had agreed to the terms and had confirmed that his niece had agreed.

'Myles,' Wesley said, using a tone that one might talk to a small child with, even though Wesley was the younger of the two of them by two years. 'I know you're set on getting married, but shouldn't it be to a woman you've actually met? Someone you know?'

'I've tried that, twice, and found myself sorely disappointed each time.' That was the precise reason Anita Crawford had been his choice. His past two attempts at marriage had inspired him to change what he sought.

Gone were the expectations of what a duchess should look like and how they should socially participate in his life. All he needed was someone to bear him children—at least two, preferably boys, so the Dukedom would be secured—and someone mature enough to understand trust.

'And you're going to be again,' Wesley said, running a hand through his dark hair. 'Sorely disappointed.'

'I don't believe so,' Myles replied. 'I spoke in depth with Brunswick, and I spoke to his driver.'

Wesley scoffed, then set his glass down on a small side table as he walked past it. 'You spoke to a man who everyone knows is a liar and a cheat. He's owed you money from a gambling debt for—what?—two years and never attempted to pay you back. And you spoke to his driver, a man who undoubtedly is loyal to Crawford, and you're saying that's enough?'

'It is enough.' Myles understood his brother's concerns. He'd had his own. Long before he and Wesley had started raising thoroughbreds, their father had instilled a love of horse racing in them. His father had often said that if it had been up to him, he'd be raising racehorses.

As a child, he'd asked his father why he wasn't raising racehorses. His father had said that it was because a man could only have so many irons in the fire. If he had too many, something was sure to fail. He would be a failure.

Not understanding, Myles had pushed for more of an answer, and that's when his father had told him about how a man has to have priorities, and he'd told him about love. About how he'd fallen in love with his mother. About how his dreams and priorities had shifted, and that Myles would understand that better when he was grown up and fell in love with a woman.

That was when he'd determined that he'd never fall in love. Never let someone make his dreams change. Never fail at anything. What may have been perhaps a silly childhood vow had become a reality when his father had grown ill and died within the week from pneumonia. The Dukedom had passed to him, and he'd felt a weight that he hadn't expected. The duties, the businesses to oversee, were manageable. He'd been confident in his ability to follow in his father's footsteps in all of them, even with the added thoroughbred business. It had been the other expectations that had weighed him down. The necessity of getting married to produce an heir.

He couldn't deny that he'd always known that he'd have to marry at some point, but having it become the topic of nearly every conversation had made him feel as if he did, indeed, have too many irons in the fire. He'd tried to meet those expectations, made the time for courting, but it had been awful. There had been nothing about it that he'd enjoyed. The women had all wanted to be his top priority, and he didn't have time for that. There had been nothing that he'd been willing to give up in order to make time for carriage rides in the park, walks in the moonlight, attending balls and the theatre and the numerous other outings that he considered merely a waste of time.

So, he'd taken the next approach. Enquired about, and found, a woman who hadn't needed any of that either. One who had the social graces to become a duchess and simply wanted to get married because it too was expected of her.

That had been Leslie Carlisle. She'd wanted to bypass all the courtship, too, get straight to the wedding, and

being the daughter of a marquess, she'd fit his standards for a wife. Until he'd discovered that the reason she'd wanted to get married, and so quickly, was because she was in love with a man her father didn't approve of. She was now engaged to that man, and Myles wished them well. It appeared that after being rejected by a duke, an earl would fit her father's needs after all.

Myles had been relieved when the engagement ended, but the expectations had still been there, so he had continued his search. Diana Brockholder had approached him with the claims of wanting nothing more than to wed and raise a family. Unfortunately, it hadn't been until after he'd given her a ring that he'd discovered she was little more than a spoiled child. He'd been glad to end that relationship, too, which is why he'd been far more diligent this time.

Huffing out another sigh, Wesley sat down in the chair adjacent. 'Myles...'

'Wesley,' Myles interrupted before his brother could say more. 'I have to get marriage behind me. We have too much at stake. We need things secured. The next generation secured. What started out as a cough ended our father's life within a few days. God forbid, if something were to happen to me, or you, we have to think of mother and the girls.' He paused for a moment, then continued, 'Redford Stables was our dream, Wes. We've already accomplished much, but there is much more we can yet do. So many more of our horses that could be winning races around the world. The competition is growing, and we have to act now to remain at the top.'

Eight years ago, when he'd been twenty and Wesley eighteen, their father had granted permission for them to

pursue breeding racehorses. The sport had been around since men had started riding, but the popularity of it was turning everyday men wealthy, and that was creating a hunger for the sport worldwide. Their timing had been perfect. They'd amassed not only a massive stable full of prime breeding stock, but their venture had ensured that Redford Stables was a name to be recognised in racing across the country, the continent.

Their goal now was to extend that reach across the ocean, to America, where the sport was doubling in participation and attraction. Wesley would travel there in the new year to meet with track owners and buyers. Men who already owned stock but wanted more. They wanted horses with pedigrees behind them. Redford Stables' English thoroughbreds not only had pedigrees; they had the drive of champions.

There had been talk of both he and Wesley travelling, promoting their horses, one to America and one to Australia, and then on to other countries, other continents, but that had been before their father's death when everything had changed. The title and role that he'd inherited included several other ventures that needed constant attention, comprising the banks and properties his family owned and other numerous duties.

All of their holdings, including the stables, had competent and dedicated employees, and though such good employees made light of his everyday workload, it didn't lessen the fact that he was responsible for every decision made. Responsible for everyone and everything.

'With you going to America—'

'I won't go,' Wesley interrupted, rising to his feet again.

'I don't have to. We can wait to expand for another few years. Goodness knows we don't need the money.'

'This has never been about money,' Myles reminded. It was about failing, and that was the one thing he refused to do. A Duke of Redford had never failed, and he refused to be the first. 'We could both sit on our assets for the next fifty years, doing nothing, and our great grandchild will still not run out of money. This is about creating something, a legacy for future generations, like our ancestors did before us. Like our grandfather did with the banks and father did with rental properties. We've created something people want, our thoroughbred horses are in demand, and it's up to us to meet that demand.'

'At what cost, Myles? Shouldn't happiness fall in there somewhere?'

'Yes,' Myles admitted. 'Redford Stables has made us both happy. It made father happy, too. This was his dream also, and one we need to continue for him as much as for us.' Understanding his brother's concerns focused on his decision to marry, Myles added, 'We'll both be happier once the family is secured.'

Wesley shook his head as he began pacing the floor. 'Will you be happy about the way you secured it? Married to someone you don't even know?'

'I know more about her than you realise, I've talked to more people than you know. Anita was the daughter of Jerome Crawford's brother, Daniel, the then Earl of Brunswick. Our father knew him. We were both too young to remember that, but he was a man of honour, nothing like his brother, the current earl. Anita is twenty-four, two years younger than you. The late earl and his

wife, and their daughter, Anita, were in a carriage acci-
dent. Her parents were killed and she was injured. That's
why she now walks with a limp. She was only four. Je-
rome Crawford inherited the title from his brother, and
a substantial amount of money and holdings, and has
lost nearly all of it. He was attempting to gamble off his
niece in a game of cards at White's on St James's Street.'

Wesley let out an expletive under his breath. 'What
kind of man does that?'

It wasn't unheard of for men to gamble with practi-
cally anything, but wagering another human being was
looked down upon by most, and Brunswick had been
thrown out of the game and the establishment. 'A des-
perate one,' Myles replied. 'From what I learned, Anita
has barely left their estate in years. It's a distance from
London, and few people have been there over the years.
Whether she remains home due to her inflictions or be-
cause Brunswick refuses to let her leave, I don't know,
but I do know that his sister-in-law chaperons his daugh-
ters around London regularly.'

Wesley pressed a hand to his forehead. 'You can't res-
cue people like you do stray animals. You've done that
with everything from squirrels to horses over the years,
but a woman? You can't do that, Myles.'

'Why can't I?' That was the very question he'd asked
himself when he'd heard about Brunswick's gambling.
He loathed seeing anyone or thing mistreated, and her
situation had resonated with him, telling him that he'd
needed to do something about it, even before he knew
about her injuries. What kind of man would he be if he
didn't help her? Not the kind he wanted to be. 'It'll ben-
efit both of us. I'll have the wife I need, children to se-

cure the Wadsworth name as well as the Dukedom, and she'll be taken care of, will never again have to worry about being gambled off in a card game. I also have access to doctors who might be able to help her.'

'What are the nature of her injuries? What if she was injured to the point that she can't have children?'

'I spoke to the doctor who examined her when she was five or so. She'd been struggling to walk a year after the accident. He said her ankle had been broken in the accident and not properly set, and that Brunswick refused to pay for a surgery that might have helped back then. Other than her leg, the doctor claimed she was healthy.'

'I still worry that you're taking a big risk here.'

'Am I?' Myles asked aloud, because he'd convinced himself otherwise. 'I'm not taking the risk that my soon-to-be wife is already plotting how to continue an affair with another man. Nor am I taking the risk that she'll throw herself into a fit of rage and mistreat the servants or my family members.' The more he'd learned about Anita, the more intrigued he'd become and was convinced that she would fit his needs. 'Brunswick's driver sang her praises. Described her as a quiet woman of dignity, perhaps a touch meek, who enjoys country life, and is the one who manages the household like clockwork. I also spoke with Brunswick's sister-in-law, the Dowager Countess of Wheyfield, who not only confirmed the driver's sentiments but added her own opinion that Anita has never been treated fairly by Brunswick.' Myles shook his head. 'I'm really not risking anything. Nor is she. All I'll ask of her is trust. That I can trust her to remain faithful to me and be kind to others.'

Wesley shook his head and huffed out a breath. 'You can't really believe this is going to work?'

'Yes, I can,' Myles answered. 'Furthermore, I do. I believe Anita Crawford is what I need. What we need. You've already put off going to America for over a year, ever since father's death. You're not cancelling another trip. I refuse to have that happen.'

Wesley shook his head, then nodded and stared across the room at nothing in particular as he asked, 'What did mother say? I'm assuming you told her, and the girls?'

'At breakfast this morning. Mother was surprised but agreed that it's my decision and will support me in it.'

'Of course she agreed with you. You're the head of this family,' Wesley said. 'But we both know her wish for us is to find the love that she and father knew.'

'Love is nothing more than a distraction, one I don't need. I need a wife who is content to not have my constant attention,' Myles said as he clamped his back teeth together. Though their mother had tried to keep it hidden, he'd witnessed how the loss of the love his parents had shared weighed on her. How it had aged her and it still was. That too increased his urgency to marry. He needed to find a wife, a duchess, to take other duties off his mother's shoulders. That, though, was not something he would share with Wesley. There was no need for his brother to worry. 'I'm twenty-eight, and the past two wedding cancellations have already given the ton all the gossip they need about us. It's time they move on to someone else.'

'Like this isn't going to create more gossip? A reclusive wife you keep hidden?'

'I won't keep her hidden. It will be up to her if she

wants to remain here, at Redford, most of the time, but I will request that she attends the Christmas Ball in London with us, as a family.' Attendance by his family was required since it would be the first ball his two younger sisters were to attend, and he couldn't disappoint them. He'd already convinced himself that he would not be throwing Anita to the wolves, which is what his brother was most likely thinking right now. He'd be at her side the entire time, the entire family would be, showing a united front.

'The ball is less than a month from now,' Wesley said. 'When do you plan on marrying her?'

'Tomorrow.'

'Tomorrow?'

'Yes, that's why I requested you here today. I'll need you as a witness at the wedding. Brunswick sent a message that she agreed to the marriage and is due to arrive before evening, given the weather hasn't delayed their travels. They should have been close to arriving before the storm rolled in this morning.'

'The roads weren't bad from London,' Wesley said, 'just cold and wet, but do you trust Brunswick to keep his word?'

'Yes, I've petitioned the courts for a loan against his holdings in the amount of his debt to me that will go into effect if she doesn't arrive today.'

Wesley lifted a brow, but a knock interrupted anything he was about to say.

'Come in,' Myles said, rising to his feet.

'Excuse me, sir,' Charles, their long-time and still overly spry butler said. 'There is a carriage coming up the driveway that appears to be out of control. I've sent Gus to the stables to get help, but I'm not sure what else to do.'

Myles wasn't sure what to do, either, other than rush outside and figure out what could be done. Wesley ran beside him, down the corridor and across the hall, and then out the door. Neither of them had grabbed coats, and the bite in the air was as cold as Wesley had proclaimed upon his arrival a short time ago.

However, the cold didn't stop them from racing down the steps and watching the carriage careen around the last curve in the road and barrel forward. A woman was driving it, with a single bright blue feather flopping atop her hat like she'd struck a bird en route and one of its tail feathers had got stuck to her head. The horses didn't appear to be out of control, but she had to be out of her mind to drive them at such speeds in this weather.

Myles couldn't tell if it was with expertise or sheer determination, by the look on her face, that she brought the steaming horses to a stop so close to the front steps that both he and Wesley had to jump back to keep from getting hit.

'There's a man freezing to death inside the coach!' she shouted. 'He fell in the river! Hurry! Get him inside the house!'

Myles leaped forward and pulled open the door of the coach. A man was huddled in the corner of one seat, so blue that if not for the way he was shaking, Myles would have thought him dead. However, he also recognised him as Brunswick's driver.

There was an older woman inside the coach, too, who looked as cold as the driver, but she wasn't blue. She was white, as if she'd lost all her colour. Even her hands that were gripping the edge of the carriage seat were white.

Groomsmen from the stable were arriving two at a

time, and Myles instructed them to get the man and woman inside the house.

As Myles stepped back, giving the men room, Wesley caught sight of the coach occupants, then looked up at the woman driver, who was telling the grooms to be careful, but hurry.

'That's her, isn't it?' Wesley whispered.

'I believe so,' Myles admitted, as a chill that had nothing to do with the cold air coiled around his spine.

Wesley slapped his back. 'I wouldn't call that meek, brother. You ever rescued a hellcat before?'

Myles ignored his brother and turned his full attention on the woman driver as the other men carried the man and other woman towards the house. Maybe all of his thoroughness hadn't been quite thorough enough. She wasn't meek. Nor was she unattractive, as he'd also been told, granted that had been by Brunswick when Myles had said he was interested in her, not Brunswick's daughters. Even with her hat askew and her hair dripping wet, the fineness of her features was enough to steal a man's breath.

'My horses need to be taken care of, too,' she said. 'Quickly. They're overheated and that's dangerous in this weather.'

Even though her words were clear and full of urgency, he heard the way her voice shivered, indicating she was as chilled to the bone as her passengers. Perhaps more so considering she'd been out in the elements.

'They'll be taken care of,' he said, stretching his hands towards her. 'Here, let me help you down.'

Chapter Two

Anita had never been so cold in her life. It wasn't just her bad leg that was stiff. Her entire body felt that if she moved anything, even a mere inch, it would break in two. Despite that, if she could move them a mere inch, she would. She tried, but not even her fingers would move so she could release the reins.

The man who had offered help, who looked similar to the one who was already unbuckling the harness from Clod, had climbed up on the step for the driver's seat. 'Here, let me help you,' he said while gently unlacing the reins from between her fingers.

Embarrassed by her inabilities, she tried to explain, 'I g-guess I—I'm ch-chilled.' The cold, or perhaps fear now that she'd arrived, was settling in fast, making it difficult to talk.

'Understandably so.' With her hands free of the reins, he grasped both of her arms. 'I'll help you stand up, then get down to the ground.'

She pushed with her good leg, forcing her bottom off the seat, but her bad leg was numb and that knee buckled. She emitted a tiny screech at the pain and at how her bottom landed back on the wooden seat.

One of his arms went around her back, the other slid beneath her knees. 'I'm going to lift you down,' he said. 'You're practically frozen stiff.'

She hadn't been carried since she'd been a small child, and couldn't be now. That was not how she wanted to arrive at Redford. The Duke could be watching out of a window, and… Maybe that would be best. Then he'd know right off that he'd made a mistake.

The man's arms were as solid as wood, and he hoisted her off the seat as if she didn't weigh more than a feather, then he climbed off the step without putting her down.

'Th-thank you. I—I c-can w-walk,' she said with effort, praying her bad leg wouldn't fail her.

'You need to get warmed up as fast as the others,' he said, already walking towards the house with her still cradled in his arms. Aunt Tilda had carried her after the accident while her leg was healing, but after a time, Uncle Jerome had put a stop to it. He'd said that her cousin Matilda was younger than her, and walking, and that she should be walking, too.

She hadn't been able to walk. It had hurt too much, so she'd started to crawl, but there, too, Uncle Jerome put a stop to it. Said that she had walked before the accident and that there was no reason she couldn't again.

If there was a point that she could remember when her determination became strong enough to push her onward, it had been then. Though she'd had to walk on the side of her left foot, and still did, she'd forced herself to do it, through the pain, and had continued to push herself to walk, and never shed a tear.

She had to do that again now. Force herself to walk and to talk through the chattering of her teeth. 'P-please

put me d-down, sir,' she said as they entered the house. 'I—I can w-walk.'

'I will put you down, Miss Crawford, after I carry you up those stairs and into a bedroom, where you'll have the privacy to get warm.'

She had purposely kept her gaze off him and continued to not look his way. The inner heat in her cheeks, which were still burning from the cold, was from the mortification of having to be carried into the Duke's house.

'That is your name, is it not?' he asked. 'Lady Anita Crawford.'

'Yes,' she replied.

'Allow me to introduce myself,' he said, while climbing the stair-steps with ease. 'I am Myles Wadsworth, the Duke of Redford.'

Mortification didn't just stay in her cheeks. It washed over her entire body. A body that was growing warmer by the heat emitted from his, no doubt, because she didn't stutter when saying, 'You're him.'

'Yes, and you're her.'

A response wouldn't form, for she was her. And he was him.

'Welcome to Redford,' he said.

She began to shake, to tremble.

'You're going to be fine,' he said. 'I promise.'

She couldn't speak. Her teeth were chattering non-stop. It could be from the cold weather, or fear, because she truly had never felt so hopeless in her life. And she'd had a hopeless life for a long time.

He carried her down a long corridor and into a bedroom, where maids were waiting with blankets to wrap around her as soon as he set her on the bed.

'We're filling a warm bath for her, Your Grace,' one of them said.

He touched her cheek softly with one hand. 'You're in good hands, Anita.'

Vocal cords couldn't freeze, so with sheer will alone, she made them work. 'Thank you, Your Grace.'

'You have permission to call me Myles,' he said, then turned about and left the room.

Anita didn't have time for even a smidgen of relief, because one of the maids was pushing aside the blankets and the hem of her skirt, exposing her boots. Although both of her boots were very old and very worn, one looked normal, with less wear and tear, while the other was severely misshapen from how she walked.

Having warmed up considerably already, which she still believed was mostly due to the heat of Myles's body as he'd carried her, she was able to move and quickly covered her boots with the blanket again. 'Please, can you check on Joshua and Olive? My driver and my maid? See how they are doing?'

'They are being assisted into hot baths, just like you,' an older woman said while entering the room through the same door that Myles had exited. 'We have to get all of you warmed up. It's a dreadful day for travelling, and I'm so glad you've arrived so we don't have to worry about you getting here.'

The woman was older, but not old, with dark brown hair and dressed in an elegant burgundy gown with a lovely white-and-gold broach pinned at the base of her neck. 'I don't want anyone to worry,' Anita said, sure that this woman wasn't another servant, although she carried a tray with a cup and a pot with steam coming

out of the spout that filled the room with the scent of fresh brewed tea.

'I'm sure you don't, dear. That's simply what mothers do, and that is who I am. Myles's mother. Mary Wadsworth.' She set the tray on a table beside the head of the bed. 'While your maid is being taken care of, Sheila and Claire will see to your needs. If there is anything you need, you just tell them.'

'There's not,' Anita replied. 'I'll be fine by myself, thank you, though, very much.'

'My dear, child,' Mary said, her brown eyes filled with compassion. 'Your dress buttons down the back and is wet, we need to get it off you.'

The wet wool cloak covering her dress was open, showing the bright blue dress with no buttons running down the front. 'Perhaps I could use some help.'

She hadn't ever had help of any kind, other than Olive during their three-day journey, and even though her foot was unsightly and she was ashamed that others would be subjected to it, she determined that perhaps it would be best for Mary Wadsworth to see it. Then she could tell her son what a mistake he was making.

The maids were swift yet gentle in their assistance, and Mary was kind as she encouraged Anita to drink not one but two cups of the hot tea.

Practically before Anita realised it, she was soaking up to her neck in a hot tub of water. Being immersed in water always made her leg feel better, but a hot bath wasn't something she'd been able to indulge in very often. Though she bathed regularly, by the time she'd carried enough hot water up the stairs to her bedroom at Brunswick, then climbed into the tub, the water had

chilled considerably. Since she'd turned eighteen and her uncle had determined her unmarriageable, she was not allowed to ask the servants to wait on her as they did Matilda and Irma, as well as her aunt and uncle.

She hadn't minded. The servants had enough to do, and she would much rather help them with the chores than sit around. Inactivity made her leg stiffer.

Claire, who was the shorter of the two maids, with shiny black hair, glistening blue eyes, and a cute button nose, used a lovely smelling soap to wash her hair and then applied a sweet-smelling oil that made ringlets form where there had only ever been fuzz.

The fuzz would return once her hair dried, it always did, but that was the least of her worries.

Once she was warmed through and through, Anita left the tub with the help of Sheila and Claire, who had to have noticed her bent foot and twisted leg, but made no comment or sign of being appalled by it. She shouldn't be surprised by that. As servants, they would have been trained not to say or react to practically anything.

Sheila explained that the clothes in Anita's trunk were still too damp and cold to wear and that others had been found for her. The under things were unlike the ones she'd removed. These were made of silk and not mended or threadbare, and the gown was velvet, the greenish-blue colour of a dunnock's egg, with delicate crocheted white lace. There was even a pair of matching slippers.

'I can't wear those,' Anita said, knowing she would ruin them in a mere a few steps.

'Your boots are too wet to wear,' Sheila said, sliding the slippers on her feet, over the silk stockings she'd already slipped on and secured with lace garters.

The slippers felt heavenly compared to her boots. Like she was barefoot, which had always been easier for her to walk, but whenever she'd been discovered being barefoot, it had been as if she'd committed the crime of the century.

'I just used a couple of combs to pull your hair back,' Claire said, running a brush to the very ends of Anita's hair, 'so it can dry thoroughly. I'll fashion it for you later, before the evening meal.'

Anita could hardly believe the person in the mirror was her. Especially not her hair. It still hadn't started to fuzz, which was highly unusual. 'Thank you,' she said, looking from one maid to the other. 'Thank you both so very much for all of your help.'

'You're very welcome, my lady,' they both replied.

During her bath, Sheila had left and returned with the news that Olive and Joshua were doing fine; therefore, Anita wasn't surprised when Sheila left the room again.

Anita was ready to leave the room, too. She was anxious to see for herself just how her companions had faired. Though achy still, due to the weather, her leg was much better and she held no worries about managing the stairs. 'Could you tell me where I would find my driver and maid?' It felt odd calling them that, but she was doing her best to sound somewhat refined.

Claire didn't answer, simply looked at the door that was opening. It wasn't the one Sheila had exited into the corridor through, nor was it the one that led to the bathing chamber. This one was on an adjacent wall. Anita hadn't noticed the extra door, because the room was so lavish, so beautifully decorated in a soft greens and yellows, that there had been too many other things to notice.

Such as the four-poster bed, the tables and chest of drawers that were made from dark brown wood that shimmered in the light coming in through the tall windows. The drapes, bedcovers, pillows and chair cushions that were all covered in the same fabric with tiny yellow flowers and green leaves. The large woven rugs beside the bed and in front of the fireplace filling the room with heat were green, and the paint on the walls, which was not cracked, was yellow.

She noticed the door now because Myles stood there. Something inside her turned a somersault. Maybe her stomach, maybe her heart, it was hard to say, but it was in that vicinity, below her neck and above her hips.

His dark brown hair was parted on the side, and a portion of it flopped over his forehead at a striking angle, right above his eyes, which were as dark as his hair. His features—nose, mouth, cheeks, chin—were clearly defined, clearly masculine, but there was also a softness to them, which added to his attractiveness.

She'd never met so many men that she truly had others to compare him to, but doubted there were many as handsome.

He was tall, too, and wearing a grey suit, with black boots that came up to the bottoms of his knees.

'May I escort you downstairs?'

Startled by his question, as much as by her own realisation that she'd been staring at him, eyeing him up like he was a horse she was checking over, she balled her hands into fists to stop their trembling. 'I—I do not wish to impose upon you for that, Your Grace. If you could just tell me where I might find my maid and driver, I'd appreciate that.' Having never had the opportunity to

speak with someone of his standing prior to today, she felt tongue-tied and completely out of place.

'After being warmed, and provided dry clothes, they are being fed,' he said, stepping all the way into the room. 'I will escort you to the kitchen to see them for yourself, then I will escort you to the dining room, where you too shall be fed, and introduced the other members of my family.'

There was that somersault again. It was definitely her stomach.

Myles felt a sense of wonder as he crossed the room. Round as coins and surrounded by sooty lashes, the eyes that looked up at him were the most amazing shade of silver he'd ever seen. More than that, they took on the hues of the colours around her. Earlier they'd had a tinge of blue to them, now it was a soft greenish blue, the shade of her dress. Her hair hung in corkscrew ringlets, down past her elbows, and it too had a silver tint to it. Not the shade of older hair, nor was it all over. Most of her hair was a soft brown colour, the shimmering here and there were strands that looked as if silver thread had somehow been weaved into the curls.

Her face was oval-shaped, with a delicacy he couldn't explain, but made a mental note to ask his mother about a cream for her cheeks, which were red and most likely chafed from the weather.

All in all, this woman was far from unattractive, and he questioned what sort of ruse Jerome Crawford was attempting to pull off by calling Anita homely. In fact, he was questioning if she was Brunswick's niece or if the man had sent someone else in her place. Giving his

throat a quick, smothered, clearing cough, he asked, 'Shall we?'

Though hesitant, she nodded.

He waited as she slowly rose off the stool in front of the dressing table, wondering if Brunswick's claim of her walking with a limp was a ruse, too.

Myles drew in a silent breath at the anger he'd felt at how Brunswick had tried to convince him to consider marrying one of his daughters instead of Anita. The man had claimed she wasn't fit to be a duchess, that she could barely walk, and when she did, it was unsightly. It had been years, not since he and Wesley used to get in fisti-cuffs when they were young lads, that he'd felt the urge to punch someone in the nose. He'd wanted to punch Brunswick that day. Not in the nose but in the mouth, forcing the man's cruelty back down his own throat.

She took a step, but as she took a second one, she stumbled slightly, grasped the edge of the dressing table. 'I—I'm sure my uncle, or perhaps your mother, told you about my leg, my foot.'

Her voice had been as soft as a whisper but also held conviction. 'My mother did not tell me anything,' he replied honestly. He had not seen nor spoken with his mother since Anita's arrival. Taking care of others is what his mother lived for, and she'd been fully occupied with the three arrivals needing immediate care.

'She saw it when they took my boots off,' Anita said as softly as before, but with her chin up. 'So did the others. Though no one commented on it, they can't be blamed if they did. It's unsightly. I was in an accident when I was young, and it never healed properly.'

The softening inside him was familiar. It happened

whenever he saw something injured or mistreated. He was like his mother in that sense. Whether it was man or beast, or even a tree or bush with a broken branch that would scar it for ever, he always wanted to help. He also noticed the way the maid kept her head down, never looked their way, as she walked to the door and opened it for them.

Not having noticed which leg had caused Anita to stumble when she'd tried to step on it, he asked, 'Which leg is it?'

'My left.'

Stepping up beside her, he held out his arm, bent at the elbow. 'Then I shall walk on your left side. I can only imagine how exhausted you are after such a journey, and I would like to offer you my arm, if you wish to lean on me.'

'That's not necessary,' she said, then added, 'Your Grace,' as if his title were something she'd just remembered.

He gently lifted her arm and hooked her hand on the underside of his bent elbow. 'Then I shall simply escort your downstairs. We have a lot of things to discuss, and we will, after we go and see how your servants are faring and after eating the noon meal with my family.'

She squared her shoulders and nodded. 'Very well.'

He let her start off walking and kept his pace slow, matching her uneven gait. It was there, but slight, he may not have noticed it if she hadn't been holding on to him, and he could feel her sway with each step.

Once they entered the corridor, he could feel her speed up, her body sway more, and wondered if her foot was so painful that she was in a hurry to get off it again. 'Does it pain you to walk?'

'Not usually, it's just—it's just what it is. I've grown used to it.'

'Is it uncomfortable?'

'*Awkward* is how I describe it, but as I said, I'm used to it.'

'Is it more awkward when you walk fast? Or slow?'

'Fast. I tend to trip more often when I have to hurry.'

Slowing his footsteps even more, he said, 'Then we will take it slow. We're not in a hurry.'

They walked nearly to the end of the corridor before she looked up at him. 'You're making a mistake, Your Grace. I don't know the details of the agreement you made with my uncle, but I'm not the kind of person who could ever become a duchess. I've had very little formal education, and my only skills are cooking, cleaning and sewing. I doubt those are things that you'd expect from your duchess.'

Disagreements to her beliefs formed in his mind, but he made no comment. Their discussion on that subject would come later. When they came to the top of the staircase, he asked, 'Are stairs difficult for you?'

'No, not as long as they have a banister.'

The staircase before them was wide, and he sidestepped, positioning them so the banister was near her right side. 'Then we shall walk on this side. You can hold the banister with one hand, and my arm with the other.'

'Doesn't this prove to you that what I just said is true?' she asked after they'd descended down a couple of stair-steps. 'I'd be an embarrassment to you, to your family. Just like I've always been to my family.'

He was no longer able to keep his comments to himself. 'The only embarrassment that I glean from your

statement is that of how you've been treated. Your uncle, your family, should be embarrassed by that, by their behaviour, not by you. The agreement I made with your uncle was simple. He owed me a gambling debt, and I told him that I'd call it even for your hand in marriage. If you agreed.'

She paused momentarily, stared up at him with a frown. 'But he needs money. Aunt Tilda said that she refuses to ask her sister Rainie for any more, and their daughters won't gain suiters without a dowry.' She shook her head as she stepped down another step. 'Forgive me for repeating things aloud that I'd accidently overheard. That was terrible of me.'

'Honesty is not something to be ashamed of.' In his mind, it proved she had more scruples than her uncle. Yet, at the same time, an odd inkling formed in the back of his mind that told him that she hadn't agreed, which would explain why her uncle and other family members had not travelled with her to attend the wedding. Again, he concluded that their conversation needed more time than they had right now.

They stepped off the stairs and he turned them towards his left. 'The kitchen is this way. In the future, if you're ever looking for me, you go in the opposite direction. At the end of the corridor behind us in my library, where my mother says I spend too much time. If you're looking for her, she's often to be found in the front drawing room. Again, behind us, but the first room on the right. For my sisters, you'll find them upstairs, second floor, the opposite direction from your room, studying, with their tutor. At least that's where they should be most days. And my brother, whom you may have briefly seen

outside upon your arrival, when he is here, he'll usually be in the stables.'

'Stables?'

The hint of excitement in her tone was the first he'd heard since he'd lifted her off the coach's driver's seat. 'Yes. We have a large stable.' There were actually several stables, and one more still being built.

'How large?' she asked.

There was definite enthusiasm in her voice, and that made him chuckle.

'I apologise,' she said. 'I didn't mean to pry.'

'You weren't,' he said, seconds before he understood why she'd apologised. 'I wasn't laughing at you, Anita, I was chuckling because I'm happy that you would want to see it. I'm very proud of our stables. We raise English thoroughbreds, the best in the country.'

'I don't believe I've ever seen a thoroughbred.'

'You will.' He refrained from saying when that would happen, because it was still snowing, and he'd wait until the pathways were clear before taking her out to the stables. 'What other animals do you like?'

'All of them,' she said.

'Then you'll like it here,' he said. 'We have three cats who roam the house, and you'll meet them eventually. On their terms. That's how cats are, and there is Roscoe, currently our only dog, who is in the kitchen begging as we speak, I guarantee that. There are also several cats in the stables, and there are barns and sheds that house horses, cows, pigs, sheep, chickens, ducks, peacocks, geese—'

'Peacocks?' she asked.

'Yes. And peahens. We have a total of six of them.'

Due to Wesley's statement that he couldn't rescue people like he did animals, and not wanting her to think the same, Myles didn't elaborate as to how he'd seen a peacock and peahen in a pen in London a few years ago that had appeared to be on their deathbeds that he'd purchased and brought home. Slowing his steps to a stop, he gestured towards the door. 'This is the kitchen.'

She nodded, but as he put his hand on the door, she touched it, stopping him from pushing it open. 'Do people eat peacocks?'

'Only the gardener.'

Her frown deepened. 'Why only him?'

He laughed and touched the tip of her nose, much like he would one of his sisters when teasing them. 'He hasn't eaten one, but threatens to each time one gets in his vegetable garden.'

The smile that flashed across her face was so natural, so brilliant that it nearly took his breath away. It was also a moment before he remembered the task at hand and pushed open the door.

The kitchen was filled with people and sound, which became muted as they walked into the room. Her maid and driver instantly rose from the table and hurried across the room.

The maid gushed, singing her praises about the kitchen, which he thought was slightly odd for a lady's maid. Her driver touched Anita's arm and asked after her condition, almost with a fatherly concern, before thanking her for saving his life.

Roscoe had rushed towards them too, but with a single look, Myles had stopped the big shaggy-haired sheepdog from bumping into Anita. The dog sat less

than a foot away and patiently waited for a greeting from her, which he got.

Myles was already observant of her every move, but the way she held on to his arm tighter as she bent enough to pet Roscoe's head, told him that bending at the waist was uncomfortable for her. He wondered just how severe her injury was and if anything could be done that might make her more comfortable.

Anita was grateful that neither Joshua nor Olive showed any ill effects from the mishap, and though it meant meeting the rest of his family, she was thankful when Myles escorted her into the dining room, where she was seated at the large wooden table with carved lion-feet legs.

Her leg wasn't hurting, but the silk stockings inside the velvet slippers were slippery, and they didn't have a sole like her boots, so there was nothing to keep the velvet from sliding on the polished wooden floors. She'd had to hold on to his arm tighter than she'd have liked to keep her footing.

She hated having to depend on anyone. She knew her challenges, lived with them every day and rarely felt sorry for herself, but there were times when she was tired. Tired of having a body that made doing the simplest things hard.

Myles, though, was nothing like she'd expected. She wasn't overly sure exactly what she had expected, but not someone as kind and compassionate as him. She'd never had someone help her down a stairway, ask her about her injury, ask if it hurt and talk to her at the same time as if she were genuinely interesting to him.

He was unlike anyone she'd ever met, and in that sense, she was sorrowful. For him. For how he'd asked for her hand in marriage without seeing first hand that she wasn't witty or worldly, or anything that a man of his standing would seek in a wife.

Before they'd left the kitchen, he'd nodded at a man, and she assumed that must have been the butler, because moments after she'd sat down at the large table, the rest of his family entered the dining room.

Myles stood beside her chair, with a hand softly touching her shoulder, as if to say she didn't need to rise as he introduced her formally to his mother, brother Wesley, whom she had seen outside, and his two sisters, Christina and Maria, who were fifteen and fourteen.

They resembled each other, all of them, with their dark brown hair and eyes, and smiles that didn't fade when they looked at her. Their smiles didn't appear fake, either.

No one at the table peppered her with questions, which she was sure they must have. Instead, they told her things about themselves and Myles and the family, as if they were sure she'd want to know. Including how she shouldn't be alarmed if she heard screams coming from outside. That was just the peacocks, which were merely pets.

She found that touching and everything they said interesting, often comical. For they were a lively bunch, laughing and teasing each other, in ways that tickled something inside her. Happiness had been one of those things that she'd long ago tied in ribbon and tucked away, but she felt it sneaking out, and couldn't stop herself from smiling, even giggling a time or two. She'd pinch

her lips together to stop the smile, and giggle and remind herself to not get too comfortable. It was hard because they were all so nice, and she wasn't used to that. Not used to any of this.

Unable not to, she found her gaze slipping to Myles more than once, understanding that he wasn't the only one who was kind and compassionate. His entire family appeared to be, and again, she wished things were different. That she was different, someone who could fit in with this lovely family. She also couldn't stop thinking about what he'd said about trading her for a gambling debt. Why would he do that? Why would Uncle Jerome have agreed to it? Something was not right, and she kept telling herself that the truth was sure to be revealed soon, and it wouldn't be favourable.

The meal was plentiful, with a variety of foods that had to have been palatable, because when she looked down, she found her plate empty. A lemon chiffon cake was served last. It was so delicate it melted in her mouth, and tasted so delicious that she knew she had one more thing to tie up and tuck away, because she'd never taste something like that again.

She'd never share another meal like this one, either, because one more thing was roiling about in her mind. He'd said if she'd agreed. Agreed to what? The marriage? She hadn't had a choice. If she had, she wouldn't be here, wouldn't hold him to any agreement with Uncle Jerome. Couldn't, because it wouldn't be favourable to anyone but Uncle Jerome.

The plates had been removed from the table, and their teacups were empty when Myles rose. 'I'm sure you will all excuse us,' he said, moving to stand behind her chair.

The family agreed and stated it was wonderful to have her here as Myles pulled her chair back and then stood at her left side so she could use his arm to assist her rising to her feet.

As they slowly walked from the room, with her still holding on to his arm, she'd never felt more self-conscious of her every movement, every sway of her hip, every slip of the velvet slipper on the floor.

Chapter Three

Each room that Anita entered seemed to be larger, more elegant, than the last one, and that included Myles's library. The bedroom upstairs had been stunning, the kitchen sparkling clean, well stocked and hosting all off the most modern appliances, and the dining room, with its sparkling candlelit chandelier and cream-coloured wallpaper had been quite beautiful, but this room… The library went beyond appealing. It was alluring. There was no other word for it.

The books lining the shelves on one wall, with their spines standing straight and dust free, called to her. Made her want to hunt through them, to find fantasies, truths and mysteries that would take her away to other worlds. Reading was the only escape she'd ever known and was the one thing she allowed herself to indulge in. It would be so easy to do that here. The chairs next to the fireplace said, *Sit here, be warm and toasty while becoming lost between the pages of a book.*

Large windows with tan-coloured drapes promised expansive views that even made the still falling snow she'd considered a traitor earlier to appear lovely.

There was also a large desk that was somewhat clut-

tered with papers and whatnots, and a sofa facing the fireplace, along with other chairs, small tables and pieces of furniture that she barely got a glimpse of before she'd sat in one of the chairs near the fireplace, which was indeed warm and toasty.

'Would you care for a stool to rest your foot upon?' Myles asked.

'No, thank you. I'm fine.'

'How about a drink? A glass of sherry?'

'No, I couldn't eat or drink anything more, thank you.'

'Very well.' He hitched up his pantlegs slightly by pinching the material over his thighs as he sat on the brown sofa that face the fireplace and her chair. 'We have some important matters to discuss.'

Anita was in full agreement but had already laid out her case while they'd been walking to the kitchen. However, that had been before he'd made the comment about her agreeing, and she truly needed to know what he'd meant by that. Before she had the opportunity to ask, a knock sounded on the door.

Without rising, Myles said, 'My apologies,' to her, then granted entrance.

'Forgive me, Your Grace, but the lady's driver is insisting that he and her maid leave post-haste,' the grey-haired butler said. 'I presumed you would want to discuss that with him.'

'You presumed correctly, Charles,' Myles replied. 'Send him in.'

'I will directly, Your Grace.' With a slight bow, as he backed out of the door, the butler nodded at her. 'Again, my deepest apologies for the interruption.'

The door closed and Myles said, 'My apologies for the interruption, Anita. Our discussions will need to wait momentarily.'

'Joshua was instructed to depart immediately upon delivering me here,' Anita explained. 'Before you had a chance to change your mind.'

Myles's response was a slight smile and nod, and Anita wasn't sure what that meant. She'd been sitting in the coach when Uncle Jerome had made the statement, speaking loudly enough for all to hear. There was no reason for anyone to be upset with Joshua for following the orders he'd been given.

'Is the maid not your lady's maid?' Myles asked.

He was frowning, and she understood why. He was beginning to see that he'd been duped. That she would not make him a suitable wife. 'No. Olive is a kitchen maid, but Aunt Tilda said that it would be unseemly for me to travel without a lady's maid, and Olive was the only servant they could spare. I have never had a lady's maid, though I believe my uncle has done his best to make you believe I am someone that I am not.'

He nodded slightly. 'Do you want her to remain in your employ?'

Anita was surprised that he remained on the subject of Olive. Then again, he was probably relieved that they all would be leaving soon. 'She's never been in my employ. I have no say in the matter.'

He cleared his throat slightly, and his gaze never left hers. 'I have not, nor will I, change my mind, nor can I send anyone out in weather like this, with horses that need ample time to rest before embarking on another long journey, despite what someone may have been or-

dered to do. Furthermore, you do have a say. As my wife, you will have the final say pertaining those in your employ. If you wish to have Olive remain here with you, all you need to do is say so, and I will see that it happens.'

Anita didn't have time to try and once again explain that she couldn't be his wife, that he shouldn't want that, when another knock sounded on the door.

This time Myles stood as he bade entrance, and walked around the sofa as the door opened and was held wide by the butler.

Joshua, with his hat in his hand, entered the room, followed closely by Olive. They were both wearing their own clothes again, and Anita doubted they'd had time to dry completely.

'You wished to speak with me, Your Grace,' Joshua said, giving a slight bow.

'I do,' Myles replied. 'With both of you.' He gave the butler a single nod.

Charles stepped into the corridor and closed the door behind him.

'First allow me to thank both of you,' Myles continued, 'for escorting Miss Crawford to Redford. It was a long and trying journey, and I would like to extend an invitation for both of you to stay until you have fully recovered and the horses have had the time they need to recuperate.'

'Thank you, Your Grace,' Joshua said, 'but we are unable to accept your invitation.'

Olive's eyes were on her, and Anita felt great empathy. They'd become close while working together in the kitchen back at Brunswick, and more so during their

travels the past three days, but she had no power or say here any more than she'd had at Brunswick.

'I understand that you have instructions from your employer to return post-haste,' Myles said. 'However, I am responsible for all persons on one of my properties, and I am not in agreement with your instructions due to the weather and the accident that occurred during your journey here. As soon as the weather permits, I will have a messenger sent to Brunswick informing the Earl as to my decision for you to remain at Redford until I see fit.' His stance was formidable, his words spoken in a considerate tone yet delivered in a powerful way that everyone in the room knew his request would be followed.

Anita's shoulders slumped and she had to swallow a moan. Uncle Jerome would not be pleased. The second thought that crossed her mind was that if Joshua and Olive did stay, at least through the night, she would have a lift back home. By then, Myles would be sure to have realised that she could never be what he expected from a wife.

The third thought that struck her was that she wouldn't be welcomed back at Brunswick. Then again, she'd never been welcome there, so it wouldn't be any different.

'If you are worried that my decision may cost either of you your jobs,' Myles continued, 'be assured that there are jobs here at Redford that each of you could fill, if that would be of interest to you.'

Both Joshua's and Olive's eyes turned to her, and Anita forced herself to smile at them. They were in this situation because of her, and though she could make no promises, she had to offer them whatever support she could.

'I agree with His Grace,' she said. 'This weather is not fit for travel.' If Uncle Jerome did fire them, which was most likely, they would be far better off being employed here, and she would be happy for them, even though she would miss them once she returned to Brunswick.

'If either of you would like to discuss this matter further, I welcome you to meet with me tomorrow morning,' he said.

Joshua was the first to speak. 'Yes, Your Grace.'

Followed by Olive, 'Yes, Your Grace.'

They both nodded at her before they turned about and exited the room.

She was used to issues that her uncle caused, but this was reaching new levels. 'I wish we were not causing you so many problems.'

'You're not,' Myles said, returning to his seat. 'How long have they worked for the Earl?'

She could argue the point that she was causing problems, but chose to answer his question instead. 'Joshua worked for my father and I'm not sure why he stayed. None of the others did. Olive has been there for less than a year. Her previous employer passed away, and my aunt's sister, who knew her previous employer, sent her to Brunswick, knowing the estate was short-handed.'

'Why was the estate short-handed?'

She didn't like talking about others yet had to be honest. 'Staff tend to not stay at a job where they are not fairly treated.'

With another slight nod, he said, 'I don't make false promises, Anita. When I stated that there were jobs here that they could fill, I meant it, and I guarantee that they will be treated fairly.' He placed his hands on his thighs

and leaned forward. 'I won't make false promises to you, either. And I'm hoping you won't make them to me. That is all I want out of our marriage. Trust. I want to be able to trust you fully, and I want you to know that you can trust me fully.'

'You can't marry me, Myles.' It was the first time she'd used his name, and she was surprised by how easily it rolled off her tongue. She should also be surprised by how easy it had become to converse with him, for he was a duke. A duke who she couldn't let make the biggest mistake of his life by marrying her. 'I told you that I have very little formal education, that my skills are more towards those of a servant. I'm simply not what a nobleman would look for in a wife.'

'Who told you that?'

'No one had to tell me.' She waved a hand from her head to her toes. 'Look at me. A marriage to me would never work.'

'I am looking at you, and I believe it will work.' He leaned back. 'Unless you're saying that our marriage wouldn't work because I won't be able to trust you?'

'I would never dishonour you or anyone else. I'm saying it won't work because you should marry a nobleman's daughter, one with no incompetencies.'

'I do not see any incompetencies in you, and you are a nobleman's daughter. Your father was the Earl of Brunswick.'

'Was. He died. If he hadn't...' She shook her head. That was something she'd thought about many times. How different her life would have been if her parents hadn't died. If that hadn't happened, she would have been honoured to be sitting where she was right now.

But her parents had died, and she'd spent the last twenty years being a burden, an embarrassment.

'His death didn't change your birthright,' Myles said. 'You are still the daughter of an earl. Despite what your uncle has attempted to make you believe, you are still Lady Anita Crawford. Still a member of the nobility and should be treated as such, should have been treated so your entire life.'

That might be true, but she didn't *feel* like a lady, and that couldn't just change. 'Why me?' she asked, flustered that he wasn't seeing her reasons. 'I don't understand.'

Myles wasn't sure he understood, either. He'd had it all worked out, had been convinced she would be all he needed, but now that he'd met her, there was more to it. He hadn't expected any dealing with Brunswick to be easy, the man was too dishonest for that. Now, he fully understood what the Dowager Countess of Wheyfield had meant when she'd said that Anita had been treated as a servant rather than family. He also believed that had nothing to do with her injuries. Injuries that surely pained her, yet she didn't complain. She had pride and strength and courage, and he liked all of that about her.

He also liked that she had a backbone, had the will and conviction to state her concerns, but that also bothered him. She was only concerned about him. How she would embarrass him. How she wasn't competent to be his wife.

She was wrong, and he didn't know how to convince her of that. Or if he should, because he wasn't certain she was here of her own free will, which is what he had requested. He certainly didn't want a wife who was being

forced to marry him. There was only one way to know for sure. 'Did you agree to come here? To marry me?'

She pinched her lips together for a moment, then lifted her chin. 'I didn't disagree.'

Reading between the lines, because despite all she'd been through, all the ways she'd been mistreated, she still had compassion for others and didn't want to hurt anyone, he asked, 'Because you weren't asked if you agreed to the arrangement?'

She nodded slightly. 'Uncle Jerome never asks, he simply demands.'

After giving himself a moment to let all of that settle in his mind, he declared, 'I won't force you to do something you don't want to do, Anita. If after we discuss this thoroughly, you still don't want to marry me, I won't hold you to the bargain.'

She looked at him for a long, quiet moment before she nodded.

He took that as a signal, an agreement to hear more. 'Why you? you asked.' He shook his head. 'Before I can tell you that, I have to explain, why me?'

She frowned slightly. 'All right.'

If he expected trust, he had to be willing to give it in return. 'I don't *want* a wife. I *need* a wife. There is vast difference. It's no secret that I've been looking for a wife since my father died. Along with the responsibilities of the title comes the responsibility to family. To the next generation. I need a wife to provide me with children. Preferably, at least one son.'

Anita didn't appear shocked by that, most likely because it was a common reason for marriage. Love, or the illusion of love, was rarely a reason two people wed.

'I pursued several women whom I thought were likely choices,' he continued, 'and offered marriage to two of them. Prior to the weddings, I discovered that I could not trust them to behave in a way that I would expect from my wife.'

'*You* broke off the engagements?'

It was no surprise that she would have heard about his broken engagements, or who had broken them. 'Yes, however, I would never purposefully tarnish someone's reputation, therefore, I requested that they break the engagements and would prefer if you kept that between us.'

She nodded. 'Yes, of course.'

'I mentioned our stables earlier today, our English thoroughbreds,' he said. 'That was a dream that Wesley and I shared, and our father encouraged us to pursue it. We've been successful, very successful. I want that to continue, and it will. Wesley is leaving for America in the new year to expand our field of buyers. While he's away, I will take over his duties, gladly, but with them added to my other responsibilities, there won't be time for me to continue to search for a wife.'

'That's why you accepted my uncle's offer?' she asked.

'No, I didn't accept your uncle's offer. He had heard, for it was no secret, that I was looking for a wife and approached me with an offer to marry one of his daughters. I declined. I was, and am, aware of your uncle's reputation, and I had no wish to become involved with him. However, then I heard about you. My father knew your father, and your father had a stellar reputation. As did your mother. They were good people, and you have every right to be proud of being their daughter.'

Her smile was soft, as was her whisper. 'Thank you.'

He gave her a nod before continuing, 'I then approached your uncle with an offer to clear a debt he owed me by giving me your hand in marriage, if you agreed to the arrangement. Prior to that, I'd spoken to several people, including your driver, Joshua, who told me about the accident. How your parents died and how you were injured. How your foot never healed properly. I also spoke to the doctor who examined you a year later, and I spoke with others who knew your family, including Dowager Countess of Wheyfield. Through those conversations, I discovered that you enjoy country life, which fits my needs. I don't spend a lot of time in London. Merely travel there when needed, and return here to Redford as soon as possible. I need a wife who understands that and doesn't need my constant attention.'

She lifted a brow, and gave a nod, but didn't comment.

'I was informed that you were kind and gracious, which I have already witnessed today. That is something else that I need. I have to trust that my staff and family will be treated with respect by my wife. I guarantee she will be by them.'

She nodded.

'I also learned that you were dedicated and competent, and again, I witnessed that already today by the way you took control of the situation at the bridge. The way you saved not only Joshua's life, but perhaps yours and your maid's as well.'

Again, she nodded, but made no effort to explain things further, which wasn't needed, he'd learned everything he'd needed to know about the accident from her driver earlier.

'Additionally, I appreciate your age. Though twenty-

four is still young, you are a few years older than my previous…' he almost said *mistakes* '…choices. I welcome your maturity.'

He was only guessing, but her grimace suggested she'd already been told she was too old for marriage. For a fraction of a moment, he wondered just how many lies she'd been told by her uncle. Things that were completely untrue about her, yet having been told them so many times, she believed them to be gospel.

'Why you?' he asked, bringing his mind back on the focus of their conversation. 'It's simple. You are exactly what I need.'

She shook her head.

He nodded. 'I believe that with you as my wife, I will be able to complete my duties unhindered. But my decision was also based upon what you need.' He paused for a moment, not sure how much she knew about her uncle's actions. 'I don't wish to upset you, but do feel the need to be honest. I first heard about you because your uncle had been attempting to wager you in a game of cards.'

She sighed slightly. 'He'd spent my dowry some time ago, and without one…' She shrugged, then frowned. 'You won me?'

'No. No, I didn't. I wasn't at the gaming house, I just heard about it and was appalled.' When he'd heard that the card game hadn't been the first time Brunswick had offered her, he'd been more than appalled. Any sort of unscrupulous man could have won her, and there were plenty in London who could have put her to work doing Lord knows what, for he highly doubted they were interested in winning a wife. Instinct to help her had kicked in and was still there, stronger than ever. 'Then I thought

about you. An innocent woman who was being egre-
giously mistreated. I couldn't let that happen. I knew
that in exchange for, or along with marriage, I could pro-
vide you with a home where you would be safe, cared
for and, hopefully, happy. I also knew I could provide
you with one more thing. Freedom. Something I'd felt
you hadn't had in a long time.'

She rubbed both of her arms as if chilled.

He rose and added a log on the fire, carefully, so no
sparks flew out, then turned, looked at her. 'If those are
not things you need, or want, forgive me for my assump-
tions. For believing that a marriage could be beneficial
for both of us. I won't force you to marry me, I won't
force you to do anything against your will.'

She made no comment, merely looked down at her
leg. The left one.

He walked back to the sofa, sat. 'What you claim are
incompetencies are not to me. Your skills are exactly
what I would expect from the Duchess of this house. The
ability to oversee that the cooking, cleaning and other
household tasks are completed. You are an intelligent
woman, that is clear to me. My mother will be here to as-
sist you, teach you anything you may not already know.'

Anita was still looking at her leg but slowly lifted
her gaze and met his. 'Thank you. I appreciate you tell-
ing me all that, for your honesty, but what I do not need
is your pity.'

His stomach sank. 'That is not what I'm offering.'

'Isn't it? You pitied me for what my uncle was doing.
For what my life was like.'

'No. I didn't pity you. If that had been the case, I'd
have gone to the authorities, seen what could be done for

you. Instead, I chose to learn more about you. I admired your courage, your bravery for all you've been through. That is why I then offered marriage between us to your uncle. I felt it would benefit both of us.'

She stared at him, silently, thoughtfully.

'I would like us to be friends,' he said, 'companion-able. I won't ask for your undying love or other such declarations, but I will ask for your honesty. I've already seen it in your concerns and beliefs as to why I can't marry you, and I would like to hear it as to why you can't marry me.'

Both of Anita's hands were on her opposite arms, and she rubbed them up and down again, still trying to chase away the chill that had arisen when he'd spoken about freedom. He could provide her with the freedom from a life in which she'd envisioned herself growing old and cracked like the walls that had surrounded her.

The other things he'd mentioned were all things she'd once hoped for, as well as other things. In many ways, she was no different than any other woman. She'd longed for a family of her own, children she could love, a home that she would manage much differently than how Brunswick was being left to fall to ruin, a husband to grow old alongside her.

She also would like to help him.

Would like to be the reason he could pursue his goals, dreams and duties unhindered. What he was asking were small things, things she could easily complete. What he didn't understand was that she could never be free. Not completely. Her foot would always be exactly like it was.

Letting out a sigh, she asked, 'What did my uncle say when you approached him about marrying me?'

'He refused,' Myles answered. 'He once again offered me a choice of his daughters.'

Even though she could not imagine that either of her cousins were mature enough for marriage, to him or anyone else, she nodded. 'Because he knew that I couldn't marry you.'

'Why can't you?'

'Because you deserve a wife who isn't maimed.'

His entire body went stiff, and he stared at her for the longest moment that time ever created. 'I do not believe that you are maimed, and neither do you.'

'It doesn't matter what we believe, it's what others believe. And they will believe it. They will say it. They will talk about it.' She'd seen it, heard it, lived with it her entire life.

'Not in my presence or yours,' he said. 'You will have my protection, and that of my entire family.'

She shook her head. 'People will still believe it and look at you, thinking, "What a foolish man for marrying someone so unsuitable."' She sighed heavily. 'And you aren't a fool.'

'No, I'm not,' he said as a slow smile formed on his face. 'Nor are you. I believe they will say, "What a lucky man for marrying such a brave and amazing woman."'

Another shiver rippled over her. She'd never been called brave or amazing, and though she was fully aware that she never would be, the way he said it was almost convincing. Or maybe it simply sparked a tiny bit of hope inside her that people could see her differently. 'I am neither of those things.'

'What would you call learning to walk, not once but twice? Saving a man's life? Driving a team of horses through a snowstorm? Living through twenty years of injustice, yet still caring more about others than yourself?'

'That's not bravery. That's just will.' The will to survive, that's what made her so determined to walk and to save Joshua and many other things over the years. She'd wanted people to believe that she was more than a distorted ankle, but if it hadn't happened within twenty years, no amount of will was going to make it happen now.

'I would be in your debt, and honoured, if you were to bring that will, that determination, into my home, my life.'

She closed her eyes against the pounding of her heart. 'I've been a burden to my family—'

'I can understand why you might feel that way,' he interrupted, 'but I see it differently. I see that your family has burdened you. Never valued you or given you the chance, or the choice, to have something different. That is what I want to offer you.'

What he offered far surpassed all she'd ever known, but she couldn't get past how that wouldn't be fair to him.

'I also understand how this must be overwhelming to you,' he said. 'I should have expected Brunswick to not give you a choice. I apologise for that and accept that you need some time to consider your options.'

Time? She eyed him directly. 'The wedding is tomorrow.'

He nodded, then shrugged. 'It could be postponed.'

She didn't like the idea of being blamed for that. Not by anyone, even herself. All of her reasonings hadn't

changed his mind, but he was making her rethink things. She was still fearful that he might someday regret it, but that flicker of hope inside her that she could have a different life kept getting brighter. A part of her wanted to grab hold of this opportunity with both hands. What he offered was more than she'd ever dared hope for. This was also the first time she'd been given a choice, a real choice about her life, and despite all that she'd been told, been forced to believe, she knew what she wanted. What she'd always wanted.

Her heart started pounding, and she took a deep breath before saying, 'No.'

'No?' he asked, with a look of uncertainty.

'No, I don't believe we should postpone the wedding.' That statement made her more breathless than climbing two flights of stairs.

'You don't?'

She would be a fool to let that happen, to let this chance of a lifetime slip away simply because of her own fears. What she had to do was put all her will and determination into his life. Make sure that he never regretted marrying her.

She felt herself nodding at her own thoughts. Trying to convince herself that she could do it. He was offering her a life she'd never expected, he was far more than she'd ever have expected. He was handsome, kind, considerate, sincere and honest. The fluttering in her stomach happened again, stronger than ever as she looked up, saw him smiling at her. She had to close her eyes because suddenly she was thinking about what would happen after the wedding. Specifically, the wedding night, and

how the flutter was now a tiny curl of heat and lower in her belly at the idea of sleeping with him.

'Does that mean you are in agreement with the marriage?' Myles asked.

At that moment, she felt as if she were about to trip, fall, but not just to the ground as she'd done numerous times. This time, it felt as if she'd stumbled off a high rocky cliff and had no idea where she would land, but couldn't stop herself because she was already in motion, falling hard and fast. Yet, she couldn't stop the smile that formed on her face. Opening her eyes, she nodded. 'Yes, I agree.'

If the rest of Myles's family didn't agree with his decision, they certainly didn't let it show. Nor did the staff. Within minutes of her agreeing, there wasn't an idle hand to be found.

A quaint parlour on the backside of the house that was decorated in the same shade of pale purple as lilacs in full bloom was turned into a sewing room, complete with a folding screen for her to step behind while changing into an ivory silk dress that would be altered to fit her. Stunningly lovely, with a fitted waist and tufted four-panel skirt and cuffs that went from her elbows to her wrists, Anita had almost protested when Mary had presented the gown for her to wear at the wedding.

Almost protested because she'd concluded that making sure Myles didn't regret his decision meant no objections from her, not on any subject. Making his life easier so he could fulfil his duties was now her job. That was the least she could do for him. He'd already made her life easier. Changed it. For the first time ever, thinking

about the future made her smile. Made her heart beat a bit faster. The impossible now seemed possible.

Mary, who was explaining the preparations taking place throughout the house, as well as Christina and Maria, who were measuring out lengths of netting and tying them into fluffy bows for decorating the house, were in the room, along with two maids, both very skilled at sewing. That was obvious by the way they were expertly marking the alterations to the dress with pins and small pieces of chalk.

Olive was in the room, too, and Anita knew the kitchen maid felt out of place with a needle and thread in her hands. 'Olive,' Anita said while standing on a short stool, with a maid on each side marking seams to be adjusted. 'I have all the assistance I need at the moment. Perhaps you'd like to see if there is any help you can provide in the kitchen for tomorrow?'

Olive's eyes widened with excitement. 'Of course, my lady.'

Only then did it occur to Anita that she may have overstepped her boundaries. Back home, being practically a servant herself, Aunt Tilda had regularly given her the duty of assigning staff to duties or positions. Though it had also been on her shoulders when things had gone wrong. When all had been in order, Aunt Tilda took the credit. Looking at Mary, which was what Myles's mother insisted that she call her, Anita asked, 'If that's all right?'

'Of course, dear,' Mary replied. 'This is your home now, and it is my greatest wish that you come to cherish it as much as all the Duchesses before you.'

Will and determination had allowed her to do a lot of

things, including to never give up, which she wouldn't do this time, either, yet she had to question if will and determination had ever turned someone into a duchess before. If not, she might be the first, because she wouldn't give up.

The alterations, bow tying, ribbon cutting and more bow tying continued throughout the afternoon. The bows would be used to decorate the front parlour for a small reception that would include a few neighbours, after the wedding. The service would take place in the chapel at the nearby village. Myles had arranged the licence and chapel a few days ago, but had suggested it could be changed to a larger affair if she wished. She didn't wish that but had suggested they ask his mother and sisters for their input, which had thrilled Mary and the girls. Myles had been happy, too, and thanked her for thinking to include them.

During all the work being done, Mary shared a great deal of information about the area and the family, including a long history. Anita held on to every word, making it stick in her brain, hoping it would help her ease into the roll she had agreed to accept.

It would be a transformation, one that she was a bit petrified about, but she was determined to rise to every challenge that came along with the decision she'd made.

When it was announced that the evening meal would soon be served, others left the room; however, Mary suggested that because Anita had been in and out of her dress so many times, there was no reason for her to go upstairs and change.

Anita was grateful for that. Not because her foot ached, but because none of the three dresses she'd left Bruns-

wick with could compare to the green-blue one she was wearing or to those that Mary and her daughters wore.

With the room to herself, Anita sank down in one of the cushioned arm chairs. She had changed in and out of the wedding dress several times, because the maids wanted to make sure that every seam was perfect, which they were.

The gown had been Mary's wedding dress, and though that meant it had to be nearly thirty years old, it didn't look old. There were ivory slippers to go with it, and Anita closed her eyes, trying to chase away the thought that had formed of her slipping while walking down the aisle at the church.

'Excuse me, my lady, would you care for me to fashion your hair for dinner?'

The door had been left open, and Anita looked down at the hair hanging past her elbows. It still hadn't fuzzed. The ringlets were just as they had been after her bath, even with all her clothing changes. 'Yes, Claire,' she answered. 'That would be nice. Thank you.'

Claire set a basket on the table beside the chair. 'You can sit right there. I have everything I need.' While removing the hair combs, Claire said, 'You have such beautiful hair. There is so much we can do with it.'

For years, she'd been told her hair was like a rag mop, and that nothing could be done with it. Even as a child, others had grown tired of attempting to brush it and tie it back. As she'd grown older, there had never been a reason to do more than wash it, brush it and pin it in bun, where it never stayed. It was always coming loose and hanging around her face like a fuzzy lion's mane.

Claire worked swiftly, without so much as a tug of

her scalp, and when presented with a small hand mirror, Anita was once again shocked by the image. Her hair was pinned in a fashionable bun, but ringlets had been left to hang from her temples, in front of her ears and the nape of her neck. Her hair couldn't have changed colour, the strands of grey that she'd inherited from her mother were still there, but they weren't as prominent, didn't make her look like she was three times her age.

'Do you approve, my lady?' Claire asked.

'Yes, Claire.' She handed back the mirror. 'I believe you are a miracle-worker.'

'No, my lady, but I am happy that you like it.'

'What was the oil you put in it during my bath?'

'Just sweet oil. My mother is the Dowager's maid and has taught me all she knows. It is my hope to become a lady's maid one day.'

Anita twisted in her chair, watching as Claire slid the mirror into the basket containing the brush and comb that she'd also used. 'Olive is a dear but is more comfortable in the kitchen. If possible, I would appreciate having your assistance.'

Pressing a hand to her chest, Claire said, 'I'd be so honoured, my lady.'

'Very well.' Then, wondering if that was something she could decide, Anita said, 'I will enquire about the change and let you know.'

'Thank you, my lady.' Claire curtsied, and then whispered, 'The Duke is outside in the corridor. Shall I tell him he can come in now?'

'Yes, of course.' Anita rose and turned towards the door.

The moment he appeared in the doorway, her insides

started doing somersaults. She understood why. Because he was so attractive. And he was the man she would marry tomorrow. It was as if she'd been dropped into a storybook. A true fantasy. If only she could read the last chapter to see how it ended.

'I hope my mother hasn't worn you out this afternoon,' he said with that Wadsworth smile, because it was always there, on all of the faces of his family members.

'No.' Though the fitting had been tedious, she couldn't remember a day when she'd done so little. Not even when it came to driving the horses this morning. She'd done that numerous times to pick up household supplies when Joshua had been in London with her uncle. Just not with the urgency of this morning. 'Not at all.'

'I am happy to hear that.' Stopping in front of her, he asked, 'May I escort you to dinner?'

'Yes.' She had to pivot enough to step around the leg of the table next to her chair, and though it was an easy enough movement, she hadn't been concentrating sufficiently, and the velvet slipper slipped on the wooden floor. She had been conscious of that happening all day and had been extra careful. Why hadn't she now?

Chapter Four

The moment he noticed her stumble, Myles stepped forward and grasped her left arm, steadying her. 'She did wear you out.' He'd been worried about that, after all she'd been through this morning.

'No, honestly, I'm fine,' she said. 'It's just the slippers. Though extremely lovely, and I appreciate the use of them, they are made of velvet and the smooth material slips on the wooden floors.'

He scanned her face, looking for a sign of distress, pain, discomfort, and found none. What he did find was a woman who kept getting prettier. Her hair outlined her face like an ornate picture frame, lovely on its own but created to make what it bordered to be the centre of attention. He hadn't wanted a wife who would turn heads, fill other men with desire, due to his first engagement, but it appeared that was what he was getting. He appreciated her beauty and was grateful that she'd agreed to not postpone their wedding. His name had already graced the printed scandal sheets too many times, but he would have accepted if that's what she had wanted. The other reason he was extremely grateful she'd agreed was even more pertinent.

She'd have nowhere to go if she'd declined their agreement. He'd thought about that while awaiting her answer earlier today and had determined that there was no way he'd let her return to her uncle.

'Truly, I'm fine,' she said.

Forcing his thoughts to return to her foot, he wondered what could be done to prevent her from falling. If he hadn't been close at hand, she may have fallen rather than just stumbled. Her safety was his responsibility. 'Shall we?' he asked, nodding towards the door.

She nodded. 'Thank you. I hope you had a good day.'

Despite her protests earlier, once she'd agreed to his proposal, she'd been very accommodating and personable, which had his mother already singing her praises. He was pleased by that and wanted to be just as accommodating to her. Walking slowly, feeling her sway in each step, he wondered if something could be attached to her slipper so it wasn't as slick. He would enquire with someone who knew more about that than him. With that thought settled, he replied, 'I did, thank you, but I'm afraid to tell you where I was most of the day. You might be upset.'

'Why would I be upset? It's your home.'

'Soon to be your home, too, and I was in the stables.' Though it had stopped snowing, he'd known she was too busy to interrupt today. He would take her out to see the horses soon. 'I know you want to see them.'

'I do, but I would never be upset for you being out there without me.'

He believed that about her, believed everything she'd told him. He appreciated her honesty.

'However, I wouldn't mind if you told me a little about them,' she said. 'I've met two of the house cats, Racer and

Shadow, who are wonderful, and am looking forward to meeting all of the other animals.'

She was smiling up at him, and he once again determined her beauty was definitely something he could live with. He felt good about the decision they'd made. Felt good that all would work out exactly as he'd planned. 'Well,' he started, 'there are four main stables, and we're building a fifth one…' He went on to explain how they kept the breeding stock separated, as well as the yearlings and two-year-olds, and several other things pertaining to the thoughtful questions she asked as they slowly made their way to the front parlour to await the rest of his family.

Charles was in the room setting out glasses and decanters of sherry and wine, and after escorting Anita to a chair, Myles asked the butler to send someone to the village that was only a few miles north and request that the cobbler pay them a visit this evening.

The conversation before, during and after dinner was consumed with plans for tomorrow, and he was grateful for how his entire family was accepting his choice. The entire household. Prior to the evening meal, his mother had assembled the household and garden staff, and introduced them to Anita one by one.

Her poise, aptitude and beauty hadn't been lost on his brother, either. More than once, Wesley had looked at him and given a nod of approval.

Not that Myles had needed that, but he did appreciate it.

He also closely watched Anita for signs of distress. He'd been surprised when she had agreed to marriage rather readily after her strong protests. Although, he

could relate. One minute he was sure he was doing the right thing, and the next he was questioning if the decision he'd made was the right one for both of them. Or if he was simply thinking about himself and his needs. He had to make sure that wasn't the case.

Dinner was over, and they were in the front parlour listening to his sisters explain how they would decorate the house tomorrow when Charles informed him that the cobbler had arrived.

'Show him to my library,' Myles said, wanting Anita to have privacy in speaking with the shoemaker. Then he walked to her side. 'There is someone I'd like you to meet.'

She nodded and rose, and he excused them from the room as they walked to the door. Though they talked during their walk along the corridor, she didn't question who was waiting for them.

Near the doorway, he said, 'I requested a visit from the local cobbler.'

'Why?'

'It is my hope that he can make you a shoe that doesn't slip.'

'I have my boots.'

He hadn't thought about her already having special shoes. 'Are they specially made?'

'No, they are just well worn and have formed to fit. They were just too wet to wear earlier.'

'I see.' He gestured towards the door of his library. 'The man has travelled five miles to get here, and I would appreciate it if we still met with him.'

She closed her eyes briefly and swallowed visibly before she nodded. 'Yes, of course.'

Though he could understand her hesitancy, he didn't

believe an injury should be something to be embarrassed about and chose not to cause more distress by mentioning that.

Myles had known the cobbler for years, and the man's thick moustache and hair were just as black as they had been when he'd been a lad. Nicholas Wainwright's smile was just as big as ever when Myles opened the door and escorted her into the library.

He introduced the two, explaining that she was his bride to be. They exchanged pleasantries and talked of the wedding for a few moments before Myles explained, 'Miss Crawford was injured in an accident and is need of a shoe that won't slip on the floors.'

'I'm sorry to hear of the mishap, my lady,' Wainwright said.

'Thank you,' she replied. 'It was a long time ago.'

'Well, I'm sure I can help,' Wainwright said, lifting his wooden box off the floor and opening the lid. Looking at him, he asked, 'Is there a stool she could put her feet on so I can take some measurements?'

Myles collected the stool from near the fireplace and set it before Anita's chair, then he stepped behind her and laid a hand on her shoulders. 'Would it be possible to receive something as soon as tomorrow?'

'Of course.' Wainwright sat down on the floor in front of the stool. 'I just need a few measurements.'

Anita lifted both feet onto the stool, and looked everywhere except at him or Mr Wainwright as the cobbler removed her slippers and stockings. If what he saw surprised him, Wainwright showed no sign of that as he took measurements, made notes and asked about the rest of the family, the horses, and shared some of the latest

village news. Wainwright included her in the conversation by explaining the people he mentioned.

Myles noticed how the side of her foot was calloused and the ankle oddly bent, and even as he felt compassion and respect for her, and how she'd overcome such adversity in order to walk, he felt renewed anger. A shocking, intense anger at how the doctor had said something might have been able to be done when she was five, but that Brunswick had refused. She was truly an amazing woman. The ankle had to pain her, but even with the bend, her feet were as dainty and lovely as the rest of her.

After placing his notes and measuring tools back into his wooden box, Wainright slid Anita's stockings and slippers back on her feet, and Myles felt a tinge of something he didn't expect. Jealousy. How could he be jealous of a cobbler? Because he wanted to be the one sliding her stockings and slippers back on? Because he didn't want any man touching her other than him? That was one of his expectations, but he had no reason for jealousy to spark over a cobbler.

'Well, now, I have everything I need,' Wainwright said. Shifting upwards, he rose onto his knees so he was eye level with Anita. 'What I have in mind, I can make tonight and have here before breakfast in the morning. However, Miss Crawford, I would like to fashion you a second pair of shoes. A pair I believe you'll find comfortable, but it will take me a few days to make them.'

She nodded. 'I would appreciate that very much, Mr Wainwright. Thank you.'

'Very well.' Wainwright stood and picked up his box. 'I have work to do, and I will see you in the morning.' With a bow, he said, 'I am honoured to have met you, my lady.'

Thanking Wainwright for his evening visit, Myles saw the cobbler to the door of the library, where Charles was waiting to walk Wainwright to the front door.

Myles turned, and was surprised to see Anita standing behind him.

'I hope you won't think it rude of me if I say that I'd like to retire now?' she asked.

Her expression was wary. It wasn't the first time he'd witness the meekness that he'd been informed of seeping out today, and he hoped in time that it would completely disappear. Especially towards him. He understood this was all new to her and would certainly give her time. There were adjustments that they both would have to make. 'Of course not,' he answered. 'You've had a full day. I'll walk you to your room.'

'Thank you, but I can manage on my own,' she said. 'I'm sure you have things you need to do, so I'll say goodnight.'

He was sure she could manage on her own—from what he understood she'd been doing so for twenty years—but that didn't ease his concern that she might slip and fall on the stairs. Yet he had been the one to say he didn't want a wife who needed constant attention, and he was certain that she was remembering that right now, too. 'Very well, I will have Charles send your maid up.'

'Actually, if it's permitted, I'd like to enquire about Claire becoming my maid.'

More than willing to grant her any wishes, he replied, 'Of course, it's permitted, and granted. I'll have them both sent up to your room.'

'Thank you, and goodnight again.'

He stepped into the corridor, giving her full access to leave the room. 'Goodnight, Anita.'

She nodded slightly as she stepped past him, and he watched as she proceeded along the corridor. Her gait was slow and her limp noticeable, but neither took away from her overall grace. She may not have had the upbringing she felt necessary for a duchess, but the way she carried herself said differently. Her shoulders were square, her head held high, displaying her pride and determination despite the odds that had been cast against her for years.

He shook his head to himself. He hadn't even known her for a full day yet felt as if he had for much longer. Perhaps because of how he'd investigated her beforehand. Either way, he liked her and felt there could be a very agreeable future between the two of them.

As she walked along the corridor, fully conscious of the slickness of the velvet slippers against the wood, Anita wondered which was worse, having people who ignored her infliction or having someone overly concerned about it. She wasn't sure how to accept having someone being concerned about it. That was new to her. Besides name-calling, which had mainly been Uncle Jerome, and her cousins when they thought it would benefit them in some way, everyone at Brunswick had ignored her leg.

As had others. They had whispered about it, given her sympathetic looks—which she hated as much as the name-calling because she didn't want anyone feeling sorry for her—when she'd gone to town for supplies or attended church. That had irritated her family, so she'd accepted absenting herself from such things, other than driv-

ing the wagon when needed, where she had remained in the driver's seat while others had completed the shopping.

No one had ever shown genuine concern. Not like Myles. She couldn't find fault or blame in that. Or in him calling in the cobbler. She believed he was merely being kind, but that kindness increased her fears of embarrassing him by tripping or falling, especially during the wedding tomorrow. Her boots were so ugly and couldn't be worn at the wedding, so she was grateful for the cobbler's visit, but she didn't want to get her hopes up that new shoes would help.

She was doing her best to keep her hopes contained, and would continue to, but it was already becoming increasingly harder. Ever since her uncle had informed her of the arrangement he'd made, she'd envisioned Myles to be a cruel, hard-headed and cold-hearted man. Why else would two women have called off their weddings to him?

Yet he was none of that. Nor had the women called off the weddings. He had but had allowed them to claim differently so their reputations wouldn't be tarnished. Those weren't the actions of a cold-hearted man.

It was understandable why he needed a wife, why he needed children and why he'd expect trust in their relationship. What had slowly crept into her mind during the dinner hour, with all the talk about the wedding, was *Could he be doing all of this, things he* needed*, because he already had a woman he* wanted*?* One who he couldn't marry because she was already married to someone else? Affairs such as that were not uncommon, and it would explain why his two other engagements hadn't translated into marriage. Perhaps those women hadn't been willing to marry a man who was in love with someone else.

It appeared as if he'd gone through a great deal of work to discover all about her prior to offering for her hand. Was that why? Because he'd needed to find someone content to stay home, to bear his children and oversee his household, giving him time to not only complete his duties but continue a relationship with a woman he loved? That didn't seem quite possible. Didn't seem like him, but what else could it be?

Anita had no idea, or reasons why she was questioning such things, other than all he was offering her seemed too good to be true. *He* seemed too good to be true. There had to be a catch. Didn't there?

At the staircase, she grasped the banister to make the slow climb upwards. It was hard to believe there wasn't a catch. So hard to trust. After years of lying in bed, deep in the middle of the night, telling herself that it didn't matter what people said, that it didn't matter that no one, shy a few servants, cared if she'd been alive or dead. It was hard to now experience kind words and actions and not question them. At the same time, it was hard to believe that anyone at Redford was anything except trustworthy, especially Myles, and it made her feel bad to think otherwise, so why was she letting her mind do it?

He'd been honest about everything, even in the fact that he'd said he needed, not wanted, a wife.

The only thing that had changed was her will, her determination to become a wife when she'd previously concluded that she never would marry, never have children.

If it was her lot in life to be married to a man in love with someone else, she would learn to live with it just as she had many other things. There was more at stake this time than before. Her uncle's ways had tarnished their

family's name, but even with the cancelled weddings, Myles's family's name had maintained its good standing, and from the conversations she'd heard since arriving, the Redford stables and their thoroughbred horses were renowned. She couldn't let being his wife destroy any of that.

More people had seen her foot in this one single day than she could remember in her life, and though none of them had reacted negatively, they had to have found its appearance confronting, hadn't they? She'd been a coward in leaving the library so swiftly upon the cobbler's departure but hadn't wanted to face Myles, knowing he'd seen her foot.

It had been as if all the name-calling, whispering and pointing of the past had exploded in her mind, making her feel so vulnerable, so ashamed, that she'd had to leave. She didn't want to believe she'd made the wrong choice, but what if she had? What if she didn't have the will and determination to be his wife?

Olive and Claire were in her bedroom when she arrived at the open doorway, and she was instantly grateful to have something else to put her mind to. She approached Olive first, with a sincere smile. 'I know being assigned as my maid was unfamiliar for you, and I want you to know that I think you did an outstanding job with the tasks. I would have had to sleep in that blue dress if not for you.'

Olive giggled, 'You almost had to, my lady.'

Recalling how hard they had laughed trying to get her out of that gown until Olive had discovered a second row of buttons on the underdress, Anita giggled herself. 'That is true.' She sighed and gave the maid a gentle

hug. 'I do hope that you and Joshua are considering the Duke's offer of remaining here at Redford.'

Olive returned the hug, and as they parted, said, 'We both are, my lady, and look forward to the opportunity to discuss a job here with the Duke in the morning. The cook says she could use the extra help in the kitchen.'

'That's wonderful,' Anita replied, truly happy for Olive.

'Perhaps you could put in a good word for me?' Olive asked.

Anita smiled. 'Of course, I will, but considering His Grace has already offered for you to stay, I don't think you have anything to worry about. He's an honourable man.'

'Yes, my lady, he is,' Olive replied. 'Everyone here is so very kind.'

'I agree,' Anita said with a nod before she turned her attention to Claire. 'I've requested that you become my lady's maid, and the request has been granted, if that is still a desire of yours.'

'It is, my lady,' Claire replied with a bow. 'Thank you so very much.'

'You're welcome, and now, if you don't mind, I would like to prepare for bed, it's been a long day.'

Prior to leaving Brunswick, she'd always seen to the tasks herself, but like other things, having assistance with such tasks was something she would need to get used to. Between Olive and Claire, in no time Anita was wearing her nightgown, which, like all of her possessions, had seen better days; her hair had been unpinned, brushed and braided; and other necessities taken care of so she could climb into the big bed with its ornately carved head- and footboards attached to the high posts at all four sides.

She knew from before, when Myles had carried her into this room and set her on the bed, that the mattress was soft and that it was wide enough for at least three people to sleep on, side by side, without bumping into one another.

Olive had already left the room, and Claire was banking the fire in the large fireplace when the door that Myles had entered earlier once again caught Anita's attention.

'Where does that door lead?' she asked.

'To His Grace's chambers, my lady,' Claire replied.

'Oh,' was all Anita could think to say.

'Would you like me to turn out the lamp beside the bed?' Claire asked.

'And expect you to find the door in the darkness?' Anita shook her head. 'Absolutely not. I can do it myself. Thank you.'

'Goodnight, my lady,' Claire said, with a slight bow.

'Goodnight, Claire.'

Anita waited until the dark-haired girl was gone from the room before she let out a long sigh and let her body sink deep into the mattress. She wasn't ready to turn out the light, because she wasn't ready to be alone in the darkness. Perhaps because once the light was out, she might wake up and this would all have been a dream.

Or perhaps because of the exact opposite. She covered her mouth with both hands, hiding the smile that formed from no one but herself. It wasn't a real love marriage, but...

She sighed as her attention was drawn to the door that led to Myles's chamber.

He could enter her room anytime he pleased, which would be his right once they were married. There was no denying she'd thought about what that meant numerous

times since being informed of her upcoming marriage. More times again once she'd set eyes on Myles. He was quite unbearably handsome, and she'd never imagined feeling so attracted to someone. Though she'd had no one explain to her exactly what took place in the marital bed, she knew the actions that a man and woman must take in order to conceive a child but had never truly felt a sense of curiosity or excitement over it. Until now.

She may not have had the formal education that her cousins had acquired, but she had read every book their tutors had assigned to them, as well as many, many others. The books in the library of Brunswick hadn't been of interest to her uncle because he'd felt they'd held no value—monetarily—therefore a vast array of volumes had been at her disposal, and it was how she'd spent her free time for years. Locked inside a novel, she'd become someone else, travelled places, learned things.

More than one of those books had in some fashion or another discussed procreation. The women in the stories often blushed and giggled and swooned with anticipation, and she wondered if that was merely storytelling or if it was more pleasurable than she'd imagined.

Suddenly, wondering if Myles might see the light on beneath the door, she sat up and quickly blew out the lamp, then pulled the covers up to her chin, and lay in the dark listening to her own heart pound in her ears.

After several moments, or perhaps much longer, she concluded that Myles would not be entering her room tonight. That wouldn't happen until they were married, which would take place tomorrow.

Knowing if she started thinking about that she'd never fall to sleep, she did what she'd done for years. Told her-

self not to think about what could have been, or might be, and to go to sleep.

That didn't work as well as it normally did, even when she tried telling herself that there was work to be done in the morning. It wasn't until she saw the faint glow of light under the door to Myles's chamber, and heard quiet sounds that stopped moments before the light disappeared, that a peacefulness washed over her. It was comforting to know he was next door. A comfort that she'd truly never known, but sleepiness consumed her before she could contemplate why.

No one had awoken her in years, so when someone said her name and touched her shoulder, she jolted upright so quickly, she nearly bumped heads with Claire.

It took a moment for her to recognise the girl and remember where she was. 'Oh, I'm sorry, Claire,' she apologised. 'So sorry. I must have overslept.'

'You didn't, my lady,' Claire said quietly. 'It's well before breakfast, but the cobbler has arrived, and His Grace would like you to meet him in his private sitting room.'

'Oh.' Shaking the sleepiness from her head, Anita threw back the covers and flopped her legs over the edge of the bed. It always took her a moment to stretch the stiffness from her leg before it would work properly, and she tried going through the motions of twisting it in each direction as quickly as possible.

'I've laid out a gown,' Claire said. 'I hope you like it.'

Considering there wasn't much to choose from in her wardrobe, Anita assured, 'It'll be fine, I'm—' Her words stopped as she noticed the gown that Claire held up for view.

Made of satin, the gown of white and raspberry-coloured stripes was one of the loveliest she'd ever laid eyes on. 'Where did that come from?'

'The Dowager,' Claire said. 'She has chests full of gowns that she's never worn. She claims to have a penchant for ordering gowns only to have them arrive and discover that she's too old to wear them, and her daughters are too young. I can find another if this one isn't to your liking.'

'No.' Anita shook her head as she stood, testing her leg. 'I like it. Very much. It's beautiful.' Her leg didn't buckle, and she slowly stood, giving her ankle and foot time to adjust.

'I have some matching ribbon to weave into your hair.'

Anita let out a sigh. As soon as a brush hit her hair, it would become a fuzzy mess. 'We'll need to hurry. I don't want to keep the cobbler waiting.'

The gown fit perfectly, and the ribbon was woven into two long braids that Claire expertly and quickly wound into a bun at the nap of her neck. There were wayward curls framing her face again, but they were curls, not fuzz.

'I truly don't know how you do it, Claire,' she said, glancing in the mirror. 'My hair has never behaved.'

'My mother taught me how to work with the curls, not against them,' she said. 'The Dowager has curly hair, too.'

Anita would never have known that. Mary's pinned up brown hair had looked as smooth as silk yesterday.

'I don't see my boots,' Anita said twisting away from the mirror. After being so wet yesterday, the boots were sure to be stiff but would eventually soften. She'd much

prefer that over worrying about slipping every step in the velvet slippers again.

'I put them in the wardrobe, but His Grace said you needn't wear socks or shoes.' Claire pointed towards the door to Myles's chamber. 'He said you were to pass through his bedroom, it's shorter that way.'

The shorter route she was grateful for; however, walking through his bedroom made Anita nervous. Pressing a hand to the knot forming in her stomach, she rose from the chair. 'Very well.'

A moment later, when Myles appeared in the doorway that led from his bedroom to his sitting room, her heart jolted hard enough that she questioned if it was a warning. She wasn't sure if it was about not getting her hopes up over the shoes or over him. He'd said he wanted to be friends, and she needed to remember that. Abide by that.

'Good morning,' he greeted, taking a hold of her hand. 'I trust you slept well.'

'Very,' she answered, feeling the warmth from his hand running all the way up her arm. 'I apologise for keeping you waiting.'

'I apologise for rousing you so early, but I wanted you to try on the slippers, so if Mr Wainwright needs to make any adjustments, he has time before this afternoon.'

'Of course.' She turned her smile across the room. 'Good morning, Mr Wainwright. Thank you for returning so promptly.'

'My pleasure, Miss Crawford,' he replied. 'I'm anxious for you to see what I brought.'

'I, too, am anxious,' she admitted as Myles escorted her to the armed chair with a foot stool sitting before it.

Once she was seated, Myles moved to stand behind

her, with one hand gently resting on her shoulder. His touch was as comforting as knowing he'd been in the room next door last night, and she smiled up at him before turning her attention to the cobbler.

Mr Wainwright settled himself on the floor in front of the stool and held up the stockings for her to see. 'We'll start with these. My wife knit them for you last night.'

'Goodness, she must have been up all night,' Anita replied, taking a stocking he held out for her to inspect.

'No, she's quick with her needles, and she knows the pattern by heart. If they work for you, as I'm sure they will, she'll make you as many pairs as you need.'

'They are very soft,' Anita said, rubbing the stocking with her palm. They were also thicker than either the silk ones or her normal ones, and she could imagine wearing one would be like walking on a carpet.

'And one looks quite different from the other.' Wainwright handed her the second stocking, which was shaped differently. 'You see, our daughter was born with a club foot, it looked somewhat like yours, and though the doctors tried to straighten it several times, nothing worked. My wife fashioned these stockings and put the little leather pads you see on the bottoms to keep Rosie's stockings from slipping inside her shoes. And I fashioned shoes for her. Several pairs over the years.'

She glanced up at Myles, wondering if he'd known all that, but could tell by the way he slightly shook his head that he hadn't.

'I'm sure she appreciates all of that very much,' Anita said.

'She did.' He let out a long sigh. 'Unfortunately, she died of a fever a few years ago, when she was twelve.'

Compassion filled her heart. 'I'm so sorry for your loss,' she replied, reaching down to touch the man's arm.

'Thank you. We cherish every memory we have of her, and both my wife and I hope that the items we made for you will help you as much as they did her. You see, when a foot is twisted, it makes that leg a bit shorter than the other one. Even just a smidgen of difference between the two legs can cause the rest of the body to adjust. Knees, hips and the leg itself, and that causes the person to limp more than the foot itself.'

'I've never heard that,' she said.

'It's true.' Wainwright slipped the socks on her feet, then held up a slipper made from soft suede, and showed her the inside of it. 'I built the inside of this shoe up to provide the side of your foot some cushion, and to make your feet level. I guessed at the amount, but I believe I've got it very close. I also have leather strips on the bottoms of both slippers to give you more traction. That will also help with stability and, hopefully, ease any discomfort you're experiencing.'

Filled with excitement, she said, 'That's sounds wonderful. Thank you.' Then she looked up at Myles. 'Thank you.'

He rubbed her shoulder as he winked at her, which was enough to send not only her stomach but her heart into cartwheels. If she tripped now, she wouldn't be able to blame her foot.

Chapter Five

Myles didn't realise that he was holding his breath as Anita took her first steps in her new slippers. It wasn't until she'd crossed the room and turned about, wearing the brightest smile he'd seen her make, that the air seeped out and he had to gulp in a new breath of air. He'd felt a flicker in his heart upon seeing her in the doorway of his bedroom this morning, but right now, it was hammering against his rib cage.

'I've never walked on anything so soft and comfortable,' she said. 'Thank you, Mr Wainwright, and please, thank your wife for me.'

Wainwright bowed at the waist. 'You are undoubtably welcome from both of us, Miss Crawford.'

'It's quite amazing,' she said, walking back towards them.

She still had a slight limp, and her dress hid if she was swaying her leg like he'd felt her do when walking beside her, but it was the smile on her face that Myles was more centred on. It made her eyes shine and her skin glow like she was filled with sunshine.

'We'll need several more pairs,' Myles said to the cobbler. 'Slippers, socks, shoes. All of them.' By God,

he'd name his first born after Nicholas Wainwright for putting that smile on her face.

There were but a few details to go over, including questions that Wainwright asked Anita, which she answered prior to them leaving the sitting room. Though Myles invited the cobbler to stay for breakfast, the man declined, claiming he'd already eaten and needed to get to get back to his workshop.

'Thank you for contacting Mr Wainwright, and for the new slippers,' Anita said after they parted ways with the cobbler at the bottom of the stairway.

Myles had noted that her hold on his arm was barely noticeable while they'd been walking down the stairs, and her pace was more even and steadier than yesterday. 'You are most welcome,' he replied, meeting her gaze. Once again, the uniqueness of her eyes, the overall attractiveness of all of her features held his attention. He couldn't fathom why her uncle had referred to her as homely. Beauty was in the eye of the beholder, but her beauty was such that anyone lucky enough to look upon her, would have to see it. Have to recognise it.

His lips suddenly tingled with the anticipation of being pressed against her naturally pink lips. He told himself that would come soon enough. There was no doubt that he was attracted to her, as a man should be to his wife. Or soon to be wife. How could he not be? She was… Why was he worried about being attracted to her? It would certainly make the act of creating an heir more pleasurable. An act that he'd spent half the night thinking about. He'd also concluded last night that having a companionable relationship, as he'd stated, would make their marriage more pleasant. For he did intend to be married

to her for the rest of his life. He'd also concluded that he'd like, at some point, if she would be attracted to him as well. In that, too, he would give her time.

He was overthinking things, contemplating things that didn't need to be contemplated. That's all it was.

Patting her hand that was hooked around his elbow, he said, 'It is my greatest wish that you are comfortable and feel at home here. If there is anything else you require, please do not hesitate to ask.'

'You've already been more than generous,' she said softly. 'And very thoughtful.'

He fully understood how those were things she wasn't used to and, as he had before, felt disgust over the way she had been treated in the past. Taking a step for them to proceed to the dining room for breakfast, he said, 'Tell me some things you enjoy.'

'Enjoy?'

'Yes. Things you like to do.'

She sighed as a serene smile settled upon her lips. 'Though not as vast as yours, there is a library at Brunswick, and I've read every book in it.'

'Do you have favourites?'

She nodded, then shook her head. 'Too many to mention, nor would I want to bore you.'

'You wouldn't bore me. Reading is one of my favourite pastimes.'

'It is?'

He nodded. 'Yes. The library here is at your disposal. If you'd like, I could point out some of my favourite books.'

'Thank you, I would like that.'

'What else?' he asked. 'Besides books, what else do you enjoy?'

After a brief moment of pause, she said, 'Animals, I enjoy taking care of them.'

He had already assumed as much. 'Do you ride?'

'Yes, I had my own horse for a time and enjoyed riding her very much.'

'I doubt we'll have time today, but soon we will visit the stables. A couple of horses come to mind that I'd like to introduce you to, and see if one is to your liking. To be yours.'

She stopped walking and shook her head as she glanced up at him. 'I was not hinting that—'

'I know you weren't. This is now your home, and I'd like to show you the property. That will be easier on horseback than by coach or carriage.'

She nodded and began walking again. 'Very well, thank you.'

He'd known that he'd need to be patient with her. Any being, person or animal who had been mistreated was cautious, skittish. They weren't used to even the simplest act of kindness. He couldn't change her past, but he could provide her with a very different future.

Anita had to keep telling herself that this was her life now. A life that she'd dared not dream about. The shoes on her feet were undeniably comfortable, and the man whom she would marry this very day was overwhelmingly attractive. Not only in looks but in his thoughtfulness and kindness. Her job was to become a competent duchess who could run his household and raise his children. She would not disappointment him in that.

She just had to keep her head about her. Not get lost in this fantasy world that she'd unexpectedly entered.

It was just that not getting lost in a fantasy was getting harder, and she'd only been here a day. Everyone was extremely nice and accommodating, but it was Myles who was causing the most upheaval inside her. Every time he looked at her, not only did things flip inside her, her heart beat faster and her stomach fluttered. She felt different. A good different. No one had ever looked at her the way he did, and it made rational thinking nearly impossible.

It also made looking away just as impossible. She couldn't help but sigh whenever the simplest thought of him crossed her mind. It wasn't a sigh of frustration or sadness, or anything else that she knew so well, and therefore had no choice but to conclude it was because she'd never had a friend before. Not a male friend. A companion. That's what it had to be. That was what he'd said he wanted from their marriage, so it shouldn't be all that confusing to accept.

Then again, maybe all her confusion was simply her, and her inability to believe she was truly getting married.

Today.

Her confusion continued as the day sped by. She felt as if she were seeing everything through a haze. The large main parlour was made even more beautiful by the pots of flowering chrysanthemums that had been carried in from the large greenhouse attached to the back of the house and placed about the room, including in front of the huge stone fireplace that, with the help of servants, and Christina and Maria, had been decorated with ribbons and bows, along with the doorways.

Pots of flowers and more decorations had also been

used to make the dining room look as festive as the parlour.

There was no greenhouse at Brunswick, but she'd always looked forward to spring and the flowers that would bloom, bringing colour and life to the gardens. She'd found joy in other things, too, other seasons. There were many things that had reminded her that her life hadn't been completely filled with gloom and doom.

Why hadn't she remembered any of them when Myles was asking her about things she enjoyed earlier? She'd felt as if her brain didn't want to work right then.

Probably because he'd been looking at her, and she'd been staring back at him, wondering if it was truly possible that she'd soon become his wife. That was all she could think about, and she'd be lying if she didn't say that it also thrilled her. Thrilled her in ways she didn't understand.

It could be because she'd been given the opportunity to prove that all the things that had been said about her were not true. It may be impossible for her to become everything that Myles may want, but she could be what he'd told her he needed. She would put everything she had into making sure of that. It couldn't be that hard. She did know how to manage staff. It was the other parts that she wasn't so sure about. Being his wife. Then again, if he was busy all the time, it could be that they'd rarely see each other.

She did feel a twinge of disappointment at that thought. It was astonishing that she'd become so comfortable around him in such a short time. Which only proved that he truly was an amazing man.

Letting out a deep sigh, she then had to swallow the lump in her throat.

There was no denying the comfort and stability of the new slippers. They helped lessen her fears of tripping at the church, which would be mortifying for all. She was grateful for the slippers, but the truth was, she was still terrified. What if she still tripped? Disappointed him on his wedding day? She could disappoint him in so many ways besides tripping.

The possibilities were endless, and the list continued to grow right up to the point when she found herself at the entrance to the church. Then she told herself to stop. Just stop thinking such terrible things and focus on walking. Walking like Lady Anita, who was about to take a husband. Focusing her eyes on only him, she lifted her chin and began the walk to the altar.

He looked so very handsome in a shimmering black tailcoat, white ruffled shirt, gold vest and black breeches. His tall black boots looked freshly shined and his golden silk cravat was elaborately tied beneath his chin. It was like looking at a portrait. A man her mind had conjured up as the most handsome on earth, but not a real person.

Yet, he was real. The warmth of his hands when they took hold of hers proved it. So did how chilled by nerves her hands were, for the church was warm.

Her heart leaped in her chest as he smiled, and his hold increased in a silent reassurance that all was well. She was sure that's how he meant it, and she smiled up at him, because she had made it. Made it all the way to the altar, to his side, without tripping. Without missing a step.

As one, they turned and faced the vicar.

The few people in the pews, consisting of his family and local friends, whom she had yet to meet, listened in silence as she agreed to be his wedded wife.

When Myles repeated his vows, he slipped a ring on her finger. A beautiful ring, with one large diamond encircled by several smaller ones. It was eye-catching but only held her attention for a moment, because the sincerity in his voice drew her gaze back to his eyes. There was a smile in them, and on his face. At that moment, she sent up a plea, a silent one, for all the help possible for her to do everything within her powers to make him never regret this decision.

The smile on his face remained as he leaned forward and placed a soft, small kiss directly on her lips. It was so brief, she didn't have time to react, other than to pinch her lips together at how they tingled afterwards. She'd never been kissed, and though she'd told herself that was not something she should expect, she had wondered if he would kiss her, and had to close her eyes as heat flushed into her cheeks.

Myles hooked her hand around his arm and slowly began the walk back down the aisle, the two of them side by side. The small congregation stood, smiled and nodded. Myles was such a gentleman in every way. Kind and considerate, thoughtful and polite. It seemed utterly impossible for her to be his wife, yet she was, and she took from his lead and smiled and thanked the well-wishers as they made their way to the doorway.

Whereas yesterday had been cold and snowy, today had been warm with bright sunshine that was still lingering in the sky when they exited the church.

'My apologies,' Myles said as they walked towards his carriage, 'but I seem to be at a loss for words.'

Guilt struck at how she hadn't considered how strange this all had to be for him, too. He didn't know her any better than she knew him, and hoping to ease his concerns over how peculiar this all was, she said, 'It is somewhat awkward.'

He frowned slightly while dipping his head closer to her. 'My loss of words was over how beautiful you look. I can't seem to find the way to tell you that I've never seen a more beautiful bride.'

Heat filled her cheeks again and her heart started beating erratically. His words were part of it, but so was how the people watching them might perceive the way he was whispering to her.

'I must, however, accept your sentiment,' he continued, 'and apologise for you feeling awkward. That is not what I'd wish for you on your wedding day. Please tell me how I can make things easier for you.'

A renewed sense of inadequacy erupted as she attempted to explain, 'It—it's nothing you did, I merely meant the idea of being married, of me being married, is awkward. It will take some getting used to.'

He didn't reply as they arrived at his carriage and he assisted her inside. After he'd climbed in, sat on the leather seat beside her and the door was shut, he said, 'I understand, Anita, and want you to know that you'll be given all the time you need to get used to the idea of being married.'

'Thank you,' she said, all the while wondering exactly what he meant. Would they not share a bed? Did he not find her attractive enough for that? Had he said she

was beautiful just to be polite? Were her other thoughts, about him loving someone else, correct? The heaviness inside her grew. This was her life. One she'd have to get used to, and she wondered if knowing more might help. 'May I ask you a question?'

'Of course.'

In need of fortification, she drew in a deep breath before asking, 'I don't mean to pry, but why did you call off your other weddings?'

'You aren't prying. You have every right to be curious.' He paused long enough to clear his throat. 'I discovered that one of my would-be brides was having an affair with another man, and though she insisted she would end it, I did not believe that would happen and felt it better to end things. For the other, I witnessed a side of her that had not previously been revealed when she mistreated her servant for something that was purely accidental, and soon determined that hadn't been the first time, nor would it be the last time. She had a very different outlook upon treating people than I have.'

Anita found both explanations understandable, yet wondered why either woman would have chosen to forsake the life of being his wife for what were selfish reasons. Anything even close to an affair was inconceivable to her, as was mistreating people. Anyone who knew him would know that he wouldn't approve of that.

'However, I must add that my ignorance was to blame just as much,' he continued. 'I had not voiced my expectations of marriage to either of them, so therefore gladly accepted the blame in calling off both weddings.'

A shiver rippled over her shoulders. 'What expectations would those be?'

'Exactly what we spoke about, honesty and trust,' he replied.

She considered those necessities in life, not expectations, which confirmed how little she knew about him and his life. A life that she was now a part of. She didn't doubt him but still needed to know more. 'Were you in love with either of them?'

'I see I am at fault again,' he said, 'in not explaining things more thoroughly. No, I was not. Love was never an expectation for marriage. It's a distraction that I don't have time for.'

He would know more about that than her, and she nodded.

'Our marriage will take some getting used to,' he said, 'for both of us, and I believe it will prove to be beneficial for both of us.'

It had already been beneficial to her, and to Olive and Joshua. They both would remain, had become employed at Redford. Whatever the future may hold, she'd grabbed onto this opportunity with both hands and was now married. She'd known love wasn't in the agreement and had lived her entire life without it, so there was no reason to start thinking about it now.

They soon arrived at Redford, where there were more guests than had been at the wedding, and as she walked beside Myles, accepting congratulations, she once again entered a dreamlike state that she knew wasn't real yet couldn't escape. The long table in the dining room was filled with platters of foods, meats, vegetables, fruits, sauces and gravies, breads and jellies, and in the centre of the table, the largest wedding cake she'd ever laid eyes upon. It was layers tall, covered in thick, white icing,

and decorated with more coloured icing in the shapes of flowers and bows.

The entire meal was nothing she'd ever dreamed of, and because she truly appreciated all of the work the household staff had taken in creating the feast, she quietly asked Myles for a moment and used that time to enter the kitchen and thank them personally. She also took the time to thank Mary and Christina and Maria. Everyone had worked so hard, and that reinforced just how much this family meant to each other. That was as foreign to her as the life of lavish wealth that was apparent in every direction.

Mealtime was a lengthy affair, during which she sat next to Myles and found herself blushing at the toasts and well wishes voiced by several. The heat in her cheeks could be from the wine she sipped during each toast, but she was more convinced it was due to the words about their marriage being fruitful.

When the meal ended, with everyone being served a slice of the wedding cake, which tasted as lovely as it had looked, everyone moved into the front parlour. Maria and Christina's diligent work on decorating had transformed it into a festive room, as did the gaiety and laughter from the guests, which was increased by Wesley and his offers of wagers as to if he'd be an uncle by this time next year.

Even in her dreamlike stupor, Anita found the ability to remain sensible. A child was expected from their marriage. Myles had made that clear. Little did he know that becoming a mother had been yet another dream she'd never expected to come true for her. It was also one she was very excited about. The idea of having a child she

could shower with love—the very love that she'd never known—thrilled her.

Her gaze slid towards Myles, sitting next to her on the sofa. He was in conversation with the man next to him, a villager named Olin Williamson who ran the feed mill. Some may have expected the room to be filled with nobility, but it wasn't. Myles said the local business owners were the backbone behind his racehorse business, and he regularly socialised with them. She was impressed by him in so many ways, and this was just one more. He wasn't haughty, nor did he look down on others like her uncle did. She couldn't help but imagine that the two women who had almost become Myles's wife—it was hard to think of herself as that, but they were married—weren't regretful at what they'd lost. Besides being extraordinarily handsome, he was so gracious and likable.

He twisted slightly, caught her gaze and smiled as his hand found hers and gave it a gentle squeeze before he turned back to Mr Williamson.

The warmth returned to her cheeks, and this time she wondered if it was because of her heart. It nearly stopped beating every time he looked at her. Though they'd only known each other a very short time, she accepted that she liked him—genuinely liked him as a person—despite the situation. Or perhaps it was because of it.

Theirs was not a love match and never would be, but it would be easy to grow fond of him.

Her stomach did a somersault as her mind went straight back to other thoughts—that of becoming a mother and how that would transpire. Love was not needed for that to happen, nor was fondness. She needed remember that. He'd sought a loveless marriage, so he

wouldn't be distracted from his duties, and her job was to make sure that didn't happen by overseeing his household. That was something she could do. She'd been running her household without love for years.

Myles was second-guessing his decision again. Not in the marriage but in the time he'd set for the service. Three o'clock had seemed fine, but now, as he glanced again at the mantel clock, which would soon strike eight in the evening, he wished he'd chosen a later time. For Anita's sake. She appeared to be fine—more than fine. A more beautiful bride would be hard to find anywhere. A string of pearls, the same shade of ivory as her form-fitting gown, had been woven into her hair, making it shimmer and shine more than usual. The gown shimmered too, and it hugged her slight frame, enhancing each and every curve, right up to where the collar was buttoned beneath her chin. He kept catching himself staring at her.

Actually, he kept catching others seeing him staring at her. Especially his brother, who once again lifted his glass in a silent salute to him.

They were now standing before the fireplace, having accepted yet another toast, and he gave Wesley a nod of acknowledgement before turning back to Anita. Concerned if her leg was hurting from so much standing and walking, he asked, 'Would you like to sit down again?'

'It's not necessary,' she whispered. 'The new slippers are very comfortable.'

The cobbler and his wife were in attendance and had sat near the sofa with them earlier, talking about little more than the weather, other than when they'd accepted

a heartfelt thank you from Anita. She was so sincere and genuine that he was sure both Wainwright and his wife were as smitten with her as all the other guests.

Myles wouldn't proclaim that he was smitten, too, nor did he want to be. He'd told her love was a distraction he didn't need or want, and still felt that way, but he felt a sense of pride in introducing her as his wife, and he couldn't seem to control the desire to touch her.

Attempting to satisfy that, he brushed aside a curl that was hanging near her left eye. 'I'm happy to hear that,' he replied, keeping his voice low. 'We should be able to make our exit soon. I believe everyone in attendance has had the opportunity to meet you, which was their goal.'

She frowned slightly. 'Why would that be their goal?'

'You are the new Duchess of Redford,' he said.

She closed her eyes for a moment and let out a soft sigh.

He took a hold of her hand, lifted it and kissed the back of it. 'The perfect addition to our family.'

A delicate smile filtered across her lips, but apprehension filled her eyes.

He brushed aside the curl again. 'I'm not the only one who believes that.'

She glanced around the room before looking back up at him. 'Everyone has been very welcoming and friendly.'

They might be off to a shaky start with this marriage, but he was up to the challenge of making things work. He was also up to the challenge of making her see that she'd been lied to her entire life. The courage she'd displayed while walking down the aisle towards him at the church was just a sample of the true Anita. He was con-

vinced of that. Her strength and resolve had intrigued him when he'd first heard about her, and was excited to be a part of the reason she could let it all come to life. Come to believe in herself. 'Would you care for another piece of cake or glass of champagne?'

'No, thank you. As delicious as they both are, I've had my fill.'

'So have I.' He took a hold of her hand. 'Shall we thank our guests and bid them goodnight?'

'We can't do that.' She tightened her hold on his hand, as if attempting to keep him from moving.

'Yes, we can. It's our house. We are the Duke and Duchess of Redford.' He'd always known the day would come when he'd have a duchess, but had never imagined that saying it would make his heart skip into a faster beat.

'What will people think?'

Leaning closer, he whispered, 'They will think that the newly wedded couple would like to be alone.'

A blush took over her entire face, and it affected him. Made his blood run faster. His pulse pound harder. What entered his mind wouldn't happen tonight. He'd promised to give her time to get used to being married, and would hold to that promise, but suddenly hoped it wouldn't take too long for that to happen.

Tucking her hand around his elbow, he verbally collected everyone's attention, thanked them for their attendance, and bid them all a goodnight on behalf of both himself and his duchess.

Enthusiastic clapping, and some cheering led by Wesley, followed him and Anita out of the room, into the corridor and to the stairway as they began to climb it.

No one in his family had let on that this marriage was less than a love match.

'Christina and Maria certainly did a lovely job of decorating the room,' she said.

Myles gave his grin the freedom to reside on his lips, knowing she was doing her best to not think about the fading sounds of excitement their leaving the room had caused.

'They did,' he agreed.

'And the kitchen staff did a wonderful job with all the food and the cake. It was enormous and so lovely. I'd never seen anything like it.'

He started to agree but instead, asked, 'Were there never any parties at Brunswick?'

'Once in a while,' she said.

'Did you not attend them?' He bit the end of his tongue, wishing he hadn't let his thought slip out, because he knew the answer. She hadn't been permitted to attend them.

'I was often needed in the kitchen,' she said, 'to make sure things went smoothly and that everyone had what they needed.'

He waited until they reached the top of the stairs before he stopped walking and waited for her to look up at him. 'That is over, Anita.'

Her eyes held a flash of wariness before she blinked.

That flash was enough to make him flinch, because it confirmed what he'd already figured, that her past life had held little more than pain and fear. He leaned forward and placed a soft kiss on her forehead, then said, 'Come. Your maid is waiting for you.'

Chapter Six

Normally Myles preferred sleeping in a chilly room; however, tonight a fire had been built in his sitting room, and he'd now spent more than half an hour doing little more than staring into the flames in the fireplace. His thoughts were on the future and what might be in store for them. Him and Anita.

Marriage would bring changes to his life, and he would be lying to himself if he didn't admit that those changes were one of the reasons, actually the main reason, he'd put it off for so long. His hope had been to control those changes as much as possible, and although Anita wasn't exactly what he'd expected, he was still convinced that their union would work.

It would take her time to become fully comfortable with the changes in her life. A single thought of how she'd been treated in the past was enough to raise his ire, and enough to make him vow that she would never suffer from such cruel actions again.

It was no surprise when both her maid and coachman had been interested in jobs at Redford rather than returning to Brunswick. He was glad about that, not just for the coachman and maid but for Anita. He liked knowing

that she'd have familiar people around her. Marriage to her was a decision he'd made, and now that it had happened, he would do his best to see that it was as beneficial to her as it would be to him.

Brunswick wouldn't be happy to lose two employees, just as he hadn't been happy when Myles had refused to marry either of his daughters. It had been evident that Brunswick had heard about the amounts of money he'd paid to the families for breaking his previous engagements. That was why Brunswick had offered his daughters, hoping the engagements would be broken, and he too would receive a large sum of money. Brunswick hadn't been happy when Myles had brought up the debt Brunswick owed him but had agreed to him marrying his niece when Myles had let the ultimatums be known. However, the man hadn't told Anita that she had a choice in the matter, and that was still greatly irritating.

The click of a door opening echoed into the quiet room, interrupting his thoughts at the same time it made his heart beat a little faster. That had happened several times today. During times when he'd caught sight of his remarkably beautiful bride. The anticipation of that happening again was what cause the uptick now, and he stood, turned towards the doorway that led into his bedroom and eventually to the doorway to her room, which had been the door that he'd heard open.

Concerned, he quickly crossed the room. As much as he told himself that she wasn't a wayward stray that he'd brought home—like he had done with a variety of animals in the past—he couldn't help but think about how similar her situation was to those he'd rescued. She was wary of the situation and he didn't want to make her

uneasy or frightened that he would request more than she was ready to offer.

His feet stalled as she appeared in the doorway leading from his bedroom to the sitting room before he'd arrived at the doorway. His heart hit another uptick, and he had to swallow at the dryness that overtook his mouth. Her beauty shone through again. She'd changed out of the wedding gown and into a pale blue nightdress and matching overcoat with lacy sleeves and tied with a single thin blue ribbon beneath her breasts.

The sudden desire to be the one to untie that ribbon had him curling his fingers into his palms. A man should be attracted to his wife, but he had to admit, he hadn't expected it to be this strong. Perhaps in time, but not this soon. They'd only met yesterday. He'd known other women for years and never felt a pull this strong. Not even with the two women he'd once considered marrying.

This time was different, and the anticipation drumming in his veins could simply be due to her beauty, for it truly was exceptional. Pushing his thoughts and desires to the recesses of his mind, he asked, 'Is something amiss?'

Her face flushed as she shrugged. 'I know what you said, about us taking time to get to know one another, and I understand that, but Claire seemed to believe that I needed to come in here, and I—well, I…'

'Come,' he said, finding his voice, for he should have realised her maid would have assumed that and how Anita would have been embarrassed to say differently. 'Let's sit by the fire.'

'Thank you,' she said as they crossed the room. 'I

won't stay long, just long enough for Claire to put away my gown and things.'

He sucked in a heavy breath of air. For a moment, while he'd been once again admiring her beauty, he'd wondered if she'd come to his room because she'd wanted to. Instead, it was the first night of their marriage, and he'd put her in an uncomfortable position. The very thing he hadn't wanted to do.

Suddenly felling unusually awkward because he had a lot to learn, he turned and gestured towards the two chairs closest to the fire. 'I will enjoy the company.' Once she was seated, he sat in the other chair and, feeling the need to become comfortable, used the toes of his opposite foot to remove his boots, one at a time, and then set them aside. He'd already removed his suit coat, vest and ascot. 'Are you warm enough?'

'Yes, thank you.'

'I'm afraid the house can be draughty at times,' he said.

'It's a lovely home,' she said.

'Thank you. It was built by my ancestor, the First Duke of Redford. I am the Seventh.'

She nodded. 'Your mother shared that with me.'

Her hands were folded in her lap, but the white knuckles said that was to keep the trembles at bay. He didn't want her to be nervous, skittish, around him, and leaned back in his chair as he let out a small chuckle. 'Am I correct in thinking that she also gave you a tour of the entire house and pointed out all the portraits along the upper gallery?'

Anita nodded, with an even more wary expression. 'I hope you don't mind.'

'Not at all. I am sorry that she bored you with such an activity.'

Shaking her head, she said, 'It wasn't boring at all. It was interesting to learn the family history.'

He chuckled again and lifted a brow while asking, 'Did she show you the closet?'

Her brows knit together. 'What closet?'

Pulling up a grin, he lowered his voice and leaned closer. 'The one filled with skeletons.'

Wide-eyed, she leaned the opposite direction in order to put distance between them. 'Skeletons?'

Teasing her might not be the most appropriate way to ease her fears, nor should he be taking pleasure in the teasing, but if it would allow her to relax, he'd continue as long as it took. Furthermore, it was helping him relax. 'Yes. Every family has skeletons in a closet.'

She pinched her lips together and shook her head, as if amused but hiding it, before a smile broke out on her lips and she covered it with hand.

'Did you think I meant real skeletons?'

'I didn't know what to think,' she admitted after lowering her hand. She also let out a little giggle. 'But I should have known you were jesting. No one would have a real skeleton in a closet.'

'Perhaps not,' he said, although he wasn't overly sure about that. He'd met some people who he'd never want to learn what was in their closets, but this wasn't the time to make a declaration like that. Shifting the conversation back to his family, he said, 'Did my mother tell you that the third Duke of Redford was a thief?'

'A thief? Heavens no.'

'Actually, he was more of a pirate. A ship's captain

who sailed under the crown, confiscating illegitimate cargo from other ships. While doing so, he stole his bride. Right off a ship, brought her home and married her.'

Her eyes were again wide, but there held the shine of interest. 'He did?'

'Yes. They had five or six children, I can't remember for sure, but years later, he stole a bride for his oldest son.'

Her smile was back and she appeared relaxed as she said, 'He did not. You're teasing again.'

'No, I'm not. He truly did. My mother will confirm it.' He waited a moment, watching her lips twitch as if they weren't sure if they should be smiling, before he continued, 'Of course, there is more to the story, but I don't want to bore you.'

'I won't be bored,' she said.

The shine in her eyes made him happy. She was not only interested; she was at ease. 'Both of those women had been stolen from their homes, and my grandfather was who the crown sent to find who stole them and return them...' He went on, explaining the entire story, including how his ancestor was practically the cream of the sailing world back then and how, besides actually rescuing the women, along with many others over the years, he'd recovered riches galore for more countries than just England. Though he didn't tell her, this story was the reason he'd sought a wife rather than love. The third duke hadn't married for love and had been very successful in having a family and business. So successful that he'd brought his son home a bride, again, where love wasn't involved, and there, too, the fourth duke had been very successful in all his endeavours.

Myles was fully aware that he may have elaborated a bit in his storytelling, for Anita's benefit. She was full of questions and so engaged in listening that she'd let her guard down. Her laughter twinkled in the air, and her eyes were sparkling as brightly as the flames licking the logs in the fireplace. He was enjoying answering all of her questions, and found himself making his way through the entire line of his ancestors, all the way to his father, before he caught her yawning.

Anita covered her mouth with one hand to hide a yawn that refused to be contained. She wasn't bored in the least. She could listen to Myles talk about his family for ever and never grow bored. He had an amazing voice and was very skilled in storytelling. Some parts had been serious, other parts very humorous, and she'd enjoyed every word. 'Excuse me,' she said, lowering her hand as the yawn ended.

'Forgive me for keeping you awake,' he said. 'It has grown late.'

She followed his gaze to the mantel clock above the fireplace and was surprised to see it was well past midnight.

'Come.' He rose and held out a hand to her. 'It's time for bed.'

A tiny shiver rippled through her, reigniting the nerves that had practically consumed her earlier. During the hours of talking with him, she'd forgotten her reason for being in his suite of rooms. She was only going to stay long enough for Claire to straighten up her room. The maid had been all aflutter in not keeping the Duke waiting, and Anita simply hadn't wanted to

tell Claire that Myles hadn't been waiting on her. That he hadn't expected her in his room tonight.

Whatever sleepiness that had befallen her, was gone now. Replaced with a nervousness that had her hands trembling all over again. More than just her hands. Her entire being was shaky as she laid her hand in his and rose to her feet. She certainly didn't want him to think she'd come to his room expecting anything, yet couldn't seem to find the wherewithal to voice that.

He wrapped her hand around his elbow and blew out the lamp on the table near his chair, leaving just the light from the fire that he'd added logs to several times to guide them as they began walking towards his bedroom.

She wasn't sure what to do. He'd said she'd have time to get used to the idea. Surely, he didn't believe that had happened during their conversation this evening, did he? Had it happened? Was she ready for this? She didn't know. It was all so confusing. And exciting, she couldn't deny that.

Or was he simply escorting her to her bedroom?

Two lamps were lit in his bedroom, one on each side of the massive bed. The covers had been folded back, and the flickering light from the flames of the lamps cast tiny shadows across the exposed white sheets and pillows. But it had been that way when she'd walked through it earlier.

She did her best to contain the sense of disappointment that washed over her as he continued to guide her past the bed and to the door that led to her room.

He opened the door, and upon spying the dark room, for Claire truly hadn't expected anyone to sleep in the room tonight, he said, 'I'll light a lamp for you.'

She slowly released the sigh that was pressing to get out. 'There's no need.'

'Are you sure?'

'Yes.'

'Well, then, I'll leave the door open until you're in bed.'

'Thank you.' She stepped into her room, but his hold on her arm stopped her from a second step.

'I regret keeping you up so late, but I sincerely enjoyed our evening together,' he said.

The way he was looking at her made her heart beat like a drum. 'I did, too,' she admitted, while finding it difficult to breathe.

'If the weather cooperates, I'll show you the stables in the morning, perhaps we can take a ride around the property, and you can tell me more about your family.'

Added excitement over seeing the stables was mixed with sinking sensation over just how different his family was compared to hers. 'I will enjoy seeing the stables and riding, but I believe you already know all there is to know about my family.'

He touched her chin, lifted it enough so their gazes met again and stared at her for so long that everything inside her grew warm. Then he leaned forward and pressed a small kiss on her forehead.

Her eyes closed at an amazing sensation that spread well beyond where his lips touched. Something warm and enticing swirled inside her from head to toe.

'Goodnight, Anita,' he said softly.

Upon realising that his lips were no longer touching her forehead and that his hand was no longer holding her elbow, she snapped her eyes open. 'Goodnight,' she said, then hurried into her room, straight to her bed.

It wasn't until she was in the bed, with the covers pulled up to her chin, that she realised she'd never taken off the lacy robe that matched the blue linen nightdress that Claire had provided for her to wear. She still had her socks on, too.

The door closed with a click, dowsing the room in darkness, and she let out a long sigh.

Confusion washed over her.

There must be something wrong with her—besides her obvious physical conditions—because she was disappointed to be lying in her own bed, alone, on her wedding night. Yet, at the same time, she was very grateful to have married a man who was so understanding. No one had ever treated her so kindly and she was thankful for that.

Would that be enough to make a lasting marriage? They were married, and there was no changing that. She'd chosen to marry him and knew love wasn't a part of it, so what was this feeling of longing inside her? She'd lived practically her entire life without love and had accepted it would always be that way.

Or was it him that she was worried about not having love? He'd known love his entire life, from his family, and therefore didn't need more. Not from her. Not from a wife.

Maybe this longing inside her wasn't love. Maybe it was the womanly desires she'd read about in novels. She squeezed her eyes shut and told herself to go to sleep. To stop thinking about him and their marriage and just go to sleep!

She tried hard, but it was hours before that finally happened.

* * *

It was that way at the end of each day that followed. She'd tell herself to stop thinking about Myles and their marriage and just go to sleep, and it grew more difficult night after night as she went to bed in her own room, alone and listening for any sounds of Myles climbing into his own bed on the other side of the door.

She couldn't help but wonder if this is what their marriage would always be like. Perhaps that was what he wanted? But they would have to sleep together at some point in order for her to provide him with an heir, and those thoughts were what kept her up at night. The more she got to know about him, the more she liked him and things about him. She liked how he held her hand and touched her shoulder, waist or the small of her back. She liked touching him, too, and even though the new shoes were wonderful, she held on to his arm whenever they walked side by side. All of that filled her with warm and wonderful sensations that made her think more and more about having his children. She grew more and more curious about that act, and other things. Like kissing. Besides kissing at their wedding, he'd kissed her cheeks and forehead, and like touching him, that all made her want more. Did that make her a wanton? Or should wives feel that way about their husbands? It was all so confusing, because everything else about her life had become so wonderful.

The morning after their wedding night, he'd taken her to the stables, where she'd chosen a pale grey mare named Starla to ride while he'd taken her on a tour of the property. He owned a vast amount of land but had only shown her a small portion of it, mainly the pasture

and stable areas closest the manor house, claiming they'd wait until it was warmer for longer rides.

She looked forward to that, because along with her wondering mind, she was finding herself restless while Myles was in the stables or working in the library. It had only been a week since their wedding, and though she would never complain about now having a lavish lifestyle that so many would wish to have, there was very little for her to do. The multitude of tasks that Mary had claimed would keep her busy took mere minutes to complete, because it mainly meant a single morning meeting with the head kitchen and household staff members. The employees were so competent, they merely needed her approval, not her help.

There had been a few additional things to keep her busy the first couple of days, when she had spent hours penning thank-you notes to wedding guests and meeting with a seamstress from the village who had been hired to provide her with a new wardrobe. Mr Wainwright had been out twice, once to deliver another pair of slippers and more socks, another time to deliver a pair of leather boots that were not only comfortable; they were lovely and shaped in a way that they didn't look distorted, like her old boots.

The new boots made her steps more even and, like the slippers, relieved the discomfort in her hip. The boots were also warm, and every step she took made her think about Myles. How much he'd already done for her. That added to her frustration. There was so little for her to do for him in exchange. She wanted to do things for him, wanted him to know how much she appreciated him.

To fill in her empty time and not wanting her leg to

grow stiff from too much sitting, she took to walking with Roscoe each day. The dog, like all animals, was non-judgemental and very good company. Walking with Roscoe helped her not think about other things, including her family. Knowing Uncle Jerome had wanted Myles to marry one of her cousins and not her was weighing on her mind, too. Uncle Jerome was never satisfied, and she feared that he wasn't done attempting to rule her life.

During her walks, she had met all the barn animals, including the peacocks, who roamed the yard at their pleasure. Two of them often followed along behind her and Roscoe, mainly because she often dropped bread-crumbs in their wake for the birds to eat.

The birds were huge, and the males were particularly gorgeous, even without fanning their tail feathers, and they could make several sounds. All loud. Startlingly loud, but their antics also made her laugh, and that made Roscoe bark.

All of that was currently happening—the birds were letting out high pitched squealing sounds and fanning out their feathers, she was laughing and Roscoe was barking—which explained why she didn't realise Myles was approaching until Roscoe ran around her, and she spun about to see why.

She bit down on her bottom lip at how her heart did another one of those little flips. One would think that after a week of seeing him numerous times every day, it would stop doing those silly somersaults. Then again, that could be exactly why those flips had become big-ger. When she wasn't worrying about Uncle Jerome, she was thinking about Myles. Naturally. That was what she kept telling herself. They were married, and *naturally*

she would want to know all there was to know about him. That she would *naturally* wonder if he would ever kiss her again, ever want her to sleep in his bed and if she'd ever giggle and blush and swoon like the women in the books she'd read.

'I apologise for interrupting your stroll,' he said, walking closer. 'I have something I think that you'd like to see.'

'Oh?' The smile on his face was leaving her breathless, making it impossible to say more, and as usual, she was having a hard time not staring at him. Simply stare and wonder.

'Yes. In the foaling stable. It's not far.' The smile on his face faded slightly. 'Unless you're tired. It can wait.'

She was not tired, and even if she was, she wouldn't disappoint him. 'No, it can't wait.' Stepping forward, she took a hold of his arm. 'You have me too curious to know what it is.'

His smile returned fully. 'Would you like a hint?' he asked as they began walking.

The other thing that happened when he was near was an uncanny sense of excitement that washed over her from head to toe. She enjoyed his company so very much but tried not to let that show because he was busy, had other things to do. 'Yes, please.'

'There are more than one.'

'More than one?' She shook her head. 'That's not a very good hint.'

'Oh? What would be a good hint?'

'Something more specific.'

'Something more specific might give it away, then it wouldn't be a surprise.'

'It doesn't have to be that specific, but it has to relate to what it is.'

'My hint relates to what it is. There are more than one.' With an even brighter shine in his eyes, he added, 'There are six. Actually, seven.'

'Seven?' She looked up at him and shook her head. 'That's still not specific enough for me to guess. There could be seven of anything.'

'True.' With a nod, he said, 'Here's another hint. One is big and six are small.'

Such a simple conversation shouldn't make her this happy, but it did. He did. In order to keep a giggle hidden, she sighed. 'You are not very good at this.'

'Oh? Are you an expert at giving hints?'

She wasn't an expert at anything and had never had anyone give her hints. What she knew about surprises— good ones—and hints she had read in books. 'No, and I don't think you are, either.'

He pressed a hand to his chest and let out a fake moan. 'Oh, you injure me.'

She knew he was teasing, and that too was something she'd never had, nor had she ever had the opportunity to tease in return, which also meant that she wasn't very good at it. 'Don't be too injured. It's hard to give perfect hints, and you are an expert in many other things.'

'I am? Such as?'

'Well…' Being wonderful and handsome came to mind, but she couldn't say either of those.

He chuckled.

Glancing at the stable now only a couple of steps away, she said, 'Horses! You are an expert on horses.'

'I'm glad something came to mind,' he said. 'For a moment I thought you were unable to think of anything.'

'No, there are lots of things, I just…' She couldn't say that she couldn't tell him about what she'd been thinking about, what she thought about all the time, because she had to be careful to not want more than he'd agreed to. That was something else she thought about often, how it was her job to make sure he had time to complete his duties.

'Just?' he prompted.

'I was *just* thinking about what there are seven of,' she said. Which is what she should have been thinking about. 'One large and six small.'

He laughed harder. 'Sure, you were.' Stopping to open the stable door for her, he gestured to Roscoe. 'You stay out here.' Then he pointed at the peacocks that were only a few steps behind them. 'The rest of you, too.'

The birds squawked and Roscoe barked, but none attempted to follow them into the stable. Anita drew in a deep breath and released it with a satisfied sigh that was loud enough for Myles to glance her way. She didn't attempt to hide her smile. She loved the smell of hay and horseflesh and wasn't ashamed of that.

He grinned. 'This way.'

They walked past the spacious stalls, slowly enough that she had the opportunity to give each horse a single pet on their elongated faces. Besides the long rows of stalls, there was a separate walled-off area with larger stalls for when it came time for the mares to give birth, and there was a large loft overhead filled with hay for the winter months. She knew this stable, and the horses in it, better than the other buildings because it was not

only the one closest to the house; it was filled with the mares who would give birth come spring. Being in the stable back at Brunswick with her father with newborn foals was one of the memories she'd tucked deep inside, and entering this stable brought the happiness of that memory to the fore front.

'Your affection for animals has become very clear,' Myles said as he led her into the large tack room. 'And I thought you'd like to see the newest ones.'

Anita drew in an excited breath so quickly she pressed a hand to her breastbone. 'Newest ones?'

'Yes.' He gestured towards a small wooden crate in the corner.

She couldn't contain her excitement and rushed forward, then sighed at the sight of a mother tabby cat and six tiny kittens. She knelt down next to the crate that held a nice bed of hay for the new mother and her babies, and instantly knew who had fixed the crate for the animals and placed it in here. Myles had a heart of gold when it came to animals. A niggling thought that she'd had more than once flashed in her mind. Was she like a stray animal to him? One he'd brought home to care for and nurture? She didn't want to be. Rather than being disappointed that there was too little for her to do, she needed to find things to do. Things for him, so he could focus on his duties. Perhaps even the duty of having an heir. A new bout of determination filled her and she smiled up at him. 'They are adorable.'

'I found them in the hayloft,' he said, crouching down beside her. 'And moved them down here so they wouldn't fall over the edge once they start walking.'

'That certainly could have happened,' she said. Be-

sides the numerous stories she'd heard about him rescuing animals, she'd witnessed his kindness towards them.

Reaching down, she gave the mother cat a gentle pet. 'I think I had a kitten when I was little.'

'You think?'

She nodded. 'I don't remember much before my parents died, but sometimes I get a feeling of things that might have happened.'

'You were very young,' he said. 'I don't remember things from when I was that small, even though my mother insists that they happened.'

They were still both kneeling beside the box of kittens, and she twisted so they were face to face and smiled at him. 'Like when you sneaked your pony into the house?' Mary had shared a story one night at the evening meal of how he'd led the horse into the house and had been caught attempting to convince the pony to climb the stairs up to his bedroom.

He laughed. 'I clearly remember that pony, but I don't remember bringing her into the house.'

She had laughed over that story, and her throat thickened a bit at not having more of her own happy memories.

Just as she was about to look away, he caught her chin, forcing her to continue looking at him. 'I'm sorry that you didn't have someone to remind you of memories,' he said softly. 'You should have had that. Should have had so much more than you did.' He released her chin and brushed aside a piece of hair hanging along the side of her face. 'From now on, I'll be here to remind you of wonderful memories.'

She had to swallow down a lump in her throat, be-

cause the warmth that was spreading in her heart wasn't from memories. He filled her with a breathless wonder like nothing ever had.

His knuckle trailed along the side of her cheek, ending beneath her chin again. The touch and the way he was looking at her stole any thoughts that might have formed, other than how perfectly his brows arched over his eyes that were so dark brown, they reflected the sunlight shining in through the window. Even his nose was perfect, and his lips.

Her heart thudded again as she recalled the soft kiss that he'd given her on their wedding day. Whether it was to cherish the memory or to keep her thoughts hidden, she wasn't sure, but she closed her eyes.

A moment later, when his lips brushed against hers, she gasped at the unexpected touch and snapped her eyes open.

He pulled his face back. 'I didn't mean to startle you.'

'You didn't.' She shook her head, because that was clearly a lie. 'I mean it was, I was…' Flustered by not knowing what to say, she sighed. 'I'm sorry.'

His hand slipped away from her chin. 'I understand.'

Chapter Seven

No, he didn't understand, and neither did she. There was so much to not understand about their marriage, but Anita did know one thing. She didn't want him to think that she hadn't wanted him to kiss her. She had. Still did.

The thought that came next struck so fast she didn't have time to contemplate stopping the impulse before she was acting on it. Grasping his shoulders so he couldn't stand up, or move farther away, she bolted forward, pressing her lips against his.

It may have been the sensation of their lips connecting or her actions that had been so fast she'd unbalanced herself. Either way, almost as quickly as their lips met, his arms went around her, held her tight as he tumbled backwards and she fell forward.

She might have pulled her lips off his, or tried to move off him, if one of his hands hadn't moved to the back of her head, holding it in place as the kiss became more than a meeting of lips.

His mouth moved beneath hers, and she copied his movements, liking how it felt and how it sent tingles throughout her system fast enough to make her dizzy. Or was she swooning? Maybe, for it felt amazing. For

the first time in her life, she forgot everything else, focusing only on feeling absolutely wonderful.

The heat of his firm body beneath her radiated through her dress, making every inch that touched him feel warm, and an unfamiliar heat swirled deep inside her, below her stomach. That heat was in her breasts, too, and being pressed against his chest made them tingle.

The kissing continued until he cupped her face with both hands and lifted her head enough to separate them.

Anita didn't know what to do, whether she should look him in the eyes or not. Her lips were wet from their kisses and throbbing, much like the rest of her. She licked her lips, swallowed.

'Thank you,' he said.

Cautiously, she glanced from the smile on his lips to the shimmer in his eyes. 'You're welcome.' Her hesitancy made it sound more like a question.

He pulled her face forward, gave her a quick kiss. 'I've been wondering which was the real you. The one who drove a carriage into the yard like the devil was chasing her or the one who barely looks at me.'

It took her a moment to collect her thoughts enough to defend herself. 'I had to hurry. Joshua could have frozen to death, and I look at you all the time.' So much that she was often afraid of getting caught staring, and that made her nervous. Almost as nervous as she was right now. She was literally lying atop him. In a stable!

He kissed her lips again. Just a small simple kiss, but it was enough to make her not want to move. Even though she knew she should.

'No, you don't look at me all the time,' he said, adding another small kiss to her lips.

'Often enough,' she answered. The heat in her cheeks said she was blushing. Swooning and blushing all at once.

He kissed one side of her mouth and then the other. 'I disagree.'

Those soft, teasing kisses were making her want more. Longer kisses. They also made her happy, so happy, she giggled. 'I can't look at you all the time.'

'Why not?'

His question included another kiss, a longer one, and that made her breathing go shallow, like short, minia-ture sighs. 'What would people think?'

'I don't care what people think.' After another kiss, he continued, 'I only care what you think.'

'What I think doesn't matter.'

'It does to me.'

His statement was followed by far more than a little kiss. It was a bout of kissing that completely absorbed her and eliminated her ability to think. Eliminated her ability to do anything except become lost in kissing him in return.

Myles had felt as if he'd been walking on eggshells for the last week. The morning after their wedding night, when she'd come down to breakfast, Anita had barely looked at him, and though he'd tried his best, that hadn't changed in the days that followed. He'd feared she'd been questioning if she'd made the right choice in marrying him. He couldn't blame her for questioning that, but the last thing he wanted was for her to regret saying yes.

He knew she'd need time, and he'd give her as long as she needed, but they also needed to get to know each

other during that time. Only, anytime they were together, she was skittish. Shy. Quiet.

Other than going for a short ride that one morning, the most time they'd spent alone together was walking to the dining room for meal times. She'd been busy, writing thank-you notes and meeting with the seamstress and Mr Wainwright, but she found time every day to go for a walk with Roscoe. Myles would never say that he was jealous of the dog, but he had been excited about the kittens today because it had given him an excuse to spend a small amount of time with her.

He needed that. For as hard as it was to admit to needing anything, anyone, the desire to be with her had been practically eating him alive. He'd never have believed that it would be so hard for a man to woo a woman into his bed, specifically, his wife. He just kept telling himself that it would be worth the wait. And it would be. If he lived that long.

The fear he'd blown his chance when he'd acted impulsively and kissed her had nearly gutted him. The last thing he'd expected was her next reaction. Her fast, wonderful, onslaught had caught him completely off guard. Yet, now, with her lying atop him, he was glad that she'd knocked him off balance.

He didn't care that they were on the floor of the tack room. The opportunity to taste her sweet lips, feel her soft curves pressed against his throbbing form, was a gift he hadn't expected, and he was cherishing every moment. It was what he wanted, and he was having a hard time forcing himself to take it slow.

He had to keep telling himself to think of what was at stake.

Nothing had changed concerning his decision to marry her. He would never expect her to fall in love with him, nor would he fall in love with her. That was not what they had agreed to. Furthermore, love wasn't necessary, nor did he want the expectation of yet another devotion. He was committed to his family, to the Dukedom and the business he and Wesley had created with the Redford thoroughbreds, and would be committed to her, forgo all other women, but he would not let marriage rule his life. Not allow himself to be distracted by it. He needed the freedom to travel between London and Redford at will, to attend Parliament as required, to focus on tasks that needed to be done, without feeling guilty that there might be someone back home waiting on him to return.

However, even knowing all that, he also knew that in order to secure the family heritage, secure an heir, companionship as well as a healthy dose of lust was needed.

That part had been easy for him, but the amount of lust filling him since he'd seen her in her nightgown and robe on their wedding night had grown unhealthy, considering how he'd been unable to think of anything but her day and night. That was distracting and made him understand that he had to get that part of their marriage behind them so he could focus on other things. The tasks that he was already fully committed to completing. The overwhelming desire he felt also made him believe that when the time came, it would be very enjoyable.

He was fully committed to their marriage, and truthfully, wouldn't call consummating it a task. More of a benefit. Kissing her was certainly a benefit, and de-

spite his best effort, it was stealing his ability to think of anything else.

Even as a part of him told him that he shouldn't take their kissing any further, he slid his tongue along the seam of her lips. A thrill sliced through him when her lips parted, giving him access to the hidden cavern of her mouth.

He'd just had his first taste of utter sweetness when an out-of-place sound filtered through the pounding of his heart echoing in his ears. Ignoring it, he focused on engaging her tongue in a game of hide and seek when the sound came again.

Louder, and much more intrusive.

It was someone making their presence be known by clearing their throat.

Flustered, he opened an eye, glanced towards the sound, and what only could be considered as complete exasperation washed over him.

Options crossed his mind, so did consequences.

Feeling as if he'd just been doused with ice-cold water, he reluctantly ended the kiss. 'We are no longer alone.'

He felt her entire body go stiff and watched her eyes grow round and her cheeks turn pink.

Anger struck. At the intruder and at himself for forgetting about the expected arrivals. He'd remembered it earlier, but upon finding the kittens and thinking of her joy at seeing them, everything else slipped his mind.

He kissed her cheek and tucked her face beside his neck before he turned his attention to the intruder standing in the tack room doorway. This certainly was a situation he never would have imagine finding himself in,

and he certainly would not embarrass Anita by being found in such a position by introductions at this moment.

Reaching out, he caught the bottom corner of the door. 'We'll meet you outside of the stables in a moment,' he told the intruder as he swung the tack room door shut.

Before he had a chance to help her, Anita planted her knees between his thighs and shot up right. 'Who is it?' she whispered, then she covered her face with both hands and let out a soft moan.

He sat up and grasped her wrists, pulled her hands away from her face. 'There is nothing for you to be embarrassed about. We are married. We can kiss wherever and whenever we wish.'

Her face had grown redder. 'On the floor of the tack room?'

'Yes, even on the floor of the tack room.'

She let out a long sigh and glanced at the door. 'Was it one of the stablemen?'

'No.' He wished it had been, any one of them would have discreetly left the building without interrupting them.

'A servant?' she asked.

'No.' Any servant would have had the good sense to leave, too.

'Oh!' Her face wrinkled as she grimaced. 'Please don't say it was your mother or sisters.'

'I won't say it was them, because it wasn't.' None of them would have made their presence be known, either. His brother might have, but Wesley had gone back to London and had sent the message that a potential horse buyer would be arriving today.

'Then who was it?' she asked.

It was his turn to sigh and grimace as he glanced at the door. 'Miss Diana Brockholder.'

'Diana Br—'

Her eyes turned as round as saucers and that told him that she recognised the name. 'Yes, Diana Brockholder.'

'The woman you—one of the women you were engaged to?'

He'd never recalled being embarrassed. Ever. Perhaps he wasn't now. It could be anger that was causing his face to feel too warm. 'Yes.'

She let out a long sigh while bowing and shaking her head. 'Oh dear. Oh my.'

He caught her beneath the chin and lifted her face. 'I apologise. I should have mentioned it to you.'

'Mentioned it?' She struggled from his hold and to stand.

He stood and grasped her elbows, helping her. 'Should have mentioned that Diana's uncle is buying a horse. I did not know that she would come with him. She hates the country.'

Anita's gaze went to the floor. 'Maybe she wants to remind you of what you could have had instead of what you have.'

His heart felt as if it had been stabbed. 'No.' He enclosed her in an embrace and kissed the top of her head. 'I have exactly what I want.'

'You mean *need*,' Anita whispered. 'You needed a wife, not wanted.'

That was what he'd said, and it still held true, yet he was greatly regretting how callous it sounded on his part when she repeated it. 'You are exactly what I need.

Everyone will see that, and see how lucky I am, at the Christmas Ball.'

She took a step back. 'The Christmas Ball? In London? The one Christina and Maria are so excited to attend?'

'Yes.'

'I thought…' She shook her head. 'We will attend?'

'Yes. The girls couldn't attend last year due to my father's death, and can't attend without chaperones, without the entire family. You'll be fine. In fact, you will wow them.' Her beauty alone would do that. He tucked a strand of hair behind her ear. 'Other than that, any balls we attend will be up to you.'

She bit her lip, then whispered, 'I don't know how to dance.'

He glanced at the door, frustrated by their interruption all over again. He'd never been one to tout fairness, but if he had been, it would be right now, because it was unfair of how quickly the air had changed between him and Anita. Taking hold of her hands, he drew her close enough to wrap his arms around her again. 'We can discuss the ball later, but know that I'll be with you the entire time, and you won't be expected to dance.'

She let out a long sigh and nodded before glancing at the door.

He gently cupped her face with both hands, forced her to look at him. 'I'm here with you right now, too.' Determined to not lose what they'd gained, he leaned down and kissed her. Not a fast, kiss, but a deep, lingering one that left them both breathless when it ended.

For the first time in her life, Anita's unsteadiness had nothing to do with her injured leg. The kisses she'd

shared with Myles before he'd opened the door had left her weak in the knees. If not for her hold on his arm, she wouldn't have been able to take a step.

Once she had taken a step, several in fact, until they walked out of the stable, she'd wished she hadn't. Diana Brockholder was a beautiful woman, with shimmering black hair and big blue eyes. Adding that knowledge to all her other worries had Anita increasing her hold on Myles's arm.

'Diana,' Myles said. 'Allow me to introduce my wife, Lady Anita Wadsworth, Duchess of Redford.'

Diana performed a graceful curtsey, while saying, 'Your Grace.'

Turning to her, Myles said, 'Anita, this is Miss Diana Brockholder.'

Something inside Anita flipped. Not her heart or her stomach this time. It was her will. The determination that she'd counted on all her life. It had waned this past week, but no more. She was Myles's wife and had to act the part. No, it was more than that. She wanted to act the part. She wanted the choice she'd made to be successful. Instead of embarrassment of being caught kissing, a sense of pride filled her. 'Miss Brockholder,' Anita said, chin up, 'it's nice to make your acquaintance.'

'Yours, too, Your Grace.' Diana then looked at Myles. 'I apologise for my interruption. I was hoping to catch you so you wouldn't be surprised to see me.'

'Why are you here?' Myles asked.

'It wasn't my idea,' Diana replied. 'I said it wasn't appropriate to visit newlyweds so soon. But I was overruled by my parents. They thought it would be a show of good grace for us to accompany Uncle Matthew here.

Mother said we could visit with your family while he looks at the horses.' Diana glanced behind her, towards the doorway of the stable. 'Your butler showed them inside the house, and I...' She shrugged. 'I am sorry. I didn't mean to interrupt you, but I did tell your butler that you were busy just a minute ago when he came looking for you.'

There was no stopping the way Anita's cheeks warmed as Myles looked down at her, but she still wasn't embarrassed. Just remembering.

'We were busy,' he said.

Diana nodded. 'Yes, well, I'll go tell them you'll be in shortly.'

'Thank you,' Myles said.

Anita held her breath as Diana turned and walked towards the house, with her lovely dark blue cape nearly sweeping the ground with each step. Despite her renewed determination, Anita had a distinct sinking feeling. Releasing the air from her lungs, she looked up at Myles.

He was looking at her, smiling. 'Ready?'

She nodded. Where there was a will, there was a way. He'd kissed her. They'd kissed. Really kissed. It had been the best moment of her life, and she refused to let anything diminish that.

That thought gave her confidence a boost. So did knowing she was the Duchess of Redford. However, it started slipping as they walked towards the house, and she wasn't sure how to gain it back.

'We'll go in through the back of the house,' Myles said. 'Your maid will meet you there to take your cloak.'

She tried harder to pull her confidence back up. 'Yes, she will.' Claire was always close at hand.

'We can freshen up and proceed to the parlour together.'

'Thank you. I appreciate that.' She did. She always felt safe when he was near.

He stopped walking, looked at her. 'I know this may appear to be an uncomfortable situation, but in truth, it's nothing more than a visit by a horse buyer. Such events occur regularly here.'

He was right about that. She was just so insecure that everything made her nervous right now. That couldn't be. He needed a wife who didn't require his constant attention so he could see to his business of raising and selling horses. She had to find a way to be that wife.

He grinned. 'I know she's in there.'

Confused, she asked, 'Diana?'

'No,' he replied. 'The woman who drove a team of horses in here like the devil was chasing them. That woman has confidence in herself and determination in what she wants.'

Anita's breath caught. He couldn't possibly know what she'd been thinking. How she needed to gain confidence. 'That wasn't confidence, that was fear for Joshua's life.'

'You handled those horses with confidence.'

'Because I've been doing it for years.'

'At high speed through snowstorms?'

'No.'

'But you had the confidence to do it because it was inside you, just waiting to be used.' He kissed her forehead. 'Just like you have the confidence to walk into that house like the Duchess of Redford. It's inside you, just waiting to be used.'

A tiny shiver rippled down her spine. She wasn't fearful for anyone's life; however, their marriage could be at stake. It was completely up to her to become the wife he needed, and she would. She would help him, support him and defend him with all she had.

The shiver was gone and her spine stiffened.

Myles was still looking at her, still smiling.

She would also need to learn all there was to know about the Redford thoroughbreds, which would be an easy and enjoyable task. 'What horse is he here to buy?'

Myles's smile increased. 'A two-year-old. He wants to train it himself.'

'Is he trustworthy? Good to animals?'

'Yes, he is. I refuse to sell to anyone who isn't.'

'Very well,' she said, taking a step towards the house. 'We shouldn't keep them waiting.'

Entering side by side, they found their guests were in the front parlour, where there were still vases filled with blooming flowers from their wedding day, and being received by Mary, who was in the midst of serving tea.

Myles introduced Anita to Niles Brockholder, the Viscount of Wilmington, and his wife, Lady Barbara, as well as Barbara's brother, Matthew Green. After the pleasantries were out of the way, Myles escorted Anita to the sofa, but when she realised that he intended to sit down beside her, she whispered, 'You don't need to stay.'

He searched her face for a moment, and she made sure to maintain a full smile the entire time.

'I'm sure,' she answered his silent question.

'Thank you,' he whispered and kissed her cheek softly

before he turned to the men and invited them to accompany him outside.

Anita sat and joined the conversation during tea which covered the weather and the upcoming yuletide, using most of the time to observe the family. Though lovely like her daughter, Lady Barbara had a coolness about her. There was no shine in her eyes, and her smile was false, and Diana was clearly bored. She didn't even attempt to hide it.

When a lull in the conversation began to turn into a heavy silence, Anita asked, 'Would anyone care for more tea?'

'No, thank you,' Lady Barbara replied, fiddling with the white lace on the cuffs of her gold-coloured dress as she looked from vase to vase filled with flowers.

Diana shook her head while letting out a sigh.

'Well, then,' Anita said, fully aware that things could grow uncomfortable, more than they already were. 'Shall we take a tour of the greenhouse?' She gestured towards the vases of flowers as she stood. 'As you can see, we have a variety of flowers still blooming, which is so wonderful when the weather turns as cool as it has.'

Perhaps because she was the Duchess of Redford, no one felt they could decline and everyone stood.

'Lovely idea,' Mary said, stepping up beside her.

Anita smiled at her mother-in-law as the women hooked their arms together. The specially made boots had lessened her limp, but her gait was still different, in part because it was how she'd always walked, and changing that would take time. Knowing those behind her could see her uneven swaying, and her slowness,

she was conscious of every step she took while she and Mary led their guests from the parlour.

If she wanted these people to believe she belonged here, she had to believe it herself. Not sure how to do that, she chose to share some history of the home. 'This home was built by the first Duke of Redford,' she said as they entered the corridor. 'And there are furnishings from around the world, brought home by the third Duke of Redford, during his sailing days.'

She continued to share small bits of information, and answered questions from Lady Barbara, who was obviously only asking them out of politeness, until they arrived in the greenhouse.

'Oh my,' Lady Barbara said, clearly impressed with all of the pots and long beds filled with blooming plants. 'I've never seen such variety.'

'Thank you. Please, feel free to explore.' Anita gave a sweeping arm gesture.

Mary flashed a smile as she moved towards the long beds that held the ivy and holly plants that would be used to decorate for Christmas.

Following her mother along the centre aisle filled with various blooming plants, Diana showed a slight curiosity in the flowers that her mother was naming, but Anita would guess it was more out of boredom than true interest.

Anita moved farther into the room to look out of the windows at the barn and a small section of one of the stables. The same stable that she and Myles had been in just a short time ago.

Where she stopped to stand may have been a mistake, because Roscoe, who was still in the back garden, in-

stantly noticed her. He barked and ran towards her, and that caught the attention of the peacocks.

The glass wall was no barrier for either the barking or the screeching. Nor did it smother the sound of screams and crashes behind her.

'My apologies for arriving unannounced,' Wilmington said as they stood next to the corral where Matthew Green was examining two particular horses. 'I felt it was an opportunity for society to know that despite the broken engagement, we are still friends.'

Myles stared at the Viscount for a moment. He'd respected the man for years, which had been part of the reason he'd thought a marriage to Diana might work. However, he wasn't overly certain that was the main reason for Wilmington's visit. He'd chalk that up to curiosity. He was sure half of London was curious about his new wife. 'I see no reason for us not to be friends,' he replied.

'I was also thinking of your best interests,' Wilmington said.

Myles lifted a brow, waited for the Viscount to say more.

'Brunswick came to see me two days ago, he wanted to know why the engagement between you and Diana was broken. Claimed he was worried about his niece.'

Myles drew in a deep breath in an attempt to control his irritation. 'Brunswick has never worried about anyone except himself.'

Wilmington nodded. 'I know. I told him to mind his business and sent him away, but I thought you should know, because I'm not the only one he's visiting. He's

claiming his niece was like a daughter to him and that he's acting as any father would. But I believe he's attempting to use your name to gain access to places he's otherwise not welcome.'

Myles turned his gaze to Green, who was still inspecting the horses. There was an ounce of truth in what Wilmington had just said. Brunswick had never treated Anita like a daughter, but he was acting like a father might. Parents got involved in their offspring's marriage plans, not because they wanted what was best for their children but because society directed that family heritage and status played a primary role in marriage, and the truth was, he was no different than Brunswick in that sense.

Those same motives had been behind his decision-making when he'd been looking for a wife. He'd almost committed himself to women he hadn't felt any real affection to because it was expected for him to marry a woman whose father had rank. In all honesty, he'd married Anita for those very same reasons.

He hadn't even met her when he'd arranged their marriage. He'd done that because it fitted his needs.

That wasn't a welcome acknowledgment, but it was true.

The other thing that was true was that Brunswick was annoyed. Angry that his niece had been chosen over his daughters. He'd hoped to gain money through marriage, and that hadn't happened.

The softening that happened in the vicinity of his heart was enough to make Myles crack a smile. He'd made the right choice. He'd found a wife who loved the country as much as he did, and animals. She had many

more endearing qualities and he would do all he could to assure she had the life she deserved.

'Thank you for your concern,' Myles said. 'But I assure you, there is nothing to worry about. Brunswick is an incompetent man who pilfered away his family's wealth and may end up in debtor's prison someday.'

'I agree,' Wilmington said. 'And your wife is nothing like he described.'

'No, she is not, nor is she anything like her uncle.' Pride filled Myles. 'Her beauty, kind nature and upstanding character puts others to shame. Which should not come as a surprise to anyone who knows Brunswick. The man rarely speaks the truth.'

'That is true, and I hope that you will not think less of me for our visit today. I felt you needed to know of the man's actions.'

The entire ton had known about his search for a wife, and now knew about his haste in marrying Anita. Many of those people he'd known his entire life, and it was of no surprise that they'd be concerned about him having any dealings with Brunswick. 'You and your family are always welcome at Redford,' he said. 'Brunswick is desperate for money and is searching for ways to find it, but this scheme isn't going to work any better than his other ones.' Myles gestured to Matthew Green, who was walking towards them. 'I believe your brother-in-law has made a decision.'

Chapter Eight

'I'm so sorry,' Anita whispered, with a hand pressed to her stomach. 'It's all my fault. I did not mean for any of it to happen, but I should have known that Roscoe would see me through the glass and start barking. It wasn't his fault or the peacocks. They are animals, simply doing what animals do.'

Upon seeing her descending the staircase, Myles had excused himself from Wilmington and Green, letting the men enter the parlour while he'd waited at the bottom of the steps for her arrival. He took a hold of her hand. 'What are you talking about? What did Roscoe and the peacocks do that has you so upset?'

She stood on the first step, making them eye to eye. 'You have not heard of the mishap?'

'No. I just came in from the stables.' He kissed her cheek. 'What happened?'

'Did you sell a horse to Mr Green?'

'I did. A filly. I'll show you which one later, because it won't be delivered to his home for a couple of days. Now, tell me what happened.'

Her gaze cast up and down the hall, before she leaned closer to him and whispered, 'After you left the parlour,

I suggested a visit to the greenhouse. Where I foolishly stood near the glass. Roscoe saw me and started barking, which made the peacocks squeal. That startled the ladies, and evidently, Lady Brockholder accidently tossed a pot in the air, covering both her and Diana in dirt.' She let out a distressed sigh. 'So much dirt.'

'Diana and her mother?' he asked.

'Yes. They are upstairs. I just checked on them. None of their clothing appears to be stained and is being brushed clean. So is their hair.'

It was not funny, for someone could have been hurt, but just the same, Myles used a single fist to hide his smile at the image forming in his mind of Lady Barbara being showered with dirt, for it seemed fitting. She hated the country as much as her daughter.

Anita didn't miss the action and gave his arm a slight slap. 'It's not funny. Someone could have been injured.'

'You are correct.' He inspected her from head to toe, concentrating on looking for dirt and not getting caught up in her beauty. 'You did not get any dirt on you?'

'No. I was near the window, and your mother was near the ivy and holly. She said she would explain the event to you and Viscount Wilmington while I was seeing to the ladies.'

He nodded, using the action as a response while he determined his options. Their options. His mother would have the retelling of the mishap under control, and the maids appeared to have everything under control upstairs, and he was just as certain others were taking care of the greenhouse; therefore, he suggested, 'Shall we go check on Roscoe and the peacocks?'

Anita's lips parted in a small O shape before pursing together as she shook her head.

'I assumed you would be worried about them,' he said. That was true, but in all honesty, he was thinking about kissing her again and would prefer a touch of privacy for that.

She drew in a breath before whispering, 'I already checked on them. Roscoe is in the kitchen and the peacocks are in the barn. Where they will all remain until our guests have departed.'

The pride, the happiness, that filled him was quite remarkable. Though he hadn't doubted it, his new duchess was certainly more capable than she imagined. 'Well, then, my dear, you have everything under control. There is only one thing left to do.'

'What is that?'

He took a step back and continued to hold her hand as she stepped off the stair, then lifted her hand and kissed the back of it. 'For me to thank you for handling the mishap so proficiently.' No longer concerned about privacy, he pulled her closer to kiss her lips, and took his time in doing so.

Anita had never been so relieved to see a carriage depart in her life. She was certain that both Diana and her mother were relieved to be leaving, too. Neither woman had looked worse for wear when they'd come down from upstairs, thankfully, but Anita could only imagine the tales that they would tell about their visit to Redford. Her mind had conjured up all sorts of versions of what happened. From past experience, she knew how easily things could be turned around and how easily people

found someone to blame. Namely her. Barely a thing had gone wrong at Brunswick that hadn't been blamed on her, but this time, it truly had been her fault.

If she hadn't suggested a tour of the greenhouse, and if she hadn't chosen to stand near the glass, and if she hadn't encouraged the animals to befriend her by offering them treats, none of this would have happened. If word of what happened spread, all of London would believe she was incompetent at being the Duchess of Redford.

Although, she did have to admit that Myles hadn't appeared to be upset over it at all, and the amazing kiss he'd given her at the bottom of the stairs had momentarily made her forget all about the calamity.

They had shared a smile, too, when Diana and her mother had barely said a word other than goodbye, which had sounded much more like 'good riddance.'

'Well, now, that was an eventful afternoon,' Mary said as the three of them turned to enter the house as the Brockholder carriage ambled down the driveway.

'Indeed, it was,' Myles said.

Having not had the chance, Anita touched Mary's arm. 'I am so sorry to have caused such an embarrassment.'

'You didn't cause it,' Mary said, patting her hand. 'You handled the situation with poise and grace. Thank goodness you were there. I was working so hard to hide my laughter that I couldn't even speak. I'm going to be laughing about it for weeks.'

Anita was taken aback by that reply.

'I was so proud of you,' Mary continued as they walked inside. 'Of how perfectly you took care of everything. I still am proud of you.'

'I am, too,' Myles said, taking a hold of her hand.

Anita felt a sense of something unfamiliar. No one had ever said they were proud of her before.

'She's a lot like you, Myles,' Mary said. 'She sees a problem and takes care of it.'

Anita shook her head, because she wasn't like him. Not at all. But she did like the idea that he was proud of her.

He was looking at her as they followed Mary into the drawing room and smiling.

'Oh dear,' Mary said as she sat down in a chair. 'Can you imagine how hard your father would have been laughing right now? He would have been chuckling about Barbara Brockholder being covered in dirt for days.'

'He would have,' Myles said.

The conversation turned to memories of Michael, his father, and Anita was glad to put the dirt episode behind them. She enjoyed hearing the stories they shared, but her mind kept going back to what Mary had said about Myles seeing a problem and fixing it.

That thought remained with her in the days that followed. Wonderful days, where Myles joined her and Roscoe, and the peacocks, on her daily walks. Those walks extended to include the stables so she could check on the kittens and the horses. She'd learned the horses' names in many of the stables, and she learned their personalities. Knew which ones appreciated a carrot and which ones just wanted to be petted. The foaling stable was her favourite, but a close second favourite was the one farthest from the house, which was where the horses were being trained to race.

They were sleek and lean, and watching them run was amazing. All of the animals were amazing, and day by day, she was feeling more at home. She'd also discovered there was more she could do for Myles in his office. She'd organised his desk and cabinets, which he seemed to appreciate.

This was her home now, and Myles was her husband, although it still didn't feel that way. They still slept in separate bedrooms, and despite kisses, too many for her to count, there hadn't been another long bout of kissing like they'd had in the stable the day the Brockholders had visited.

She'd read another book, a romance novel, hoping to discover a way to make him ask if she was interested in sharing his bed, but none of them worked. They'd only been little things. Like touching his hand while batting her eyelashes, which only made her eyes water, and bringing him something to drink while he was working, and having the cook make his favourite desserts. He seemed to appreciate all that, but all it did for her was make her wonder how much time he'd meant when he's said that they would take time to get to know each other. Get used to the idea of being married.

The once unusual urging to want more than single kisses had become very familiar and left her with an ache that often made her hold her breath while waiting for the ache to ease. It truly never went away.

She wondered if all that was because she'd become much more familiar with him. It was so easy to be around him, to talk with him and to laugh. There was always something amusing. The animals, the teasing and joking between family members, which she was now a

part of, or a memory that someone would bring up, and the entire family would join in to tell her more about it. Her favourites were about Myles.

The only memories that made her cringe inwardly were the ones about Christmas. Christina and Maria were very excited about being old enough to attend the Christmas Ball.

Their dresses had arrived this morning, along with hers, and Mr Wainwright had also delivered yet another pair of shoes. Once again, made of soft leather, his special design fit her feet perfectly, and this pair he'd dyed dark green to match her dress.

It was odd how, at times, she nearly forgot about her foot and her hip. Nothing hurt like it used to, but it hadn't changed. She still walked with a sway and a limp, and her foot was still ugly. All of that made her think about Myles. She'd told him about the velvet slippers being too slippery, and he'd found a way to fix that by requesting a visit from the cobbler. She was very grateful for that but couldn't help but wonder if he was also wondering how to fix her. There wasn't a fix for her foot. A fix for her.

A knock on her bedroom door had her responding, 'Come in.' She closed the door on the wardrobe where the new shoes sat beneath the green gown that she would wear to the Christmas Ball and turned about.

'Excuse me, Your Grace,' Charles said upon opening the door. 'His Grace would like to see you in his library.'

She couldn't stop a frown that formed. Usually, Myles just found her wherever she was if he had something to ask her. 'Very well, thank you, Charles.'

Concerned and, as she had been nearly every day,

grateful for the shoes that allowed her to hurry, she made her way to the first floor.

Knocking with one hand, she turned the knob with the other and was already entering when he verbally granted entrance.

He laughed while rising from his chair. 'That was fast.'

She closed the door behind her. 'You wanted to see me?'

'Yes, I wasn't sure if you were still busy trying on your new dresses,' he said, walking towards her.

Her heart had taken to thudding so loudly it echoed in her ears when he looked at her like he was right now. The sparkle in his eyes was making it difficult for her to recall that several dresses had been delivered, along with her ball gown, more than she'd owned in her life. 'I tried them on this morning, before the seamstress left, and thank you for them. They're lovely.'

His hands started on her upper arms and slid all the way down to her hands, making her breath catch and a significant desire come alive.

'You are very welcome.' He gave her a short, soft kiss. 'I received a message from London, and there are some things that I need to go take care of. It will take a few days.'

Messengers arrived almost daily with packages of paperwork for the banking and other businesses he oversaw. When he'd been unable to find a specific letter one day last week, she'd helped locate it. That's when she had offered to organise his cluttered desk and drawers and shelves. She'd enjoyed having tasks to complete and had been amazed by the number of businesses that he did oversee.

She knew how busy he was every day, so she shouldn't be surprised that he'd have to go to London, yet felt uneasy about him not being here. Which was something she would have to get over, because he'd made it clear in the beginning that he needed to be free to focus on his duties. 'When will you leave?'

'This afternoon. I've set up a meeting for first thing in the morning.' He released one of her hands and used his free hand to run a knuckle over her cheek. 'Would you like to go with me?'

Her first impulse was to say yes, but luckily, she had enough sense to remind herself that he needed to be able to focus on his duties. Her second impulse was to ask him if he wanted her to go with him. There again, she was able to remind herself why she couldn't say yes. She bit down on her bottom lip, telling herself that she knew what she needed to say. 'I probably should stay here.'

He released her hand and took a step back. 'I understand. I'll be gone four or five days, and then we'll all travel to London the following week.'

She wanted to take his hand, tell him—what?—that she did want to go with him? That she was petrified of going to London for the Christmas Ball. There would be dancing there, and she couldn't dance. Would it disappoint him to see others twirling to the music? The idea of disappointing him in any way twisted her heart into a knot.

'It's all right,' he said. 'I'll be so busy that you'd just be at the London house alone all the time.'

She could live with that but had already said no. Holding in a sigh, wondering if she'd made the wrong choice this time, she asked, 'Is there anything I could do

while you're gone? With tasks here?' Knowing the stablemen gave him reports on every thoroughbred horse, she suggested, 'I could record the reports on the horses in your ledgers and the feed reports and any post deliveries and—'

'Yes,' he said, stopping her, 'that would all be very helpful.'

She clapped her hands together as happiness burst inside her. 'Wonderful. Thank you.'

Chuckling, he shook his head. 'Had I known making notes in ledgers would make you so happy, I would have asked you to do it before now.'

'I like doing things for you.' It made her feel needed, like she was part of the family, and that was something she hadn't had in a very long time. She owed all that to him. The desires that lived inside her were so strong she couldn't stop herself from stretching on her toes and kissing his cheek. 'I'll miss you.'

'I'll miss you, too,' he whispered before his lips captured hers.

As Myles climbed into the carriage for his trip to London, the disappointment filling him was confounding. He had exactly what he'd wanted. A wife who didn't mind staying home in the country with the animals while he focused on his duties, yet he had truly hoped that she'd want to go to London with him.

He'd been hoping for more than that. Never in his life had he imagined that he could want someone as much as he wanted his wife. Their kissing and caressing was wonderful and was pushing him to the brink. There had been so many times that he'd wanted to ask her to join

him in his bedroom. Even though he believed that she'd agree, something was holding him back.

That something was guilt. She was working so hard at pleasing him. Every day she did things for him. Little things, nice things, and he appreciated all of them, but those acts made him realise that he didn't want her saying yes to joining him in the bedroom just to please him.

He wanted her to join him because it was what *she* wanted.

He'd thought rescuing her from her uncle would be enough for her to be happy, but he'd truly only been thinking of himself. Of what he needed and not what she needed. Or wanted. Or deserved.

She deserved to be loved, cherished beyond all else. The very things he could never give her.

Pulling back the heavy curtain, he looked at the house, at the porch where she stood. The taste of her goodbye kiss was still on his lips, and he pressed two fingers to them at how they tingled. She saw that and touched her own lips, then blew him a kiss before waving.

His chest constricted as he waved back, then let the curtain fall back into place. Letting out a sigh, he accepted that he didn't know how to fix this.

He couldn't just all of a sudden decide to love someone—her. That didn't fit within his plan, nor did he have time for it. Love was a distraction that he couldn't afford.

Both he and Wesley had been dedicated to making Redford Stables work, but starting it hadn't been easy. Their father had said it was because they were getting distracted, that a house was built one board at a time, one nail at a time. He'd encouraged them to focus on one

thing that needed to be done and how they were going to do it, then move on to the next and the next.

That was what they'd done, and it had worked, was still working, and now he needed to hold up the venture here at home while Wesley went to America. That's why he'd wanted the whole marriage thing behind him, so that one task was completed, and he could dedicate his time to the next.

Why, then, wasn't it that easy?

Chapter Nine

'You've been in London for two days, and I feel as if I've been talking to myself that entire time.'

Sitting behind the desk in the study of the London house, Myles didn't lift his head. 'You've never been one to hold your silence.'

Wesley stood and crossed the room to refill his glass.

Glancing back down at the paper he'd been writing on, Myles used his left hand to cover where he'd written Anita's name. His mind had been distracted, but he had been engaged in all of his duties, including listening to Wesley, because he wanted these tasks over with so he could get back home. 'I agree. He will make a good addition. We need someone here in London to continue engaging prospective buyers as you've been doing.'

Returning to his seat, Wesley rested one ankle on his opposite knee. 'What's his name?'

Myles laid the pen in his right hand on top of the paper but kept his left hand in place. 'Jonus. Jonus Hawthorn. You've been friends with him for years. He's been out to Redford more times than I can count, but most importantly, he's well known in the racing circles and knows his horseflesh.'

Wesley nodded. 'I was just making sure you had been listening.'

Myles wasn't surprised that Wesley had caught on to his inattentiveness and knew it wasn't doing him any good. The more he thought about Anita, the more he was distracted, and convinced that he'd done her wrong. 'I also agree with your choices of horses,' he said, pushing other thoughts aside. 'Those three are ready for the track. I'm just wondering if three is enough.'

'I could only secure three stalls on the ship,' Wesley replied. 'Carl and I agree that three are enough. The horses are highly strung, especially Prince. It's hard to say how well they'll adjust to travelling on the water.'

'That's true,' Myles said. 'Carl is an excellent groom. I'll miss having him at Redford.'

'His excellence is exactly why he's the groom I chose.' Wesley chuckled. 'And he asked me to choose him years ago, when we first discussed taking horses to America.'

'I know. I wasn't sure if you'd changed your mind.'

'More like you were hoping.'

Myles nodded. 'Perhaps.'

'One groom isn't going to be missed at Redford.'

That was true, but he wasn't thinking about the grooms or the trainers or the stablemen at Redford. He was thinking about Anita and how excited she'd been to help him by recording the reports from each of the stables. He missed her and wondered what she'd think about the necklace he'd commissioned to be designed for her. He was sure she'd like it. She loved horses. She loved animals.

Wesley set his empty glass on the desk. 'Does this

have something to do with Wilmington's visit to Redford?'

Myles lifted his head, squared his shoulders as every muscle went stiff. 'What are they saying?' Diana and her mother only had themselves to blame for getting covered in dirt. If they were saying one disparaging word about Anita, they would hear from him.

'Easy there, big brother,' Wesley said. 'Wilmington's saying that Anita is beautiful, that the two of you are happy, and that no one should listen to Brunswick's tales.'

Myles felt the tension easing from his shoulders.

Wesley went on to say, 'Diana has stated that she caught the two of you kissing like every woman wants to be kissed.'

The tension didn't return. Instead, Myles wondered if that was true. If Anita wanted the deep, long kisses they'd shared in the stable that day rather than the soft, undemanding ones he'd given her since then. He wanted those long, heated ones but hadn't wanted to push her too far too fast.

'Did she catch the two of you kissing?' Wesley asked.

Myles replied with his own question. 'Does anyone in the ton have anything else to talk about apart from my life?'

'Yes, but everything else is quite boring.' Wesley wiggled a brow. 'Did she catch you?'

Myles huffed out his answer, 'We are married.'

With a raised brown, Wesley asked, 'So your plan is working well, then?'

Myles was ready to defend his marriage, but this was Wesley, and his brother would see through his justifica-

tions as easily as he himself did. Letting out a suffocating sigh, he said, 'I may have made a mistake.'

'Is that why you keep writing her name over and over?'

Myles lifted his hand off the paper and used it to rub his forehead. 'She is so much more than I expected and deserves so much more than...'

'Than what?' Wesley asked.

Myles stood. 'Than I can give her.' He walked over to pour himself a glass of brandy.

'I'm not following you,' Wesley said. 'What can't you give her?'

Myles emptied his glass in one swallow and considered refilling it. He also considered leaving the room, but neither of those options would help him figure out what to do. Neither had thinking about it non-stop. 'She's been mistreated her entire life, and I can't do that to her.'

Wesley twisted in his chair to look at him. 'You? You've never mistreated anyone, anything, in your entire life, other than me at times, when we were younger and would fight.'

Myles shook his head but then nodded, because it was true. The two of them had fought plenty when they were younger, and being older and bigger and stronger, he'd always been the winner. Huffing out a breath, he said, 'I would never physically mistreat her, but she deserves someone to... Well, to put her first. Above all else. I can't do that. I have commitments. Duties.' He shook his head. 'I've never felt guilty coming to London for work before, but I do right now.'

'So this is about you, not her,' Wesley said.

'No, it's about her. About what I can't give her.'

'Then find a way to give it to her,' Wesley said. 'What-

ever it is, find a way. You're good at solving problems. Furthermore, what's your other option? You can't break this engagement, you're already married.'

Myles knew that, and he knew that he didn't want Anita trapped in a loveless marriage. She'd been trapped in a life without love for too long already. So, what was he going to do about that? He had to fix it.

'I have a meeting.' Wesley rose to his feet and walked towards the door. 'But I am wondering if you've asked her if she wants to be put before everything else or if you are just assuming that because that's what other women want.' He stopped at the doorway to add, 'From what I've seen, she's not like the others. But you know her better than me. I'll see you later.'

Myles stared at the empty glass in his hand. Could it be that simple? Did he simply need to ask her what she wanted?

Anita had never felt the level of excitement that was pumping through her this morning as she found her seat at the breakfast table. It had only been four days, but she'd missed Myles like he'd been gone for years. The message he'd sent yesterday said that he'd be home this evening, and she couldn't wait to see his face. To see all of him. To talk with him, laugh with him, walk with him. To know he was sleeping in the room beside hers.

She'd visited every stable, every day, and made meticulous notes in his ledgers, as well as neatly arranged the mail that had arrived for him by date, and she'd made sure all of his fountain pens were full of ink.

'Good morning, dear,' Mary said, and paused long enough to place a small kiss on Anita's cheek.

'Good morning,' Anita replied.

'Excited?' Mary asked while sitting down.

Anita swallowed at the heat that filled her cheeks.

'Oh, darling,' Mary said, waving a hand. 'Missing your husband is nothing to be embarrassed about, nor is being excited that he'll be home this evening.'

Anita busied herself by spreading jam on a slice of toasted bread. 'I do hope he's had a good trip.'

'I'm sure he has,' Mary said. 'Just as I'm sure he wants all his business completed before we go to London for the ball.' Using her fork, she gestured to the empty seats. 'I'm also sure the girls are still sleeping, because they've been up half the night packing for London.'

'They were very excited to hear that you are leaving tomorrow instead of next week.'

'First balls are very exciting, although they can become boring rather quickly, so I hope the girls aren't overly disappointed. The Arlingtons are wonderful hosts, and one of the few who invite younger girls to their balls. It's something they all wait for. By going to London early, the girls will have time to get reacquainted with a few other girls their age who will also be attending, and hopefully that will help it become all that they are dreaming about.'

The love this family had for each other would never fail to amaze Anita. It was like she was living in a different world. One she was still attempting to get used to. The Christmas Ball had been the topic of conversation for weeks, and though she'd been included in those conversations, she hadn't admitted to never having been to a ball herself. That was something a duchess should

have done from an early age, and she was still attempting to figure out what she could do about that.

'Besides,' Mary said. 'I should have considered the option before. You and Myles deserve some time alone.'

Anita's face grew warm again.

'When Michael and I were first married, we lived in the London house and his parents lived here at Redford.' Mary took a sip of tea and let out a long sigh. 'Relationships can feel so uncertain in the beginning. It takes time to get used to living with someone. Takes time to get to know them.'

'Yes, it does,' Anita agreed.

Mary reached over and laid a hand on Anita's arm. 'Sometimes we don't realise how much we care for someone until they are absent.'

Anita truly didn't know what to say.

'I must be honest with you, dear,' Mary said. 'I was concerned when Myles told me about your fast marriage, especially after two broken engagements. Of which I let out great sighs of relief after each. He may be a duke and the head of this family, but he will always be my son, and I will always worry about him.'

'Of course you will,' Anita replied. 'And you had every right to be concerned.'

'Until you arrived.' Mary's smile grew. 'When I saw you drive that coach up to the house, I rejoiced and sent up gratitude for my prayers being answered. I knew at that moment, before I'd even met you, that my son was marrying a woman who could be his match.'

Why did everyone think she was someone she wasn't all because of one coach ride? 'That woman was scared for the life of her employee,' Anita said, even as what

Myles had said echoed in the back of her mind. The confidence was in her. She just had to use it.

'Rightfully so, without you, Joshua may not have lived. Can you imagine what would have happened if Miss Diana Brockholder's coachman fell in the river? She would never have done what you did. You see, it's when we are scared that our true selves come out, because we are fighting. Fighting for something we want. But I don't have to tell you that, you've had to fight your entire life.'

Anita's throat had grown thick. Though she'd never spoken of her past life with anyone other than Myles, it wasn't a surprise to know that they all knew. Had known from the beginning.

'My son is a stubborn man,' Mary said. 'I know. I raised him. Don't be afraid to fight him. To fight for what you want. Lord knows that I fought his father, and it made our marriage, our love, stronger.'

Mary's hand was still on her arm, and her fingers wrapped tighter around it. Anita almost choked trying to swallow. She couldn't tell Mary that Myles didn't want love in their marriage. And that she didn't even know what love was. What it felt like. Or what it meant. She'd been too young when her parents had died to remember any of that. Although, she had remembered more wonderful memories since coming here, and she loved those memories. A tiny shiver coiled around her spine, making her wonder if what she was feeling for Myles was going in that direction. In the direction of love. She'd certainly never had such strong feelings for anyone else.

'I've seen you blossom since you arrived here,' Mary said. 'Seen the light come into your eyes, the shine on

your face. It's been like watching a flower opening up in May.'

Anita had to admit that life here had made her feel safe, secure, comfortable in ways she never had before, and that could all be attributed to Myles, but none of that was love.

'You aren't the only one who I've seen changes in,' Mary said. 'Myles has always claimed to know what he wants, even though I've told him that sometimes we don't know what we want until we find it.'

Anita looked down at her plate, trying to make sense of what Mary meant. Myles hadn't wanted a wife.

'Oh, I guess the girls aren't still sleeping,' Mary said, referring to the giggling filtering in from the corridor. Before removing her hand from Anita's arm, she whispered, 'Everyone deserves to feel the power of true love. It's worth whatever it takes to get there.' Then Mary turned her attention to the doorway. 'Well, good morning, girls.'

Anita's attention was on the sinking inside her. Myles would never feel the power of true love married to her.

Long after breakfast, the conversation with Mary was still replaying itself in Anita's head. Myles had married her because he didn't want love. He hadn't wanted a wife. He'd *needed* a wife.

She lifted her head, looked at the sky overhead. 'Not being married had been a problem for him and he solved it. Just like Mary said. My boots were a problem and he fixed that, too.'

Roscoe let out a bark, and she looked down at him. 'I wasn't talking to you, but thank you for listening.'

The dog barked again and one of the peacocks behind them let out a scream. She laughed. As crazy as it seemed, she loved those silly birds with their ear-piercing screams. She loved everything about Redford.

Arriving at the stable door, she told her furry and feathered companions, 'You wait out here. I won't be long.'

Snorting and stomping and whinnies met her as she stepped inside the stable. Mr Gorman, the main groom for the foaling stable, was in the centre aisle. The concerned look on his normally friendly face made her heart race. 'What's the matter? Was it the peacocks?'

'No, Your Grace.' He shrugged his shoulder and lifted his hands. 'I don't know what it is. They've been nervous all morning. There's nothing in here out of the ordinary. Not even a bird. I've checked every stall and there's nothing. The mother cat and kittens are all in the tack room.'

Anita stretched out an arm to stroke the nose of one of the horses, but it threw its head back, away from her touch, which was abnormal. 'Something is wrong.'

'I know. It's odd for all of them to act like this. I've never seen it before.'

Knowing something had to be done, but not sure what, she suggested, 'Let's look again, everywhere, or maybe we should put them out in the corral.'

'That's exactly what I was getting ready to do,' Mr Gorman said. 'Once they are outside, I'll take another look around.'

'I'll help release them,' she said.

'I can do it, Your Grace. There's no need for you to trouble yourself.'

'With two of us, we'll get them out faster.' There were two doors leading out to the corral, one at each end of the stalls. 'I'll start down here. You start on that end.'

He didn't argue, and she knew it was only because of her title but truly didn't care. The horses were not acting normally, and that worried her. She opened the corral door, then walked to the first stall.

As if grateful to be led out, away from whatever had them all so nervous, as soon as Anita opened the stall, the horse walked straight to the corral door. So did the second and third ones.

The fourth one, a beautiful brown horse with a white slash down its nose, backed farther into the stall rather than walking out.

'It's all right, Dolly,' Anita whispered while wishing she'd remembered to stop in the kitchen for carrots this morning, but her mind had still been on her conversation with Mary. 'Nothing's going to hurt you.'

The horse tossed her head and stepped sideways. Anita instantly noticed something in the bedding of straw. It was small, the size of a coin, but bright red. 'Mr Gorman, come here please,' she said, keeping her voice as calm as possible.

He arrived instantly. 'What is it, Your Grace?'

'Look, there.' She pointed to the bedding. 'Is that blood?'

Quickly, he inspected the bedding and horse. 'She's spotting. The rest of them could smell it, and it made them nervous. I must have missed it when I looked in her stall.' He shook his head. 'It's too early for her to go into labour. She could lose the foal.'

'I'll get the rest of the horses outside,' Anita said.

'You take Dolly to a birthing stall so she'll have more room and seclusion. I'm sure the rest of the horses were making her nervous, too.'

'I'll get someone else to help me, Your Grace.'

'That will be fine, later. I'm here now, so let's get her to a stall and the rest outside.' Certain he would protest again, she added, 'Now, Mr Gorman.'

He gave a quick bow before sliding a rope around Dolly's neck. 'I'll be right back to help you.'

'Get her settled and comfortable,' Anita said. There were only two more horses to put outside, and they exited as easily as all the others. She then closed both corral doors before she made her way into the room that held the larger birthing stalls.

Because they wouldn't be used until next spring, there was no bedding in any of the stalls, and Mr Gorman was using a pitchfork to put fresh straw from a wheel barrel into the stall he'd put Dolly in. 'She's young,' he said. 'This is her first foal.'

'Poor girl.' Anita grabbed another pitchfork and stepped around him into the stall. Using the fork, she spread the hay he was pitching into the stall into the far corners.

She also gave him a look that said, *Don't protest. It won't do any good.*

Dolly already appeared calmer, most likely because the other mares weren't making her nervous with their stomping and snorting. Over the past few weeks, Anita had read several of the books in the library about horses and more than one section about breeding and giving birth had explained that miscarriages were not uncom-

mon. 'Wouldn't a miscarriage normally happen earlier than this?'

'Yes,' Mr Gorman replied. 'Long before now. In the early weeks. I'll have Mr Walsh examine her. He handles all the foaling.'

'You go and find him, I'll finish this,' she said.

'I couldn't, Your Grace,' he said.

'Yes, you can, and you will.'

Apprehension wasn't just in his eyes. It took up his entire face.

'My apologies, Mr Gorman, but now is not the time to worry about what is or isn't appropriate. We need to have Dolly examined, and the sooner the better. Now, please, go and find Mr Walsh.'

'Yes, Your Grace.' He set aside his pitchfork and raced out of the room.

Anita finished spreading out the straw, then put away the pitchforks and the wheelbarrow before re-entering the stall. Dolly nudged her with her nose, and Anita wrapped an arm around the horse's neck. Pressing their cheeks together, she said, 'Everything is going to be fine, Dolly. This is the best stable in all of England, maybe in all the world. I've seen other stables, and if I was a horse, this is where I'd want to be.'

She went on, talking low and slow, telling the horse that Redford was a nice place to live at for a person, too, and serval other things, until she heard a door close.

Mr Gorman was back but alone. 'I sent someone to get Mr Walsh, Your Grace, and please, you should step out of there.'

'She's calm now,' Anita replied. 'I think I'll wait here until Mr Walsh arrives.'

'But—' He stopped talking at the sound of another door closing.

'That must be Mr Walsh,' she said.

Mr Gorman shook his head, and a moment later, Myles walked into the room.

Her heart leaped with joy inside her chest, and she opened her mouth to say hello, but she didn't get a chance.

Myles was too distracted by what she was doing in the stall. He shouted a warning that she could trip, fall, get trampled on if the mare spooks, at the top of his lungs while rushing into the stall and grabbing her around the waist.

She'd never seen him acting so irate. 'Myles, stop! You're going to make Dolly nervous again.'

'Nervous?'

'Yes!' She batted at his hands as he carried her out of the stall. 'Put me down!'

'No, with all that straw, you could trip!'

'I can trip when there's nothing in my way!' she shouted her thoughts aloud. 'Now put me down!'

He didn't. He not only carried her out of the stall but out of the room, while grumbling aloud about how he'd never expected a groom of his to be so careless.

He was holding her by the waist, flush against him.

'It wasn't Mr Gorman's fault!' Using her good foot, she kicked out, catching him on the shin, which hurt her toe more than it hurt him, no doubt, because it didn't slow his steps at all. 'Put me down right now!'

'I'll put you down when we are outside, where the dog and peacocks are waiting for you! That's where you should be, not inside a stall with a horse that weighs ten times more than you do!'

At that moment, one thing that Mary had said this morning stuck in her mind. *Don't be afraid to fight him.*

She wasn't afraid. She was furious.

As soon as they were outside, she shoved against his chest, hard, with both hands. 'Put me down!'

He lowered her until her feet were firmly on the ground but didn't release his hold on her waist. 'What were you think—'

'Stop right there, Myles Wadsworth! I don't care if you are a duke or not, you have no reason to blame to Mr Gorman for anything!'

'Yes, I do! With your foot and all that straw—'

'My foot!' She'd never been so mad in her life and shoved his arms, forcing him to release her waist as she stepped backwards. 'It's my foot! And I've walked on straw my entire life!' The idea that she—that her foot—had caused problems for the groom, who had been following her orders, was tearing her up inside. Putting another step between them, she continued, 'And you know what else about my foot? You can't fix it! It's not a problem for you to solve! That's what you do! You see a problem and you want to fix it. Well, I can't be fixed! Never!'

'I never tried to fix your foot! I never said it was a problem!'

'Oh, so you called in the cobbler for no reason?'

'I summoned him because I didn't want to see you in pain!'

She did know that, but she was so angry her mind didn't want to work. Or maybe it was him. He just overwhelmed her at times. Not only his kindness and concern, but him. All of him. She shook her head and said

the first thing that came to mind. 'Without the pain, I don't know who I am!' That was true. So very true. Without the constant pain to think about, she'd started thinking about other things. Him. And being married and a duchess and…love. Tears were stinging her eyes, which made her madder. She never cried. Never. She couldn't cry. But she was. 'The only thing I do know, is that I don't like you very much right now!'

Spinning about, she started for the house.

'Anita! Wait!'

One of the peacocks let out a scream and she screamed back at the bird, 'Tell him to leave me alone! Just leave me alone!'

Chapter Ten

Myles told the squawking, fanned-out peacock to shut up, but it didn't listen. Just squawked louder. He pinched his temples with one hand, not because of the bird, but because he was trying to make sense of all that had just happened.

He'd seen Roscoe and the peacocks waiting at the stable door as soon as he'd stepped out of the coach and had known that's where he'd find her. Inside the stable.

But not in a stall. His heart had dropped to his ankles at the idea of her falling in that enclosed space and getting stepped on. Getting hurt. He'd never lost his temper as fast as he had at that moment. He'd never feared something so much.

He'd never said that her foot was a problem, either, or that it needed to be fixed. There was nothing about her that needed to be fixed.

A shiver raced over his shoulders. Was she right? Is that how he'd seen it?

It was his responsibility to solve all the problems for his family, for his businesses, for his life.

He let out a curse. That was how she'd seen it.

That was exactly how she'd seen it.

He felt sick to his stomach.

She was at the house, rushing in the back door, and he took a step to follow, but the peacock fanned out again and squawked, as if saying it wouldn't let him pass. The bird was probably right. He should give her a moment to calm down before he tried to explain that finding her in a foaling stall had made his heart stop. The memory of it practically did the same thing, until the image in his mind made him pause.

Why had she been in a foaling stall?

He twisted about, stared at the stable for a moment.

That made no sense. He'd take the time to find out, then he'd go talk to her. Explain the dangers had little to do with her foot. Anyone could trip on hay.

Mr Walsh was in the foaling pen when Myles arrived, and Mr Gorman quickly described what had happened, showing extreme distress while explaining that he couldn't disobey the Duchess.

Myles had felt like a heel before and felt even lower after hearing the entire story. He apologised for his behaviour and questioned the horse's condition, because he knew Anita would want to know.

Mr Walsh's examination found no signs of labour, but the man insisted that the horse remain separated from the other horses to keep her calm and said that he'd remain with her, watching for any changes.

Myles requested updates be sent to the house and left the stable intent upon finding Anita.

His mother met him at the back door. 'Hello,' she greeted, 'we didn't expect you until this evening.'

Not about to explain to anyone how he'd kept others working until late last night so he could leave this

morning, he said, 'I finished early.' Taking a step to walk around her, he said, 'Excuse me.'

She stepped at the same time, blocking his path. 'No.'

He stepped the other direction, and so did she.

'No, I won't excuse you,' she said. 'I don't know what happened out there, but you need to let Anita be. She doesn't want to see you right now.'

'I need to see her.'

'To further upset her?'

Frustrated, he grasped his mother's upper arms, lifted her, and set her down out of his pathway. 'No, to explain what happened.'

'If you think that's what she needs right now, you're a bigger fool than I ever thought.'

Shaking his head, he walked past her.

'Sometimes, jumping in doesn't solve the problem,' she said. 'Because sometimes all that is needed is a little time, and things will work themselves out.'

He stopped and closed his eyes as he shook his head while everything about him dropped even lower. He'd never regretted something as much as he did right now.

'Why don't you go to your office,' his mother continued, 'and look at the notations she made in your ledgers and the notes she left for you? She was very happy to be helping while you were gone.'

He pivoted to face her. 'Mother, I respect you, but this is between Anita and me.'

'I respect that and would like to remind you that I was married to a man much like you for almost thirty years and learned a few things over the years. There are times when a woman needs to be left alone.'

She hadn't interfered in his actions so boldly since

he'd been young, but he still had to talk to Anita. Therefore, he turned and walked towards the back stairway.

He stopped before stepping onto the first stair and drew in a deep breath. His mother did know much more about women and marriage than he did, and he'd never been one to overlook knowledge and experience. Against what he considered his own better judgement, he walked past the stairway and along the corridor that would eventually allow him to arrive at his office.

There he reviewed his ledgers. Read every notation Anita had made with neat, perfect penmanship that was much easier to read than his hastily written entries. He also read notes she'd left atop piles of mail, sorted by the dates they had arrived. She'd also left him notes about other things that had happened in his absence. Nothing major, but things he appreciated knowing, like how one of the racehorses beat its own best time.

He leaned back in his chair and stared at the desk that used to be cluttered but was now neat and tidy. So were the desk drawers, the shelves and the cabinets.

People kept telling him he was a problem-solver. That was a part of his duties, but he sure couldn't solve the one that was plaguing him now and had been the entire time he'd been in London.

They were married and would remain married. Not because of society or rules or anything else, because he truly didn't care about any—

He stood up and paced the floor. Her. He cared more about Anita than anyone else. He wanted to take care of her. Provide her with everything she needed for a good life. Provide her with other things, too. Little things she

might like, such as the gift he'd ordered for her while in London.

Caring for someone wasn't the same as loving them, but maybe he could make sure she was happy in every other way. She had agreed to marry him knowing love didn't play a part in their marriage. Maybe he was the only one who had determined that was a problem. Whereas it truly wasn't.

Could that be true? Could he be jumping to conclusions that weren't there?

Could his mother be right, that sometimes things just needed time to work themselves out?

That was possible, but right now, he still felt the overwhelming need to speak to Anita, to let her know that he'd never wanted to fix her. He would take Wesley's advice, too, and ask her what she wanted.

He left the library, and upon arriving upstairs, saw a single person outside of Anita's bedroom door. It was Olive, who rose from the chair as he approached.

'Is the Duchess in her room?' he asked.

'Yes, Your Grace.' The woman lifted her bowed head to meet his gaze. 'She cried herself to sleep. Perhaps it would be best if you let her rest.'

He couldn't stop the gut-wrenching sigh that escaped.

'She never cries,' Olive said. 'In all the time I've known her, no matter what someone said to her or did to her, she never cried. She just—' shaking her head, Olive looked down at the floor '—took it and never cried.'

He hadn't thought he could sink any lower, but he did, and he'd rather have taken fifty lashes than being the one who had made her cry. 'You can leave, Olive. I won't disturb her.'

'Thank you, Your Grace, but I will remain in case she needs anything.'

'Where is her maid?' he asked but immediately shook his head. 'Never mind.' The younger Claire would have been afraid to face him, to block him from entering Anita's room, whereas the older Olive had been willing to put her position on the line for her duchess.

He walked down the corridor to his room and entered. Removing his coat, he tossed it on a chair and remembered the excitement that had been bold and bright inside him this morning when he'd put on the coat in London. He'd been looking forward to coming home, to seeing her.

Not one to ever go back on his word, he struggled with his impulse, but it was too strong to overcome and he walked to his bedroom, past the bed to the door to her room. His hand balled into a fist as it reached for the knob. Would it be locked?

There was only one way to find out.

A flutter of relief washed over him as he turned the knob, then slowly, quietly, opened the door, and a wave of something he couldn't explain filled his chest as his gaze landed on her.

She was lying on her bed, on her side, facing his door, with her head on the pillow and eyes closed. Her slow, even breathing said she was asleep. A single blanket covered her.

Roscoe was on the bed, too, lying with his head on her thigh. The dog opened his eyes and looked at Myles with such sadness that he felt his shoulders droop.

His gaze went back to her face as he quietly pulled the door closed. He waited until he heard the latch click,

then he rested his forehead against the door. There was nothing about her that needed to be fixed, and it pained him to think that she'd thought that was what he'd been trying to do.

Pained him in a way he'd never known.

'Thank you, Claire,' Anita said, glancing at herself in the mirror. The maid had repaired her hair, which had been messed from her nap. Her dress had been wrinkled as well, and her face had been puffy when she'd awoken, but a cool cloth had helped with that.

She'd been right about crying. Once she'd started, she hadn't been able to stop, but she'd felt empty upon waking up. Or maybe cleansed.

Her thoughts had certainly been clearer than ever before. She knew what she had to do. Myles hadn't been trying to fix her. That was up to her, and she had to know if there was even a chance of that happening. Myles had said he'd talked to the doctor in London who had examined her as a child. It was time she talked to that doctor.

Twisting in her chair, she said, 'I've decided to go to London with the Dowager Duchess and the girls tomorrow. Would you mind packing a trunk for me?'

'Of course,' Claire replied.

'Thank you.' Drawing in a deep breath, Anita stood and took a final glance at herself in the mirror. She was not the same woman who had arrived here. Maybe it was more accurate to say the woman she used to be she'd left at Brunswick and had arrived as someone else.

The transformation had continued during her stay here. Not only had her looks changed, with the help of Claire, and her limp wasn't as noticeable, thanks to

Myles and Mr Wainwright, she'd changed on the inside, too. It was odd that what she'd always considered to be a strength had indeed been a weakness. The will she'd prided herself on for forcing herself to forge forward despite obstacles had actually been a crutch.

She'd never stood up for herself. Instead, she'd accepted what was thrown at her without question. Without objection.

The question she had to ask herself was what she would do now that she understood that? Now that she knew she could stand up for herself.

The other question screaming in the back of her mind was if she was truly brave enough to fight for what she wanted.

Twisting the ring on her finger, she determined that she had to be. It would take confidence, and it was bit frightening.

More than a bit.

Drawing in another deep breath, she held it until it burned inside her, then let it out and walked to the door. This wasn't going to be easy, might not even be possible, but if it was, it would be worth it.

She was wearing one of her new dresses. A soft rose-coloured gown with a neckline that was much lower than she was used to, but the seamstress had insisted that Myles would like it. The full skirt had scalloped layers that were highlighted by tiny bows, and there was another tiny bow in the centre of the neckline. That seemed to really highlight how low the neckline truly was, and it left her feeling a bit exposed.

However, it also made her feel attractive in a way she had never felt before. Probably because she'd never

thought herself attractive before coming here. Another thing she had Myles to thank for. His attention and kisses. She sighed. She'd been looking forward to his kisses and instead had yelled at him, accused him of things that she shouldn't have. He'd been nothing but wonderful since her arrival.

She proceeded down the corridor and the stairway to the front parlour, where the family had already gathered.

It took all she had to stop her gaze from lingering on Myles overly long. They needed to speak, but it could wait until after the meal. 'Forgive me,' she said, turning to Mary. 'I hope I haven't delayed dinner.'

'Not at all, dear,' Mary replied, smiling. 'Would you care for a glass of sherry?'

'Yes, please.' She took a seat in a chair near the sofa where the girls sat.

Myles provided her with a glass and clearly noticed the bow on her neckline while handing her the sherry.

Finding the ability to speak was difficult. His gaze made her breasts feel heavy and her face warm. 'Thank you,' she finally managed to say.

'I would like a moment to speak with you,' he said.

Ironically, it wasn't difficult to smile at him. 'I would appreciate that. After dinner?' She placed her free hand on her stomach. 'I fear I awoke quite hungry.' Actually, she was so nervous she wasn't looking forward to eating but was sticking to her plan of finding the confidence to do what was needed.

'Of course,' he said.

Turning her attention to Mary, Anita held her breath as she said, 'I've decided to—' she had to let the air out

'—travel to London with you tomorrow, if that wouldn't be a problem.'

'Not at all,' Mary said. 'I think that is a brilliant idea. I could introduce you to some of the extended family who were unable to attend the wedding. They'll all be at the Christmas Ball, but meeting them ahead of time would be wonderful.'

'You are going to love Aunt Tina,' Christina said. 'I'm named after her. She's Mother's oldest sister and so delightful.'

'So is Uncle Norman,' Maria said. 'He loves doing magic tricks, and they are so funny.'

The girls and their enthusiasm over the trip and the ball dominated the conversation until dinner was announced. Myles had been standing next to Anita's chair since handing her the glass of sherry and took a hold of her arm as she rose to her feet.

'You look very lovely, as always,' he said.

'Thank you,' she replied, amazed by how confident she felt. Truly confident. 'I hope your trip to London was productive.'

'It was, and now you are going there.'

'Yes, there are some things I'd like to see to.'

'Anything I can help with?'

'No, thank you.' She was doing her best to not look at him, even though she felt his eyes on her, and that made her want to at least glance his way. 'I hope you found your ledgers in order.'

'Indeed. Thank you. I appreciate your thoroughness. I'm sure you'll be happy to hear that Dolly has shown no signs of going into labour.'

'I was very relieved when Claire shared that with me.'

'Mr Walsh will remain with her and keep her separated from the other mares for a time.'

'That's good. She calmed considerably when separated from the others.'

'I heard as much.' He paused in the doorway of the dining room. 'Anita, I—'

'If you don't mind,' she interrupted. 'I think we should wait to continue this conversation until after dinner.'

'Of course.'

It wasn't easy, because the way Myles kept looking at her took her breath away, but she managed to eat a sufficient amount of the meal before the true test of her new-found confidence was but minutes away. Fear trickled down her spine as he escorted her from the room. There was no guarantee what she had to do would change anything, but she had to try. Had to take the risk.

Neither of them spoke during what seemed to be a very long walk to his library.

Once there, he clasped a hold of the hand she attempted to slide off his elbow.

'One thing was foremost on my mind when I left London this morning,' he said, 'and is still there.'

Her ability to not look at him disappeared. Biting her tongue, she lifted her gaze and felt as if parts of her were melting by the way he looked at her. Forcing herself to speak, she asked, 'What would that be?'

He cupped her chin with one hand, and his gaze roamed her face. 'Kissing you. May I?'

More melting made her knees weak. 'Yes.'

His lips met hers softly, but only momentarily, until the pressure increased. Her arms wrapped around him, because she might end up on the floor without him to

hold on to. Their lips parted, then collided together with an urgency that stole her breath. She gasped for air and felt a tiny moan rumble in the back of her throat when his tongue slipped inside her mouth.

It was like the kiss in the stable, the one she'd wanted a repeat of for what felt like years. It was utterly divine, and she pressed herself up against him as an exhilarating ache overtook her inside and out. She'd never felt so alive or so...wanted.

She could have gone on kissing him for ever and felt dizzy when his lips left hers.

His arms kept her pressed up against him as he held her in a tight hug. 'I am so sorry, Anita. There is nothing about you that needs to be fixed.' He leaned back and framed her face with both hands. 'I had no idea that is what you thought.' Shaking his head, he said, 'I didn't like knowing you were in pain. If there was something that could help with that, I wanted to find it. And I apologise about how I reacted in the stables. It scared me to see you in the stall, and I overreacted. It won't happen again.'

More than her heart was pounding, and the sensations filling her confirmed the decision she'd made after waking up today was the right one. 'I'm sorry, too,' she said. 'I shouldn't have yelled at you. Or kicked you. I've never done anything like that before and am quite appalled at myself. I know you weren't trying to fix anything, but in a way, you did. The shoes you purchased for me have helped tremendously. I rarely feel the pain that I used to, and I owe that to you. Thank you.'

'I wish that you'd never had any pain.' He kissed her forehead.

Closing her eyes to completely absorb the feeling of his lips, she smiled to herself. She used to wish she'd never had any pain, but without it, she'd never have met him. Now she had to do everything she could to be the wife he needed. He didn't need to love her. She could live without that; being his wife would still be the best life she could ever hope to have. But this wasn't about her, it was about him, and she wanted to see him happy.

'I'm sorry I made you cry,' he said, leaning back to look at her.

'I'm not. I needed to get that out of my system. I think I did for a long time.' She drew in a breath before saying, 'I also hope you don't mind that I need to go to London. There's something I have to do.'

'I don't mind. I could go with you.'

She shook her head. 'No, you have things to do here, and the ball is next week.' That still made her nervous, even more now, because it didn't give her much time. Holding up one finger, she said, 'I would like a message or two about Dolly if possible.'

'Definitely possible.' He touched her cheek. 'What do you want, Anita? From our marriage, what do you want?'

She looked at him for a long moment, then smiled. 'I want what you want.'

Myles wasn't done with regrets. Watching as the carriage rolled away, he regretted not asking Anita to join him in his bed last night. He'd struggled with the decision, because every part of him wanted her. His desire for her had already been throbbing through him, but the dress she'd worn had made him hotter than a smoking gun. He wasn't even sure why he hadn't invited her

to his room, other than her answer. She wanted what he wanted. He didn't know what that meant and hadn't wanted to ask.

He'd already coerced her into marrying him, and from now on, what happened in her life was her decision. Including joining him in his bed. He wouldn't ask that of her. He'd wait until she offered it.

She deserved that.

Letting out a long sigh, he watched until the carriage driven by Joshua, who was officially the Duchess of Redford's driver, and the second carriage, which was filled with luggage and servants, both disappeared. Then he turned about and let out a grunt. For a man who found himself too busy for a wife, he wasn't looking forward to being alone for seven days.

There was work to be done, but his will to complete it wasn't there. Probably because his mind was too focused on Anita. He hadn't asked what she needed to do in London. It did seem odd that she had anything to do there, but he'd sensed that she didn't want him to know what that was.

That made him all the more curious.

Which was no help in motivating him to focus on work.

He was at his desk that evening, doing nothing more than looking at the notes Anita had made for him while he'd been gone for the hundredth time, when the door opened.

Myles did a double take upon seeing Wesley walk into the room. 'What are you doing here?'

'When the London house became overrun with women, I decided to leave,' Wesley said, sitting down in a chair.

Myles lifted a single brow, because company had never bothered Wesley.

'Naw,' Wesley said, waving a hand and laughing. 'I'm meeting a buyer here tomorrow.'

Myles leaned back in his chair. 'I could have taken care of that.'

'I know, but it's just one more of the loose ends I want tied up before I sail to America.'

'What horse did they buy?'

Wesley shrugged. 'Pick of the litter.'

'Already trained?'

Wesley nodded.

Myles opened a drawer and pulled out the horse ledger. 'Got one who keeps breaking his own best times, and they're good times.'

Leaning forward, over the desk to look at the book, Wesley shook his head. 'That's not your handwriting.'

'Anita wrote in the ledgers for me while I was gone.'

'Interesting how you arrive home one day, and she leaves the next.'

Myles bit his back teeth together at how he was already missing her. 'She had things to do in London.'

Wesley sat back in his chair. 'You know I was shocked when you told me about your marriage to her, and I was worried, until she arrived, then I got a feeling that the two of you would make a good match. We both know I'm rarely wrong.'

Myles shook his head at his brother's conceit.

'Did you ask her what she wants?' Wesley asked.

'I did,' Myles replied, but wasn't any less confused now than he had been in London.

'And?'

Myles didn't want to elaborate on the details of his thoughts. That would be impossible, since he didn't fully understand them himself. 'She's—she's more than I expected.'

'So, there's still a problem?'

'I—' Myles stopped himself from saying there wasn't a problem and changed his answer. 'She's a very endearing person.'

'You consider that a problem?'

'Neither of us entered into this as a love match. I needed a wife, needed to get married, and she needed to be taken care of. Treated with respect and…'

'Love?'

Myles couldn't answer that aloud, but his answer was yes.

Wesley started laughing. Too hard for comfort.

Leaning back, Myles crossed his arms, waiting for his brother's bout of unjustified humour to pass.

Still laughing, Wesley slapped his thigh. 'I should say that I hate to tell you this, but I can't lie. I'm happy to be the one to say it.'

'Say what?'

'That you, big brother, have fallen in love.'

Myles shot out of his chair, crossed the room while rubbing his chin. That was impossible. He couldn't have fallen in love. He didn't feel an undeniable need to give up his dreams, to want to focus on no one but…but Anita. Smothering a curse, he pointed at Wesley. 'Is there really a buyer coming here tomorrow? Or did you just come here to torture me?'

Wesley was still laughing, but it was more of chuckle now. 'Yes, there are buyers. They'll arrive around two

tomorrow afternoon. Torturing is just a…a gift I hadn't expected.'

Myles walked to the cabinet, picked up a glass and used it to point as his brother. 'Don't you think I'd know if I was in love?' He would know. He was sure of that.

Wesley shrugged. 'Can't say. But I do know it won't happen to me. I'm the lucky one. The one who isn't required to marry and produce an heir. I'll never be expected to love anything more than our horses.'

Myles poured them each a drink, knowing he didn't feel unlucky. He wasn't. He was very lucky to have married Anita. Carrying a glass to his brother, he said, 'She said she wants what I want, which is not love. However, I am the lucky one. When I said she was more than I expected, I meant because she discovered a mare who may have had a miscarriage if not for her quick thinking and action.'

Wesley smile faded. 'Oh?'

'Yes.' He proceeded to tell Wesley about Dolly and how Gorman said Anita was the one who discovered the blood in the stall and most of the rest of the story. He left out how he'd physically removed her from the stall. However, he also pointed out his desk, ledgers and files, where things had never been so easy to find, and how she knew the horses as well as either of them.

'Well, I'll say one thing,' Wesley said with a chuckle. 'If you don't love her, I think I do.'

Chapter Eleven

'Where to now, Your Grace?' Joshua asked while holding her hand to assist her into the luxurious carriage that was parked in the driveway of the surgeon's terraced house. The very same doctor who had examined her as a child.

'Home,' Anita answered, taking a seat on the plush cushion. She couldn't even muster up a smile. Her hopes had been shattered. They had been too high, and she shouldn't have done that to herself. It had been an impossible dream, and she'd never been a dreamer. 'Thank you.' She nodded for him to close the door. Shut her inside. Alone. Where she could wallow in her pity. She'd refused to do that for years, but things had been different back then. She hadn't experienced something that she wanted.

Wanted more than anything possible.

That was the problem.

It wasn't possible. The doctor had said that nothing could be done with her foot. The injury was too old.

Joshua started to close the carriage door but then pulled it back open. 'I'm sorry, very sorry. I should have done more when you were young. I was afraid. If I'd said anything more, done anything more, I would have

lost my job, and then there wouldn't have been anyone to watch over you. The others who had been at Brunswick then couldn't tolerate it when your uncle moved in, and left.'

His words, his sorrowful expression, pushed through her own sadness. She pressed a hand over the softening of her heart. Confounded, she asked, 'That's why you stayed employed at Brunswick? Because of me?'

'Yes, Your Grace. I pulled you out of the wreckage that day, took you home and helped take care of you until your aunt and uncle moved in. A doctor examined you after the accident and said you were fine, but when you refused to walk, I begged your uncle to take you to another doctor. He refused and threatened to fire me if I asked again. After a year, when you still weren't walking, I brought you here. To Dr Potter. He'd said that he might be able to fix it, but there again, your uncle refused. I should have paid for it myself.'

'No.' She laid a hand on his arm, truly touched by his dedication. A dedication that she'd never realised had been there. 'You can't take any blame, Joshua. You did far more than I ever knew.' Her heart was aching for him. 'Please know how much I appreciate what you did. For all you have done for me over the years. I'm sorry for never realising it. I—I never knew any of that.'

'I know you didn't. I was instructed to stay away from you.' He looked over his shoulder at the house. 'And I'm sorry the surgeon couldn't help you now.'

The way her uncle had treated people over the years had angered her many times, but she'd never done anything about it. Never said anything because there had been nothing that she could do about it. But she should

have tried. Should have said something. 'I'm the one who is sorry,' she said, 'for the way you were treated.'

Pulling up a smile, wanting a way to make him feel better, she said, 'It's all right, Joshua, I was just curious if anything could be done, but it doesn't matter. The new shoes I have are wonderful. My foot rarely hurts any more.'

'Perhaps another doctor,' he said.

She shook her head. 'No, let's just go home.' Patting his arm, she said, 'But thank you, for all you've done, and for keeping this visit just between us. Your support, you being here with me, means so much to me. It's time to leave. Go home. We both have a much better life now than we ever did.'

'We do, Your Grace.' He bowed his head while stepping back, then stopped. 'Perhaps His Grace—'

'No,' she said before he could say more. 'No.' She didn't want Myles to know what she'd done. How she'd tried to fix herself after she'd accused him of trying to do that very thing.

Joshua closed the door, and she leaned back against the soft, thick velvet padding. Myles had done so much for her. Given her, and Joshua and Olive, a life that was the complete opposite of what they'd known, and she'd wanted to do something for him in return. She truly had hoped the surgeon would be able to do something so she could become a wife that he wouldn't need to worry about tripping over hay or anything else. It had been too great of a hope, and she should have realised that.

It had been a foolish idea. She just didn't ever want a repeat of their argument about her being in Dolly's stall. Never wanted her foot to be the reason someone lost their job. Though Myles hadn't said that, she had

been worried for Mr Gorman because of how employees had been treated at Brunswick.

The sinking in her stomach made her groan. Joshua had almost lost his job years ago for that very reason. Her injury had been affecting others since the day it happened.

A knock sounded on the coach door, and she pulled back the velvet curtain that had been blocking the cold December air and spied the surgeon, Dr Potter, whom she'd just seen.

'Pardon me, Your Grace,' the doctor said through the window. 'I have an idea I'd like to discuss with you. It might be of some help.' Opening the door, he continued, 'Would you mind coming back inside?'

She accepted the hand he held out but told herself to not get excited, to not expect too much. 'Certainly, thank you.'

Once again in his exam room, she sat on the chair while Dr Potter removed her shoe and sock. He twisted her foot in ways that once in a while caused a shoot of pain before he looked up at her, raising both of his bushy grey eyebrows at the same time.

She raised her brows, not to copy him, but in anticipation of what he might say. Nothing had changed in the few minutes since he'd examined her the first time.

He first scratched the shiny bald spot atop his head, then rubbed a hand over his whiskered chin. 'As I said earlier, surgery could cause more problems than it would fix, and I still wouldn't advise risking that. But with some concentrated exercises, you might gain more flexibility.' He held one hand up. 'You'll never walk on the flat of your foot, so I don't want to give false hope, but with more flexibility, especially with the support of these

specially made shoes you have, your limp, your chances of tripping, might be diminished.'

'What sort of exercises?' she asked, tamping down the hope that was attempting to renew itself.

'I need to do some research, but if I was to suggest you coming by for an hour or so, for the next few days, for me to show you some ways to move your foot to regain muscles that haven't been used in a long time, would that be of interest to you?'

He spoke so low and slow that she replied, 'Yes,' before his last word was out. 'Yes,' she repeated. 'I'm willing to try anything.'

He gave her a slight smile. 'Shall we say in the afternoon? Around two, starting tomorrow?'

'I'll be here.'

'Very well.' He replaced her sock and shoe while saying, 'Please don't expect miracles, and you'll have to continue to practise the exercises regularly.'

'I understand, and I will.' It wasn't what she'd hoped for, but she would try anything if it would ease Myles's concerns. He needed a wife who he didn't have to worry about so he could focus on his duties. She wanted to be that wife. Wanted that more than she'd ever wanted anything in her life. Not just for herself. The life he'd provided her was wonderful, and she wanted him to have one just as wonderful.

'Thank you, Dr Potter, very much.' The excitement inside her was growing, and she had to remind herself to be conscious that nothing had changed with her foot as she stood and balanced herself. 'I'll be here tomorrow at two.'

He walked to the door of his exam room. 'Alfred will see you out, and I will see you tomorrow.'

'Thank you,' she said, and smiled at the older house-man waiting in the short corridor.

'Good day, Your Grace,' Alfred said a few steps later while he opened the outside door for her.

'Good day,' she replied.

Joshua was standing on the stoop, waiting for her with expectancy looming in his eyes.

Smiling at him as they walked to the coach, she said, 'He thinks some exercises might help. I have to come back for the next few days.'

'That's wonderful news, Your Grace. Just wonderful.'

Not wanting to get his hopes up, either, she said, 'It might not help, but it's worth a try.'

'Indeed, Your Grace, indeed.'

Her heart felt lighter when he closed the door of the carriage this time. For a moment. Then another sensa-tion made her stomach flip. She'd never kept secrets, and that's what this was. It would have to remain a se-cret, too. It had been difficult to not tell Myles why she'd wanted to go to London with Mary and the girls, but she hadn't wanted to disappoint him if her plan failed.

The kisses they'd shared before she'd left still lived inside her. To tell the truth, if only to herself, she wanted him to kiss her like that all the time. Every day. She now could relate to the giggling, blushing and swoon-ing women in the books she'd read. Every time she thought about him, that ache in her lower belly made itself known. She couldn't help but speculate if all wives felt those sensations when thinking about their husbands or if it was just her. If she was just odd, because some-times, when she was in bed, thinking about him, she had to admit the things she thought about doing with

him were not ladylike. They were quite lustful, and she wasn't certain that a woman should feel that way.

The jolt of the carriage as the wheels began rolling brought her back to her senses. She would have to come up with another excuse to leave the house tomorrow, and possibly over the days following. Today, she stated that she needed to see about purchasing a few Christmas gifts. Before she'd left Redford, Myles had given her a significant amount of money, and had informed her that he had added her name to charge accounts at stores throughout London.

Mary had told her about a favourite store, Fortnum & Mason's, before she'd left the house today.

Reaching up, she pulled the curtain back and tucked it behind the hook to keep it back as she leaned her head out the window. 'Joshua?'

'Yes, Your Grace?'

A hint of dread washed over her, because she'd rarely gone shopping. Practically never, but she would have to, because that is what she'd said she was doing. 'I'd like to stop at a store, Fortnum and Mason's, please.'

'Very well, Your Grace.'

She would have to tell Myles about Dr Potter eventually, to account for the money she'd spent, but hopefully, by then, the exercises would have done some good.

She also hoped that nothing was planned for her to attend over the next few afternoons. Mary had invited her sister and husband for dinner last night, and just as Christina and Maria had said, Uncle Norman and Aunt Tina, as they instructed her to call them, were great company. So were their two daughters, Abigail and Deana,

who were close in age to Christina and Maria, and all four of them were very excited to attend the ball.

The ball was still a looming dread in Anita's future. She had nightmares about tripping, having all of London laughing at her, and a look of disgust on Myles's face had jolted her awake more than once. She told herself he wouldn't act that way. He was too kind, too wonderful, but her dreams didn't seem to understand that.

Pressing a hand to her stomach, she closed her eyes and sent up a prayer that Dr Potter would be able to help her keep that nightmare from coming true. Just that alone would be a miracle.

As luck would have it, an afternoon visit to the doctor each day was very easy for her to attend. No one questioned her desire to go shopping for a couple of hours each afternoon. In fact, Mary said that was smart, because it was impossible to see all the store had to offer in one trip. Or even one day.

Dr Potter had certainly done his research and had shared it with her by pointing at drawings of ankles, legs and feet in a book. For over an hour, he would manipulate her ankle in all directions. It was painful at times and left her ankle aching, but she didn't complain. The pain was simply a reminder of why she was doing all of this.

By the third day, her ankle was more than achy, it was sore, but that did not stop her. She could already tell that she had more flexibility, and that was exciting.

That was also the day he included walking in her exercises. Not just regular walking, but sideways, backwards and in circles.

'You've trained yourself to take small steps,' he said, watching every step she took. 'I want you to take the biggest steps you can. Think about dancing and taking long, smooth steps.'

'I don't know how to dance,' she admitted.

His bushy brows drew together as he frowned. 'Surely you've seen others dancing?'

'No, I haven't.' She shrugged. The few times there had been parties at Brunswick, she'd been in the kitchen. Out of sight. Which hadn't bothered her. That part of her life was over. She could no longer hide. 'I did see my cousins pretending to dance, but that was more just fooling around.'

'But you will be attending the Christmas Ball?'

'Yes.' She huffed out a breath. 'I won't dance.' Myles had said she wouldn't be expected to, but she did worry what others would think or say about that.

Dr Potter looked at her thoughtfully. 'Would you like to?'

'I don't think it's possible.'

'I think it might be, if you'd allow me to teach you. It could be part of our treatment.'

'The ball is only four days away.' She was counting, not due to the ball, but because Myles would arrive the day before the ball.

'I'm a very good dancer, a very good teacher.' His smile was a mixture of pride and teasing. Holding up a hand, he said, 'Wait here.'

Normally, they stayed in his exam room, but with the walking today, they were in the front parlour of his home. It wasn't nearly as large as the Wadsworth home, nor as finely furnished, but it was a bright and cheery

room, with windows that overlooked the street out front and provided several potted plants plenty of light.

'Your Grace,' he said, returning to the room. 'This is my wife, Martha. Martha, this is Lady Anita Wadsworth, the Duchess of Redford.'

'It's my pleasure to meet you, Your Grace,' the grey-haired woman said, with a slight curtsy.

'It's lovely to meet you,' Anita replied.

'Martha has agreed to play the piano so I can teach you to dance,' Dr Potter said.

That was how her doctor visits turned into dance lessons. Each afternoon, when she arrived home, she went upstairs to her bedroom, which, like back at Redford, was connected to a room that Myles would occupy when he arrived.

There, she would lie on the bed with a wet, cool towel wrapped around her ankle until the aching eased. She clearly remembered how badly her ankle would hurt some nights at Brunswick and wished she'd known about the towel back then, for it truly did help. Dr Potter had suggested it, and he'd promised each day the pain would get better. That the muscles were only sore from not being used for years.

He was right. The aching wasn't as bad as it had been, and she felt a difference, too. In her stride, her balance and in her confidence.

She was still careful to not get too excited, and she was diligent about not taking tiny steps and rotating her ankle as often as possible. Barely a moment went by when she didn't think about rotating her ankle or walking even just a few steps.

To make leaving the house each day honest, prior to

her appointments, she went shopping. It had been intimidating at first, but no longer. So far, she had gifts for the girls, Mary and several servants hidden in her trunk for when they returned to Redford to celebrate Christmas, but she'd yet to find anything for Myles.

Anxious to get to London as quickly as possible, Myles chose to ride rather than take a carriage. It was a long, cold journey, despite the afternoon sun. He'd planned on leaving first thing this morning but had discovered his horse, Donovan, had a loose shoe. Knowing the risks of that, and how losing a shoe during his trip would cause an even longer delay, he'd requested Donovan receive four new shoes.

Then an unexpected buyer had shown up. He half wondered if Wesley, who had returned to London a few days ago, had sent the buyer out purposefully, knowing he was leaving for London today.

The buyer, who had purchased two horses, had been sent by a mutual friend in Cambridge, so Wesley was off the hook, but it had been close to noon by the time Myles departed Redford.

What felt like days rather than hours later, as he entered the city, he was glad to be on horseback rather than in a carriage. It made navigating the traffic far easier, and quicker.

The sooner he set eyes on his wife, the better.

He'd come to the conclusion that he was not in love. He would know if that had happened. However, he was distracted and overly frustrated and had concluded why. He was in lust. Plain and simple. He was very attracted to his wife, and she had said that she wanted what he

wanted. His plan was to ask her to consider sleeping with
him. More than sleep. He wouldn't request, simply ask
her to consider it, and if she was agreeable, which was
his greatest hope, a hope that went beyond all else, he
would ask her to come to his room. If she chose not to,
he would wait. He would tell her that, too. The choice
would hers.

His optimism, one that continued to grow inside him,
that she might agree, came from the way she'd returned
his kisses, especially the night before she'd left for Lon-
don. He could still taste the sweetness of her lips, how
they'd felt softer than velvet, and how they'd danced in
concert with his, until her lips had parted, inviting him
into the heat of her mouth. He could still feel the way
she'd pressed the perfect curves of her body against him.
The way her arms had been looped around his neck and
how his hands hand roamed up and down the sides of
her body. He'd had to fight hard to not cup one of her
breasts, feel the firmness and weight in his hand.

A groan rumbled in the back of his throat, and he
shook his head to dilute the memory and shift his seat
in the saddle against the blood that had started pound-
ing in his veins and had rushed to his groin.

He also told himself that his patience would be worth
the reward. Even if she said that she needed some time
to think about it.

However, he also hoped that she didn't need too much
time, because he might die from the desires that filled
him day in and day out.

Steering Donovan around yet another slow-moving
carriage, he espied a coach taking a corner several blocks
ahead. One he knew well. It was his mother's coach.

It took a second for the next thought to hit. Then his heart nearly leaped from his chest. That was no longer his mother's coach, it was his wife's coach. He urged his horse to move faster through the traffic, but as if the world were against him, at the next crossroad, two huge and very slow-moving freight carts blocked his path.

He was cursing aloud by the time the carts got out of his way, and then he had to figure out exactly which corner it had been where Anita's coach had turned and then gone from there.

Convinced he was on the right street, he rode slowly, looking up and down each crossroad, which now made him the slow-moving traffic that others steered around.

Catching a glimpse of a black carriage with a gold crest on the doors and gold-painted wheels, he spun Donovan around for a second look. He was in an unfamiliar neighbourhood. The modest terraced houses all looked the same.

Turning down the street where the coach was parked a distance ahead, his heart lurched into an erratic beat. That was Anita walking from the coach up to a house. He was certain of it, due to the new dark blue cape she'd worn when leaving Redford. The white fur on the hood had stood out then and stood out now.

He urged Donovan into a trot, but not for long due to the narrow street and the traffic, including a slow-moving milk cart directly in his path that didn't care if he hadn't seen his wife in nearly a week or not. The longest week of his life, no less.

By the time he arrived at the house, he was certain she'd entered, her coach was turning the corner at the end of the block. She wouldn't have had time to walk

to the house and back to the coach. It hadn't taken him that long to get here.

He stared at the house. Why would Joshua have left her here?

Just then, a man, young and tall, with curly blond hair, exited the stable beside the house and practically ran to the house as if in a hurry to see someone. Unless stablemen in the city had started wearing ascots and embroidered frock coats, that man didn't work here. He lived here.

The very house where Anita was inside.

Donovan snorted and stomped a foot. The horse knew he was in the city and was ready for their journey to be over. The horse was probably also frustrated that others were moving past him and he was forced to stand still.

Myles didn't know what to think and scanned the houses, the street. He had half a mind to go knock on the door, ask what his wife was doing here, but what if that hadn't been the house?

It looked very similar to the ones on each side of it. He couldn't just start knocking on doors, demanding to see his wife. Perhaps this is what she'd meant about needing to do something in the city. Visit an old friend.

As far as he knew, she didn't have any old friends.

She certainly had never mentioned any.

Joshua would know. He would know which house she was at and why.

Myles scanned the house again, finding that it had a black hitching post in the driveway that was different from any others. Saving that information to find the house again, he gave Donovan his head and began searching for the coach again.

He found it readily enough. Less than eight blocks away, there was a small tavern. A joint that looked as if it were one that drivers visited while waiting for their employers, due to the large gravelled area next to the building, which was where Anita's coach was parked.

Stopping next to it, he noted the block had been set for the horses, which meant that Joshua intended to be inside for longer than a few minutes.

Myles climbed off his horse, tethered it, and made his way to the door. The place was neither large, nor busy. Joshua was at a table near a window with a newspaper laid out on the table and a tankard sitting beside it.

The driver looked up, then jumped to his feet as Myles approached the table.

'Your Grace,' Joshua said, pulling the hat off his head. 'You've arrived. The Duchess will be so happy to see you.'

'Where is she?' Myles asked.

Joshua's Adam's apple looked as if it had gotten stuck as the man swallowed. He held up a finger and reach down, lifted the tankard and took a drink. 'Tea,' he said, followed by a cough while holding the tankard out for Myles to look inside.

Myles couldn't care less that it looked and smelled like tea; he was still waiting for the man to answer his question.

'They don't have proper teacups, but they do make a strong cuppa,' Joshua said, setting the tankard back on the table. 'Would you care for one, Your Grace?'

'No, I would like to know where the Duchess is.'

Joshua shifted his feet. 'Oh, well, you see, Your Grace, she is shopping.'

'Shopping?'

Joshua nodded his head while wringing the hat he was holding with both hands. 'Yes, shopping.'

'Where?'

A sheen of sweat was forming above Joshua's brows. 'Well, um… Fortnum and Mason's, Your Grace.'

Myles was familiar with the department store but was far more curious to know why Joshua was lying to him. The man had not shown incompetency of any sort since arriving at Redford but, like Olive, was very dedicated to Anita. So dedicated he was clearly lying on her behalf. 'That is a distance from here.'

'Yes, Your Grace, it is indeed. She asked me to return for her in an hour, and I came here, on account of how good their tea is. Bought myself a paper to read.'

'I see,' Myles said, while deciding how to proceed. He wanted to demand the truth, yet, a part of his memory was reminding him of the last time he'd acted without thinking and how his behaviour had made Anita cry. He didn't ever want a repeat of that.

'The Duchess will be home by four, Your Grace,' Joshua said. 'All done shopping by then.'

'Will she?' Myles asked, still contemplating his next action.

Joshua's head was bobbing like an apple in a barrel that had just been shaken. 'The Duchess knows you are arriving tonight.'

He had mentioned it would be evening by the time he arrived in his last message to her about Dolly, so it wasn't out of the realm for her to be shopping this afternoon. But he knew she wasn't shopping. He needed

more information. 'Did you visit this establishment while working for Brunswick?'

'On occasion, Your Grace.'

The hair on his neck quivered. 'Why? Did Brunswick have family, friends, in the area?'

Joshua shook his head. 'No, Your Grace. His Lordship was known to visit an establishment just up the road.'

Myles nodded. 'The gaming house.'

'Yes, Your Grace.'

'What about the Duchess? Does she know anyone who lives in this neighbourhood?'

A single bead of sweat trickled down the side of Joshua's face.

Perhaps it was compassion or that Myles didn't want to know the true answer, because Joshua was clearly going to continue lying for his duchess. 'Never mind. It doesn't matter,' Myles said. 'I will see you and the Duchess at home.'

'By four, Your Grace,' Joshua said.

'By four,' Myles said, then pointed at the tankard. 'Enjoy your tea.'

As he left the establishment, he contemplated his options. There were several, including knocking on doors to find his wife. He had to think this through, for that might not be his best choice.

In the end, after much contemplation, he did what any man who wanted to know the undeniable truth would do. He returned to the house with the black hitching post, found a discreet spot to hide Donovan in the alley and one for him to hide in the bushes beside the stable of the house across the street.

His nose felt like an icicle, and he was blowing into

his hands to keep them warm by the time Joshua arrived. The driver nearly fell off the coach steps in his hurry to get down and get to the house door. Anita exited that very door almost immediately, and the way she grasped a hold of Joshua arm, told Myles that the driver had informed her that her husband was in town.

The two of them practically ran to the coach.

Myles then had another decision to make. Once again, it included knocking on the door of that house. Actually, he was more in the mood for kicking it in. Still, though, he had the common sense to refrain from such actions until he knew more.

Therefore, he ran to Donovan and nearly caused several accidents during his somewhat wild and fast ride to his London house.

Ironically, his mother shared the same lie with him. That Anita was shopping at Fortnum & Mason's and would be home by four. She also assured him how excited Anita would be to see him and told him that his second cousins, Lord and Lady Ashton would be joining them for dinner. His cousin Dafne was pleasant enough, although a bit feather-headed, but her husband, Gibb, was an arrogant man who pretended he'd been the one who'd brought money into the marriage rather than Dafne.

In other words, Myles now had two things that he wasn't looking forward to. A dreadful dinner with his cousins and finding out the truth about what Anita had been doing at that house. He wanted to believe it had simply been a visit to an old friend or family member, but was having a hard time accepting that would be true.

Chilled to the bone, he used the time it would take

Anita to get to the house to change into warm clothes and then stood before the fireplace in the study until his fingers and toes no longer stung.

He saw the carriage roll past the window, and though the house was large and it was clearly possible that he hadn't heard anything, he was positive he heard when Anita entered the house.

Moments later, when a knock sounded on the study door, he took a moment to tell his heart to stop acting so foolishly before he said, 'Come in.'

A second later, he had to momentarily close his eyes, because somehow, Anita had become more beautiful than the last time he'd seen her. Opening his eyes, he noted that she wasn't wearing the blue cape.

'I'm sorry I wasn't here when you arrived,' she said, quickly entering the room. 'I was shopping.'

'I was told that,' he said.

She set a paper-wrapped package on the desk while asking, 'Would you like to see what I bought at Fortnum and Mason's today? But it's a Christmas present, so you have to promise not to tell.'

He still wasn't over the sight of her, nor was he prepared to answer, because he was also thinking that she didn't have time to stop at Fortnum & Mason's after leaving that house.

Without him having said a word, she folded back the paper and lifted up what looked like a colourful rug. 'Isn't it pretty?' she asked.

'A rug?' he asked, with a headshake to get his eyes and mind working correctly. 'As a Christmas gift?'

'Yes, for Roscoe.'

'You bought the dog a Christmas present?'

'I hope you don't mind,' she said. 'I'd seen it the other day and thought it would be nice for him to lie on in front of the fireplace on cold days, so I had to go back and buy it today.'

He had to smile. She was so kind and thoughtful that she would buy a present for a dog. That was just one of the things about her that was so endearing. There were more. So many more. Whatever she'd been doing at that house today had to be a minor thing, one she'd tell him about, and he'd feel foolish for wondering about it. He took a step towards her. 'You have seen how much hair he has, right?'

Smiling, she set down the rug and took a step towards him. 'Yes, I have, and I bet he still would like a rug to lie on.'

'Do you want to know what I'd like?' he asked, taking another step.

'I would,' she replied.

'A hello kiss.'

It was as if she flew across the room and landed in his arms. Hers looped around his neck as their lips met. For the next several moments, he was lost in the world that he'd been dreaming about. Her lips dancing with his, her body pressed up against his. He'd missed her so much. The taste of her. The feel of her. The smell of her.

He wasn't sure what clicked first in his mind, that she smelled different or that the difference was that she smelled of men's cologne, and it wasn't the scent he used. Either way, he stopped the kiss and took a step backwards.

She had on a blue-and-white dress that buttoned all the way to her chin, but that didn't stop him from no-

ticing her breasts, how they heaved up and down with her hard breaths.

He was breathing hard, too, from kissing her and from the darkness that was filling his chest.

They stood there for a moment, a very long one, looking at each other. Her beauty was still captivating him, but so were dark thoughts. He'd never expected her to betray him in this manner. His chest constricted, several times, and the pain was damn near unbearable. It spread, too, like it had fingers, long fingers that were almost strangling him. He tugged at his shirt collar, but it didn't help. He'd never felt anything like this. The pain was making it hard to breathe. Hard to think.

Hard to… Hell! It couldn't be. He couldn't be in love with her. He refused to be. Refused!

Turning, he looked at the fire blazing in the hearth. He bit down on the tip of his tongue until his focus was only on the pain of that, then he said, 'We're having guests for dinner. You'll want to go to your room and change.'

'I have plenty of time—'

'I don't,' he said, needing her to leave before he said things he shouldn't. 'I need to get some work done.'

'Oh. Is there anything I can help you with?'

'No.' Making his lie viable, he walked to the desk.

She did, too, and picked up her rug and the paper. With a bright smile, she said, 'Dog or not, I think Roscoe will appreciate his gift.' The she turned and walked to the door.

He sank into his chair, watched as she walked into the corridor, even gave a one-fingered wave when she fluttered her fingers at him before she pulled the door closed in her wake.

Throwing his head back he stared at the ceiling. This was impossible. He was in lust, not love. But lust wouldn't hurt like this. The pain was all-consuming. Head to toe, but focused on his heart. So focused.

It was a hell of a lot more than a distraction.

When had it happened? How had he not known?

How had he not known that he was madly in love with his wife?

And jealous as hell!

He slammed a hand down on his desk. Who the hell was that blond man at that house? How long had she known him? Was she in love with him? A slew of other questions hit him like bullets being fired from a gun— several guns, all at the same time.

Some weren't questions, they were statements. She'd never looked more radiant. Her face had shone. Her eyes had held a twinkle. Her steps had…

A shiver raced down his spine and he snapped his head forward, stared at the door again. Her steps had been longer than usual. It was an odd thing to notice, but not for him. He'd been aware of her steps, her walk, since the first day they'd met. Even with the fitted shoes, her steps were still short, circumspect.

Was she so happy, so in love with someone here in London that she practically had a spring in her step? She'd never had that with him.

This couldn't be happening! But it was. There was no denying that. There was no denying the utter despair washing over him, either.

Chapter Twelve

Anita entered her bedroom and twirled about in a tiny circle. A bit of an uneven and ungraceful circle, but she did it anyway, because she'd never been able to twirl until recently, and she was so happy to see Myles that she wanted to twirl around, over and over again.

So very happy. She was a bit disheartened that their time together had been so brief, but that was part of being his wife. He was a busy man, and she fully understood the importance of that. She just wished there was more she could do to help him.

Furthermore, the way he'd acted said that he wasn't any happier about having to see to some tasks than she was. He'd appeared to be quite frustrated about it. But if he got them all accomplished now, then they would be able to spend a longer amount of time together later.

She sincerely hoped that was the case. Seeing him had reminded her of exactly how much she'd missed him. And missed kissing him!

She completed another twirl and landed on the bed with a giggle and pressed her hands over her fast-beating heart. Her insides were twirling with happiness, just like she had twirled her body.

Even though she'd always had one good foot, she'd never been able to twirl because of her balance, and fear. Dr Potter had suggested that not walking until a year after her accident had been so painful because when she had started walking, she'd been walking on her ankle bone. As a child, she'd found a way to take tiny steps that caused the least amount of pain and had continued to walk that way out of fear of the pain returning until that had become the way she walked. With the special shoes and the therapy, so many things had changed. The pain, her balance and stride, and the trust she had in herself. The belief that she could do more than she'd ever imagined.

It had only been one week, and it had taken a lot of work, and not just during her sessions with Dr Potter. She'd kept doing the exercises all day, discreetly, and would continue to for the rest of her life. It was worth it. Though her foot would always look like it did, Myles wouldn't have to worry about her tripping. He wouldn't have to shorten his strides to match her—well, maybe a little bit still, for he had very long legs—when they walked side by side.

Another bout of happiness washed over her. Or when they danced! She would dance with him at the Christmas Ball! It was amazing how easy it was to move to the music. Her feet could just glide across the floor. She had to make sure that she was leading, as Dr Potter called it, with her right foot, but she could dance!

That would never have been possible if she hadn't gone to see Dr Potter. Would never have been possible if— She let out a sigh and shook her head. None of

it would have been possible without Myles. She owed him so much.

When Joshua had told her about seeing Myles at the tavern near Dr Potter's house, she'd been scared for a split second. That had diminished when Joshua assured her that he hadn't mentioned the doctor or her therapy. Then she'd simply been overjoyed. So excited to see him that she'd thought the carriage ride would never end.

She'd known he'd laugh about her buying Roscoe a Christmas gift. The rug had caught her eye yesterday, but knowing she'd need to go to Fortnum & Mason's again today, she'd waited to buy it. That store was astonishing. It had everything that a person might ever need or want.

Thank goodness, because she'd stopped there every day to buy another present. She'd finally found a gift for Myles there, too. It was hidden in her trunk along with the others and was the one she was most excited to give on Christmas. She hoped he liked it as much as she thought he would.

Though she could lie here on the bed, staring at the ceiling and thinking about him for hours, feeling happier than she'd ever thought possible, she sat up, got off the bed and walked to the wardrobe to pick out a dress to wear for the evening meal.

There, too, she had to sigh—a joy-filled sigh—at how her life had changed.

Her inner joy continued to climb throughout the afternoon. With Claire's assistance, her hair was refashioned into a braided coil at the crown of her head, with long curls left loose to fall around her face. A gold ribbon that matched her white-and-gold dress was wrapped

around the braided coil, and another piece of the ribbon was around her neck and tied in a bow as a makeshift necklace.

Made of two layers, the underdress was white silk, and the top layer was made from a shimmering sheer gold material. White lace decorated the square neckline that revealed plenty of skin, and lace was also on the puffy short sleeves. The gown was so lovely, it made her feel lovely, and she relished the idea of Myles seeing her in it.

Dinner wouldn't be served for a couple of hours, and their company, a niece and nephew of Mary's, were not due to arrive for at least another hour when she left her room to go downstairs and hopefully spend that time with Myles. His daily messages had kept her up to date on Dolly, but she was curious to know about other things at Redford. The racehorses and kittens, Roscoe and the peacocks, but mainly, she merely wanted to be with him. Talking, laughing, just enjoying each other's company. That's what she'd missed the most. It had been nearly two weeks since they'd taken a walk together, since he'd told her a fun or amazing tale about a past duke, since they'd sat side by side on the sofa and he'd touched her hand or rubbed her shoulder.

She pressed a hand over her heart, which was so overfilled with bliss it was close to bursting as she made her way downstairs. The house wasn't nearly as large as the one at Redford, but it could not be considered small or modest. Exploring the house over the past week had not only given her knowledge of the entire home, it had given her the opportunity to continue her therapy. The lower floor consisted of the kitchen, dining room, two

parlours, a study and the tiled hall, as well as the utility rooms for laundry and storage. The second floor contained family bedrooms and sitting areas and several water closets, and the uppermost floor was dedicated to space for the servants. There was also a cellar where the coal for the many fireplaces was stored.

The home boasted a curved staircase off the hall in the front of the house, and a narrow set of stairs off the hall near the kitchen at the back of the house. She no longer considered steps an annoyance, they were now an opportunity to build her resilience. Dr Potter said the objective was to make the muscles in that foot as strong as possible.

She had walked, including up and down steps, her entire life, but she'd never really walked on that foot, she'd used it more like someone would use a cane. Just to hold her weight as she did most of her walking with her right foot. All that he'd said made so much sense, and she was excited to tell Myles all about it. She would have told him after showing him the rug she'd purchased for Roscoe if he hadn't been so busy.

From the stairway, she could see inside the parlour, but just the fireplace. She would check there for him first.

'Anita, dear, you look absolutely radiant,' Mary said.

Forcing herself to not let disappointment show that her mother-in-law was the only one in the room, Anita held her smile in place. 'Thank you. I'm astonished daily by Claire's ability to make my hair behave.'

Mary touched the nape of her neck. 'Few of us know what a curse natural curls can be. I've looked like a scarecrow a time or two in my life. I would have scared

off far more birds than any stuffed one standing in the field.'

Anita was still in the doorway and let out a small laugh at Mary's tale while searching for a way to excuse herself so she could look for Myles in his study.

'Myles went upstairs a short time ago. I'm sure he'll be down presently,' Mary said.

Anita had been listening for any sounds coming from his bedroom, but evidently, not closely enough. She entered the room and chose to sit on the sofa.

'Did you complete your shopping today?' Mary asked.

'Yes, I did.' There would be no gift-buying, nor would she be going to see Dr Potter tomorrow. Today had been her last session. He'd promised that he'd make time for sessions whenever she visited London in the future. It had been hard to say goodbye to both the surgeon and his wife after all they had done for her.

'I have, too,' Mary said. 'After the ball, we can return home and focus on the yuletide season and family celebrations. It might be the last one that Wesley is with us for a time, and the first one with you. I'm looking forward to it.'

The conversation easily flowed into the decorations, special meals and treats, and traditions that would occupy Christmas Eve, Christmas Day and Boxing Day. Such days had been celebrated at Brunswick in a much smaller manner. She no longer cared that her participation had been very different there than here. It was simply how things used to be and, because of Myles, never would be again.

As if she somehow had the capability to conjure him

up out of nowhere with a single thought, Myles strolled into the room. A tiny shiver rippled over her, not from a chill, but anticipation of him sitting down beside her.

He crossed the room, placed a tiny kiss on his mother's cheek, then walked towards her, and Anita wondered if there would ever come a time when he didn't make her breath stall or her heart thud.

Leaning down, he kissed her cheek, then turned about and walked to the fireplace, where he placed a hand on the wide, wooden mantel, as if he intended to lounge there and not sit next to her. She kept her disappointment hidden. Looking at him was just as exciting. He looked overly handsome, as usual, in his dark blue tail coat, gold brocade vest and dark pants. She especially liked the way he had that one cluster of dark hair that always hung at an angle over his forehead.

'Still chilled from your long ride?' Mary asked him.

He held his other hand towards the flames. 'Yes.'

Anita rose. She'd been so focused on how happy she was to have him here she hadn't thought of the cold ride he'd experienced during his journey to London. 'Would you like a snifter of brandy?'

'No, thank you, I have already had one.' He tucked one hand in his pocket, but kept the other on the mantel. 'You'll be happy to know that Dolly has been returned to her stall, and that all of the kittens have their eyes open and are walking more than crawling.'

'That's wonderful,' she replied, lowering to sit on the sofa again. 'The racehorses? Has Maximus beat his own record again?'

'Maximus has been sold,' he answered. 'He'll be racing at Chester in May.'

A tiny prick struck her heart, even though she knew all of the horses, less a few personal ones, were for sale and would eventually be gone from Redford. 'He'll be amazing on the track. A winner. I'm sure of it.'

'We should plan on attending the race,' Mary said.

'That would be too far to travel just for a race,' Myles answered.

The smile on Anita's face was becoming difficult to maintain, because there was something very different about Myles. His tone and clipped answers were not only uncommon; they were cold.

'We could take the train,' Mary said. 'It would be fun to watch a Redford thoroughbred race.'

'And win,' Anita said cheerfully, hoping it would spread.

He pushed himself off the mantel and walked to the chair next to Mary's, the one farthest away from where Anita sat on the sofa, and she felt her cheerfulness and smile fade even more.

'Mother, if we start travelling to watch our horses race, we won't have time to raise any others.'

The expression on Mary's face said she found his short temper as unusual as Anita did.

His mood didn't get any brighter throughout the evening, and though she thought Dafne and her husband pleasant people, the arrival of the guests seemed to sour Myles even more.

Until she realised it was she who was souring his mood. Every time she looked at him, he'd look the other way, as if he didn't want to face her. Nausea swirled in her stomach, growing stronger as the evening pro-

ceeded. It wasn't just her stomach that was upset; her heart started to ache, as if it were as damaged as her foot.

When was she going to learn to not get her hopes up? His expression wasn't that he didn't want to face her. He was disgusted by the sight of her. She knew, because it was the same expression that she saw in her nightmares about tripping at the Christmas Ball. Learning to walk, learning to dance, didn't change who she was. It wasn't going to change how he felt about her, either. She'd never be able to give him a wonderful life. One where he was happy that he'd married her.

Why had she thought she could? Furthermore, why had she been so foolish to believe that she could have what she wanted?

As much as he hated the gulf that he was creating between him and Anita, Myles knew it was what needed to happen. He had to put some distance between them so he could figure out what to do next.

More than one look, more than one touch, had sent him close to breaking his resolve and deciding that it didn't matter if she was in love with someone else. He didn't hate her. Just like he didn't hate Leslie Carlisle for loving someone else. In fact, he should have expected it. He'd been engaged to a woman who loved someone else, so why shouldn't the one he married love someone else, too?

There was no reason for her not to.

Hell, he wasn't even mad at her about it. He'd told her that love wouldn't be a part of their marriage.

That's what he was mad about. Mad at himself. Mad

that he'd succumbed to love. Why anyone would want something that could hurt this badly was beyond him.

He'd been right about one thing. He was in lust. The cleavage that Anita's dress exposed was not what he'd needed tonight. He'd not only fallen in love with the most beautiful woman on earth, he'd married her and never consummated their marriage with her. The idea of her doing that with someone else was gutting him.

He'd never cared for Gibb, had barely tolerated the man's arrogance, but tonight, it wasn't Gibb's unending boasting that got to him. It was the way Gibb wouldn't stop staring at Anita that galled him no end. The man already had bug-eyes, and tonight they looked like they were about to pop right out of his head. Myles was sure he'd seen the bounder lick his lips a couple of times, too. Myles knuckles stung from being balled into fists so many times throughout the evening.

If that was the case with just his cousin's husband, what was going to happen when he met her lover? Would he kill the man? End up in prison?

He would find whosever's cologne he'd smelled on her, because it was not a minor thing. They were married. He hadn't asked for her undying love, but he had requested her honesty, trust and faithfulness.

If she couldn't give him that, then—what?—a failed marriage?

He sucked in a deep breath, let his gaze roam to the other side of the parlour, where she stood talking to Dafne. Her gold-covered white gown fit her as perfectly from the back as it did from the front. It hugged her slender back, fanned out over the slight swell of her hips.

His palms tingled, wanting to feel those swells, and his groin throbbed with its own wants.

'You have more restraint than I,' Gibbs said.

Myles clamped his back teeth together as he slowly turned his neck to look down at the man standing next to him.

Gibbs shrugged. 'Rather than standing here thinking about seducing my wife, I'd haul her up to our bedroom and perform the act.'

Myles gritted his back teeth together so hard it hurt. He was close to reaching his limit. Very close. Too close. 'I'll have the butler get your coats,' he growled.

He left the room, and after informing the butler that the guests would be leaving soon, he went to his study, where he shut the door and cursed aloud at how Gibbs had hit a bull's-eye. He had been thinking about seducing Anita. Thinking about performing the act.

The mistake he'd made was not doing that on their wedding night. He wouldn't be in this position if he'd done that, she might already be carrying his child, because that act wouldn't have happened just once. She would be well and truly secured to him then.

What the hell was he thinking? He didn't want her secured to him. He wanted her...

Undying love.

He let out a long, heavy sigh.

That's what he wanted.

That's what he'd always want, because he'd never known a desire so great, and he knew himself well enough to know that it would never wane. Never go away.

If there was the slightest chance that he could ever

gain her love, he had to know more about his opponent. Maybe she wasn't fully in love with that man yet.

Within minutes, he was on Donovan, travelling across the city. Traffic was minimal and didn't impede his travel. Not that it would have stopped him.

He hitched Donovan to the black post and mounted the steps, hand out to knock on the door. A gas lamp flickered next to the door, and a profound sense of shock struck, stopped him from knocking as he read the sign beneath the light.

Dr Harmen Potter.

The door opened before he had a chance to decide if he should knock or not. Before he had a chance to determine anything.

'Are you seeking the doctor?' a man asked.

The man wasn't Dr Potter. At least not the Dr Harmen Potter that he had summoned to his London house to question about seeing Anita when she'd been a small girl. The older man standing there wasn't the blond man he'd seen earlier today, either.

'Who is it, Alfred?' The owner of the voice who'd asked that question appeared a moment later, next to the door opener. 'Your Grace.'

Myles recognised that man. It was the same doctor who been at his house. 'Dr Potter.'

'Won't you come in?' Dr Potter asked.

'If you don't mind,' Myles replied. He truly needed answers.

They walked through a small entrance area and into the doctor's exam room, where Myles was invited to take a chair.

'I'm assuming you have questions about the treatment I've been providing the Duchess,' Dr Potter said.

Myles hid his obliviousness about treatments by simply nodding.

'I'll tell you what I told her,' Dr Potter began. 'Surgery could cause more problems than it's worth. Of course, someone else might hold a different opinion, but my belief is that the pain and suffering she would need to endure would not be worth the surgeries. It would take more than one operation, and with each one, there would be the chance of doing more harm than good. She could end up with one leg considerably shorter, or be left completely unable to use her foot. Those are risks I wouldn't suggest she take.'

Hell! This was why she'd come to London? This was what she'd had to do? See about having surgery? Because of him. She still thought he wanted her fixed. Myles felt sick to his stomach. Very sick.

'I know she was disappointed,' the doctor continued, 'which is why I suggested the treatments we've been completing each day. The first few days were painful for her, and I offered her some medication, but she refused. She said the cold cloths helped ease the pain. She's an amazing woman, but I'm sure you know that.'

'I do,' Myles said, sounding hoarse because his throat was thick. She was amazing and perfect. He was the one who had faults. He'd asked for trust and honesty in their marriage, yet he hadn't given that to her. Twice now, he'd betrayed her, wrongly jumped to conclusions. Foolish conclusions because he was a fool. An idiot for comparing her to anyone else. She was different, unique. Special. Very special.

'I'm sure you've noticed how well she's responded to treatment,' Dr Potter said. 'Better than I had expected. Her stance and balance has improved tremendously. So has her gait. The increased flexibility in her ankle took some getting used to, and I'm very impressed by how well she's managed that. How well she's started using that foot. Truly, I'm shocked over her progress in such a short time.'

A mixture of feelings was filling Myles, everything from regret that he'd been the cause of more pain to her, to shame that he'd thought the change in her footsteps had been for reasons that were abhorrent, ridiculous and totally irrational. 'She does seem to have a spring in her step, now,' he said.

'Exactly. Isn't it amazing?'

It was, and he was a lout for not paying more attention to that. For thinking about himself when he should have been thinking about her. 'Very amazing.'

'She's looking forward to the Christmas Ball, and I believe the dance lessons vastly aided our treatments. I'm sure she mentioned that I asked my son to join us today, to be her dance partner, because he's about your height and build, so she could practise her steps with someone whose stride would be closer to yours than mine. It means so much to her to be able to dance with you and not stumble.'

Myles hadn't thought he could be more regretful, but it grew again at learning the blond man was the doctor's son. 'I wouldn't care if she stumbled,' he said. 'I wouldn't care if we didn't dance at all.'

'I'm sure you wouldn't, but it matters to her,' the doctor said. 'She wants to make you happy.'

Myles had never felt more humbled. 'I was already happy. She was perfect just the way she was. Nothing about her needed to be fixed.'

Dr Potter met his gaze, then glanced away and nodded. Looking at him again, he smiled. 'Your Grace, if I may, I'd like to tell you what I think.'

Myles nodded. 'Please do.'

The doctor scratched his bald spot, then ran a hand over his chin before he began, 'Imagine a young woman who had spent her entire life being told that she was worthless. That no one would ever love her. That she would never amount to more than an old maid. Whether it was true or not, that became her belief because she heard it over and over again. Then, all of a sudden, she becomes a duchess. It sounds like a fairy tale, but to the young woman, it's more of a nightmare. Because now she has to become something else, someone else.'

Myles shook his head. 'No, she doesn't.'

'She believes she does. She believes she needs to find a way to go from being unworthy to being worthy. Damaged to being repaired.'

A shiver rippled over Myles from head to toe. He looked at the doctor. 'She doesn't need to be told that she doesn't need to be fixed,' he said, thinking of the conversation between him and her after the stable episode. 'She needs to be told that she has been fixed. Because for her entire life, she has believed that she was damaged and couldn't be repaired.'

The doctor nodded, smiled. 'She wants to be a duchess you can be proud of, but she has to be proud of herself first.'

Myles knew he'd never be able to repay Dr Potter for

the profound thankfulness he felt, or the knowledge he'd gained. 'These treatments, is there a chance they could cause further injury to her? Make things more painful?'

'No, it's simply been a matter of stretching and using muscles that had grown, well, dormant due to the way she had been walking. Let me show you.'

Their conversation continued for some time, with Dr Potter pulling out a medical book and showing him drawings and pictures while explaining his findings and treatments in full detail. When the doctor closed the book, Myles fully understood that any changes to her foot weren't as significant as the changes about how she felt about herself. That was something he could help her with, and he was excited about that.

By the time he untied Donovan from the hitching post, it was the wee hours of the morning, but he felt like a new man. A new man with a plan.

A plan he would put in place the following morning.

A plan that would start with him kissing his wife.

Myles found Anita in her bedroom dressed in a green-and-white-striped gown and sitting on a stool as her hair was being fashioned. Their gazes met in the refection of the mirror before her as he rested a hand on the bedpost at the foot of her bed.

The apprehension in her eyes could have gutted him if he'd have let it. Instead, he smiled, giving free rein for the happiness in his heart to come through. 'Good morning.'

'Good morning,' she replied. Twisting, she glanced up at Claire.

Before she could dismiss her maid, he said, 'Please finish. Don't mind me.'

She met his gaze in the mirror again, then nodded at the maid to finish her hair.

Her beauty was not only skin-deep; it went clear to her heart. Her big, wonderful heart that he had no right to ask for a piece of, but if she found a way to trust him enough with it, with the love it contained, he would never take it for granted. Never put anything before her and their love. Never stop proving to her how perfect she was, even after he'd convinced her of that.

He now understood what his father had said about love. About priorities. Love changed what was most important, and that was her. Would always be her.

Claire was swift in completing her duties. After a few soft words were spoken between the maid and her duchess, Claire bowed at him, then silently left the room.

Anita rose, and he stepped forward, slid the stool she'd been sitting on aside and wrapped his arms around her from behind so they were both staring into the mirror.

Dipping his head, so his face was next to hers, he said into the mirror, 'I find myself in the position of needing to apologise to you yet again. I am very regretful for the way I behaved yesterday, and if you will forgive me, I promise that I will work harder at curbing my jealousy.'

She frowned.

He smiled. 'It's difficult being married to the most beautiful woman in the world.'

Rolling her eyes, she shook her head. 'Stop right there. Jealousy was not what was wrong with you yesterday.'

'Yes, it was.' He pulled her back tighter against him and ran his hands over her stomach and rib cage. 'I was jealous that you might have found someone who made you so happy, they'd put a spring in your step.'

Her eyes grew wide and she squirmed enough to loosen his hold so she could spin around and face him with an expression of disbelief. 'You noticed?'

He kissed the tip of her nose. 'Of course I noticed.'

Smiling, she pressed a hand to her breastbone and shook her head. 'I did that. Put a spring in my step. There wasn't anyone else, well, there was, but he's a doctor. Dr Potter. I was going to tell you last night, but, well, I came here, to London, to see if anything could be done about my foot. Dr Potter said the bones have been the way they are for too long, that surgery wouldn't help, but he created some exercises, therapy he calls it, that have helped. They've really helped.'

The happiness on her face, in her voice, was so great, his heart could feel it, too. 'I'm so proud of you.' He planted a soft kiss on her lips. 'So very proud of you.'

She blinked several times. 'No one ever said that to me before I met you.'

He could tell her that they should have. She'd done a lot to be proud of, but should-haves and could-haves were things from the past. This was their future. 'You've never had a husband before me.'

She giggled softly. 'No, I haven't.' Looping her arms around his neck, she said, 'I think I'm getting used to it.'

Desire struck so hard he had to tighten his leg muscles all the way to his toes as their lips met. It would be so easy to ask her if she wanted to join him in his bed, and he would ask her that. Just not right now.

Not.

Right.

Now.

He repeated that several times again as their kissing became more ardent, and it took a will power that he hadn't known existed to end the kiss. This was about her, what she needed, and he was excited to be the one to help her find it. He was also excited to give her the necklace he'd had commissioned for her to wear to the ball. 'As enjoyable as this is, we have things to do today.'

'We do?'

He stepped back and took a hold of her hand to lead her to the door. 'Yes, we do.'

'What?'

'You'll see.'

Chapter Thirteen

Anita's footsteps had never felt lighter, and she'd never felt warmer than being snuggled next to Myles in the coach as they traversed the city traffic. He refused to say where they were going, and she didn't mind in the least. It was exciting. An adventure, and that added to her happiness. The joy filling her heart was indescribable. She'd hoped to become someone he could be proud of, perhaps feel tenderness for one day, and was so very glad that he was happy that she'd come to London, gone to see Dr Potter.

The carriage rocked as the horses stopped, and she lifted the thick curtain blocking the cold air. She didn't recognise the stores. 'Where are we?'

'Hatton Garden.'

'What are we doing here?'

'We are going to visit a jeweller that I know.'

'Oh, Myles, you have already provided me with so much, I truly don't—'

He pressed a finger to her lips. 'My duchess needs some jewellery.' He then tapped on the ceiling of the coach.

The footman riding atop with Joshua opened the door for them, and a few steps later, they entered a small but

brightly lit store with a glass counter that was filled with sparkling jewels.

'Ah, the Duke of Redford has once again graced my humble establishment,' a tall dark-haired man said.

'Anita, my love, please pay no attention to the rake coming our way,' Myles said loudly enough for the man to hear, while tugging her a bit closer to his side with the arm he had around her. 'He is the worst sort of scoundrel. A thief in all honesty.'

She was aware the two men were teasing each other, but the echoing of the pounding of her heart was muffling her hearing. That had happened as soon as he'd called her 'my love.' He'd called her his duchess before, but never my love. He probably didn't even realise he'd said it, not like she did.

'Allow me to introduce myself, since your husband appears to be too busy calling me names,' the man said to her. 'Perhaps he is jealous that you will favour me over him, no?'

'No,' Myles answered for her.

She giggled, because he was correct.

'I am Jillian Voss.' The man gave her an exaggerated bow. 'At your service, Your Grace.'

'Kiss her hand and we'll be in the back alley,' Myles said.

The jeweller laughed. 'It would be worth it.'

'If you fancy a broken nose,' Myles said.

The two men then shook hands and slapped each other on the back.

'We've known each other since the cradle,' Myles told her. 'I wouldn't really have broken his nose, just bruised it.'

The conversation between the two had happened so

fast, it had been impossible for her to get a word in before now. She gave Myles a playful little slap on the arm and nodded at the jeweller. 'It's a pleasure to meet you, Mr Voss.'

'The pleasure is all mine, Your Grace. Come, the necklace I have designed is right over here.'

Myles once again placed an arm around her waist as they followed the jeweller across the store. She liked Myles's arm being around her. Liked knowing that he didn't feel that she had to hold on to his arm in order to keep from tripping.

Mr Voss walked behind the glass counter and lifted a black velvet-covered box out of a cabinet below the counter, then set it atop the glass. With a nod, he said, 'Open it.'

She glanced at Myles, who also nodded.

Having no idea what to expect, she used both hands to carefully open the lid and gasped at what she saw. A pearl necklace shimmered brightly within. Each perfectly formed pearl was full of tiny colourful prisms, but it was the pendant that hung from the pearls that held her full attention. A horse's head and neck carved from a glossy black stone, with the horse's flowing mane made from fine, individual strands of gold.

'I've never seen anything more beautiful,' she said.

'Neither have I,' Myles said.

He was looking at her, not the necklace, and she shook her head at him.

Mr Voss pushed the necklace closer towards her. 'Try it on.'

'Allow me,' Myles said, picking up the necklace.

She untied the bow of her cape and let the heavy ma-

terial slide onto her shoulders so he had access to the back of her neck. The treatments from Dr Potter had definitely worked, because she could feel her toes curling, the ones on both feet, as Myles's fingers touched her neck while he clasped the necklace in place. The strand of pearls was just long enough that she could look down and see the gorgeous horse.

Turning to look at Myles, she said, 'It's so lovely. So very lovely.'

'I'm glad that you like it.' He gave her a soft kiss on the lips, before he looked at Mr Voss. 'You created exactly what I wanted.'

'Did you have any doubt?' Mr Voss asked.

'No.' Myles's eyes were back on her. 'Not a single doubt.'

Her heart was completely uncontrollable today. It was not only pounding; it was swelling to twice its size. Not getting her hopes up that he could someday care for her was growing more difficult by the moment.

Myles thanked the jeweller and apologised for not being able to stay any longer, because they had another appointment.

Back in the carriage, she said, 'Thank you for the necklace. It's exquisite.'

'You're very welcome,' he replied, touching the necklace with a single finger. 'I wouldn't object to a kiss of appreciation.'

She wouldn't mind, either, and showed him that with more than one kiss. Those sensations that she wondered if all wives felt were making themselves known low in her belly. Not wanting them to grow stronger until she squirmed in her seat as she sometimes did in her bed at

night, she ended the kiss and sat back in her seat, tried to act normally.

Her gaze went to her necklace again. The design of the horse reminded her of something, and when it struck, she lifted his hand and pushed back his coat sleeves. 'The horse on my necklace is exactly like the ones engraved on your cufflinks.'

'It is.'

The significance of that touched her very soul. She treasured the idea of how that connected them, made them a pair.

'Jillian designed the cufflinks for me several years ago. Wesley has a similar pair, but his design is of an entire horse.' Myles went on to explain how their father had encouraged them to start breeding racehorses and several other stories about things that had gone well with the business and hiccups that had happened along the way.

She was more than interested; she was enthralled to learn so much more about him, his family and the horses, and practically peppered him with questions, right up until the coach stopped again.

Then, when she lifted the curtain, she stiffened with confusion. 'We are at Dr Potter's house.'

'We are.'

'Why?'

'When I said I was jealous last night, I was telling the truth. I'd seen your coach on the road yesterday upon arriving in town and followed you, to here.'

She pressed a hand to her throat. 'That's how you found Joshua at the tavern.'

'Yes, and I wondered why he lied to me. Told me you were shopping.'

Grasping his arm, she shook her head. 'Don't blame him. Please. I asked him to not tell anyone.'

'I know, and I don't blame him for protecting his duchess. For following her orders.' He cupped her cheek with one hand. 'I will never question a servant or employee for obeying you.'

Guilt swirled in her stomach. 'I was going to tell you, I truly was.'

'I believe you, but I didn't give you a chance. When you came home with a rug for Roscoe, I decided it didn't matter why you'd been here, but then, my jealousy struck.'

Confused, she asked, 'Because of a rug?'

'No, because I smelled men's cologne on you.'

'Oh.' She hadn't noticed the scent of cologne, not even while dancing yesterday. Perhaps because she'd been pretending to dance with Myles. 'That was Dr Potter's son, Adam. He's tall and—'

'His strides are closer to mine for you to practise dancing with.'

'Yes.'

'My confession is not over. After almost punching Gibbs for staring at you non-stop last night, I came here to confront the cologne owner. Instead, I found Dr Potter.' Rubbing her cheek, he continued, 'You've amazed me numerous times over the past four weeks. You have become the Duchess that I need, one who has helped me in so many ways. With the horses, animals, guests, paperwork, and now I want to do something for you.'

'But you already have.'

He shook his head. 'No. I've given you things, but I haven't helped you achieve something you want.'

His eyes were truly amazing. So dark brown that the depths of them seemed endless, and right now were full

of something she didn't recognise but felt, yet she had to admit, 'I don't understand.'

'I've asked Dr Potter if we could have a therapy session together so I can learn to help you with your exercises and so we can practise dancing together. I want to be the one who helps heal your wounds.'

To anyone else, it might seem foolish, silly, but to her, what he was giving her, was the most precious gift she'd ever receive. Ever.

'I'd like that very much,' she said. 'So very much.'

Myles stood in the parlour, resting a hand against the fireplace mantel and staring at the door, waiting for a glimpse of Anita on the stairway. He'd never been excited for a ball before. They were a waste of time as far as he was concerned, but tonight was different. He was eager to show off his duchess.

How they'd spent the entire day together yesterday had made it the best day of his life. Every moment of it. During their dance lessons, Dr Potter had shown him how to keep a hand on Anita's hip, how that would aid her ability to control her movements. That of course was paramount, but he'd be lying if he didn't admit that he liked how that was more intimate than placing a hand on her back.

He also learned how to make sure she was always stepping with her right foot first, so the left one merely had to glide along while they danced. The lesson appeared to grow her confidence even more. It had also increased his. He liked knowing what he could do to help her.

Dr Potter had also shown him the foot manipulations exercises, which he'd performed for her this morning, greatly enjoying the feeling of her silky-smooth skin.

'Good evening, big brother.'

Myles nodded as Wesley entered the room. 'I was beginning to question if you'd already left for America.'

'Nope, not yet,' Wesley said. 'Sorry I wasn't able to make the dinner with our cousins the other night.'

'No, you aren't,' Myles replied.

'You're right, as usual.' Wesley grimaced. 'I'm not sorry. I have too few nights left in London to be stuck spending one of them with Gibb.'

'You are the lucky one in that sense.' Myles wrapped his left hand around his right fist. 'I almost hit my limit with him.'

'Aw,' Wesley groaned. 'You're making me wish I'd been here.'

'No, I'm not.'

Wesley nodded in agreement.

'Mother says she's barely seen you the past week,' Myles then said.

'Well, I was at Redford for a few days, as you know, and I am tying up loose ends before I leave.'

'I do hope those ends won't result in something I need to be concerned about,' Myles said with a large portion of serious warning.

'Don't worry, big brother, I will not be leaving any maidens sobbing about my departure.' Wesley slapped his shoulders. 'The next generation is your job, not mine.'

That was a job Myles was looking forward to and had a strong belief it would happen tonight.

Wesley laughed. 'It appears as if you no longer consider that a burden.'

'I don't,' Myles admitted.

'I can see why.'

Myles turned in the direction of Wesley's gaze, and

his hand slipped off the mantel so unexpectedly he stumbled slightly.

His brother laughed.

Myles shook his head but silently chuckled to himself. If he hadn't stumbled, he'd still be standing there, staring as his wife descended the stairway outside of the parlour's doorway; instead, he was now walking towards her, hand out for when she reached the bottom step.

Her green gown was probably lovely in the eyes of many, but his eyes were on her face, seeing how it glowed, how her eyes glistened. A beauty like no other. He was also an honest man and had to admit that his eyes also caught on her necklace, how the horse pendant settled nicely just above of the top of her cleavage.

He wouldn't mind being that horse's head right now.

Drawing in a breath that was unsteady due to several reactions taking place in his body, he took a hold of her hand as she stopped on the last step. 'You look extraordinarily beautiful, as usual.'

She smiled. 'You do tend to exaggerate, but thank you. You look quite charming yourself.'

'Charming, is it?'

'Yes.'

'I was going for handsome.'

The way she laughed was exactly what he'd been truly going for. The sound was amazing and he wanted to hear it all the time.

'You are always handsome,' she said, 'even when you aren't trying.'

A groan sounded as Wesley followed him into the corridor. 'My dear sister-in-law, please do not make his head any larger than it already is.'

'Oh,' Anita said, with a fake frown as she patted the

top of his head. 'I had not thought of that. The ceilings can't get any taller.'

'Exactly!' Wesley then gave her a bow. 'However, he, my big brother, was right. You are extraordinarily beautiful.'

'Thank you, Wesley,' she said. 'And you look very handsome as well.'

Giggles filtered from the corridor atop the stairs but then faded.

'Thank you,' Wesley said. 'It sounds like we might as well get ourselves a refreshment. For girls who have been looking forward to this ball for months, it might end before they are ready to go.'

Myles nodded. 'You might be right.'

Anita shook her head at both of them as she stepped off the stair. 'They will be ready soon. Just be patient.'

Myles nodded, but he was not thinking about his sisters. His mind was counting how many weeks they'd been married, and how patient he'd been during that time. There had been times that he'd felt as if his manhood had been twisted in knots and hoped that would all soon be over. The twisting part. The wonderful parts would go on for ever.

It wasn't long before his sisters and mother made their way downstairs, and though he would never understand such enthusiasm for a ball, he was happy for his sisters. They both looked very pretty, and perhaps a bit older than he would like.

Anita must have noticed that, because she whispered, 'Don't worry. They are good girls.'

'It's not them that I'm worried about,' he said. 'It's who will be looking at them, and why.'

'You have a few years before that will come,' she said.

'I hope so.' He glanced at her. 'Ready?'

She nodded. 'Yes, I am.'

The two of them rode in her coach while the rest of the family rode in a separate one, and he used the privacy for them to share a few kisses, because such opportunities would not be prevalent during the ball.

The two coaches arrived, one after the other, and the entire family entered the Arlington home together, where they were met by housemen offering to place their coats and capes aside until needed later.

His sisters were still giggling as they climbed the stairs to the second floor, and Myles waited until his family entered the glittering ballroom and were announced before he smiled down at his wife. He had the greatest desire to tell her that he loved her. So great it almost slipped out the second before he placed a tiny kiss on her temple.

With her arm hooked on his elbow, he led her forward through the wide double doors with pride filling chest like never before. The quiet that followed their announcement wasn't unexpected, nor were the stares coming from all directions.

Stopping before Donald Arlington, the Viscount Wakefield, and his wife, Myles made the introductions. There was a small amount of friendly chat, where Anita joined in, before they moved on so the next partygoers could greet the hosts.

The ballroom was full of groups of young girls dressed in their finery, clustered together and giggling, while being closely watched by other clusters of mothers, fathers and various family members. The fact that

events such as this truly only had one ultimate goal—marriages between members of the ton—was the very reason he'd avoided them as much as possible.

'The decorations are very lovely,' Anita said. 'Don't you think?'

He glanced around at the greenery and flowers, the bows and ribbons, including those casting down from the ceiling and looked at back her. 'I'll concede to your opinion, for true beauty doesn't come from adornments. I see that each time I look at you. It makes no difference what you wear, your natural beauty outshines it all.'

She let out a sigh that also held a slight, throaty groan. 'I now understand that your silver tongue is the part of the reason women quickly jumped at the chance to marry you.'

'What's the other part?' he asked.

'I'm not sure.' She cast him what he considered an appreciative head-to-toe gaze. 'Perhaps your charm.'

He gave her a much more thorough and appreciative gaze that lingered longer than necessary where the pendant of her necklace rested. Her ample bust was part of the reason; the other was the necklace. It was like a brand, his brand, and he liked that. 'Is that why you married me? My charm?'

She giggled. 'I married you because you needed a wife, and still do. Someone to tell you that we shouldn't be standing here blocking the pathway.'

He leaned down and whispered in her ear, 'Shall we find a secluded alcove and share a few secret kisses?'

The breath she sucked in made her bust line rise out of the neckline of her dress just a hint more. 'No. Don't be silly.'

'I'm not—' A slap on his back stopped his words.

'Redford.'

'Trimble,' he replied to the grinning, red-headed man. 'I see they'll let anyone in tonight.'

Trimble laughed. 'I sneaked in through the back door.' He then looked at Anita. 'I'm only joking, Your Grace.'

Myles introduced Robert Trimble, who would one day become the Duke of Hamstead, to Anita. After the pleasantries were exchanged, he explained that Trimble loved horse racing and owned two Redford thoroughbreds.

'What times are your animals running?' she asked.

Trimble lifted a brow.

Myles grinned and held his silence. In a very short time, Anita had learned more about horse racing than some of his grooms. Her notes in his ledger proved it, but their walks before he'd come to London the first time had included tons of questions from her about the animals.

'In the quarter mile,' she clarified.

Trimble rattled off a couple sets of numbers, the seconds it took his horses to run a quarter mile, and she responded with a thoughtful nod.

'Is that good or bad?' Trimble said. 'Do I need a new horse?'

'Everyone could use a new horse,' she said. 'A Redford thoroughbred, but those numbers are close to what our newly trained horses are running.'

Trimble glanced from her to Myles. 'Where did you find her? I need one just like her.'

Myles tucked her a bit closer to his side. If his pride in her continued to grow, he'd soon be popping the buttons off his vest. 'She's one of a kind, and she's mine.'

Chapter Fourteen

For weeks Anita had expected to find herself either scared to death or quite bored at the Christmas Ball, but she was, in fact, neither. The whole reason was her husband, of that she would never hold a doubt. The people she'd met so far were friendly and enjoyable to converse with, albeit many of them were close friends of Myles's or the family overall.

A large number were men, but many of them were married, and their wives were just as pleasant. Furthermore, the main subject always seemed to be the horses, or animals in general, subjects which she found easy to converse about.

After slowly strolling around the room, a small group of them, herself and Myles included, had found a generally quiet area in the supper room, a distance enough away from the massive buffet table and the crowds it drew, to speak without needing to raise their voices over the noise of so many people and the music that was being provided by the orchestra on the far side of the ballroom next door.

Lovely displays of bright ivy and holly were placed strategically, along with red and white flowers, giving the room a festive feel without taking up too much space. There were also red and green ribbons and bows, includ-

ing a few trailing down from the ceiling with red paper bells attached to the bottoms.

She grinned as Wesley walked past and winked at her with, once again, a different woman holding on to his arm. There certainly would be a large number of women disappointed when he left for America after the new year. The Redford brothers were handsome men and could steal a heart without even knowing it. Myles hadn't stolen hers, for he didn't want love, and though that saddened her a touch, she refused to let it overshadow her otherwise happiness. Being his wife, even without his love, was more than she'd ever dreamed, and she could live with that.

'Would you care to dance now?' Myles asked, leaning close to her ear.

A trickle of anxiety caused her to shiver slightly.

'It's all right.' He kissed her temple. 'We can later, or we don't have to at all.'

'No.' Shook her head, feeling foolish that she'd let any amount of anxiety unnerve her even briefly. 'I mean, yes, let's dance. Now.'

His eyes were full of compassion. 'We don't have to.'

'I know, but I want to.' She did want to dance, with him. Only him. She also knew that he was aware of how long they had been standing. He must have completely memorised everything that Dr Potter had said, because every so often throughout the evening, he'd suggested they move a small amount.

'All right, then.' He excused them from the others in their group, and then he slid his arm further around her, cupping her side as they began walking.

She loved the way he touched her, the way he made her feel so safe. At the same time, his gentle, soft caresses

had her body humming with sensations that made her want to close her eyes and just let the wondrous feelings consume her. That should make her uncomfortable, because they were surrounded by people, but she wasn't. She was happy. So happy to be the Duchess of Redford. Myles had given her so much; she couldn't ask for more. Wouldn't ask for more, even though she wondered what it would be like to be loved by him.

As they made their way around the large buffet table, they had to stop in order for several people to walk past carrying food-ladened plates towards a seating area.

'Anita?'

A shiver tickled her spine at recognising the high-pitched voice of her cousin Matilda. She turned. Smiled.

'It is you!' Matilda said. 'I barely recognise you. You're pretty. How did that happen?'

Anita's heart wanted to sink, but Myles's hand rubbed her side, letting her know she was not alone. 'Hello, Matilda.' Looking at Myles, she said, 'This is my cousin, Miss Matilda Crawford.'

'Your Grace,' Matilda said, giving her blond curls a shake. 'I'm sure you recall that we've met before. At the Pennington Ball last year.'

'Miss Crawford,' Myles replied.

Saving him from having to say more about remembering or not remembering Matilda, Anita asked, 'Is Irma with you? Are you visiting your aunt in London?' In her opinion, neither Matilda nor Irma were homely. In fact, with their blond hair, creamy complexions and faded blue eyes, they were quite pretty. It was their high-pitched voices and personalities that caused them to not maintain friends. Much like their father.

Matilda popped a confection in her mouth before answering, 'Yes, Irma's here somewhere, and we are all living with Aunt Rainie.'

Surprised, Anita asked, 'Living with your aunt? Why?'

Letting a sigh hang in the air, Matilda asked, 'Well, what did you expect after you stole away all of our servants?'

Anita's first impulse was to apologise, but she stopped herself. She also stopped Myles from stepping forward and speaking with a quick shake of her head. 'Olive and Joshua were hardly all of your servants.'

'Well, the rest quit within a week of you leaving.' Matilda popped another confection into her mouth. 'With no one to cook for us, we moved to London. To Aunt Rainie's. She's not happy about it. Neither is Father. He says it's all your fault. That he should never have let you leave.'

'Excuse us, Miss Crawford,' Myles said, and gently tugged on Anita's waist for them to walk away.

Anita gladly complied.

'Hey,' Matilda said in their wake, 'why aren't you limping?'

'I will have them removed,' Myles said.

'No,' Anita replied. A part of her was embarrassed, but a large part of her wasn't going to let it affect her, or him. Hopefully, he wasn't affected. Oh, how she hoped he wasn't affected.

'Would you like me to contact your uncle?' he asked.

The shiver that rippled over her was far from tiny. 'Why?'

He stopped and turned so they faced each other. 'I

could enquire if Brunswick is for sale. I could purchase it for you. It is your family home.'

'Not any more,' she said.

His lips turned up into a smile. 'No, it's not. Redford is.'

She nodded and was very thankful he'd replied exactly as she'd hoped he would. 'I'm sorry about—'

'There is no need for you to apologise about anything,' he said.

His face truly was dashingly handsome. She wished they were alone so she could kiss him. Instead, she would settle for being in his arms. 'Can we dance now?'

'Yes, we can.'

A sweet thrill filled her, making her realise that she still wasn't nervous, not even after encountering Matilda. She did feel sorry for the servants who had lost their employment, but in all honesty, no one had ever stayed long at Brunswick, other than Joshua. She was doubly grateful to Myles for providing Joshua and Olive positions.

Myles led her onto the dance floor with one hand, then bowed, and kissed the back of her hand before stepping forward and placing one hand on her hip and clasping one of her hands with his other one.

She set her other hand on his shoulder.

With a smile, Myles stepped closer, much closer than he had at the doctor's office, and a whole lot closer than either Dr Potter or his son had been during her lessons.

'Is this proper?' she asked. The feelings surging through her weren't proper. She wanted to press herself against him, like she had during their kisses. Or like in the dream she'd had last night that had woken her up and left her writhing in her bed, heart pounding.

'We are married,' he said.

'All right.' She nodded and threw propriety to the wind while sliding her arm around his neck rather than resting it on his shoulder.

The first notes of music began to fill the room. 'Ready?' he asked.

'Yes.' Gracefully smooth, they took the first step together.

The then next and the next. Dancing had been so much easier than she'd imagined. All she had to do was let the music in, let her body feel the rhythm. That's what Dr Potter had said, and it worked.

It worked even stronger with Myles. Besides feeling the music, her body could feel him, and that didn't leave any room for her to worry about tripping as he led her across the floor. All she had to do was follow his lead, step with her right foot and let her left foot slide. Step and slide. Step and slide.

Myles kept their steps in time with the music, and he kept his eyes on her, the entire time. Giving her mind even less room for worry.

'I feel as if I'm floating on air,' she admitted.

The twinkle in his eyes grew brighter. 'Are you saying that I'm sweeping you off your feet?'

She knew the meaning behind that, and even though her mind didn't want to work, she still had enough sense to not speak of love. He didn't want it, and she wasn't going to do anything to ruin what they did have. 'I didn't know you knew how to sweep,' she said. 'I've never seen you use a broom.'

He laughed. 'I know how to sweep. I've swept out plenty of stalls.'

'Does that mean I'm going to end up in a wheelbarrow?'

He laughed harder. Then the gleam in his eyes grew stronger and made the heat in her belly feel fiery as he brought them even closer together so her breasts were touching his chest. A tiny moan at the pleasure rippling through her rumbled in the back of her throat.

'No,' he said, close to her ear, 'but I might try a haystack.'

The music stopped before she could think of a reply. Considering how hard it was to think, that was understandable. He kissed her neck right beneath her ear before he stepped back. 'Thank you, my dear. That was the most enjoyable dance I've ever had.'

'Thank you, Your Grace,' she replied. 'It indeed was delightful.'

As they walked off the floor, she felt eyes on them. She hadn't while they had been dancing, but did now. Coming from all directions. A hint of fear rose up inside her. Had she stumbled and not realised it?

'Did I stumble?' she asked him, needing to know the truth.

'No, not at all. People are simply amazed by how I chose the perfect bride. And they're jealous,' he said. 'So very jealous that there's only one of you.'

She doubted that, but as long as she hadn't stumbled, she wasn't going to argue. Instead, she laughed. 'You jest.'

'Hardly. You impressed Trimble with your racing time knowledge, and it's grown from there all night. I couldn't be prouder of you. Prouder to be married to you.'

She couldn't be happier.

Until she noticed the man directly in front of them.

In all the years she'd lived at Brunswick, she'd never known Uncle Jerome to attend a ball. He looked the same. Ruddy-faced, thick black sideburns above his jowls, a suit that was too small for his barrel shaped body.

Myles's arm stiffened beneath her hold, telling her that he'd noticed her uncle, too. She wanted to stop walking, turn around, anything, but Myles kept walking forward with even strides, so she did, too.

'Brunswick,' Myles said as they came face to face with her uncle.

'Redford,' Uncle Jerome replied. Glancing her way, he said, 'I don't like being duped.'

'You weren't duped, Brunswick,' Myles said. 'Step aside.'

Curling his nose into a snarl, Uncle Jerome kept looking at her. 'Pretending to be lame so you wouldn't have to do any work. You're disgusting!'

Anita felt everything she'd gained slipping away. Her happiness, her confidence and more. An ugly darkness that used to shroud her was moving back in.

'Unless you don't want to keep your teeth,' Myles growled. 'I suggest you stop talking now.'

Uncle Jerome squared his shoulders. 'You know the cost of a good brood mare verses a nag. You owe me—'

Anita heard no more because the room erupted as Myles leaped forward. Wesley and Robert Trimble appeared out of nowhere, each one grabbing one of Myles's arms, and several other men rushed to stand between Myles and her uncle, who was still shouting, but others were shouting over him as several men grabbed him by the arms and dragged him away.

It all happened within a matter of seconds, minutes at the most, but the shame inside her would live for ever.

She'd rather have tripped than having it announced that Myles only married her to be a brood mare. But, in truth, she wasn't even that.

There would come a time when he'd thank Wesley and Trimble for stopping him from reaching Brunswick and making the scene worse, but right now, Myles still wanted to shred the man to pieces. The look of mortification on Anita's face had been the only reason he hadn't broken the holds on his arms to follow the men who'd hauled Brunswick away.

When he'd wrapped his arms around her, she'd been shaking as hard as she had the day she'd arrived at Redford, driving the team of horses through the snowstorm.

Both Lady and Lord Wakefield had apologised profusely for allowing Brunswick to attend and for his vile words, and encouraged them to stay for the rest of the ball, but Myles had thought it best to take Anita home.

She didn't say a word until they climbed into the coach, then she said, 'This isn't going to work, Myles.'

His anger at Brunswick was still just below the surface—and at himself. She'd worked so hard and had done so much in order to attend this ball. All for him.

This beautiful, amazing woman with a heart the size England, who'd bought a Christmas present for a dog, had done it all for him. She'd been enjoying herself, and he'd ruined it for her. He should have steered her away from Brunswick, left before the man had the chance to say a word.

Would she ever trust him again to protect her, keep

her from getting hurt? 'Yes, it will work,' he said. 'We'll make it work.'

'Why?'

It was dark inside the coach, but he could see that her face was turned from him. Hiding the tears that he could hear in her voice. He almost said that it would work because he loved her but wasn't sure she'd believe that, not after claiming he didn't want love. 'Because we're married.'

'Are we? Or are we just pretending?'

'No, we aren't pretending.' He reached for her hand.

She folded her arm across her body, turning farther away from him. 'Aren't we? I knew who I was until I met you, and now...'

'Anita.' He reached for her again, but she flinched before his hand touched her shoulder.

'Please, don't,' she said, burying herself farther into the corner of the coach.

He didn't know what to do or say. The desire to make Brunswick pay for what he'd said, for the way he'd always treated her, flared again as the carriage rolled thorough the quiet streets, and deep thoughts of revenge formed. Multiple ways he could see that Brunswick got his due. There were things he could do, things he could pay others to do, as well. The man would never be able to show his face in public again by the time he was done. He'd force him make a public apology to her, too.

When the coach rolled to a stop, he opened the door himself rather than waiting for the driver and escorted her inside, down the corridor to the entrance of the parlour. 'Would you like a glass of sherry or some brandy?'

'No.' The sorrow in her eyes was massive. 'You don't want to be married to me, and I—'

'Yes, I do.'

She backed away from him. Hands held up as if defending him off. 'I thought I could do this, but I can't. I just can't.'

The colour was gone from her face, the shine from her eyes. The woman before him was not the same one he'd gotten to know. This was the meek version of Anita who had appeared now and again, briefly, when she'd first arrived at Redford. He didn't know what to do, how to get the other one back. The one with determination and backbone. 'I'm sorry this happened. Your uncle is looking for an easy way to make money. I didn't think he'd stoop to—'

'Telling the truth?' she interrupted.

'No!'

Shaking her head, she turned, grasped a hold of the banister. 'Yes, he did.'

He shot around her, leaped up the steps. 'No, he did not.'

'I'm tired,' she said. 'And if I could run, I'd already be upstairs. Away from you. Away from everything.'

Not knowing what else to do, he stepped out of the way, let her walk up the stairs.

It felt as if he was watching his life walk away. A life that he hadn't known he wanted but did. He wanted to spend the rest of his life with her. Loving her. Unable to stop himself, he said, 'Anita, I love you.'

She paused for a moment, then let out a sob that echoed in his ears as she took the last few steps faster than he'd ever seen her move.

Regret, remorse and worse filled him as she disappeared into the upper corridor. Why had he said that? Because he did love her. There was no denying it. Maybe he should start over with her and, this time, do it right?

Ask her to marry him because he loved her. But did she want that? It didn't appear so.

He heard the click of a door, her bedroom door, and he slapped the banister rail. Hell! He wished that Wesley and Trimble hadn't stopped him from reaching Brunswick tonight.

Calling her a brood mare! Of all the nasty—

He sank onto the stairs. Brunswick was a vile, cruel and sick man, but there had been an ounce of truth in what he'd said. A terrible truth.

Feeling as if he'd just been shot in the heart, Myles hung his head. He had arranged the marriage in order to secure an heir. He'd told her that he didn't want a wife, that he needed one. Needed a brood mare.

He was such a selfish lout and didn't deserve her, but he wasn't going to lose her. Determination shot him off the step. If his mother was here, she'd probably tell him to leave Anita alone. Give her some time. That had been the right advice last time, but not this time. Anita had to know that he didn't want a brood mare. He wanted a wife. Her. That he'd wanted her as his wife for weeks.

He spun about but froze before climbing a single step. If she could run, she'd already be away from him. That's what she'd said.

Turning, he walked into the parlour.

Love wasn't a distraction. It was devastating. Devastating to all those involved.

He had no idea how long he'd been in the parlour wallowing in self-pity but knew sitting here wasn't going to solve anything.

And this was a problem that needed to be solved.

He took the stairs two at a time. Even if it took all

night, he had to make Anita believe that he loved her. Wanted her.

There was no light coming from under the door of her room. Had she fallen asleep already, or was she lying in the dark, crying again all because of him?

His hand shook as he reached for the door-knob. Out of fear. He was afraid. Scared to death that he, not her uncle, had hurt her beyond repair. She might never be able to love him. Might never want to see him. Might want to leave for ever. What would he do?

He'd have to let her go. Have to. He couldn't force her to stay, hold her against her will.

Releasing the knob, he tugged at the cravat around his neck that felt as if it were choking him. He pulled it off and unbuttoned the collar of his shirt, sucked in air. Ah, hell, he might as well get rid of his coat and vest, too, and pulled them off. His cufflinks caught his eyes, the carved horse-head exactly like the one he'd given her.

Her love of animals, of the horses, was just one of the things that had surprised him. One of the things they had in common and one of the things that made her the perfect Duchess of Redford. A duchess who he didn't want to live without.

He unhooked the cufflinks and dropped them in his pocket, all the while deciding that he needed to spend some serious time thinking about what he was going to say. How he was going to convince her to stay. How he would beg her to give him yet another chance. This could be the greatest failure of his life.

Reaching the door to his room, he grasped the knob. Unlike at Redford, his room here didn't have a separate bedroom from the sitting area; it was all one large

space, and several lamps had been lit for his arrival. He wouldn't have minded the darkness, wouldn't have minded the— His thoughts and footsteps stalled.

'I have something I need to tell you,' she said from where she sat in his bed. In, not on, because she was under the covers. Well, they were up to her waist, revealing that she was wearing a thin—so thin it made him swallow—white nightgown. One long, thick braid of her shimmering hair hung over one shoulder, down to her elbow, and her eyes, those unique colour-changing eyes that held so much emotion, were looking at him with a bit of unease, but he also saw confidence in them.

'I have something I need to tell you, too,' he answered, while kicking the door shut with his heel. He tossed the jacket, vest and cravat on to a chair and crossed the room. He'd dreamed of this, wanted this, but not this way. Not because she believed she was a brood mare. Rather than climbing on the bed, an act he wanted to do so badly, he knelt beside it and took a hold of her hand. Searching for the right words—God he needed the right words right now—he kissed the inside of her wrist.

She cupped the side of his face with her hand. 'I sat down on the stool for Claire to remove the pins from my hair, and when I looked into the mirror, all I could see in the reflection was the necklace you gave me.'

He turned his face enough to kiss the inside of her palm, still searching for the right thing to say. He couldn't just blurt out that he loved her again, he had to explain, beg her forgiveness.

'Then I saw the rest of me,' she said. 'The person I've become, not the person I was. I almost became that person again. Actually, I think I did, for a short time. Became

the old me. The sound of Uncle Jerome's voice made me feel dark and ugly. I didn't want to feel that way, but I couldn't seem to stop it.'

'You aren't that person,' he whispered, cursing himself for not ignoring Brunswick. He could have simply steered her in the other direction and avoided all that, but hadn't because he was so proud of her. He'd wanted Brunswick to see how beautiful and perfect she was in every way.

'No, I'm not,' she said. 'The moment you hugged me, the darkness began to fade, but the memories were still there, telling me I was useless, lame, not someone anyone would want, until I saw the necklace in the mirror. It was so bright. So beautiful. Then I knew that I had the ability to never be that old me again. I will not allow a man who is such a failure that he takes his anger out on everyone else because he can't stand to see someone be successful, happy, to take that from me. To take anything from me. Nor from you. I won't apologise for him. He doesn't deserve that. He's always blamed others, when it was his fault. It was all his fault. He inherited so much, and now Brunswick sits empty because of him. I will not accept that blame.' Her lips curled into a tentative smile. 'I know I have my faults, things about me that can never change, but if you are willing, I promise I'll do everything I can to be the wife you need.'

He wanted so much to climb onto the bed, hug her, kiss her, tell her that she had no faults and didn't need to change, but he couldn't. Not until she knew the entire truth. This was his chance to start over with her with a clean plate. 'It was all Brunswick's fault, and you shouldn't accept any blame,' he said. 'Nor do you have

any faults. But I do, and though I am beyond willing, I can't ask you to stay, can't expect you to stay with me until you know the truth. The whole truth.'

Frowning slightly while nodding, she said, 'All right.'

'When I was young,' he started, 'my father told me that a man has to have priorities, that if he had too many irons in the fire, he would fail. I decided that I was never going to fail and, in my young mind, determined that if I never put love into my fire, I wouldn't fail, because then my dreams, my priorities would never shift. When my father died and I had to take over the Dukedom, it became apparent that marrying, having an heir, was a priority whether I wanted it to be or not. I thought I could manage it as long as I didn't let love in there. When I discovered that Leslie was in love with someone else, I didn't care. I almost married her anyway, until it was brought to my attention that I would never know if any child produced between us was mine, and that would have been a failure.'

She was looking at him with such compassion, such understanding, he hated to go on, hated for her to know his motives had been so self-centred. He had to. She had a right to know. Deserved to know.

'Then, as you know, there was Diana. I didn't care that she wanted the esteem of being a duchess, wanted to do nothing more than flutter around London, until I saw her in a childish fit of rage that was beyond embarrassing. Having a duchess with such low regard of others and self-control would have been a failure on my part. Breaking a second engagement was easy. I'd done it before and didn't consider it a failure, just a mistake that I needed to correct. I was also relieved, because I hadn't

wanted to marry either of them.' Shaking his head at his selfishness, he continued. 'When I heard about Brunswick offering you up in card games, I thought someone needed to stop him. Rescue you from him. A couple of years ago, we'd been at the same horse race, and he'd ended up owing me a considerable amount of money that I'd written off as a bad debt, but then I decided to use it to stop his maltreatment of you.'

He wrapped both hands around her wrist. Kissed her fingers. 'I didn't go to him to buy you. I went to hold the debt over his head, but shortly into our meeting, I knew that wouldn't stop him. I left, but I couldn't get you out of my mind. I talked to Joshua and Dr Potter, the Dowager Countess of Wheyfield and others, and knew I had to do something. I never once thought of you as a brood mare. I just couldn't let you stay there any longer and thought that you'd be so grateful to me for rescuing you that you'd agree to become my wife. I was wrong for putting you in that position. Wrong for not giving you a choice.'

Never taking her eyes off him, she scooted closer to the edge of the bed. 'You weren't wrong,' she said. 'You did rescue me, and I will be grateful to you for ever for that. And you did give me a choice. The first choice I'd ever had.'

'Not much of one. You were already at my house, and I, well, I wouldn't have let you go back to your uncle. I couldn't. You deserve so much more than that.' He loved her. Loved her so much that he had to give her what she should have had. 'You also deserve a choice of who you marry, the opportunity to find someone worthy of your love.'

Chapter Fifteen

If she had still been her old self, the one who never stood her ground, never fought for what she wanted, Anita might have been scared right now, worried that Myles didn't want to remain married to her. That meek and un-confident Anita was gone and would never return. The one sitting on his bed not only had confidence; she'd learned so much about this man before her. This amaz-ing man who had seen her at her worst, freezing cold and wet, unable to walk, yet had still asked her to marry him. Who had seen her injury, yet focused only on find-ing her relief from the pain it caused. Who had seen her insecurities yet pointed out her strengths. Who knew she couldn't be fixed yet helped her to heal. Who had never asked anything of her yet gave her so much.

All of that was admirable, so very admirable, but it was his heart that she'd truly come to know. He was afraid to give it out freely, because he didn't want to fail. Neither did she. Yet, somehow, without knowing it, that's what they both had done. Given away their hearts, without failure.

When he'd said that he loved her while she'd been climbing the stairs, running away from him, she'd thought

he couldn't love her. No one could. But then, she'd seen the necklace in the mirror. In that moment, she knew. Knew he did love her. Because she knew him. He hadn't said it before, but he'd shown her. He'd been worried about her falling, worried about her pain, admitted his jealousy, learned to dance, gifted her with a personalised necklace and so much more, all because he loved her.

All of that was crystal-clear now. It hadn't been before, because she'd thought that she would never experience love. But she had. He truly had rescued her. In so many ways. Living at Redford had allowed her to unlock her old memories of being loved. He'd demonstrated his love in so many ways, but she hadn't recognised it as such because she had forgotten what it looked like, what it felt like. It had become buried beneath the pain that had become her crutch, until he'd shown her that she didn't need a crutch. Not when she had him. Not when she had his love.

Mary was right. Feeling the power of true love was amazing, and was worth whatever it took.

Leaning forward, she softly touched his lips with hers. 'I choose you,' she said. 'Of all the men in the world to marry, I'd choose you over and over again.'

He grasped her face with both hands and leaned back, stared at her.

Those incredible brown eyes of his were searching hers, looking deep, and she didn't mind that he could see clear to her soul. She welcomed it. 'You are worthy of my love,' she said, 'and you have it. You've had it for weeks. I love you, Myles Wadsworth, Seventh Duke of Redford. I love you very, very much.'

His lips met hers in a hard, almost desperate kiss. 'I love you, too.' He kissed her again. 'So much.'

'I know.' She also knew that she sounded smug, because she was, would always be about being loved by him. Others could only wish to be her. That was a bit conceited, too, but she was the Duchess of Redford and very proud of that. Proud of him.

He laughed. 'I'm glad you know that, and I do. I will love you until the end of days.' He combed his fingers into her hair. 'I was wrong about it. About love. About not wanting it. You changed my mind. You changed my life.'

'You changed mine.' She ran her hand up his chest, to his shoulders. Her newfound confidence held no bounds. 'We aren't going to fail at this or anything else. We are going to succeed. All those irons you have in the fire, I'm going to help you with them.'

'And I will help you with all of yours.'

Feeling so free, so alive, so confident in who she was and in their love, she kissed the tip of his chin. She wasn't as good at teasing as he was, or the rest of his family, but she was working on it. 'Good, because I can't figure out what to buy the peacocks for Christmas.'

Laughing, he grasped her waist, pushing her across the bed as he climbed on it. She knew what was about to come, and she wanted it. Wanted it so very much.

He held the back of her head as his lips descended upon hers in a kiss that reached the very depths of her soul. A kiss where her love for him was strong and true and, like his, would last until the end of days.

She wrapped her arms around him and retuned his open-mouth kiss with all the passion she'd experienced

only in her dreams. Those wanton, wifely dreams that were about to come true.

His hand slid up her side to her breast and cupped it. She didn't attempt to smother the moan that rumbled in her throat at the pleasure, and at the sweet, hot desire that spread far beyond her lower belly. It was everywhere. Her entire body was alive, wanting to be a part of loving him. A part of sharing their love.

Dreaming about something wasn't nearly as intoxicating as the real thing. It was breathtaking, and knowing she could have this, could kiss him whenever she wanted, was addictive. They'd only just begun, yet she already felt like she'd won. Won the greatest prize life had to offer.

Feeling emboldened by the power of their love, she pushed up the material of his shirt to feel the heat of skin, the hardness of his chest. The idea of exploring his naked flesh thrilled her as she ran her hands around to his back, where she let her fingers and palms explore at will.

'Berries,' he said, while running a line of kisses down the side of her neck.

Questioning her hearing due to how hard her heart was pounding, she repeated, 'Berries?'

He leaned back, smiling and nodded. 'Yes, we'll give the peacocks berries for Christmas. They constantly try to break into the garden to eat them off the bushes.'

Her life had already become wonderful, and that was just going to keep happening, because he just kept being more wonderful. Reaching up, she slid a button on his shirt through the buttonhole, then another one. 'Where do you plan on getting berries in the middle of winter?'

'Cabbages?' He grinned. 'There are always plenty of cabbages in the cellar.'

She reached for the last button, unbuttoned it. 'You don't like cabbage?'

'I like you.' He pulled off his shirt and threw it over the side of the bed.

His bare chest, sprinkled with dark hair, looked so powerful, so lean and muscular and enticing. 'Cabbages it is,' she said and ran a hand up the centre of his chest. 'Thank you for solving that problem.'

He caught her hand and folded his fingers around it. 'Is there anything I can help you with right now?'

The sensations he aroused in her were nothing short of wicked, and she wanted to explore those feelings to the fullest. Not embarrassed by that, she replied, 'Yes.'

'What would that be?'

She wasn't shy in her request, either. 'I have the over-whelming desire to be your wife in every way.'

The smile on his face was not only dashingly hand-some; it was filled with promise. 'That will be an easy request to fulfil.' He lifted her hand, kissed her fingers and then swung his legs over the edge of the bed. 'But I must warn you, it will take some time,' he said, tugging off his tall boots.

No, it wouldn't! She'd already waited four weeks! While he removed his boots and breeches, she tugged her nightgown over her head and tossed it to the floor so that when he turned about, she was as naked as him. Except for the bedcovers that came up to her waist.

They stared at each other, exploring with their eyes. Hers narrowed in on his hips, and lower, the area where

she'd only seen such images in crass drawings in books. The artists definitely had never seen her husband.

Excitement reverberated through her as he climbed back onto the bed, his gaze still roaming from her face downward. Every inch of her tingled, begging for his touch, and the appreciation in his eyes left her feeling as if she might never be able catch her breath again.

He placed a finger beneath her chin and, with a slow smile, covered her mouth in a long, dreamy kiss. 'We are in no hurry, my love,' he said. 'We have all night. The first night of the rest of our lives.'

Coming out of the depths of a deep sleep, Anita stretched her arms, covered a yawn and kept her eyes closed as a smile overtook her mouth. It hadn't been a dream. She'd had her wedding night, a month late, but it had been worth the wait.

So worth the wait.

She let out a deep, satisfied sigh at the happiness fully shrouding her. It was as if she were floating on a cloud, basking in bright sunlight, without a care in the world. Glory be, but becoming Myles's wife had been a glorious occasion. It had surpassed her dreams, her expectations. The things they'd done hadn't been wicked. They'd been divine acts of giving and receiving pleasure, of cherishing and possessing one another.

He had certainly fulfilled her request. More than once. He'd made her feel so complete, so loved, so blissful. She didn't even regret that it hadn't happened before last night. The weeks they'd shared falling in love had created a deep devotion that she would now spend the rest of her life basking in. Rejoicing in. Reliving.

'Are you going to lie there all day, pretending to be asleep and smiling?'

Giggling, she kept her eyes closed, even as her heart thudded at the sound of his voice. 'Maybe.'

The lips that touched hers were warm and tender, but what she loved the most was their familiarity. He'd used them proficiently in demonstrating how spectacular it was to be his wife in every way many times last night, and again this morning as the sun was raising.

Stretching her arms out, she wrapped them around his neck, keeping his lips against hers. Feeling the collar, then the back of his shirt just to confirm things, is what made her end the kiss and open her eyes. 'You're dressed.'

He grinned. 'Yes, I am.'

'Why?'

'Because I didn't want to shock the entire household by walking around naked.'

Waking to such a handsome face each morning added to the bliss inside her, and she let out a sigh of satisfaction. 'Others are awake?'

'Yes.'

'I suspect that means I should get up, too.' She'd never been one to lounge about, but she'd never had a loving husband to share a bed with, either. Pressing a finger in the middle of his chin, she let out a little moan. 'Get dressed…'

He chuckled and kissed her lips. 'Only if you want to travel to Redford today. The others have already left.' He kissed her chin, then her shoulder. 'We could stay another day. If you'd like.'

She contemplated that as he kissed the swell of her beasts, right above where the blankets covered her. The

thrill that shot through her would be so easy to give in to, yet she had to admit, 'I want to go home. To Redford. See Roscoe, the peacocks and the horses.'

'Then that's what we will do,' he said, tugging the blanket down to her waist. 'Later today.'

His mouth found one of her breasts, and she arched her back, ran her fingers in his silky hair, fully welcoming his actions. 'Yes, later will be just fine.'

It was mid-afternoon by the time they left London, the two of them riding in the luxurious coach with Joshua driving and Donovan ambling along behind them, tethered to the back. City traffic was slow, and there was a nip in the air, but neither bothered Anita. She had her husband beside her and his love inside her. Both kept her warm.

They had yet to reach the outskirts of the city when the coach steered to the side of the street and came to a stop. She looked at Myles. He shrugged and pulled back the curtain covering the window at the same time the coach door opened.

'Sorry to intrude,' Wesley said, stepping inside. 'I was hoping to catch you before you left the house.'

'Why?' Myles asked. 'You'll be coming to Redford tomorrow for the yuletide season. Mother will have your head if you don't.'

Wesley sat on the seat opposite them. 'Oh, yes, I'll be there, but I heard some news this morning that I wanted to share with Anita.' Wesley smiled at her. 'Just so you are prepared if there's a message waiting for you at Redford.'

'Concerning what?' Myles asked.

She felt the way he stiffened and patted his leg. No one would be contacting her for anything of importance.

'From what I've discovered, and it's taken me most of the morning and afternoon to confirm it all with several sources, Brunswick has had a mishap.'

She was far too content for any news of her uncle to overly disturb her and simply asked, 'What sort of mishap?'

'Along with having Brunswick removed from his property last night,' Wesley explained, 'Arlington also requested that the Countess Brunswick and her daughters be removed, as well as her sister Rainie, the Dowager Countess of Wheyfield. That was the final straw for the Dowager, who reportedly has had little tolerance for Brunswick. She had him removed from her house as well, during that removal, he tripped or fell, or something, and broke both ankles.'

Anita would never be happy about someone being injured, but she wasn't sad, either. Just neutral, which surprised her. She glanced at Myles, who gave her hand a gentle squeeze.

'A constable called in a doctor,' Wesley continued. 'Dr Potter. He reportedly told Brunswick that nothing could be done. However, due to his oath, Potter summoned another doctor, who suggested that Brunswick be admitted to a hospital.' Wesley shook his head. 'No hospital would take him due to his debts.'

Anita knew well that hospitals could choose their patients. More than once her uncle had told her how none of them would even look at her foot due to her lack of coin.

'So he was admitted to a Poor Law Infirmary in the West End,' Wesley said.

Anita glanced up at Myles. Everyone knew the West End consisted of the worst slums of London.

He gave a slight nod. 'It appears that in time, some problems do work themselves out.'

She nodded but wasn't sure how the new her should handle this information. The old her hadn't had any means to help anyone, including herself, but the new one did.

'I didn't want you to be surprised if you receive a message from the infirmary,' Wesley said. 'When his wife and sister-in-law refused to help him, Brunswick said his niece, the Duchess of Redford, needed to be contacted to get him out of such a hell hole.'

'I see,' Myles said. 'Well, thank you, dear brother. We will be prepared if a message arrives.'

'You're welcome.' Wesley reached over and patted her knee before he opened the door and made his exit.

Unsure of herself, Anita looked up at her husband, seeking his wisdom. His help.

He tugged her closer to his side and kissed her temple as the wheels on the coach began to roll again. 'You are not responsible for him.'

She nodded. Just last night she'd determined that she'd never have anything to do with her uncle again, but even all that wasn't helping her confliction.

'No one can fix all the problems of the world,' Myles said, 'but they can do what feels right. If it will make you feel better, and because it was due to him that I met you, the love of my life, we could send a donation to the infirmary.'

The softening in her heart had nothing to do with her uncle. It was all due to her husband. He was right.

Her uncle wasn't her responsibility, but she wasn't uncaring, either. A donation to see that he did receive care was fair. She laid her head on his shoulder. 'I think that would be fine. A stay in the infirmary might be good for him. Sometimes all it takes is a new place to live to change a person.'

Myles lifted her chin, pressed his forehead to hers. 'I love you.'

'I love you more,' she said. 'Every day, I love you more and more.'

Epilogue

One year later...

The large yule-log burning behind the grate of the fireplace in the front parlour snapped and crackled as flames ate away at the wood. Ivy and holly were strung along the mantel, with draping red bows on each end, and mistletoe, his now favourite plant, hung in the doorway to the room that also hosted the large decorated Christmas tree.

An entire wall next to the fireplace was covered with Christmas cards they'd received in the post, and Myles was very sure that his beautiful wife had sent out hundreds the past week. The Duchess of Redford had captured the hearts of the ton, and the horse-racing world, as quickly as she had his.

She was standing at the wall, tacking up yet another colourful card. He walked up behind her, wrapped both arms around her waist and pulled her back against him. 'One more?'

She leaned her head against his shoulder. 'Yes, from Aunt Tilda. I don't believe she's ever sent out cards before.'

'Are you surprised?' He wasn't. Brunswick, claiming

it hurt too much to walk, was homebound, and Tilda had taken over the family finances. She may have received help from her sister Rainie, no one knew for sure, but Tilda had managed to reopen the Brunswick estate and was doing a fair job at refilling the family coffers, even after paying off numerous debts.

'No, I'm not surprised,' she replied, 'and I do hope Uncle Jerome appreciates all that Aunt Tilda is doing.'

Myles had his doubts but kept them silent.

Anita twisted her neck enough to look at him. 'We can always hope for the best.'

He laughed and hugged her tighter. 'Yes, we can.'

She wiggled from his hold and turned about, rested both hands on his shoulders. 'I was just thinking about the past year,' she said, 'how wonderful it's been, how much we have to be thankful for, and thinking of the new year to come.'

'It has been a wonderful year.' He used the stopwatch she'd given him for Christmas last year almost every day when timing the horses, and for a few other reasons, but the gift she'd given him this year didn't compare to anything he'd ever received. It had arrived two months ago. Their son, Michael, named after Myles's father, was the sum of their love.

Pulling an envelope out of his pocket, Myles handed it to her. It was just one of the gifts he'd give her for Christmas this year.

'What's this?' she asked.

'Open it.'

She lifted the flap and pulled out the slip of paper, frowning slightly. '"Belmont Stakes Raci—" Oh! Oh! A horse race! We're going to a horse race! In Amer-

ica!' She flung her arms around his neck and jumped up and down.

He held on to her waist to steady her. There would never come a time when he didn't worry about her re-injuring her foot, because he loved her just the way she was, whereas she seemed to have completely forgotten about her old injury. 'Yes, in June,' he replied.

'And we'll meet the Duchess!'

'You're the Duchess,' he reminded.

'Of Redford! We'll meet the Duchess of Manhattan! Oh, your mother and sisters have to come with us! They'll perish if I meet the Duchess and they don't!'

Keeping his laugher silent, he asked, 'You do know you're talking about a horse, right?'

She gave his chest a playful slap. 'Of course I know I'm talking about a horse! It'll be wonderful to see everyone!'

He agreed with that. It would be wonderful to see his brother and the American facility he'd created for the Redford thoroughbreds.

'Oh! I can't wait for June,' she said. 'I just can't wait.'

Leaning forward, he touched her lips with his while pulling her closer. 'I have an idea of something we could do while you're waiting.'

Her giggle was soft and throaty as she rubbed her body against his. 'We only have about an hour before Michael's feeding time.'

As he swept her off her feet and into his arms to carry her to their bedchamber, he said, 'That will do. That will do.'

* * * * *

HISTORICAL

Your romantic escape to the past.

Available Next Month

Penniless Until The Earl's Proposal Helen Dickson
The Truth Behind The Governess Carol Arens

..

A Wager To Win The Debutante Eva Shepherd
The Lady's Proposal For The Laird Jeanine Englert

Keep reading for an excerpt of a new title
from the Historical series,
ACCIDENTAL COURTSHIP WITH THE EARL
by Samantha Hastings

Chapter One

Hampford Castle, England—
1817

The snake slithered down the steps before her in the secret passageway. Lady Helen Stringham preferred it that way. She didn't like mice and her pet snake, Theodosia, ensured that not a mouse could be found in the dark hall. Turning the corner, she realised that she was not alone.

It wasn't a mouse—it was her little sister, Rebecca.

Helen breathed in sharply. 'What are you doing here?'

Becca shook her head in the dim light. 'The same thing you are. Eavesdropping on Mama and Papa.'

Helen sat next to her sister, near the secret door that led to her mother's dressing room. The door that neither of her parents knew about. They both leaned against it, pressing their ears close to the age-old wood. Linking arms, they eagerly waited to hear what their parents had decided about their London Season.

'Why must they go to London at all?' Papa asked from the other side. 'I don't see why they need to get married. I would much prefer that they stayed with us for ever.'

'You didn't mind when the older children left,' Mama pointed out.

'Because they weren't half as interesting as the two youngest.'

Helen nudged Becca and they both grinned at each other. *Dear Papa.*

They heard Papa clear his throat. 'I...uh... Well, the thing is...you see... Becca is not getting any younger... and she is very mature for her age...certainly...uh...more mature than most debutantes. I do believe with all of my— *head* that it would be a marvellous idea. Or was it a great idea? It's both! For her to accompany Helen this Season.'

Helen couldn't hold in her smirk. Papa had just ruined Becca's carefully prepared speech that she'd composed for him.

The word was supposed to be heart, *darling Papa.*

'I see that Becca has put you up to asking me if she can go with Helen to London and debut at the same time.'

Mama had seen right through the charade and their father had no guile in his scientific soul.

'That's the ticket,' he admitted.

'The answer is still no.'

Both Helen and her little sister groaned. Becca rubbed her eyes and Helen's throat felt dry and sore as if her disappointment was stuck inside it. She adored her little sister's company and Becca accompanying them to London would have been like bringing a piece of home with her. They were both peculiar girls and they belonged together.

Mama set down something that clattered on the table, making Helen jump. 'A pair of Bow Street Runners couldn't keep track of them both in London. You know it would be a complete disaster. I dare say the Great Fire of 1666 would dim in comparison.'

Helen shrugged. 'Unflattering, but fair.'

Becca pursed her lips to one side and nodded.

Papa cleared his throat again. It was now time for Helen's speech for him. She hoped her father would do better at hers than he had at poor Becca's.

'If two girls are too much to bring to London,' he said, 'why doesn't Helen stay home with me and Becca can go and have her very own presentation? Helen has no interest in it and she would be happier here studying her reptiles. She feels out of place in London and loves being at home where she belongs.'

Helen sat up straighter. Papa hadn't flubbed her speech. *She* had made him repeat it at least a half-dozen times.

'Helen put you up to that, too, I suppose,' Mama said. She grimaced.

Why did Mama have to be so shrewd?

Hopefully, Papa remembered the second part of their argument. She waited a few moments before he said, 'Her book is coming out this summer and that is enough stimulation for this year. Scientists believe it is unwise for a young female to feel too much excitement. It can quite overturn her delicate constitution.'

They heard their mother get to her feet. Never a good sign. It usually signalled the end of a discussion. 'There are porcupines that are more delicate than our second-youngest daughter. She doesn't want to stay home for her book or her reptiles. Helen wants to stay home and make eyes at Jason, who needs more to do than being his father's curate and grinning at all the young ladies in the parish. Helen should have the chance to meet a man with better prospects than Jason. Besides, Becca must stay here as I've already arranged for a young scholar from Oxford to visit Hampford and help Becca with her spelling. I am sure if she applies herself, her reading difficulties will be over.'

Helen let her head fall on Becca's shoulder and they both groaned.

'Do you mean Helen likes Mr Robertson's eldest son? The one with the large canines and the ears that stick out?'

Jason Robertson's ears *did* stick out a trifle, but there was nothing wrong with his teeth. They were straight and strong. Perhaps they were slightly large. Oh, dear, thanks to Papa she would now think of the line from *Little Red Riding Hood* every time that she saw him: *Oh, what large teeth you've got.*

'I believe that they may be secretly engaged,' Mama said.

How did she know that?

The only person Helen had told was Becca.

'Mama must have second sight,' Helen whispered into her sister's ear. 'There is no other way that she could have known.'

Becca sighed and then bit her lower lip. 'I really am applying myself to spelling and reading. The letters on the page just don't stay in the right places.'

Her little sister's difficulties with reading and writing were of long standing and none of the eight governesses they had previously engaged could help her overcome it.

Helen held up a hand to silence her sister. Her parents were talking again.

'You'd better take Helen to London after all,' Papa said. 'We don't want her marrying a curate whose ears stick out. It's a hereditary trait that he'd probably pass on to all of their children.'

Helen could have screamed in frustration. But she was unsure if Papa objected to his lack of fortune, or his ears more. She was the daughter of a duke and Jason was only the son of the local rector. It would be an unequal match. But it wasn't as if Helen was young and impressionable.

She was one and twenty. She had briefly and disastrously attended school, where she had not made even one friend. She had travelled abroad to Greece and failed to create new acquaintances. And at home, the only humans who seemed to like her were her own family and Jason. She was simply too different from other people.

London society would be a nightmare! She would perpetually be the one fiddle that was out of tune with the rest of the chamber orchestra. No matter how hard she tried, she was simply odd. And was abysmal at pretence. Even in their family theatricals, she'd never been given a speaking role and sometimes her sister Frederica had made her be a part of the background set so as to not ruin the play.

Helen could never fit in with the *ton*, nor become a peer's wife. Her suitors would expect her conversation to be on normal feminine topics like the weather and fashion, not about the natural sciences and the mating habits of different species of snakes. And a peer would expect her to be obedient to him, which was never going to happen. Helen was bossy like her mother. She wished to be a scientist, not a hostess. The thought of planning social gatherings— which she hated—for the rest of her life was enough to make her feel queasy.

No. She couldn't marry an aristocrat with a title.

Jason didn't mind that she was peculiar and, if they married, she would not have to suffer through the London Season. They could stay in Ashbury village near Hampford Castle. Her natural habitat and where she was the happiest.

Helen was old enough to make her own decisions and it grated on her that she wasn't allowed to. She stood up and grabbed her little sister's hand. 'Come on, Becca. It's not over yet.'

* * *

Mama set her wine glass on the table. 'This discussion is over.'

Helen grumbled. 'I don't wish to have a London Season. I am simply not the debutante type. I am a naturalist. Papa, tell her.'

She cast a look of entreaty at her father.

Papa, bless him, looked from her to her mother and shrugged. Mama, the Duchess of Hampford, was the alpha of their family. Not that Papa was the beta—that was Wick's wife, Louisa, who was too kind for her own good—but he wouldn't go up against her. She was the queen bee and Papa didn't want to get stung.

Her father cleared his throat. 'Helen, I think your mother is right. Why don't you go to London and meet more young men…with ears that don't stick out…you might decide that you like them better after all?'

'And if I don't?'

Her father looked to her mother and waited for *her* to answer. Thirty years of marriage made him wise enough to know when not to speak.

Mama took another sip of her wine. 'We are not heartless. If you do not find another man whom you like better, we will not oppose an engagement to Jason.'

Helen pulled at a loose curl in her coiffure. 'Can I get that in writing? Like the contract you had with Grandfather when you married, Papa?'

'You write it up and I'll sign it. But you must promise, Helen, to smile and attend every single event whose invitation I accept. You will dance with whomever I choose and you must promise to keep an open mind with your suitors.'

Becca cleared her throat and gave Helen a speaking glance.

'And Becca,' Helen said stoutly. 'Becca must be allowed to come with me for the Season.'

Her mother set down the goblet. 'Absolutely not.'

'You let Frederica debut at nineteen,' Becca protested. 'The same age that I am.'

'Yes, but she had no elder sister who was unmarried,' Mama said, giving Helen a penetrating glare. 'Becca, you will have your turn next year.'

Becca harrumphed, but Helen held her tongue. Once Mama made up her mind there was no moving her. And if Helen went to London and was agreeable, her parents would approve her match with Jason. Then she would never have to leave Ashbury and Hampford Castle again. It was more than she could have hoped for. Now all she had to do was ensure that every eligible young man in London wanted nothing to do with her.

That shouldn't be a problem.

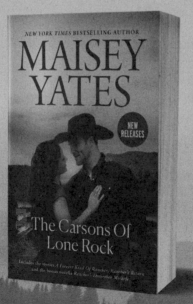